Kathleen Rowntree grew up in Grimsby, Lincolnshire, and was educated at Cleethorpes Girls' Grammar School and Hull University where she studied music. Her other novels are *The Quiet War of Rebecca Sheldon*, *Brief Shining*, *The Directrix*, *Tell Mrs Poole I'm Sorry* and *Outside, Looking In* and she has contributed to a series of monologues for BBC2 TV called *Obsessions*. She and her husband have two sons and they live on the Oxfordshire/Northamptonshire borders.

Also by Kathleen Rowntree

THE QUIET WAR OF REBECCA SHELDON
BRIEF SHINING
TELL MRS POOLE I'M SORRY
OUTSIDE, LOOKING IN

and published by Black Swan

Between Friends

Kathleen Rowntree

BLACK SWAN

BETWEEN FRIENDS
A BLACK SWAN BOOK : 0 552 99506 1

Originally published in Great Britain by
Victor Gollancz Ltd.

PRINTING HISTORY
Gollancz edition published 1992
Black Swan edition published 1993
Black Swan edition reprinted 1993 (twice)
Black Swan edition reprinted 1994 (twice)
Black Swan edition reprinted 1995

Set in 11/12pt Linotype Melior by
County Typesetters, Margate, Kent

Black Swan Books are published by Transworld Publishers Ltd,
61– 63 Uxbridge Road, Ealing, London W5 5SA,
in Australia by Transworld Publishers (Australia) Pty Ltd,
15– 25 Helles Avenue, Moorebank, NSW 2170,
and in New Zealand by Transworld Publishers (NZ) Ltd,
3 William Pickering Drive, Albany, Auckland.

Printed and bound in Great Britain by
Cox & Wyman Ltd, Reading, Berkshire

To Lili Rance

Part One

OCTOBER

1

There was nothing to suggest an earth tremor occurring in Tessa Brierley's kitchen, or a maverick surge of electricity, or a tidal wave sweeping through. Sunlight continued to fasten on blue and white plates lining the dresser and to make the dust dance above rugs lying askew on the stone-flagged floor. From the hall came the stolid beat of a long case clock and faintly, somewhere overhead, Mrs Cloomb bumped a vacuum cleaner over floorboards towards a soothing carpet.

Nor was there any hesitation on the part of the two women there. Tessa, standing at the huge pine-wood table, continued to pour the coffee and, when she held out a mug, Maddy leaned calmly over the cat she was nursing to reach for it. Then Maddy sank back in the wooden rocking chair and Tessa took her own mug to the oak settle by the side of the Aga and sat with her back against the arm and her feet up. This was how they invariably arranged themselves for coffee in Holly House. Maddy talked vigorously and Tessa listened. This was as usual, too, for Maddy was active in village life and so knew all the gossip, whereas Tessa spent most of her time working in her attic studio and relied on her friend to keep her up to date. When hoofs clattered outside in the street and the horse-rider, Celia Westbrook, stared in frankly as she bobbed past the window, Maddy interrupted herself just long enough to say, 'G'mornin', Squire,' and tug an imaginary forelock, and Tessa laughed as she would normally laugh at one of her friend's witticisms. The cat on Maddy's lap rose, arched her back, unfurled her tail in Maddy's face and settled down again. All was peaceable and unremarkable.

It could be virtually any morning during the past decade, Tessa reflected. Here were two friends – close friends, she amended – having coffee together in the kitchen. Yet her heart was banging as though she had been violently disturbed. And it had been such a simple remark. She had been bringing the coffee to the table when Maddy made it – 'What rotten luck about Paul.' Blankness had come over Tessa as she set down the tray, and creeping, foolish bewilderment; then, as she poured the coffee and Maddy fell over herself to change the subject, suspicion. How can she know? she thought wildly. Her hand stayed steady, but her heart thundered into overdrive and the lining of her mouth turned to sandpaper. It was as though the answer were there, nudging her, and she refusing to notice it.

And Maddy, without pausing in her report of the feud between Mrs Burrows and Mrs Frogmorton, thought, Christ, I've given it away. She's guessed – oh God, I think she's guessed.

When Maddy had gone, Tessa carried the coffee tray into the scullery, ran water into a bowl and began to wash up. Soon, her hands fell idle in the water and her eyes went to the window over the sink. In the autumn garden there were roses still in the bed by the wall, and a pink mass of them on the trellis archway. If she stood on tiptoe and looked to the left she would see fuchsias trailing over the stone steps to the door – a feature she often opened the back door on purpose to view at this time of year; but now she was unable to stir an inch; pink roses had transfixed her. When the blooms blurred out of focus, she was not aware of it, for her mind had begun to recall every detail of every happening and conversation that had occurred since Paul telephoned with his news late yesterday afternoon.

Her son's voice had been bleak. 'Mum, I'm out of the tournament. Left knee's in plaster. Dislocated.'

'Oh, Paul! What happened?'

'Bit of a ruck; got stood on. It's going to take ages to mend – no, Mum, it won't be permanent. I'm just thoroughly pissed off. Tell Dad, will you? Obviously, I won't be in the team when we play his lot on Saturday week.'

'He'll be very disappointed. And you must be, bitterly. So am I, darling,' she added duplicitously, aware of unseemly maternal relief at the thought of no more university rugby for her son this season.

The risotto had been ready to go into the oven when Nick telephoned. She knew it would be her husband before she lifted the receiver; this was not the first time recently he had rung to say he'd be late.

'Sorry, love. Don't bother getting dinner for me – I'll grab something in the pub. I'm going to the hospital tonight – got to see Colin about those papers.'

'Is it fair to bother Colin, do you think?'

'Hell, Tess, it's for the department. Colin'd be the last man to see the department undermined.'

She had been about to say, Give Colin my love, when she recalled that the conversation was probably a charade and the visit to Colin a fabrication summoned in aid of Nick's latest adventure. Instead, she reported the news of Paul's rugby accident.

'Poor lad! He's been living for the chance to play in the tournament. We'll have to think of something to cheer him up – talk about it later. Don't wait up,' he advised, needlessly.

She had spooned some of the risotto into a smaller dish, put this into the oven, then covered the remainder with foil and slammed it into the fridge. While her dinner was cooking she sat in the wooden rocker, sipping a glass of red wine, wondering, Who's the lucky lady this time? An undergraduate, a fresher who missed the warnings to be on her guard against the too-handsome senior lecturer in the psychology department? A new secretary, bowled over by his charm? Or someone he'd met on his travels – like the air stewardess he flew with to the Boston conference?

11

She'd discover soon enough. Nick's flings were usually of short duration and afterwards he was full of remorse and a need to confess the details. Once, these episodes had made her wretched. Nowadays, they merely irritated.

This was not strictly true, she corrected herself, setting the wine glass down on the table in order to consider the matter more rigorously. She was irritated, all right, by their pathetic predictability, but beneath her irritation lay heart-ache. She thought of a night following one of Nick's broken-hearted confessions; she and he lying hand in hand in the dark like two small children afraid of the bogeyman, weeping as they acknowledged it would probably happen again (for it seemed to be an incurable impediment), comforting themselves that it was possible to be borne, promising one another that it would never ever part them. Feeling safer, they imagined themselves bound by an impregnable web woven by time.

Sometimes she imagined what other people said about them – people at the university who knew what Nick got up to – but always mentally stopped up her ears. It was nobody's business but their own, she stoutly told herself. Of course, she had made it Maddy's business, too, in a way, by confiding in her so thoroughly. But telling Maddy was a safe indulgence.

The risotto had burned round the edges by the time she had remembered to take it out of the oven. She had eaten some of it, then gone into the sitting room and turned on the television. There was nothing worth watching, of course, and she was too tired to read having worked non-stop in her studio from breakfast time until Paul's telephone call. A longing stole over her to tell Maddy. She always told Maddy. Maddy was one of those women able to hear the worst about a friend's husband and still look him in the eye and be matey. Her reactions were sensible – she never urged divorce or paying Nick out in kind – and her judgement – whether to give a sympathetic hug and pass the tissues or a snort of laughter and get out the whisky – sound. Telling Maddy always buoyed her up.

Unluckily, Robert, Maddy's husband, had answered the phone. Tessa was not surprised to hear his voice, for even as she dialled the Storrs' number, she registered that it was not yet nine o'clock and there were numerous claims on Maddy's time of an evening – the WI, the parish council, the Friends of Wychwood Church, or any meeting called to consider a matter of village concern. But last night, Tessa had learned that Maddy was not expected home until late. 'It's her creative writing class in Fetherstone, and afterwards they go for a drink,' Robert said.

'Of course, I'd forgotten. But it doesn't matter, it's nothing that won't keep.'

'You and Nick will be coming to the harvest supper? We've plenty of tickets to get rid of.'

'I'll certainly come. And Nick will, if he's here.'

'Come with us, anyway.'

'Thanks, Robert. I'll phone Maddy in the morning.'

She had poured herself a second glass of wine and looked forward to having Maddy round for coffee. She had imagined making it (Maddy chatting in the background), then pouring it out, settling herself and beginning, 'Guess what? I think Nick's at it again.' And Maddy's close scrutiny as she gauged her response; Maddy putting down her coffee mug to indicate that for her friend she had all the time in the world. It had been a comfort just picturing it.

Nick had not come home until after she had gone to sleep. The alarm woke them at six and there followed half an hour's rush to get Nick packed and breakfasted in time for her to drive him to the airport. Zipping on her anorak, she had dashed into the barn, started the car and backed it out. Nick slammed the front door and ran down the steps.

Up to this point her recollections had come at a gallop. Now they slowed. She lingered over the short journey to the end of the village as if creeping through

fog. Wychwood had felt dead, she remembered, its tall
stone houses and huddled stone cottages – so mellow
in sunlight – loomed stark as moorland outcrops in the
dank chill air. Black yews fronting the churchyard
hulked menacingly over the street; even a lighted
cottage window glowed balefully, like a warning,
rather than as a token of life. Life, when it appeared,
erupted rudely: a Jaguar car shot out of The Glebe – a
small estate of executive houses near the T-junction
with the Manor. Tessa braked. Nick swore. 'Used to
having the road to himself at this time in the morning,'
she guessed. The cowman was crossing the yard at
Manor Farm, and a paper girl unlatching the gate to
one of the tied cottages. Tessa was waving to the girl
when Nick said, 'What rotten luck about Paul,' and
they began, at last, to discuss it.

Her recollections came to a halt. This was the point
she had been aiming for. Nick's voice, and Maddy's
voice, saying, 'What rotten luck about Paul.' Had the
coincidence of their using the same phrase put the grotesque idea into her mind? Because it was grotesque –
and impossible. But how else could Maddy have
known of Paul's accident, if not from Nick? Perhaps
she and Nick had bumped into one another innocently
– though Maddy's class was in Fetherstone and Nick,
presumably, had spent the evening thirty odd miles
away in the city. And if they had met, why hadn't
Maddy said?

'I must be mad,' she told herself, starting to scrub the
coffee pot. 'There's something I've overlooked – bound
to be.'

Dolly Cloomb stood in the doorway and said, 'Er,'
and Tessa jumped out of her skin. 'I've done. Your bed
were a mess – that dog were on it again. I tried to shift
'im, but he growled.'

'Sorry, Mrs Cloomb. I was up early this morning and
we were in such a rush I forgot to make it.'

'Well, I didn't like to disturb you with a visitor an'
all.'

14

'Only Mrs Storr,' Tessa pointed out – hardly 'a visitor', just an old friend and a very familiar figure about the village.

'Mm,' said Dolly.

Tessa dried her hands and hurried to the kitchen to get her purse. 'Scrap's getting to be a crotchety old fellow. I'll take him for a good brisk walk later on – wake his ideas up. Thanks, Mrs Cloomb. See you on Thursday.' She unlatched the door and held it open.

'Right you are, me duck.' Dolly, having tied on her headscarf, picked up her shopping bag and went down the steps to the street where her friend Rose Fettle was waiting.

2

'She kept yer,' said Rose when Tessa had closed the door. 'Yer ten minutes over.'

'It were me. I lost count thinking about our Arthur.'

'Oh – 'im. Well, come on, or they'll be shut; I'm peckish.'

They linked arms and turned right into a road running between two broad swathes of turf known as the Green.

On Monday, Wednesday and Friday mornings they worked together for Mrs Westbrook at the Manor and this they regarded as their proper work. Should Mrs Westbrook require it, they abandoned work of a secondary nature (Dolly's at Holly House and Rose's at the Rectory) to hurry to her aid, to pluck game birds, perhaps, or clean up after a party. This was hard on Tessa and on Eleanor Browne, the rector's sister, but was the sort of thing one learned to accept in a village.

At the village shop, Rose pushed open the door, then stiffened.

Brenda Varney, who was behind the wire partition in the post office section attending to Maddy Storr's parcel, stiffened too, and called nervously, 'Good morning, ladies.' The sight of Rose Fettle and Madeleine Storr both in her shop at one and the same time always made her nervous, for it put her in mind of a dreadful incident over a decade ago when Mrs Storr – as she was then known, being a newcomer with unclear social status – had stood at the counter and marvelled over the amazing number of people who had once lived cheek by jowl in what were formerly Numbers One to Five Back End Row and was now her spacious home, Jasmine Cottage. The Storrs had recently bought the terrace of empty and dilapidated dwellings from their owner, Major Westbrook, and renovated them as one good-sized house. Unknown to the newcomer, a former inhabitant of Number Three Back End Row in the person of Rose Fettle was at that moment waiting her turn at the counter and taking in every word. Afterwards, Brenda wondered how she had managed to avoid a nasty accident with the bacon slicer.

Maddy turned. 'Good morning, Rose. Good morning, Dolly.' (She was friendly to everyone and was no more put off by surliness from the lower orders than by frostiness from the grand; if people chose to be peculiar, that was their problem.) 'Shan't keep Brenda a moment. We're trying to work out the postage for Mexico.'

'Be as long as yer like fer me,' said Rose, turning to inspect a display of soup cans. 'D'yer fancy mulligatawny, Dolly?'

'All right.'

'And a doughnut? My treat.'

'Ooh, yeah. You are good, Rose.'

'See you all tonight,' called Maddy, going to the door.

And with different degrees of enthusiasm they agreed that she would, for Tuesday evenings in Wychwood were devoted to the WI.

Tessa put her head through the kitchen doorway into the hall and yelled: 'Get down here, you little wretch.' Then she went into the scullery to collect her wellingtons. When she padded back in her socks, Scrap had arrived in the doorway; he stood on the step, head on one side, one ear raised enquiringly. Black, shaggy and imperfectly formed, he was the least fortunate consequence of an unscheduled mating between her aunt's cairn terrier bitch and the neighbour's small black poodle dog. He had inherited his father's tenacity. Between the ninth and eighteenth months of his life, he drove the Brierley household mad with relentless howling at street or garden door whenever a neighbourhood bitch came into season. A surgeon's knife restored their peace, but Scrap continued to exhibit an obsessive nature by entertaining only two goals in life: his mistress and food.

Tessa, sitting on a chair to pull on her boots, gave him a piece of her mind. 'How dare you growl at Mrs Cloomb? Next time she orders you off the bed, jump to it. D'you hear?'

His tail went from side to side in three precisely measured movements. He was not given to wagging, but found it a useful corrective to an unpleasant tone of voice. His tail was an instrument of encouragement to be used sparingly; compliments raised it not one jot, but when Tessa grumbled, a few wags served to show that he, at least, knew how two beings who were all in all to one another should conduct their intercourse.

'We're going for a walk, you blighter,' she said – unnecessarily, since Scrap could plainly see, in spite of the hair over his eyes, that she was donning her wellingtons. He went to the street door and waited patiently.

Down the steps and into the street – Church Street, the main village thoroughfare. On the left, the churchyard; on the right and rounding Holly House, the Green. For centuries Holly House had been the village inn and coaching house, the latter facility provided by the barn on Church Street which now housed the Brierley cars. The house had an impressive frontage on to the Green, though its front entrance was seldom used by the Brierleys who preferred the kitchen door on Church Street for its proximity to the cars and the kitchen flags for their tolerance of mud. Towards the end of the last century the inn fell into disuse and a rival, the Red Lion (and village pub to this day), was set up in a cottage on the opposite side of the Green next door to the village shop. In the twenties, the former inn was gentrified as Holly House, but by the end of the war it was again sliding into disrepair. Then, seventeen years ago, it was saved by Tessa and Nicholas Brierley who turned it into a family home and work place for Tessa.

Tessa did not turn right into the Green but left into the churchyard where, from a kissing gate in the far wall, a footpath led into fields skirting the wood. Sighting no sheep in the field, she unclipped the leash; Scrap raced towards an ancient hedgerow where he had often savoured rabbit droppings. Tessa stuffed the leash in her pocket and strode on, over a stile and into a further field. The path rose steeply over tufty pasture. At the edge of the wood there was a stile worn shiny, for it was a favourite place to sit and admire the view: Wychwood in the foreground, Steeple Cheney beyond, and the little market town of Fetherstone grazing the horizon. This was Tessa's country; she was no newcomer in the true sense of the word. Her father had been a land agent in Fetherstone until, at her mother's death, he had been persuaded to retire and make his home in Yorkshire with Tessa's brother who owned a riverside hotel with good fishing. Aunt Winifred, her father's sister, had been the Wychwood school mistress for many years and though the school closed down on Aunt Winifred's retirement and village children were now bussed to school in Fetherstone, many villagers had been taught by Miss Hodson. She

18

was also remembered as the church organist; Tessa could never hear the instrument without her throat constricting. Her aunt died four years ago in the little cottage she bought in Honey Lane after moving out of School House, which had been sold and turned into a modern home with rather too much enthusiasm. Some years ago, Tessa and Aunt Winifred had gone there to Mrs Burrows' bring-and-buy coffee morning – a miserable experience; chiefly, Tessa remembered trying to utter polite praise while staring at the platform where once stood her aunt's desk and now stood a drinks bar decorated with horse brasses.

Chance had returned Tessa to Wychwood, the chance of Nick accepting a job at the city university. At first they lived near the campus in a three-roomed city flat comprising the ground floor of a Victorian villa. Then Paul was born, and when Tessa, a painter, started to make money as a book illustrator and they could afford more extensive accommodation, Nick surprised her by suggesting they live in the country. Always keen to initiate a trend, he imagined himself in thorn-proof jacket and deer-stalker, gun under arm, labrador to heel – and the flattering amazement of friends and colleagues. Of course, once installed in Holly House, he entirely forgot the fantasy, and Tessa often thought that were it up to Nick they would move back to the city. But it was not up to Nick. She had built a perfect studio in the attic of Holly House with a skylight and every possible convenience, and these days her earnings more than matched his. In any case, she had not the tiniest inclination to leave Wychwood. It was her territory.

Behind her the wood pressed close. She gripped the stile and remembered climbing it as a child, eager for bluebells and blackberries; and vaulting it with her brother and friends, hell-bent on terrifying one another with their whispers, rustles, and sudden leaps from overhanging branches. Echoes had magnified their whooping races through the trees, and sometimes in the midst of a game (she recalled a mysterious phenomenon) they would fall unaccountably still as though mesmerized by the hidden watchfulness of other creatures. On winter Saturdays she had helped Aunt Winifred haul fallen logs over these fields to the School House yard. She could see the roof of Old School House now, and the remaining sections of the school which had been turned into the village hall and meeting room. Leaving Wychwood was unthinkable – not because of memories and fond familiarity – rather, that the place had become her notebook, its nooks and crannies the stuff of her work.

Casting her eyes over the view, past paintings came to mind: an interlace of twisted tree roots, wind-strewn grasses blowing silver and mauve. And the church had provided richly – a crumbling pillar, a wooden lattice, a jutting gargoyle leering under a puffball sky. There was also a cherub on a Victorian memorial which would fit beautifully into her present scheme of work. The thought galvanized her. 'Scrap!' she called.

Scrap heard, but ignored her. Fields and ditches were dogs' business of which his mistress had but limited understanding. He darted, nose down; swivelled, and shot his head into a grass thicket.

Tessa thought, Too late for work today. I'll get up early tomorrow and make a good start. 'Come on, Scrap,' she called, then walked on, taking a path along the wood's circumference.

Thinking of work put Maddy in mind, for Tessa's paintings had precipitated their friendship. On the face of it, Maddy was an unlikely friend, but the friends she had acquired more predictably had often hurt her with their peculiar attitudes. Village friends were embarrassed by her occupation, made polite noises if they saw her paintings in print and changed the subject if ever Tessa referred to them. Gardening, hen and goat-keeping, prize jam and cake-making, teaching, shopping, organ-playing, hunting and dressmaking, these activities and more featured in animated conversation between the enterprising women of Wychwood. But painting put a damper on things. 'Our lady artist,' she had once heard herself described in a facetious tone by the chairman of the parish council. She was sitting beside him on the platform at the time, having been asked to judge a Keep Wychwood Tidy poster competition. There was a nervous titter. No-one in the audience met Tessa's eye. Friends acquired through Nick's work at the university had also disappointed her, though in a different way. They were excited to learn she was a painter, imagining works hanging in galleries and articles about her in magazines. Her commercial success came as a blow; one day, they consoled her, she would produce a masterpiece. Maddy's response came like a breeze through mist. She had noticed Tessa sketching in the churchyard and strolled across to investigate. Soon they were clambering up the Holly House attic stairs and sorting through portfolios; examining, discussing, enthusing. It was astonishing to find this town-smart newcomer so completely on her wavelength, but when the Storrs' house, Jasmine Cottage, emerged from its former dilapidation, Tessa understood the matter: Maddy, too, was an artist, not with pencil and paintbrush, but with objects, interiors, and her own self. Over the next ten years, more than an understanding of matters artistic bound them. Tessa began to guess at the sense of waste which propelled Maddy's compulsive organizing, and Maddy to comprehend why Tessa put up with Nick. At times, each felt the other had saved her sanity.

Suddenly, Tessa was crouching down, grabbing fistfuls of turf as pain sliced her. It was nothing to do with Nick – it was Maddy. Dear God, if Maddy . . .

Scrap saw her and came trotting, but stopped several feet short to view the situation which did not suggest, so far as he could judge, continued happy gambolling or a stride in the direction of a tin-opener. But, wait! (his tail rose cautiously) she had lifted her head and appeared to be recovering her senses.

A thought had come to Tessa with stunning clarity. It couldn't be, couldn't possibly be, because Maddy wasn't Nick's type. Nick had confessed repeatedly – and she had witnessed its truth with her own eyes; once by spying on him, once accidentally in a pub, and once when he had taken to bed a colleague whom she knew – that all Nick's inamoratas resembled herself, each one tall and dark with masses of long hair. 'She reminded me of you, darling – not consciously, of course, but looking back, that's what I found irresistible. Believe me, I can't get enough of you, Tess,' he had said about the air stewardess. (When she repeated this to Maddy, they had fallen back in their chairs and laughed like drains clearing.) But Maddy was not at all like Tessa; she was petite with gamine features and the sort of immaculately cut ash-blonde hair that women admire and men don't because it looks untouchable. She recalled Nick scoffing at Maddy's outfits: 'I see your chum's mowing the lawn in her designer gardening gear.' And Nick spotting Maddy on a rainy day in Fetherstone market, dressed bright as a canary amid the dun thorn-proofs and navy anoraks, calling, 'Morning, Maddy. Love the deep-sea trawling outfit!' Nick was amused by Maddy, not attracted to her. The relief was so great, the feeling of foolishness so hot, that she unzipped her anorak and began to stride home.

This time, Scrap stayed to heel. Her purposefulness looked very good indeed, and would undoubtedly lead to a dog's dinner.

3

'You *are* in a rush. Hurrying back to work?'

Tessa's over-laden mind went blank. She registered that she had arrived back in the churchyard at the point where a path running round the side of the church was crossed by a path linking church and Rectory. There was a tall gate in the Rectory garden wall; Eleanor Browne was standing by it, watching her. It was a moment or two before Tessa could answer.

'Not really. I'm having a stupid sort of day – just wool-gathering.'

'Then come and have tea.'

'But you're busy,' she objected, looking at the grubby linen draped over Eleanor's arm.

'I shan't tackle this now. Tomorrow will do. I thought on Sunday what a poor colour the amice had got. Timothy never notices. And I'm afraid we're both becoming rather *forgetful*.' The last word was dwelt over. Eleanor had a measured way of speaking, pronouncing each word precisely and important ones dramatically. As always, Tessa hung on them. Eleanor was spell-binding – and not just for her diction. Equally hypnotic was her style of gesture and movement, a way of hugging herself as if to ward off desolation, and maintaining bony knees and ankles in close touch with one another to occupy the minimum body space. A dewdrop often bejewelled the end of her nose, conjured, no doubt, by the Rectory chill; when this dropped and thereby drew attention to itself, she would root in her cardigan pocket for a handkerchief and apply it with an air of conceding fruitlessness. For as long as she could remember, Tessa had associated Eleanor with extreme age and fragility (and her memory went back a long way, for Timothy Browne had been rector of Wychwood for the last thirty-eight years). That in fact Eleanor was as strong as an ox, had outlived many of her friends – Winifred Hodson, Tessa's aunt, for one – and still housekept for her brother with minimum assistance, visited almost daily in the parish and kept a diplomatic eye on the team of ladies who tended the church fabric, added to her mystery and fascination. She featured in several of Tessa's paintings – a figure hunched over a fire, a narrow shape disappearing through a gateway, a kneeling shadow in a flower bed – though no-one but the sharp-eyed Maddy had spotted this and Tessa had sworn her to silence. Eleanor inspired her curiosity; Tessa could not observe her enough.

'Well then, I'd love to. But I must drop the dog off and change my footwear.'

'Good. Don't be long. I'll put the kettle on.'

In the scullery of Holly House, Tessa was scarcely able to remove her wellingtons for the dog's frantic jig at her feet. She decided to feed him to forestall an outbreak of furious barking. From the window ledge, the cat glared as Scrap hurled food into his throat.

Tessa put on her shoes and thought that were she Maddy going to tea at the Rectory she would at least comb her hair and change her jeans for a skirt. I'm beset by idleness, thought Tessa, and a desire at all times to be comfortable. She recalled being persuaded by Maddy into attending Mrs Davenport's recent bring-and-buy coffee morning at Hilltop Farm, how, with virtuous intent she had put on a smart jacket and skirt and then, at the last minute, rushed upstairs to swop skirt, tights and shoes for trousers, socks and sneakers. 'Sorry – skirt creased and no time to press it,' she panted, belting herself into Maddy's sporty little car. 'You look fine to me,' said Maddy, not looking at Tessa but at non-existent traffic in the driving mirror. Anyway, Tessa excused herself as she headed for the Rectory, people expect me to look 'arty' and it would be a shame to disappoint them.

(Eleanor, had Tessa known it, did not notice what people had on, and would be perfectly satisfied to see Tessa installed in her chintz armchair indeterminately clad in dark blue to match her eyes and look well with her long dark hair. Tessa was a favourite of hers, niece to her dear dead friend, and someone she had seen grow from a tomboy into a Rossetti-style beauty. And there was a quiet thoughtfulness about Tessa, which Eleanor found attractive. Her only regret was that she was not a proper church-goer. Winifred had often brought her young niece to church, but when Tessa returned to Wychwood as Mrs Nicholas Brierley, she confined her church going to village occasions such as the harvest festival and the carol service.)

Tessa walked up the left side of Church Street, passed the church gate and turned in at the Rectory entrance marked by a five-bar gate kept permanently propped open. The drive was of sparse gravel stones; mossy earth and small weeds mounded along its centre. On the left of the drive and filling the space to the church wall was a shrubbery of laurel and bay, on the right a copse of tall trees where rooks nested. Through the copse was a subsidiary drive to the old stables which now functioned as a garage, and at the side of the copse was a path to the kitchen door. If this had been a different occasion – a helper's visit to prepare for the church fête, for example – she would have taken this path, but today she continued along the main drive which ended in a circular sweep at the front door. Evidently, she had judged correctly, for Eleanor had left the door open and pinned it back with a wrought iron doorstop.

She stepped inside. In the hall, loose floor tiles under thin Persian rugs clicked beneath her feet. Passing the wide staircase, she recalled a childhood visit to old Mrs Browne (now deceased), mother of Eleanor and Timothy, bedridden for years in a cavernous upper room overlooking the garden. It had been an ascent into a region of frost. With each stair climbed, the cold

25

clasped more of her, raised the hair on her head, slipped icy fingers between her shoulder blades. Even now, as she looked up, chill air glanced across her forehead. Why this house should be always full of restless, freezing air was a puzzle. True, there was no central heating, and the grates, installed in all the rooms, remained empty. (Sam Parminter, now in his nineties and resident in one of the village almshouses, had been boot boy at the Rectory during its affluent days at the turn of the century. Boot-cleaning, it appeared, was the least of his chores; his prime occupation was to run from room to room with a coal scuttle, stoking fires.) These days, only the drawing room fire was lit at four o'clock on winter afternoons. But could empty grates adequately explain an icy turbulence ruffling even the warm days of summer, wondered Tessa, or were there ghosts up there constantly churning the atmosphere?

Eleanor came out of the kitchen, bearing a tray. 'Oh good, you're here. We'll sit in the drawing room as it's such a nice day.' She meant in preference to her little sitting room with its one-bar electric fire. Tessa followed her. Rays from a low sun were pouring in through the bay window overlooking the lawns; they sat in sun-warmed chairs, the tea tray on a low table between them.

'Did Dolly Cloomb appear well this morning?' asked Eleanor, pouring tea.

'Yes, I think so.' Tessa searched her memory.

'I'm relieved to hear it. I was visiting in Orchard Close this morning. Whether it was just village gossip, I can't say, but apparently Arthur Cloomb made a particular nuisance of himself after closing time last night. There were sounds of upheaval in number seven.'

'Oh dear. Now I come to think of it, I believe her face was swollen.'

'Of course, when I got back here and tried to broach the subject with Rose Fettle, not a word would she

26

utter. A very *retentive* person, Rose. So you think it's possible Dolly was the worse for wear?'

'I can't be sure. I was a bit – you know – mind on other things this morning.' She regretted her self-absorption. Not because she would have raised the matter – she would not have dared; but because she liked to show solidarity with Mrs Cloomb when she arrived bearing war wounds – a gentler tone of voice, a light touch on the victim's arm. And then Mrs Cloomb allowed Tessa to cosset her, accepted a longer coffee break, and chocolate instead of plain digestive biscuits. I suppose that's why she was sniffy about my 'visitor', Tessa thought; I didn't give her due attention. She sighed and said, 'Poor woman. She's so shabby, so lacklustre. I don't think she's properly nourished. I bet that man drinks her wages – beats her if she doesn't hand them over.'

Eleanor became agitated. 'You're not thinking of putting her money up again? You will give us notice next time, dear?'

'Us' delineated Eleanor and Mrs Westbrook of the Manor. Tessa had caused them anguish some years ago by unilaterally raising the domestic pay rate. She had been startled into guilt by an advertisement in the university paper for cleaners. 'You should be getting a pound extra at least,' she told an astonished Mrs Cloomb. 'Here it is, and there's something extra to make up what you've lost. I couldn't do my work without your help in the house, and I can't bear to think of myself as exploitative,' she explained as Dolly continued to gape. Mrs Cloomb's colleague, Rose Fettle, had lost no time in familiarizing Rectory and Manor with the new rate at Holly House. 'This is what you get when the wrong sort of people move in,' fumed Celia Westbrook to Eleanor. 'People like the Brierleys don't understand how we go on in the country.' Eleanor understood her implication: Tessa had usurped the Manor's prerogative, for the Manor led, and others followed; understood, too, that for the

Manor to discuss these matters with Holly House was an impossibility and any future negotiation must be channelled through the Rectory.

Tessa smiled and shook her head – to Eleanor's huge relief, for though she had appreciated Tessa's scruples as well as Celia's outraged *amour propre*, extra money for Rose Fettle had been difficult to extract from her budget. 'No,' Tessa said, 'I'm not thinking of a rise; I just wish she'd use what she earns for her own benefit. Really, she ought to leave the man.'

Eleanor answered her and went on talking, but her own words hung in Tessa's ears and made her blush. I bet people have said that about me, she thought.

Eleanor passed the cake dish. 'Have another slice.'

'Thanks. It's jolly good.' She was starving, having eaten nothing today but a slice of toast. She broke small pieces from the rather tough sponge slab and savoured them slowly to make them last.

Tessa was looking strained, Eleanor thought, and soon, concern for her favourite's physical well-being passed on to concern for her spiritual health. She rejoiced whenever she discovered Tessa sketching in church, sure that its aura of holiness must eventually capture so sensitive a person. Tactfully she encouraged these visits. Now, taking up her teacup, she remarked innocently, 'Your friend, Mrs Storr, has made the most beautiful arrangement in the chancel – yellow roses and cream chrysanths mixed up with dried things, corn and bulrushes and so forth. Most original, and so pretty. You must pop in, Tessa, and see.'

Tessa seemed startled, and Eleanor wondered whether she had been too obvious.

'She's clever at that sort of thing,' Tessa mumbled, but made no promise to go and see for herself.

'Did I ever show you my scrap book from our years in Hong Kong?' Eleanor asked to fill the silence. 'Because it would interest you, Tessa; there are some exquisite prints and water colours.'

'You did, Eleanor, but I should love to see it again.'

28

It was a good answer — truthful, exact. Pleased, Eleanor rose and went to fetch it.

'Come and sit on the sofa,' she said, returning. She opened the book at page one and spread it over their knees.

This is so soothing, so safe, thought Tessa, looking anew at the yellowed, dog-eared pages. It was her sixth or seventh viewing, but the prints with their stylized blossoms, misty hills and tiny people were endlessly fascinating, and almost as addictive were the faded photographs and newspaper cuttings. Eleanor's voice lulled her, and soon both women were lost in an antique Anglican perspective of old Hong Kong.

When, half an hour later, Timothy came in and turned on the light, they looked up, disorientated. 'Don't know how you saw a thing. And it's cold. Good Lord, Eleanor, you'll freeze the girl.' And he bent down and put a match to the fire laid out in the grate. 'That's more like it,' he said when it was blazing, and — not out of perversity but from long habit — promptly prevented any heat from reaching the women by standing in front of the fire to warm his bottom. He was tall like his sister, but whereas Eleanor was bony and sallow, Timothy was plump and pink.

'A good day, Timothy?'

'Yes, yes.'

'Timothy has been visiting friends at The Elms in Fairminster,' Eleanor explained. 'It's a sort of residential club for retired clergymen. The bachelors and widowers are particularly fond of it; they can stay for so many weeks per year and invite their chums over to lunch or dinner. It makes a nice change; they meet up with old cronies and enjoy a little modest luxury. Any, er, *changes*, dear?' she enquired.

'Yes. Two more gathered,' he reported happily: 'Peter Thornton from Greatworth — which was more or less expected, funeral's on Thursday; and a chap I didn't know from the south of the diocese — courtesy of influenza, I believe, three or four weeks ago.'

'Oh dear,' sighed Eleanor, 'Peter was very frail, and I suppose at our age we have to expect . . .' And then – looking on the bright side – 'But they gave you a good lunch?'

'First class.' He rocked on his heels. 'Jugged hare, apple pie, Stilton, claret – good, robust fare.'

This talk of food made Tessa feel faint. She closed the book on to Eleanor's knee, and stood up. 'I must go. We'll finish the scrap book next time. Promise?'

Eleanor saw her to the door. 'The nights are drawing in. I hate that.'

'Me too. I flourish in the light.' She kissed Eleanor's thin cheek and clasped her hand. 'You know, I feel so much better for this afternoon.'

Eleanor was touched. The remark was a gift, for although it confirmed her suspicion that something was amiss with Tessa, it warmed her to learn she had helped.

'I'll phone you next week and ask you to Holly House. Mind you bring the scrap book. Goodbye.'

'Goodbye, Tessa, dear. Do take care.'

4

At half past six, Rose Fettle went upstairs to change out of her workaday clothes into her second-best dress. When this was accomplished she squinted in the dressing table mirror and smote herself four times – on nose, cheeks and chin – with a powder puff. As the dust cleared, she drew a line of lipstick over her upper lip, clamped both lips together and held them thus for a count of five. The hat came next – brown felt in preference to glossy navy straw – and with this pinned securely to her corrugated hair she returned to the living room, where, on a dining chair in front of the television, she sat and cast her eyes alternately over

Midlands Today and her cuckoo clock. At ten minutes to seven, she rose, switched off the television, collected handbag and carrier bag from the dining table and went into the hall passage for her coat.

Orchard Close was deserted, its twenty-two council houses bolted and curtained for the night. There was one street lamp, but this was outshone by the moon. It's as light as day, marvelled Rose, tripping smartly down her neat garden path. She closed the little gate behind her and looked over the road to Number Seven. All serene, it appeared, at the Cloombs'; nevertheless, her footsteps became a touch cautious as she approached the Cloomb gate – open as usual and half off its hinges. Dolly only used the front door for ceremonial excursions, to a christening, perhaps, or a wedding or funeral; the front door was Arthur Cloomb's means of ingress, Dolly's was at the rear. Rose, therefore, gave the front door a miss and – tiptoeing now – went round the side of the house to the kitchen door. This she opened and put her head round.

'All clear?' she hissed.

'Oh, come in, Rose.'

Rose came in. 'He's still here, then,' she observed, jerking her head towards the hall passage.

'He's staying in. He's been banned.'

'No!'

'He has. Terry King told me. He were having a drink in the Lion last night and saw it all. Accounts for Arthur's paddy when he came home, I suppose.'

Rose snorted. 'He can't say he's not been warned. John's got his licence to think about.'

Dolly took the coat which was lying on a kitchen chair and pulled it on. 'D'you think I should tell 'im,' she asked, tying on a headscarf.

'Tell 'im what?'

'That I'm off out.'

'He's quiet. I should let sleeping dogs lie.'

Dolly sighed and picked up her shopping bag.

'Got your spoon for the competition?'

31

'Yes, me dear; but it's no good. Yours is bound to win. Yours or hers.' (At the WI, Rose Fettle or Madeleine Storr invariably won any competition containing an artistic or handicraft element, as did tonight's for Dressing a Wooden Spoon.)

'She'll win, I'll be bound,' said Rose, pulling her friend out of the back door. 'Wonder what sort of get up she'll have on tonight.'

They passed, arm in arm, beneath the street lamp, crossed Fetherstone Road and turned right into Church Street, where, a little further along on the right between Old School House and the Rectory stood their destination, the village hall.

Maddy Storr's get up was revealed when, as WI president, she slipped off her coat and called the meeting to order. She gained immediate rapt attention. Nineteen pairs of eyes took in an overall impression then got down to details: a red corduroy skirt – revealed, when the wearer obligingly stuck out a knee, as culottes – red silk shirt and red sleeveless V-neck sweater, all this redness set off by a plain gold chain looped round her neck and over her tiny bosom. Most members were struck with admiration. Mrs Storr, it was felt, was an asset, particularly when speaking on their behalf at county meetings or welcoming visitors from neighbouring institutes. Some of those present had made a similar sartorial effort but with less success, notably, Mrs Burrows of Old School House in voluminous blue and Mrs Dyte from The Glebe in smart grey worsted. Most ladies, the farmers' wives, the cottage and council house dwellers, were dressed unremarkably, neat or comfy according to taste. Only Miss Browne from the Rectory had made no effort at all, merely dragged her quilted nylon zip-up over her baggy tweed skirt. Her pockets bulged; everyone was familiar with their contents – scraps of paper, church magazines, envelopes, pens, purse, scarf, dusty cough drops – which tended to erupt in a heap with a dragged out handkerchief.

'What *does* she look like?' Rose scoffed in Dolly's

ear, referring to Maddy Storr. She was indignant, having read in her magazine that reds could on no account be worn together: how galling to see the president getting away with it.

'Jezebel,' whispered Dolly, who had other ideas about the wearing of red.

'What?'

'She looks like a Jezebel.'

This piece of original thinking impressed her friend. 'You could be right, there, me duck; you could well be right.'

The remains of the risotto, heated through, were quite good; she ate every scrap with relish. Then she saw to the cat's needs: shut Scrap outside in the garden and put down a saucer of milk and some meat in a shallow tin dish. The cat paced sniffily round these offerings then at last crouched low to eat. The back door rattled furiously until Scrap was readmitted and free to race upon the cat's dish and propel it with his tongue over the flagstone floor. 'Wretched dog,' said Tessa, removing the dish to the scullery sink. When all was clean and tidy, she put out the kitchen light and went through the hall to the sitting room.

Having nothing further to hope for in the food line, Scrap proposed to devote the remainder of the day to his mistress. He waited courteously to see where she would sit and, when she had settled herself on the settee beside the inglenook, glass of wine, newspaper and remote control to hand on a low table, he jumped up beside her and lay with his head on her thigh. She fondled him absently with one hand and with the other worked the television control. Her body was pleasantly relaxed, her mind reasonably blank – though in the background provocative thoughts hovered threateningly. Viewing would be a safer occupation than reading, she judged, for the television would go on transmitting however insistent became the dangerous thoughts.

She was still successfully repressing these when, an hour later, the telephone rang. She switched off the television, collected the phone from its resting place on a pembroke table, returned to the settee and lifted the receiver. 'Hello?'

'Hello, Tessa.'

'Colin!' she blurted, hearing the unmistakable baritone – then felt foolish because it couldn't be. 'Colin?'

'Yes, it's me. I'm home.'

'Wonderful! Oh, Colin, that's marvellous news. Did you come out of hospital today?'

'No, no. They let me out at the weekend – decided I'd got a remission. That's what they call it, but I'm really hopeful this time. If I can build myself up I reckon I'll make a fight of it.'

'Of course you will. I'm so glad.' But joy for an old friend was alloyed by a more selfish consideration: so Nick *had* been lying – well, of course he had.

'Nick's not there, I suppose?'

She jumped guiltily. 'No. He's in Oslo for the conference.'

'When does he get back?'

'Friday – all being well.'

'Will you give him a message? Jerry and Viv came to see me before I left hospital. Jerry was anxious about some papers I was preparing before this business struck me down. Unluckily, Sophia was there. She made a scene – accused Jerry of pestering the mortally sick! So I thought it'd be better to tell Nick rather than Jerry: the papers are here in my study, on the bottom shelf of the recessed cupboard at the side of the fireplace. You know where I mean, Tessa?'

'Yes, I remember.'

'Sophia's out, which is why I'm ringing. She's furious with the university over my sick pay, and furious with the department for what she calls pestering. It's not, of course; I like to be kept in the picture. But you know what she's like. The department's desperate to lay hands on those papers before the funding council inspection, so I thought if you and Nick came round one evening, he could pocket them while you divert Sophia.'

Tessa's heart sank. Sophia was a fearsome prospect. 'Perhaps Jerry and Viv could get round sooner.'

'Lord, no. Sophia's furious with Jerry, and Viv's never been her favourite person. You're good with her, and Nick could charm the devil.'

'If you say so. I'll tell Nick, certainly. But you shouldn't be worrying about the blessed department. There are more rewarding things, I should think.'

'Yeah. Tessa?'

'Mm?'

'Where are you? I want to picture you.'

'Just sitting on the settee in the sitting room – you know? Got the dog next to me.'

He laughed. 'And I've got Puss on my knee. Aren't we quaint? I bet you're wearing that mirror-work skirt.' He sounded wistful.

She looked at her jeans and said, 'How did you guess?'

'I always think of you in that.'

'Fancy you remembering.'

'I couldn't forget. You're lovely, Tessa.'

'So're you. It'll be great seeing you at home instead of . . .'

'In hospital. Mm. I'll be a person for a change, not an object. Believe me, I'm going to beat it this time.'

'I know you are.'

'Ta-ta, love. See you soon.'

'See you soon, Colin.'

For some time she was motionless. Her mind dwelt on Colin, moved briefly to Nick and the business of the papers – which depressed her, for it entailed making obvious to Nick that she knew he had lied – and back again to Colin. Gradually, the quietness of the house drew her; she found herself listening to it – the hall clock's steady pulse, a far-off humming, the merest rustle and intermittent click, but overall a velvet stillness. I've wasted today, she told herself, hearing the clock, seeing an image of Colin. But not tomorrow. All worry, all supposition, would become peripheral once work was under way. The alarm clock had been set at six for today's early start; it could stay at six; she'd have an early night and make the most of the morning. 'Bed,' she said, dislodging the dog. She returned the telephone and unplugged the television.

There was something to be said for an absent husband, she decided, going to the scullery to collect her radio: she could do as she darn well pleased. Nick objected to a radio in the bedroom.

He also forbade dogs. Every morning, Scrap waited for the man to leave and for the moment when he could rush upstairs and possess the resting place favoured by his mistress. Now, he stood in the bedroom doorway, watching her pad to and fro, wondering whether he had read the runes correctly. 'You're OK,' she confirmed, noticing him. 'He won't be back tonight.' In a single sweep he was across the room and up on to the bed where he lay with a weight so mighty that ten men would scarcely shift him.

When the plumbing fell quiet, the bath drained, the tank filled, soft sounds from outside reached the bedroom. She put out the light, went to the window facing the Green and pulled the curtain back a small way. Mrs Dyte of The Glebe was sitting in her car with the engine running, having dropped off Mrs Joiner of the Old Forge. Their conversation continued through the open passenger door. WI members on their way home, deduced Tessa, and at once visualized Maddy arriving higher up the street at Jasmine Cottage. I won't think about her, she vowed, and to banish the image, quickly closed the curtain and went to a second window overlooking Church Street. This time when she drew back the curtain, moonlight flooded. Opposite was the churchyard; looking to her right (in Maddy's direction) she could just see the east end of the church. Looking to her left she saw two moon-cast cottages and the long shadows of trees screening The Glebe development. Moonlight was everywhere, yellowing stones, greening slates, casting a lake in the road. I'm lucky to be here, she thought, lucky to be me. No problems of mine compare with that terrible hope of Colin's. If you do exist, God, let him recover. She left a slit between the curtains and followed the flaxen line of moonlight over the carpet to bed.

5

The next day went as planned. She made an early start in her studio. Larry, her collaborator on a series of books for children (he provided the text, she the art work), phoned mid-morning and they held a useful conversation. During the afternoon she went for a walk with Scrap and was enjoyably detained on the way home by Mrs Frogmorton of Honey Lane. It was Mrs Frogmorton's dog (now deceased) who had fathered Scrap, and despite the scandal of that incident, for the poodle had burrowed beneath the shared garden fence in order to ravish Aunt Winifred's terrier, Mrs Frogmorton had ever after treated Tessa as a sort of relative. This afternoon, having greeted Tessa effusively, kissed Scrap indulgently and quietened him with a piece of chocolate produced from a pocket of her quilted nylon jacket, Mrs Frogmorton became confidential over the latest doings of her neighbours, an uninhibited young couple recently installed in the cottage which was once Aunt Winifred's. Refreshed by this brush with the outside world, Tessa returned to her work and continued until she was stiff and in need of a drink.

It was not until she was reclining in the kitchen rocking chair, glass in hand, that a certain silence, a certain emptiness, confronted her. Looking back, she knew it had been there all day, hovering spectre-like at her shoulder while she worked, stalking her steps during the afternoon's excursion. Only now, when she had no means of distraction, did it assert itself and demand acknowledgement. Very well; she knew exactly what it was: Maddy's silence, a lack of contact from Maddy – though it was a mystery how a lack of something could exert such ominous presence. You won't hear from Maddy until she and Nick have had a chance to concoct a story explaining how she came to know of Paul's accident, a voice had prophesied at some point during the day, though she had refused to admit it fully into her consciousness. Now she told herself how foolish this was. She and Maddy were not in the habit of seeing each other daily; if a week elapsed before they set eyes on one another again it would be nothing out of the ordinary. But the idea refused to budge and, as if wearily admitting the grip of an obsession, she began to long for a call from Maddy to prove her suspicions wrong.

The next day, Tessa found supplies were low. She decided against driving to the supermarket in Fether-stone – ostensibly on the grounds that it would take up too much good working time, but really because Maddy might call in her absence and thus Tessa would miss having her mind set at rest. Instead, she put the doorlatch on the snib and made a dash for the village shop. By this time, her obsession was sufficiently undermining to allow the most wild supposition – for instance, that Maddy was not only avoiding Tessa, but skulking, out of shame, from the sight of the whole village. Utter nonsense: nevertheless, she could not resist probing Brenda Varney.

'Did you have an interesting speaker at WI?' she asked, emptying the contents of a wire basket on to the counter. 'And half a pound of Cheddar, please.'

'It was that Dusty Dean from Shutterworth – the folk-singer – going on about old songs from hereabouts. Quite interesting, I suppose, if you like that sort of thing.

I was dying to ask why he sings with a hand over his earhole as if he can't stand the sound of his own voice. But I didn't. Seven and a quarter ounce, all right?'

'Fine. And a pound of tomatoes. Good turn out was it? I suppose Maddy was there?'

'Of course; she's president.'

'Um, and a cauliflower. No, I just thought . . .' She had been about to justify the enquiry by saying that Maddy had complained of a troublesome throat on Tuesday morning, but stopped herself in time – Brenda might pass this invention on to Maddy. 'She's such a worker, puts me to shame. I bet she'll be turning out for something else in the village tonight.'

'I dare say she will; the harvest supper committee meeting's tonight. I'm sending me apologies. I've got the post office books to do. Anyway, they know I'm giving the ham. Is that it? Er . . . nine pounds thirty-seven, please.'

'Thanks. Gosh, yes; harvest supper already.'

'And before we know where we are it'll be the Christmas bazaar. Doesn't seem five minutes since the church fête,' said Brenda, who felt her position as shopkeeper was often abused when contributions in the grocery line were required for village functions.

'Yes – time flies. Must dash. 'Bye, Brenda.'

She hurried across the Green and round to the side of her house on Church Street. The door appeared blank and unruffled, untampered with; there was no note stuck in the letter box, no-one had opened the door to wait inside. Scrap barked at her nastily.

'Not yet,' she snapped. 'In fact, you might not get one today.' But by two o'clock she had relented and was in the scullery pulling on her wellingtons.

When Dolly Cloomb arrived in the morning – Friday morning, the day of Nick's return – Tessa forbore to mention the subject uppermost in her mind until she had examined Mrs Cloomb for signs of woe. 'How are you? Everything all right at home?'

39

'Yes,' said Dolly with an extended sigh; 'not too bad I 'spose.' She looked droopy rather than bruised.

'Have a cup of tea before you start.'

Dolly brightened. 'Don't mind if I do, me duck. Shall I pour you one?'

'Thanks. Then I must go upstairs. Got a lot of work to get through today. I wonder,' she said musingly, taking her cup, 'whether we shall see Mrs Storr this morning? She may bring round my tickets for the harvest supper.'

'Shouldn't think so,' said Dolly, maddeningly.

'No?' Tessa prompted.

'She was getting her car out when I went by. That big basket of hers was on the back seat – you couldn't miss it.'

No, you certainly couldn't miss it. Most people, these days, used shopping bags or carrier bags, some pushed trolleys, many relied on a cardboard box between check-out and car boot; only Maddy sported a Provençal basket over her arm. 'Going to Fetherstone, I expect,' said Tessa her mind making much of the fact that Maddy hadn't phoned, as she sometimes did, to ask if she needed anything from town. 'I must get on. Help yourself to coffee and biscuits – give me a shout when you've done.'

She went up to the studio and arranged her tools for work. A great deal of effort seemed required this morning; her mind was sluggish, her hands cumbersome. Force yourself – it's the only way, she admonished. The silence continued to menace her; even so, by the time Mrs Cloomb yelled, 'I'm off, then,' up the stairwell, she found she had been surprisingly productive.

By late afternoon she was listening, not for Maddy's call, but for Nick's. He had arranged to get a taxi from the airport to the university, look in on a meeting there, and give her a call to say when she should drive in to collect him. It was six o'clock when he rang.

'Tessa?'

'Nick! You're late. Shall I come in straight away?'

'Uh, no. Look, I've got one of my postgrad students here. He's got a problem, so I've agreed to give him an extra tutorial in exchange for a lift home.'

'All the way out here?'

'He's not local. He'll be making for the motorway.'

'Who is he?' she asked, playing for time.

'Jim Butcher – don't suppose I've mentioned him. I'm supervising his PhD.'

Suddenly she was enraged, caught her breath, said, 'Sure, fine,' and put down the receiver. He's keen enough on honesty afterwards, so why not be honest while the thing's going on? she asked herself furiously, sitting still as stone with her ears banging.

The phone rang again almost at once. 'Tess; what's up? Look, if you want me home straight away – OK. No problem. Tess?'

She gave a long sigh.

'Is that it? Is that what you want? For Pete's sake, it's not worth upsetting you for – you hear me, Tess? God, I *love* you.'

There was fear in his voice. She'd heard it before. ('Fear of losing Mother' was how she once disparaged it to Maddy.) And now an echoing protective fear made her hurry to be pacifying.

'I know you do, Nick,' she said wearily. 'I'm tired, that's all – been working full tilt. Shall I keep something hot for you?'

'Don't bother,' he said, chirpy again. 'We'll go to the pub.'

'Well, don't let Jim drink too much, as he's driving.'

There was a pause while he recalled who 'Jim' was. 'Right! Don't worry, we'll be eating, not supping. See you later. But, Tess . . .'

'I know, Nick; I won't wait up.'

All this time Scrap, legs splayed, head down, had been watching her from under his eyebrows. He continued this unwavering observation as she continued to sit beside the kitchen window sill with her hand on the telephone. When at last she rose, he took a hopeful step forward, but she swept past without a word, into the hall and out of his sight into the sitting room. Depressed, he remained stock still. Then optimism rose in his breast encouraging him to trot after her in the expectation of life having righted itself. Still she failed to notice him, just sat slumped on the settee, staring at the wall. He was done. This glumness was exhausting: he jumped up beside her, pressed his back into her thigh and buried his head so that he was no longer obliged to look at it.

A painting on the wall had riveted her attention – probably her favourite possession; the one thing, after husband, son, dog, cat, she would risk going back for if the house caught fire. It was a Dorothea Sharp, a study in oils of children on the sands at dusk. She had seen it in a gallery in Stowe and had gone back and back to examine it. Without telling her of his intention, Nick had withdrawn the small inheritance left him by his father and sunk the lot on purchasing it for her. The lot. The only bit of money ever to have come his way without effort and ever likely to. Oh yes, he loves me, she thought.

She got up and went closer to peer at it – the pink-flecked sandy brush strokes, the raised blue-green of gorse put on with a palette knife, the chalky pigment of an evening sky; and the time she first saw the painting on her own sitting room wall came back to her – a calm time, the years of fighting Nick, of willing him to change, years when he vowed to change, behind her. Why had the heat suddenly dissipated? Growing confidence in her work, she supposed, and the fact that every passing year made her son less dependent. Also, because other facets of Nick became more important to her – his tenderness to her dying mother, his delightful teasing of Aunt Winifred. 'Nick's such a charmer,' her aunt would say with fond indulgence. They all loved him. It would have been a loss to others as well as herself if she had turned him out. One or two of his adventures would have passed unnoticed had he not been desperate to confess the moment they were over for fear she would somehow learn the truth and threaten his precious security. For above all things he feared to lose her.

Once, four years ago, he came close to it. It was soon after Aunt Winifred's death when she had inherited the cottage in Honey Lane. Stung by his affair with someone she knew at the university, it occurred to her that with the proceeds from the sale of the cottage she could buy Nick out of Holly House. He had never actually humiliated her before and she was beside herself with anger. 'You've made a fool of me in front of your university friends and you're damn well not getting the chance to do the same on our home territory,' she swore.

The thought of losing her made him frantic. It brought on repeated attacks of the nightmare.

She always knew when he was having it. Moaning, wide-flung arms, kicking, wrestling, would jolt her from sleep and she would wait – knowing it was useless to wake him – for the inevitable choked-sobbed cry. He had recounted what had happened to him so often that when he relived the scene in dreams, she saw it all in her mind's eye as she lay beside him.

Nick, eleven years old, nose in his *Eagle* comic, was sitting beside his mother on the number eight bus returning home after a Saturday shopping trip to buy his new grammar school uniform. His mother was tired but excited. Her son had passed the eleven-plus and was going up in the world. The bus was damp and steamy; it had been raining steadily for days. His mother nudged him – 'Our stop next,' and unravelled her plastic head covering and tied it under her chin. He went on reading. 'Nick, put it away and put your cap on.' Grunting, he folded the comic and stuffed it into a pocket of his gaberdine mac. From another pocket he pulled a damp cap and stuck it sulkily on his head. 'You'll have to help me with all these,' said his mother, becoming anxious for the precious purchases to be carted home in the wet. Off the bus and across the road, both of them weighed down with shopping bags. Then, passing the high retaining wall surrounding the banked-up earth of St Joseph's churchyard, they were felled, lacerated by an onslaught of masonry, buried by a rushing tide of earth: the wall and much of the bank had collapsed. Nick scrambled out severely cut but not maimed. There was nothing to indicate his mother's presence save an inert hand clutching a shopping bag. He scrabbled, yelled. People arrived. Someone raised a lump of bricks. They pulled him away but not before he had a clear glimpse of her, his mother with her smashed-in face. Nick went to live with his dead mother's sister and her family. His father took a job abroad. Nick learned to make himself appealing, to fit in, to get on.

When he woke from the nightmare he always clung to her. 'Don't leave me, Tess. Promise you never will.'

Following the nearly disastrous affair with a colleague, Nick reformed. As far as Tessa knew there was only one further dalliance (with the American air stewardess) the existence of which she may never have known were it not for a sudden spate of excuses and absences culminating in heart-broken confession. Nothing else. Not until now.

A thought, hovering at the back of her mind, swooped like a sparrow hawk. Her warning four years ago rang in her head: 'Don't ever do it to me here, at home. Or that'll be it, Nick; I mean it.' Was his insecurity so great, so unbearable, that he was compelled to test her? Had she, by threatening him, precipitated this crisis? Oh, nonsense, nonsense; things usually happen by accident, she countered wearily.

An overwhelming need to clear her mind made her restless. Looking round, seeing the telephone, she thought briefly and ridiculously of calling Maddy which was her habitual means of safe release. She pulled herself together and dialled the Rectory number. Not that she would confide in Eleanor. It would be an outrage to disturb someone as jejune as Eleanor with a mess like this. She just needed to hear a friendly voice, a voice she could be sure of.

'Oh, hello, Tessa,' Eleanor said with customary enunciation and resonance.

'Eleanor, I wondered whether there were any jobs left to be done for the harvest supper,' she improvised. 'I know I'm a bit of a sloth, but . . .'

'There aren't any that I can think of – though it's nice of you to ask. Madeleine Storr would know, though I dare say she'd have asked you already if there were. You know, Tessa, I sometimes think there are too many chiefs in this village and too few Indians. If everyone insists on organizing, who will be left to organize *for*? No, dear; you will lift our spirits simply by being there. And Nicholas is such a favourite with the old ladies. You're both coming, I hope?'

'I, er, think so.'

'Oh, tell Nicholas he *must*. Otherwise Mrs Bull will want her money back. Do you remember him teasing her last year? He's a naughty fellow, but there's no malice in him. Tessa?'

For a second she couldn't say a word. Tears were pricking her eyes. 'Oh, Eleanor, I'm sure we'll be there,' she got out in a rush. 'Come to tea on Wednesday.'

'Not Wednesday. Wednesdays are my hospital visiting days.'

'Thursday.'

'Yes, Thursday will do.'

'Bring the scrap book.'

'Very well, though I'm sure you've had enough of it.'

'No, do bring it. See you on Thursday.'

Your trouble, she admonished herself as she replaced the receiver, is not getting out enough. Everyone else in this village is involved in something or other, whereas you shut yourself away absorbed in the works of your own hands. It's disgusting. No wonder you get things out of proportion. Good grief, girl, you'll survive! And one day it won't matter a toss. Someone else will be here in Holly House, worrying her head off as though now were for ever and no hereafter. 'Budge up,' she said to Scrap. She clasped him, felt the warm sturdiness, the relaxed slide of skin over bone, and a sensation of safe anchorage stole through her hands, her body, her mind.

6

At half past three in the morning, Tessa woke from a hectic dream and sat bolt upright. Maddy'll come round this morning, she thought, aghast; now they've synchronized their stories, she'll be here first thing.

At her side, Nick was breathing evenly. She lay back, drew the covers up to her face and stared at the paler square of dark made by the window opposite the foot of the bed. She wondered how to conduct herself during the coming exposition. Where should she look? (Anywhere but at Maddy's face.) Should she stand up and appear attentive, or sit at the table and fiddle abstractedly with cutlery? Trying to picture it, she almost cringed under the sheets, embarrassed by the lies that must fall between them. On the whole, Maddy's role seemed preferable: far easier to deliver untruths than to passively receive them. Perhaps she shouldn't go through with it. Escape – no breakfast – let Nick see to the dog – just dress, get the car out and scram. Objections surfaced, such as that Paul might phone and she wanted to know whether his injured knee was improving, that there was shopping to do, and something else which she couldn't for the moment recall . . .

When she woke again it was because Scrap was pounding the bottom of the door. It was nine o'clock.

Nick was still oblivious, worn out, no doubt, by the travelling yesterday. It would be mean to disturb him. She slipped a dressing gown over her silk pyjamas, tied it at the waist, pushed her feet into mules and noiselessly turned the door knob.

'Shh,' she warned the dog. He harried her heels as she padded along the corridor and down the stairs.

'Want to go out straight away?' she asked, undoing the back door.

He stepped back. Of course he didn't; his morning dog biscuit was overdue. She tossed him one, and when he had bolted it, shooed him outside. The day, foggy and cold, seemed hardly worth getting up for.

'Hello, cat,' she called, going through the kitchen. A newspaper was stuck in the letter box. She pulled it out, hesitated, then drew back the bolt and put the doorlatch on the snib. Then she began to make life cheerful with marmalade on the table, and butter, and soon a pot of tea and slices of toast.

She was eating toast and reading the newspaper when the knock came. 'It's unlocked,' she called nervously. The door opened and sunlight bounced in – or so it seemed – in fact it was Maddy in livid yellow donkey jacket, navy cord trousers and bright blue muffler.

'Crumbs,' said Tessa with spontaneous appreciation. 'That's new.'

'Don't say it,' cried Maddy, unwinding the scarf and flinging herself on to the nearest chair. 'I'm in the doghouse; well in – door locked and bolted, key thrown away.'

'Overspent again?'

'Been handed a vurry tight budget. Got to stick to it for months, or until Robert calms down.'

Robert uncalm was hard to imagine, though more than once Tessa had seen him long-faced and exasperated by further evidence of his wife's extravagance. Maddy could not resist good clothes. A new colour, a new shape, seemed able to convey itself to her through

47

the ether; she got 'a feeling' about an unseen garment and set off to track it down in one of the shops that had previously proved reliable. She had similar hunches about articles for the home. A bare patch of wall, an empty shelf, a hitherto unregarded corner would suddenly cry out to her for a particular embellishment; to discover just the thing and leave it unpurchased would be a cruel denial of destiny. Sometimes, returning from a shopping trip, she would stop off at Holly House to show Tessa her latest acquisition and then, her courage ebbing, beg her friend to accompany her to Jasmine Cottage. 'Come and see if it's right. If it's wrong I'll take it straight back; I trust your judgement, Tessa.' Robert, who worked mostly from home as a designer of computer systems, would come out of his study to watch as Maddy, head on one side, carefully positioned her new trophy. If she had been really reckless, he might invite her into the study to inspect the bank statement. Once, following a prolonged binge, he confiscated her cheque book and credit card for a month and doled out the housekeeping.

'You must have been bad if it's come to a budget,' Tessa said. 'Cuppa?'

'Thanks. Actually, I've brought these.' She pulled two tickets out of a pocket and put them on the table.

'How much do I owe you?' asked Tessa, handing her a cup.

'Six quid.'

Tessa took her purse from her bag on the settle and found the money.

Maddy folded it away. 'I presume Nick'll be coming' (she mentioned him smoothly), 'but Robert said, call at Jasmine Cottage either way. I shall have to go early, of course, so you'll be company for him – and you can save me a seat.'

'That'll be nice, What time shall we call?'

'Oh, ten or five to. It's only a step across the road. Let's hope Robert's cheered up by then.'

'I've never known him put out for long.'

'That reminds me. I never told you, did I? – whew, it's cosy in here!' – she unbuttoned the coat and shrugged her arms from the sleeves, thus revealing a favourite method of clothing her upper portion: silk shirt and sleeveless pullover, today's version in toning shades of blue.

Tessa, feeling like one of those creatures born without fur or feathers, secured the front of her dressing gown, which had slipped, and waited to hear what it was that Maddy had never told her.

'A group of us from the creative writing class bunked off last Monday night. We drove into the city to see *Dangerous Liaisons* – hated it, actually, but afterwards we went for a drink, and guess who was in the pub?'

Tessa didn't say, though her anticipation was acute.

'Nick! He was a bit down, I thought; but he'd been visiting that friend of yours in hospital. Isn't his a desperately sad case? Only forty-nine, Nick said.'

Tessa looked into her empty cup. She could certainly spike that one if she chose to, but on the whole thought it more comfortable to keep quiet.

'Thing is, Tessa: will you ask Nick not to mention it to Robert?'

Surprised, Tessa raised her head.

'Well, seeing as I'm on this budget, supposed to be watching every penny, I'd rather not confess to a night out. I can just see him totting it up – petrol, cinema, food, drinks . . .'

'So there was food, too?' she asked, following closely, and then thought what a fool she was, pouncing on an irrelevant detail. And it had visibly boosted Maddy's confidence.

'Absolutely! Steak and chips and gungy gâteaux. So tell Nick to keep schtum, there's a sport.'

'Oh – right,' mumbled Tessa, thinking that of course Maddy would not be so crude as to underline the crux of the matter ('So that's how I knew of Paul's accident – Nick told me about it while we were chatting.'); she had far too much delicacy and taste to over-egg the

49

pudding; it was enough to have established the opportunity. 'You didn't care for the film, then?'

'*Vile*,' said Maddy, and was about to enlarge when the sound of a door banging overhead, very soon followed by the clomp of feet on the stairs, caught her attention.

Tessa wondered why they had stopped talking. It was as if their brains had atrophied, or the atmosphere in the kitchen become too laden to move a muscle.

Their silence brought Nick to an abrupt halt in the doorway. 'What's up?'

'I've brought the tickets for the harvest supper,' Maddy said, her voice cracking as though her throat had dried. Her eyes were like flames, darting at him. (Tessa guessed she was stricken with doubt over his ability to match her own deftness.)

Hesitating, they teetered on the edge of collapse. Maddy dropped her eyes to the tickets on the table while Nick and Tessa looked to her with the frozen terror of forgetful actors whose prompter has lost her place in the script. Horror rose, and Tessa foresaw her warm and friendly kitchen with its old wood and treasured china, its homely smell of polish, dried flowers and toast, its air of steadfast stability underscored by the faithful hall clock, filled with the mess and carnage of wrecked relationships; and the role she would then be obliged to play – abused wife, betrayed friend – the mantle of which drew suffocatingly close. It was an outcome at all costs to be averted. She clenched her hands beneath the table and took control.

'You'll come won't you Nick?' she asked lightly. 'To the harvest supper next Saturday? Robert wants us to call for him because Maddy's got to go early to organize things, of course. According to Eleanor Browne, the old ladies have set their hearts on your being there.'

Relief broke over Nick's face. 'Sounds as if I've no choice. Can't disappoint my public. What's on the menu?'

'Oh, the usual – you know how conservative people are,' said Maddy in a rapid discharge of breath.

The phone rang. 'I'll get it in the sitting room,' said Nick.

'If it's Paul, call me when you've had a word,' Tessa shouted after him. Then to Maddy, 'Shall I make us some coffee?'

'Good Lord, no. I'll let you get dressed.' She stood to button the coat and wind on the muffler. 'Anyway,' she said with a self-deprecating grin, 'when I've been to the market, I've a pile of notices to deliver to my ladies. Got to stump up entries for the county exhibition. Your Aunt was such a wiz at jam-making; we haven't won a thing in the cooking line since.' She put her hand on the doorknob. 'Come round to me next week.'

'OK. I'll see how the work's going and give you a ring.'

'Oh, this fog! 'Bye, Tessa.'

' 'Bye, Maddy.'

7

Rose Fettle, in stout shoes and gloves, went briskly down her garden path. At the gate she met Gail Partridge from Number Eleven. Gail was shoving her fourth child along in a pushchair with number three hanging on to the handle. The fifth, and as yet unborn, protruded between the unbuttoned edges of her grazed leather coat. And never a hint of a husband, said a voice in Rose's head. 'Hello, Gail,' she said aloud, reprovingly.

Gail, who had already passed by, did not look back. 'Arternoon, Missus Fet-ul,' she all but spat into the still, chill air.

Three lads were kicking a ball in the road with

desultory Saturday afternoon aimlessness. Picking her way through the scrummage, Rose crossed over and went in at Dolly's. In the Cloombs' front room a sports commentator was expounding men's business, his confident tone assuming for his sex a natural possession of the airwaves. Rose curled her upper lip and went along the side of the house to the back door.

Dolly was standing in the kitchen with her coat on.

'Ready?' asked Rose.

'Dolly?' yelled Arthur Cloomb over the voice of the know-all on the television.

Dolly, looking apprehensive, went along the passage; she did not venture inside the living room, but hung in the doorway and looked back to her waiting friend.

'I'm goin' woodin', Arthur.'

'What?'

'Me and Rose is goin' woodin'.'

'That weren't our Barry in the kitchen, then?'

'No. Rose. Shall I bring you a cup of tea before I go?'

'Tea!' scoffed Arthur.

When, after a decent interval, nothing further was said, Dolly gingerly returned to the kitchen. 'Let's be off, quick.'

'Is your Barry coming over, then?' Rose asked, once they were clear of the Cloomb gateway.

'He promised to put in a word with John this dinner, about ending Arthur's ban.'

'That's a pity.'

'Oh, I dunno, Rose. At least it gets him out of an evening – gives me a chance to get near the fire. Makes me sick the way he hogs it.'

'But while he's banned you ent worrying about closing time.'

They had turned out of Orchard Close, crossed over the end of the road leading to the chicken farm and were now going along Fetherstone Road by the side of the allotments. Ken Tustin, chairman of the parish

52

council, was hauling a bag of manure from the back of his pick-up.

'Good afternoon, ladies.'

'Good afternoon, Mr Tustin.'

'We shall see you at the harvest supper, I hope?'

'All being well, Mr Tustin, though the tickets is dear.' Rose was glad to have made this point.

'I'm sorry you think so, but I'm assured it'll be a very ample spread.'

They walked on and Dolly, who had been thinking, said, 'I still owe you 50p for mine, Rose.'

'You can pay me next week. I was in the shop this morning, and that Mrs Burrows was complaining the tickets weren't dear enough. "Oh dear, Miss Browne," she says, "you'll never get enough to mend the church roof at this rate. They ought to be five pounds at least." Five pounds! How they think the old 'uns could afford to pay that out of a pension, beats me. Always the same in this village, the newcomers want everything to be in aid of summat, never just for folks to enjoy theirselves. Not like the old days, eh, Dol?'

'You're right there, Rose,' said Dolly obediently. The subject was one of Rose's hobby horses.

'Never mind. It'll soon be our do — the Christmas whist drive. Should be better than ever this year. Ooo!' She sucked in her breath and put a hand on Dolly's arm. 'You see that?' she hissed. 'Over there.'

Following Rose's direction, Dolly looked to the fields on their left. A horse raced across the horizon then vanished in the dip containing the Peck farmhouse. Even from this distance its rider conveyed abandonment. She wore no hard hat, but a scrap of scarf from which her hair streamed, and she leaned over the horse's neck, her arms embracing it. 'Wild,' said Rose.

After a pause, Dolly made the conventional remark concerning Phoebe Peck, the remark automatically uttered by all those with roots in this place whenever an example of Phoebe's eccentricity was observed (for the Peck name was an ancient name and much revered in Wychwood). 'It's Roy and them kids I feel sorry for, and old Sam and May.'

'He should never have married her,' said Rose, making the correct reply. 'It's a wonder all them Pecks don't rise outta their graves in Wychwood church-yard.'

In the church, Eleanor and Timothy were preparing for Sunday's services. Eleanor was refreshing the flowers. It had been decided not to put in new flowers this Saturday, for next week the church would be comprehensively decorated for the harvest festival. The flower ladies had been granted a Saturday afternoon off and Eleanor had promised to top up the water and remove any seriously deteriorated pieces. Just in case, she had brought with her a few blooms from the Rectory garden.

Timothy was putting everything in order for the morning. There was much to do: notices to arrange on the pulpit book-ledge, little scraps of paper to mark places in the books on his desk, the numbers to be changed on the hymn board, the silk marker of the lectern Bible moved to mark the first lesson.

It was dim in the church and the lights were on in nave and chancel. It was chilly, too, though both were warmed by the other's industrious company. Timothy liked it particularly when only he and Eleanor were here. Sometimes the flower ladies fell out – not that they shouted or behaved in an unseemly manner – but he could always tell when there was an upset by the change in Eleanor's voice. Eleanor on her own was all busy, decorous calm. She reminded him of their mother going about the traditional Saturday afternoon tasks in church. He and Eleanor had been bred to this work as their parents were before them; Anglicanism was in their bones. All over England, in village churches and town minsters, he imagined a similar loving duty performed – a scene that had gone on for

54

centuries and would go on still when he and Eleanor were dust. These thoughts fathered cheerfulness; so much so that he began to hum. But before he had hummed the first line of 'Far down the ages now', a woefully unpleasant catarrhal noise marred his tunefulness. Timothy turned towards his sister and said urgently in the muted tone they employed in God's house, 'I think this awful mist we've been having's got into my tubes.'

'Oh dear,' said Eleanor, straightening up. 'I do hope it won't affect your voice for tomorrow.' Timothy's voice, as a servant of the liturgy, was an instrument both held in awe.

Timothy crossed the chancel, inclining his head to the altar as he went, and pushed up the shutters covering the organ console. He pressed the switch, waited until the bellows were full, then struck a bass C.

'Mmumumm,' sang Timothy, taking the note's measure. Then, standing tall, expanding his chest and rounding his lips to produce mellow Anglican roundness, intoned, 'O Lord, open thou our lips.'

'And our mouth shall show forth thy praise,' Eleanor dutifully responded.

'Ye-es,' said Timothy judiciously, and to make sure, struck a bass G. 'O God, make speed to save us.'

'O Lord, make haste to help us,' quavered Eleanor.

'Well?'

'I can detect no fault, Timothy. But to be on the safe side, I'll make you up a gargle. That usually clears the passages.'

'Indeed. Thank you, my dear.' His happiness restored, he closed the organ and returned to his desk, though for the time being, to give the voice every chance, he eschewed humming.

Ten minutes later, their quiet industry was rudely interrupted. The church door was flung open and booted feet strode in.

'Thought I'd find you here as I couldn't raise you in the house,' called Celia Westbrook, modifying her penetrating tone not one whit in deference to the Almighty.

Sister and brother winced and looked at her in stern enquiry.

'Come to ask you t'make up the table for lunch tomorrow. Got the Laughtons coming' (she referred to the local MP and his wife), 'and the Ferribys from Castle Belford, and Daphne Addinbrook with current swain. Drinks from twelve-thirty.'

Eleanor shot Timothy a glance. Celia never troubled to disguise her opinion of the Rectory pair as fit only for lunch or dinner party make-weights. As far as Celia was concerned this was precisely what the Rectory was for – to house a couple possessing the essential qualification of gentility conveniently close at hand. And, since they were poor, Celia assumed they owed a duty to their stomachs to be obliging.

The Brownes had come to dread these summonses to dine. They were often made uncomfortable by the assumptions of fellow guests and the off-handed treatment of their hosts, not to mention Major West-brook's temper which grew yeastier as the wine flowed and prompted an airing of his uncharitable views concerning the fitness of certain sections of humanity to live. And the food, as Timothy pointed out, simply wasn't worth it – tough meat, lumpy gravy, frozen vegetables, bought puddings. Eleanor agreed and wondered how Celia got away with it.

Now, rather flustered, Eleanor cast her mind over Plan A (which was that one or other of them was indisposed), and rejected it in view of Celia standing there observing them in rude health. Plan B (that they had a prior engagement) would serve but required some on-the-spot refinement, for no-one could seriously suppose a parson would travel far on a Sunday between morning service and evensong. Inspiration, like a blessing, descended. 'I'm afraid it's impossible, Celia. We, too, expect friends for lunch.'

'Oh?' said Celia sharply. 'Who?'

The woman is shameless, thought Eleanor, and so deserves this prevarication. 'No-one you know. Church people.'

Celia frowned. Was it worth widening the planned extent of her luncheon table? she wondered. The Brownes, she knew, were well-connected; their father had been a canon, and there was a colonial bishop somewhere in their background. But Browne glory was a faded glory, and 'church people' these days could mean anything – ghastly blokes with accents like coal miners or people with the right accent but hideous bolshie ideas. God, no; bound to be a horrid mistake. 'Right,' she said, slapping a jodhpured thigh, 'your funeral.' With which she turned and strode away.

Silence crept in as the noisy departure faded, stole towards them in Celia's vacated footsteps. With a look of guilty dismay, they moved instinctively towards one another until they were side by side in the chancel. Eleanor, still holding a pair of scissors, thrust her free clenched hand deep in the pocket of her long cardigan. Timothy's hands were clasped on his cassocked stomach. Their stillness lent them permanence, like that of the carved knight and Elizabethan benefactress set in stone in the sanctuary, and their opposing shapes –hers angular, stick-like, his smooth and round – were belied by the uniformity of their attitudes; both slightly inclined their heads, both looked to the altar. Their eyes dwelt on the Lamb of God emblazoned on the altar frontal.

'He will forgive us,' said Timothy.

Celia Westbrook, having retrieved her bicycle from where she had thrown it against the church porch, was about to mount when she caught sight of Rose Fettle and Dolly Cloomb coming through the churchyard hauling two fallen branches.

'You've saved me a journey,' she declared. 'I was about to go to Orchard Close. Will you do me a couple of hours tonight or first thing tomorrow morning? Got a dinner for ten this evening and people for lunch tomorrow. It's the washing up.'

Rose let go of her log. 'You know we don't do evenings or Sundays, Mrs Westbrook,' she reminded her employer severely.

'I should have thought *you'd* be glad of the work, Mrs Cloomb. You can speak for yourself, I take it?'

Full of fright, Dolly dropped her branch and stepped back.

'It's against our principles,' said Rose.

'Oh, good Lord!' Celia was disgusted. 'I don't know what's happening to people these days. Well, it was you I was thinking of – it'll still be there waiting for you on Monday morning. I shall just chuck a cloth over the dinner table and serve lunch in the billiard room.' With which she jumped on her bike and pedalled to the gate.

Gravel spat up at the wheels' spokes. She did not dismount at the churchyard step, but braked, free-wheeled down with a bang, then turned left and vanished behind the yews.

When she had gone, Dolly said, 'I suppose it'd kill her to wash up herself.'

'Wouldn't get 'em clean if she did, me dear; though I wish she'd scrape 'em and put 'em to soak. But she ain't been brought up to it,' Rose said, making allowance. 'Still, we'll hear a bit of gossip. She's always full of it after a do.'

'Ooh, yes. That Mrs Addinbrook's had her picture in the *Echo* again. Wonder if she's coming.'

'Bound to be, Dol. They're thick as thieves, her and Mrs W.'

8

Celia Westbrook, bicycling back to the Manor, was passed by Maddy Storr's nippy little car travelling in the opposite direction. Maddy had completed her delivery of notices to WI members living within the village, and had two remaining, one for Phoebe Peck at Peck's Farm and one for Mrs Davenport at Hilltop Farm. She had decided to leave the more outlying farm, Hilltop, till last. Whizzing along Church Street, she passed the familiar places, principally Holly House, the Green, Peck's Lane and her own home on her right, the church, the Rectory, the village hall and Old School House on her left. Then, having paused at the crossroads, she turned right into Fetherstone Road, drove past the allotments and turned left on to the Peck's Farm track.

It was rutted and pot-holed. She grimaced and dropped down to second gear; into the dip, and the track widened, became a yard surrounded by farmhouse, stables, cowshed and barn. A collie came skidding to a halt, ground its belly into the dust and barked dementedly. Maddy remained in her car and honked the horn. Roy Peck looked out of a barn doorway, raised an arm in greeting and hollered for his dog. Reassured, Maddy took one of the notices from her basket on the passenger seat and sprang out of the car.

'Good afternoon, Roy,' she called, making for the house.

'Arternoon – bit of a dull 'un,' called back the invisible Roy.

'Phoebe about?'

'Aye. Somewhere.'

Maddy rapped on the door. After a substantial pause, the door was opened abruptly.

'Oh, it's you,' said Phoebe.

'Can I come in? I've brought something to show you.'

Phoebe led the way.

The kitchen looked set for a jumble sale, pots and dirty plates piled high in the sink, the table covered in clutter – food, piles of washing, an iron, horse tackle, newspapers. Children's toys and a heap of boots littered the floor, dogs' baskets and a cat filled the inglenook.

'Sit down, then,' said Phoebe without indicating where. Her face stayed blank.

'We've missed you at WI these past few weeks. Problems with the children?'

'Oh, no. Roy's mum has 'em most of the time.'

Mr and Mrs Peck senior lived in a newish bungalow on Peck land further along Fetherstone Road. Roy's younger brother and family also lived in a modern home, built at the farm's extremity two miles distant. Phoebe and Roy and their two daughters occupied the old farmhouse.

Maddy felt kindly towards Phoebe; village people could be so nasty. When Maddy was newly arrived in the village, Phoebe was still Phoebe Mullins, a groom at the livery stables in Steeple Cheney. (Her ancestry, rumoured to be gypsy, remained unknown; if the Pecks had discovered who the Mullinses were, they had not troubled to pass on the information.) At the livery stables, Phoebe was constantly in trouble with her employer for taking horses out for illicit gallops. Dismissal followed the warnings, and arson (committed at a safe distance from the horses) followed Phoebe's dismissal. Nothing was proved, but there were no doubts in the district as to the fire's perpetrator. Then Phoebe had some sort of breakdown characterized by wild and frantic behaviour, and became a patient in a mental hospital. After her release, she went from farm to farm in search of work. Eventually, Roy Peck took her on and within a year married her. Contrary to local expectation, their first child was not born until two years later. Her pregnancies disturbed Phoebe's fragile equilibrium necessitating return visits to the hospital, and even now, every six months or so, Phoebe went away for 'a rest'. It was a blessing for the two little girls that the Pecks were such a close-knit family, Wychwood folk had frequent cause to remark.

'I've brought you some information about the county competition,' said Maddy, handing Phoebe a leaflet. 'There's a creative writing section this year. It can be prose or poetry . . .'

'That's what you're studying on Monday nights, isn't it? Leastways, that's what Robert said you was doing when Roy saw him in the Lion the other night.'

'Well, yes. But I've got enough on my plate, and I expect I'll show willing in the arts and crafts section. Anyway, between you and me, I'm not too wonderful at creative writing.'

'No?'

'No. It was you I had in mind. Why not enter one of your poems? Or write a new one. Let's see – what's the title . . . ?'

'Oh, that'd be no trouble. When I'm in the mood they come easy as thinking.'

Phoebe's poems were a well-known phenomenon in Wychwood. What had prompted her to start writing, nobody knew, though Maddy thought Tessa's suggestion – that she had been encouraged by a hospital therapist – sounded likely. In her capacity as Mrs Roy Peck, wife of Sam Peck's elder son and heir to Wychwood's most ancient dynasty, Phoebe was often called upon – when able – to hand out prizes, declare functions open, or deliver a vote of thanks. She usually took the opportunity thus afforded to air her latest work. Such was the awe attaching to the name of Peck (the Pecks had owned land in Wychwood since

61

records began; there was a Peck's Lane in the village and a portion of the wood was Peck's Wood) that Phoebe's poems were heard with evident respect and only disparaged in private. (To real village people, the Pecks were Wychwood's finest; whereas the West-brooks, whom the uninitiated took to be the premier family, were mere interlopers, having bought Manor Farm – or 'bought the village' as Celia liked to refer to the purchase – after the war to give Major Westbrook an occupation.)

'"My Longest Day",' said Maddy, finding and reading the title.

'"My Longest Day",' echoed Phoebe, and at once went into a trance.

'Not very inspiring, is it?' Maddy commented, becoming nervous at her companion's prolonged silence. 'But at least it's vague – you could write about almost anything.'

Still Phoebe said nothing, just sat at the side of the table, her legs spread out straight and propped on the heels of her boots, her hands curving emptily in her lap. Long lank hair framed her weather-beaten face. From a distance, Phoebe appeared a slip of a girl, but closer inspection dealt a shock; the face was lined, ravaged, the eyes sunken, lost.

'Phoebe?'

Phoebe sighed. '"My Longest Day". I've had 'em, I suppose – longest days. Yes, I've had 'em all right, but I kept falling asleep.'

With horror, Maddy suddenly guessed at some of the particulars of Phoebe's longest days – needles, white walls, possibly even a strait-jacket.

'I dunno if I'll write about 'em, though.'

'Ah, well,' said Maddy, casting round for a cheerful topic. 'You and Roy are coming to the harvest supper on Saturday, I take it? And Sam and May. Who's going to baby-sit?'

'Keith's eldest girl. Yes, whole family'll be there. Tell you what,' she said, brightening, 'I could give the vote of thanks, if you like. I could easy write a poem about harvest.'

Maddy made a prevaricating sound, but Phoebe seemed struck by the idea. 'Yeah – the combine going round and all the rabbits running out . . . It'd be good, that. But there's only a week. I'd best get on with it.' And to Maddy's amazement, she pushed aside some of the clutter, pulled open a drawer and smacked a notepad and biro on to the table.

'Just – just a short one, then,' Maddy conceded weakly. 'They'll be full of food; we don't want them to drop off.' She looked at her watch. 'Heavens, is that the time? I've got Hilltop Farm to visit yet. Look, do come to WI on Tuesday,' she said, going to the door. 'I'll come and pick you up if transport's a problem.'

'Oh, no, it's not that. It's just I forget.'

'Really? In that case I'll give you a buzz.'

'A buzz?'

'A phone call to jog your memory.'

'Oh,' chortled Phoebe. 'When you said "buzz" I thought of a bee – suits you, don't it; a busy little bee?'

'Mm,' said Maddy. 'See you on Tuesday.' She waved and went out and got into her car. 'Sod,' she said, switching on the engine.

She crashed the gears while she was backing and then accelerated too fast over the ruts. The car bumped and jarred her spine. Adopting a more ponderous speed, she became philosophical. At least it perked her up, she thought. And if anyone smirks on Saturday, I'll just quell 'em with one of my looks.

After Celia Westbrook's departure from the churchyard, Rose and Dolly were not inclined to retrieve their burdens immediately, for their fallen branches, possessed of a tendency to twist while being dragged along, were tiring to handle. Rose said she would just pop over to husband Jack's grave and check the freshness of his dahlias, and Dolly clomped over the grass and stood glumly in front of her parents' resting place.

Then Rose joined Dolly and they moved along the rows, reciting names and recalling old times, bemoaning examples of neglect and sniffing at ostentation.

'"Mother of Susan and Reginald. Sorely missed",' quoted Rose. 'Huh, that's nice. Never came near her; not even when she was in the 'ospital.'

'Your mum and dad's is wearing well, Rose.'

At length they trooped back to the path. They had begun, rather wearily, to gather up the branches when Tessa came through the yard from the kissing gate.

'That looks hard work. Let me give you a hand,' she called. She hauled up both branch ends and tucked one under each arm.

'Mind you don't hurt yourself, me dear,' said Dolly.

'Two'll be too much,' protested Rose.

'I'm balanced like this. Dog's a nuisance, though. When we get to Holly House I'll drop him off if you can hang on a minute.'

They waited meekly at the bottom of the Holly House steps, glad of her help, though renewing their protests as soon as she reappeared.

'Are you both coming to the harvest supper?' she called conversationally as they went along, wheelbarrow fashion.

'We are, aren't we, Rose?'

'I dare say. Three pounds is steep, though.'

'Is it?' asked Tessa, who had thought it a bargain.

'It's very hard for folks with just their pension to lay hands on that sort of money.'

'Dear me, I suppose it is.'

When they had crossed over Fetherstone Road and turned into Orchard Close, Dolly explained that both branches should be taken into her back yard where her son, Barry, would eventually chop them into logs. Getting them through the gate of Number Seven and along the side of the house was quite a performance. They shunted to and fro, calling advice to one another above the blare of the television. Dolly, who had detected a similar though fainter noise going on within

Holly House said conspiratorially, 'Can't get 'em away from it on a Saturday, men.'

'My Jack didn't waste his time; he always went down the allotment,' Rose said, preeningly.

'Phew – all right here?' Tessa let go of the branches.

'Aye. And it were good of you to give us a lift. Weren't it, Rose?'

'It were. Ta kindly, me duck.'

They watched her go. 'She's good hearted, that one,' said Dolly.

'Pity she's so thick with *her*.'

Hurrying back along the pavement, Tessa decided that Orchard Close, built to rehouse the poorer cottagers whose ancient dwellings by the end of the war were no longer fit for habitation, had been conceived in a spirit of meanness. She imagined the officials responsible searching out the cheapest bricks, the thinnest wood, the most pinched and depressing design. Its very location was punitive, away from the heart of the village on the far side of Fetherstone Road – a striking contrast to the welcoming setting of Wychwood's other modern development, the 1970s cluster of executive homes built on the former Glebe Farm near the Manor and Rectory.

Her mind was so taken with these thoughts that she failed to register the car coming along Fetherstone Road until it was almost level with her. With a screech of tyres it stopped dead, and Maddy wound down the window.

For Maddy it had been an instantaneous reaction. Out of the blue and quite out of place, stood Tessa, and the possessive curiosity reserved for one's closest friends dictated an immediate checking of the driving mirror and hard pressure on the brake.

'What're you doing here?' she called. 'Something up with Mrs Cloomb?' – for Dolly Cloomb's troubles, like those of most villagers, were common property.

'No.' Tessa went to the car and leaned a hand on the window ledge. 'I found her and Mrs Fettle struggling to lug home some wood – gave them a hand. You're not still delivering notices?' Taken by surprise, they had fallen at once into their easygoing way, as if the horror of this morning's meeting had never happened.

'I stopped a bit at Phoebe's.'

'She all right?'

Maddy looked doubtful. 'Not as good as a few weeks back. I've a nasty feeling she's on the slide again.'

'Tch. Poor thing.'

'Oh, and I landed myself in it. I wanted to persuade her to enter one of her poems for the county competition. She wasn't too keen about that, but suddenly latched on to the idea of writing a poem for the harvest supper. What could I say? I mean, it brought her to life; she started composing then and there. Trouble is, it'll be such a downer – or worse, some of that lot from The Glebe'll start sniggering.'

'You'll handle it. I can just see you – clapping your hands, starting the music. You're a born stage manager. Trust yourself.'

Maddy mock-punched Tessa's arm. 'Thanks, chum. See you.' She put the car into gear, wound up the window and speeded off.

They parted, cheered. Over the years they had developed a knack of finding the right few words to boost the other's morale; a two-way boon, as invigorating to the creator of the fortunate phrase as to the one who had needed the boosting. Tessa's step along Church Street was almost jaunty, and her mind, in tune with her raised spirits, took an optimistic turn. The happy thought occurred that it was utter rubbish to suppose Maddy could be having an affair with anyone, because Maddy simply didn't have time. At what point in her frenetically busy schedule would she fit it in? And how, given there was no sign of her work-rate flagging, would she find the energy? Because – let's face it – sex took energy: all that wanting it like mad, dreaming of it, scheming for it, enduring hideous inconvenience for it; Tessa felt limp just totting it up.

66

Take today, for instance. Maddy would have been on the go from the moment she stepped out of bed this morning, tidying Jasmine Cottage as she always did first thing, then rushing over to Holly House, and on to Fetherstone market to fill her basket with good fresh produce for the wonderful meal she would set before Robert tonight; then delivering all those notices and badgering people into doing things they'd never dream of doing left to their own devices: it all took energy, certainly more than Tessa's idea of a day's worth. And if any small thing remained undone in Wychwood this Saturday night, you could lay money on Maddy Storr being out there doing it.

'You're wasted here,' she had once said to Maddy in the early days of their friendship. 'You should get a qualification and go into management – lick some organization into shape.' Later, on reflection, she regretted the remark, which seemed to belittle both the village and her friend whom Tessa visualized as a bright thread weaving through the lanes and byways, lending colour, drawing people in. She regretted the remark even more when she learned how the Storrs had come to live in Wychwood.

Born into a poor family, Maddy had left school at sixteen and started work as an office menial. Within eight years she rose to become the managing director's personal assistant (and married Robert and suffered two miscarriages along the way). Her boss, who liked a long lunch hour and an afternoon on the golf course, left an increasing portion of the work to his capable assistant, and during the five years preceding his retirement, Maddy alone managed day to day affairs. Things went well – she was fulfilled, the business prospered – until the arrival of his successor, a new broom. This younger man preferred to keep control of the tiniest detail, and of women in the office he had but two requirements – that they be decorative and breathlessly deferential. Maddy's final undoing was to recommend for dismissal a spectacularly slothful (and incidentally beautiful) member of the typing pool, for whose favours, it later transpired, the new boss was ambitious. Maddy's life was made miserable until she admitted defeat and resigned.

The move to Wychwood was an escape engineered by Robert to save his wife from the resulting savage depression. And it was an instant success. There were a few early hiccups, typified by Maddy's comment in the village shop about the cheek by jowl circumstances endured by the former occupants of her new home, but Tessa was able to be helpful here, warning her as to whose toes she might be treading on, and where to guard her tongue. Maddy soon got a feel for village politics, and set about utilizing her talents for Wychwood's benefit. As the years passed, she proved to be more than an inveterate committee woman. She could sniff out human need like a pig truffles. When Annie Seymore, a widow living in a poor way in Peck's Lane, needed treatment for breast cancer, it was Maddy who organized a rota of people willing to drive her to and from the city hospital, thus saving Annie a day spent in an ambulance travelling half-way round the county collecting and dispensing patients, and from the loneliness of submitting to an ordeal without a friendly hand to hold. And it was largely due to Maddy, after years of grumbling and worry about the state of the church tower, that sufficient money was at last raised to repair it. Wychwood would be a sadder place without her.

And Tessa, shut up in her eyrie, would be sadder, too. Maddy's garnered titbits brought spice to her sometimes solitary existence. It was a heady pleasure being Maddy's confidante. Of course, were he so inclined, Robert would be the main beneficiary; but though endlessly willing to serve as the committee woman's obliging husband – setting up the trestle tables, putting out the chairs, manning the bottle stall, taking tickets at the door – the human minutiae involved did not fire his imagination as a new computer system did or the latest digital recording of a piece of chamber music. When his wife was in the mood to reflect aloud on all that she had heard and seen, Robert would say, 'Mm', and 'Really, dear?' and reach for the latest issue of *Gramophone*. Soon, the telephone would ring in Holly House. 'Tessa – doing anything? Fancy a drink?'

Her thoughts were full of Maddy as she ran up the steps to her door. She was quite startled when it opened before she had time to put a hand to it, and Scrap dashed out barking and Nick said: 'Where've you been? Fantastic news . . .'

'Arsenal five, Southampton nil?' she asked flippantly.

'Nil nil draw,' he snarled. 'No – listen. Colin's home. I've just phoned the hospital. They said he's improved enough to go home. Isn't that bloody marvellous? Only a week or so ago we'd given up hope.'

She went past him into the house. 'I know. Colin rang while you were away.'

'He *rang*?'

'I'm sorry.' (Trust me to be the one apologizing, she thought.) 'But you were back so late last night, and then we overslept . . .'

'I'll ring him straight away. We could go there tomorrow.'

'Shut *up*, Scrap – all right, come here.' She bent down to acknowledge and fondle her dog and to give herself time to think. It came to her that she might test her new-found optimism. 'Oh – Nick . . .'

'Yes?' He was going through the hall and did not turn round.

She went after him. 'I thought you and I might do something tomorrow.'

'We will. We'll go to Colin's and Sophia's.' He went towards the telephone.

'I mean just us. We could drive out, have lunch somewhere. Maybe go to a film. We've seen so little of each other lately. If you could get away early on, um, Monday night, we could go to Colin's then.'

She'd got his attention now, all right. He put down the receiver. 'Didn't I say? Monday evenings are out until further notice. Course development team meetings – it's the only time everyone can make it.'

'No, you didn't.'

'Sorry. Look, aren't you burning to see Col?'

'Of course I am.'

'Well, we'll do something together next Sunday.' After a moment, he began to dial.

She was angry. Not hurt, not disappointed – angry. She thought of their lies and smiles. How dare they make a fool of her, discount her from their calculations? An image of Maddy jumped into her mind and juddered there like a puppet; and all her admiring affectionate thoughts jangled in her ears like a magpie's screech. She stared at her husband as if through glass, seeing him, but cut off from him. While she was watching, he suddenly clapped a hand over the mouthpiece and hissed, 'Cow!'

Jolted, she went and stood beside him, and he held the receiver at an angle which would allow her to overhear. Sophia was shouting to someone – not to Nick, but to someone with her. 'Are you sure? Because it's been nothing but people people people from that blessed place ever since you got home. You're supposed to rest, dar-ling.' ('Darling' as pronounced by Sophia sounded ominous.) 'All right. But don't blame me if you have a relapse.' (They jerked back their heads, looking at one another in horror.) 'Nick? He says it's OK. But look, I've no time to cook. I'm exhausted, utterly exhausted. You can't imagine what this is like for me. I mean, don't run away with the idea that he's not still practically helpless.'

'Of course, Sophia, we don't expect a thing. We'd just like to see you, er, both. About three?'

'OK. But don't stop long. And no talk about papers or theses. And I hope you're not going to ask him to write a reference.'

'Wouldn't dream of it.'

'That one with a beard did. Can you believe it? My husband at death's door and the man comes pestering for a reference.'

'Shocking. But we're old friends of Col's and we'll be good as gold, promise. See you tomorrow.' He crashed down the receiver. 'Well! You heard her? – "relapse", "death's door" – Col was sitting there for Pete's sake. God, that woman. If only . . .'

She walked away, out of the room, through the hall. 'If only Colin hadn't met Sophia.' They had all said it, she and Nick, Viv and Jerry. When the children were small, they four plus Colin and Lucy had been close friends; but Lucy had left Colin, had taken the children and gone off with a visiting Australian professor. Years later, Colin met Sophia at a conference in Budapest. How romantic they had thought the couple's escape together, and how thrilling the exotic Sophia when she had only a minimal knowledge of the English language.

It was terrifying how life could run away with you, thought Tessa. One moment you were dealing with a minor catastrophe, such as your wife leaving you, or your husband having an affair, and the next, wham – all hell had broken out. See where life had landed Colin: ridden with cancer and tied to a termagant. As for Sophia escaping from the drab tramlines of totalitarianism: life had stuck her with an ailing husband and his cold, unfathomable friends.

Nick was still complaining when he joined her in the kitchen. 'And it'll be hell tomorrow, I'll bet; impossible to get a word with him.'

'She's terrified,' said Tessa.

'What?'

'Sophia's terrified of losing him, terrified of being marooned here without him.'

Nick was struck dumb. Evidently it needed thinking about.

Opening the fridge door to peer inside, Tessa noticed that her hand was shaking. I'm weak as a kitten, she thought, closing the door and going to sit on the settle. And it won't do. A great deal of strength must be summoned in aid of Colin by tomorrow afternoon.

'What are we going to eat?' asked Nick, noting her retreat from the fridge.

'I was going to make a fish pie' – she sighed – '*am* going to make a fish pie. But I need a cup of tea first. Make me one, will you?'

He went into the scullery and filled the kettle. 'We could go to the Lion,' he called hopefully. 'The food's not bad at the weekend. Or the Green Man in Budbrook if you fancy something posh.'

Any excuse to get to a pub, she thought. But perhaps it wasn't such a bad idea. 'The Lion suits me fine. Debbie White does the cooking on Saturdays.' She felt better suddenly. 'I'll go and have a bath.'

'I'll bring up the tea.'

Heavens, how cosy we sound, she thought, going upstairs.

Maddy's cheerfulness was of even shorter duration than Tessa's. She had travelled no further than a quarter of a mile when her sinuses swelled and her eyes smarted. At first she thought it was a reaction to something sprayed on the land and closed the car's air vent; then that it was the onset of a cold; and then, as a hard lump formed in her throat, that it was particularly virulent indigestion. But, God, no. She was crying. Any second now horrid mascara-stained tears would cut disastrous channels through her immaculately applied blusher and glitzer, then splodge on to her brand new jacket. Thankfully, there was a lay-by ahead. She pulled into it and switched off the engine, leaned forward to squint in the driving mirror and pull a tissue from the glove compartment. A corner of tissue applied to either eye, some careful through-the-mouth breathing, and the danger was averted. She sank back in her seat and blew her nose.

It was no good. Dammit, she was going to bawl.

Within seconds her eyes had become taps and her mouth and nose as rheumy as old Ben Sculley's when he'd had a few and lost his key and spent the night in the village green telephone box. Through the flood she had a vision of Tessa leaning in at the car window, lifting back a hank of hair, gazing at her, dark-eyed and earnest. Her face was not as pale as usual, there was a gleam in her cheeks from the exertion of hauling Dolly Cloomb's wood. Typical, that, of Tessa. She'd help anyone. She was so natural, so kind on the spur of the moment – nothing planned, just immediate warm response. 'Oh, Tessa,' she growled through her teeth, as if trying to ward her off. Then, despairingly, 'Oh, help, Tessa.'

When it was over, she blew out her breath and blotted her face. Then she examined herself in the driving mirror, spat on a tissue and rubbed at the gunge beneath her eyes. Dare she go on to Hilltop Farm looking like this? It was nearly dusk, and she wouldn't stop, just shove the notice through the letter box.

Fortunately, when she got there, Hilltop Farm was deserted. Ten minutes later she had arrived back in Wychwood. A street lamp lit the corner of Fetherstone Road and Orchard Close, and a second lamp shone through the murk outside the village hall opposite her own home. She drew up a little way before Jasmine Cottage, but left the engine running.

There was a light on in the sitting room. Robert had not yet drawn the curtains. It hit her forcibly that she didn't want to go in. Of course, she must, there was nothing else for it. The first, busy part of the evening didn't loom too threateningly – preparing the meal (paupiettes of beef, a salad of endive and chicory, orange soufflé), eating it, helping Robert wash up. So long as she could keep busy she was all right. It was the next bit she dreaded, when Robert would expect her to go and relax in the sitting room while he made and brought in the coffee. Then he would play his latest acquisition, a recording of some Bach sonatas if she remembered correctly. And there would be no getting away from it then – she would have to nod and smile, look frankly into his face which was very dear to her but which, because of her guilt, had started to frighten and depress her. After a bit, he probably wouldn't mind if she picked up her tapestry frame. And then she wouldn't have to look at him, and it might stop her counting the hours . . .

She looked swiftly at the dashboard clock. How many hours left now? Fifty-two. Maybe fifty-one and a half. Her stomach tightened and her pulse quickened. Oh, God, she was at it again. She crooked her left index finger, put the knuckle between her teeth and bit. Hard. Harder.

9

Nick switched on the outside light. It was misting with fine rain, not heavy enough to warrant an umbrella. Tessa ran down the steps. Behind her, the door slammed, then Nick was at her side, linking arms. They turned the corner of their house and there was the Red Lion glowing across the dismal expanse of the Green – she sensed how the sight raised his spirits and his eagerness as he pushed her ahead of him on the path cutting through the greensward. Single file, they arrived at the pavement along the pub's frontage, crossed it and made for the front entrance where a light illuminated the announcement: 'John and Linda Maiden, licensees'. The opening door wafted a frowsty smell of stale tobacco and ancient beer spills.

Neither John nor Linda were in the lounge, though John's voice could be heard in the public, hectoring some unfortunate. 'And only when Barry's here to keep an eye on you, right? Till the end of the month, then we'll see. But first sign of trouble and you're out, mate – don't say you haven't been warned.'

In the lounge, the sharp, cleansing odour of a log fire cut through the staleness and faint fatty smell of chips. Nick jangled the bell on the bar top and called 'Shop!' and at once John appeared, rubbing his hands, re-arranging his face. 'Nick!' he called in an altered tone, very much mine host. 'How's yourself? Oh, and the lovely Tessa – we *are* honoured this evening. And what is your will, kind sir?'

'Pint of the best, John, and have one yourself. Tess?'

'Um – brandy and soda, please.'

Tessa looked round.

There were people eating already, a couple she knew by sight and nodded to, and four strangers. Beyond the tables set out for diners was an area of easy seating and low tables for drinkers. From here, someone raised an arm and jabbed a gnarled finger in her direction. 'Tessa Hodson!'

'Hello, Mr Bultitude,' she said, going over to him. Years ago he had been the bailiff on the Rochford Estate and so knew her father, but Tessa remembered him as the retired man who had helped her aunt with the garden.

'Sit down, sit down,' he spluttered.

Wishing 'Good evening' to his companions, she sat down. On a week night Mr Bultitude would take a drink in the public, but tonight, in honour of Mrs Bultitude and two elderly neighbours, he had put on his good jacket and polished shoes for the lounge. Mrs Bultitude – a stout, well-preserved woman – and her female friend were both dressed up for the occasion and eyed Tessa's old sweater askance. Mr Bultitude, too, seemed struck by Tessa's appearance. Ignoring her question as to his health, he again smote the air with a finger. 'Spangled,' he got out. 'You're spangled.'

Tessa raised a hand and felt how surprisingly damp her hair was, and Mrs Bultitude burst out with a disclaimer. 'Don't be silly, Fred. It's just rain.'

'She's spangled,' the old man insisted, and his hooded eyes were alight with some inner imagining whose essence Tessa caught though she remained ignorant of the particulars. She smiled, and their eyes locked. For a few moments, fanciful images danced between them, elusive, fleeting, dew-beaded, while in their ears Mrs Bultitude poured scorn. 'The things he says. You'd think he'd gone soft in the head – spangled! Fred, June's ready for another, aren't you, June? Another packet of crisps, Harry? Nuts, then? Some photos came this morning of our grandson getting his degree. Pass us me handbag, Fred; perhaps Mrs Brierley'd like to see 'em. Fred!'

Mr Bultitude tore his eyes away and groped for the bag. Mrs Bultitude snatched it and rummaged within.

'Here. That's Toronto University. And here's our Pat. Get 'em in, Fred, June's gasping.'

Tessa took the photographs and Mr Bultitude collected the ladies' glasses. ('Nick's getting mine, thanks.') 'Very nice, Mrs Bultitude. Pat must be proud.'

'Paul getting on all right, is he?'

Tessa reported Paul's rugby injury. But Mrs Bultitude had not tricked herself out this Saturday evening to waste time on other people's relatives. At the earliest opportunity she cut in and reverted to the subject of her grandchildren. Tessa leaned back in her chair. Her eyes followed Mr Bultitude's rather stooping figure making slow progress to the bar. She recalled how upright he had once been standing at Aunt Winifred's side in the School House garden to bemoan the presence of couch grass in the rockery.

'It'll all have to come out, every stone.'

'Yes, it'll have to be thoroughly cleaned. Leave it to me, Miss Hodson.'

'So obliging, and such a superior sort of man to be helping one in the garden,' Aunt Winifred had confided with a sigh. During the school holidays she always baked scones on Mr Bultitude's afternoons and insisted on his eating them fresh out of the oven with a pot of tea in her kitchen. Once Tessa caught her standing behind the curtain peeping at Mr Bultitude working in the flower border.

As Mr Bultitude edged through the small crowd by the bar, Tessa's eyes fell on Nick at the group's centre. He was lolling back, sometimes turning his head to gather John's attention, mostly holding forth to those about him. He was a picture of relaxed charm, one hand in trouser pocket, the other holding a pint glass, a foot propped on the bar rail. A roar of laughter went up. Nick lowered his head modestly to his glass as though an ability to draw eyes and raise uproariousness was of no particular matter to him. In fact, Tessa knew they were as food and drink; for wherever he was, whatever the circumstances, Nick lived to seduce. For this purpose he could adapt his manner instantly; become grave for a ceremony, mean and sharp for an academic argument, conciliatory in support of a vice chancellor obliged to decide between the claims of fiercely partial groups, intimate for the shyly sensitive, naughty for those who liked a bit of fun. By his elbow stood her brandy and soda. Murmuring 'Excuse me,' she got up and went to claim it.

His eyes shot to her at once as though he had been desperate for her to come and rescue him.

She smiled and sipped her drink.

'Take a look at the menu,' he urged. 'John recommends the trout.'

'Trout, then. No chips.'

'John – ah, good man: two trout, one with chips, one without.'

'Peas and tomatoes?' asked John, pencil poised.

Tessa nodded. 'And a bread roll, please.'

Nick took Tessa's arm. 'Do you know Martin and Paula from The Glebe?'

Tessa found that she did vaguely. Martin was the early morning driver of the Jaguar car.

'Crazy man drives to London every day,' Nick reported.

77

Tessa expressed her amazement and asked Paula how her children liked Fetherstone school. Nick, feeling that the zest had gone from the gathering, cast his eyes about the room for a further challenge. 'Shall we go and get a table?' Tessa suggested, before he could slip away.

'Yes, let's,' he agreed, gratefully squeezing her arm. 'Thought I was trapped there. Martin tends to go on a bit.'

While they were waiting for their food, Mr and Mrs Frogmorton came in and placed an order at the bar. They greeted the Brierleys, then took the last free table on the far side of the fire. Their presence prompted Tessa to marvel over the changed eating habits of the past seventeen years. When she first came to live in Holly House, no-one of standing dreamed of eating in the village pub. Fetherstone's Ram Hotel and Tudor Café were the only acceptable local dining places. Aunt Winifred had never set foot in the Red Lion, and until a few years ago, Tessa was sure the same could be said of her equally respectable neighbours. Yet here sat the Frogmortons, preparing to eat among smokers and drinkers, put off not at all by drooling music piped – mercifully quietly – through loudspeakers perched on the picture rail. Recently, Eleanor Browne had remarked to Tessa on the modern-day acceptability of the pub – not in so many words, but obliquely, by reporting Mrs Erskine's recommendation of the Red Lion for lunch. Tessa could tell that Eleanor was not entirely reassured by Mrs Erskine's example, even though Mr Erskine was a retired and locally revered physician; her close scrutiny of Tessa's face betrayed her desire for a further opinion. 'Nick and I have a bite there now and then,' Tessa told her calmly. 'Debbie White does the cooking on Saturdays.'

'Really?' exclaimed Eleanor, evidently convinced. 'I must say it seems a splendid idea. Think of the electricity saved, and the bother. When there are just the two of you, cooking can be a frightful fag.'

She had looked wistful Tessa remembered, resolving to take Eleanor out to lunch one day soon.

John came to their table bearing the preliminaries – knives and forks wrapped in paper serviettes, and a small tray containing salt, pepper, tomato sauce, vinegar, mustard. 'Tartar sauce'll come with the trout,' he promised.

Behind the bar, a door opened and Linda sidled in. She crossed her forearms on the bar top and over them rested her bosom. Nick saw her and waved. She fluttered her fingers at him keeping the rest of her still. ''Evening, Linda. Chef's night off?' called Nick, and to Tessa he said in an undertone, 'Good job, too. A bit heavy on the grease is our Linda.'

Then Debbie White bustled in with two over-filled plates and set them down on the table. 'Mind, they're hot.'

Nick smacked his lips with relish then jumped up to refill their glasses.

When they had eaten, Tessa put her hand over his to secure his attention and proceeded to pass on what Colin had told her concerning the whereabouts of the departmental papers. 'He wants you to get them if you can – without upsetting Sophia, that is. But promise to be careful, darling. Don't give Sophia cause to have one of her fits; it would be so bad for Colin.'

Nick was excited. 'Thank heaven! If I can pick them up tomorrow, we'll have plenty of time to study them and make a good case for the department before the funding council's inspection.'

'When's that?'

'Oh, mid-December.'

'Then you've loads of time. They'll be other opportunities if it's dodgy tomorrow. Do promise not to risk upsetting Sophia – for Colin's sake.'

'Sure. Don't worry. Pud?'

'No thanks. I'll have a coffee, though.'

'This is jolly nice, right on our doorstep,' Nick remarked, after ordering two coffees and a portion of treacle pudding at the bar. 'Nothing like your own friendly local.'

'Isn't it?' she agreed, guessing he was storing the evening up to regale his colleagues with – the friendly atmosphere, the homely fare, the honest traditional bitter.

While they were drinking their coffee, the Bultitudes and party got up to go. Tessa waved, and Mr Bultitude came over for a few parting words. 'Mind you come over and see my chrysanthemums. My "Yellow Raga-muffin" won first prize at the horticultural a few years back. I don't bother with shows these days, but they're still worth a look. Some rare beauties. Your aunt used to admire them.'

'A nice old buffer,' said Nick when he had gone.

'He was Aunt Winifred's gardener. I think she was sweet on him.'

'Go on. Like another brandy?'

'No thanks, but you go ahead.'

Whereupon he scraped back his chair and hurried to join the men lined up at the bar hanging on to their drinks and staring into Linda's cleavage.

Seeing Tessa left alone, Mrs Frogmorton beckoned her. 'Draw up a chair, dear. How are you? How's my little rascal?'

'Greedy. He ate the cat's dinner today before I could stop him.'

'Just like his father. My poor Benji was such a character, the dear fellow, though your aunt didn't care for him.' Then, lowering her voice she confided, 'Terrible about the Harrison boy.'

'Is it?'

'Oh yes, dear, haven't you heard? You know he went off to college? – let me see – it was the same time as Paul, I believe. Well, he's back. Expelled, or whatever they do to them. And you should see him – shaved head and a long bit sticking out of the middle, earrings, paint on his face, knees hanging out of his trousers. And, my dear,' – she craned her face closer and

80

mouthed – '*the smell*. Mrs Dyte was in the village shop when he came in for some cigarettes. It was overwhelming. Brenda wondered whether she ought to fumigate.'

'Poor Mrs Harrison.'

Mrs Frogmorton pursed her lips. 'I'm not too sure about "poor". There were goings on in that house while those children were growing up – according to Marjorie Hume who lives opposite, and she should know. I wouldn't be at all surprised to hear they have trouble with the daughter.'

'Dear me. Have your neighbours settled in yet?' Out of the corner of her eye, Tessa was watching Linda who had sauntered from behind the bar and was now moving between tables collecting glasses. She looked sulky. Her former audience had dispersed and regrouped in a corner where Nick, in the course of an impromptu and animated lecture, was pointing out the finer details of an old sporting print. The chaps were agog; it was marvellous what you could pick up in a pub, they would no doubt confide later to their wives. Perhaps Linda resented the competition.

Mr Frogmorton had been bursting to get in a word for some time, but his wife was unstoppable and it was not until Tessa rose to go that he seized her arm and said urgently, 'Never mind that chap's "Ragamuffins". Come and see my "Korean Sunrise". Twelve inch diameter, some of the blooms. Fellow came the other day – said he'd seen nothing like 'em in forty years of visiting Kew. There now. Don't forget.'

'Good gracious, Mr Frogmorton, I'll bear it in mind.' Having bade them good night, she went over to Nick and said ruefully in his ear, 'I'm fit to drop. Give me the key. You stay on if you like.'

He wouldn't hear of it. Enough's enough, his sly wink said, but he'd better say good night to the Frogmortons.

She waited at the door, saw him slip an arm round Mrs Frogmorton's shoulder, heard her pleased throaty chortle.

It was still drizzling outside. They picked their way over the narrow path to the road then ran hand in hand to the house. Nick leapt up the steps ahead of her to unlock and hold open the door. She went to pass him, but he caught hold of her, tipped up her chin under the beam of the carriage lamp and kissed her moisture-speckled eyelashes. 'That were a reet good evening,' he said happily. 'Weren't it, our lass?'

'Oh-ah,' she said.

10

The church bells were ringing. They woke Tessa, but not Nick, in their bed in Holly House. Tessa rolled on to her back and paid attention. On some Sunday mornings with a full complement of bell ringers, including – and this was vital – Davey Partridge and Mr Frogmorton, the peals were exemplary; the chimes spaced evenly, the changes achieved smoothly. But this was not always the case. Sometimes, with a depleted, less expert team, the peals rang joltingly and Nick and Tessa lay holding their breath as the ringers lost the beat and a lurching pause followed discordant collision followed lurching pause. Not this morning, though. Tessa counted six ringers pulling sonorously. With confidence she pictured them, shirt sleeves rolled, feet firmly planted, under the reliable leader-ship of Davey Partridge and Mr Frogmorton.

At her side Nick stirred, made a noise like a rusty hinge, gasped, 'Shunday,' and went back to sleep. The Brierleys had always been Sunday morning lie-abeds. Features of past Sundays flitted through her mind, love-making to the accompaniment of church bells and Scrap's furious pounding of the base of the door, cosy talks about the future, giggles, cups of tea, the odd row. She propped herself up and squinted at him. 'Love you,' she silently told the only visible bit of him – some black hair, a pink ear and a portion of unshaven chin. A pang hit her; she would love to nuzzle close, but now, for the time being, it wouldn't do at all. She turned away and lowered her feet to the floor.

She had just finished dealing with Scrap and put the kettle on when the phone rang.

'Get over here, quickly,' said Maddy. 'I've unlocked the front door.'

'What? I'm not dressed.'

'Then get dressed, booby. Only hurry. You'll be sorry if you don't. Come quietly – oh, and leave that blasted dog behind.'

It was a surprisingly pleasant morning, Tessa found as she hurried along Church Street a few minutes later in track suit and trainers. She opened the Storrs' gate noiselessly, as instructed, and likewise the front door.

The string of five cottages from which Jasmine Cottage had been fashioned was still evident inside. Numbers One and Two, with upper storey partly removed and stone work and roof rafters exposed, formed a stunning sitting room; Number Three was now a spacious hall and small cloakroom, Number Four a dining room, Number Five a kitchen. Upstairs there were two bedrooms and bathrooms and Robert's large study. From the hall, Tessa saw Maddy appear in the kitchen doorway, a finger to her lips. Tessa slipped through the dining room and joined Maddy at the kitchen window overlooking the garden.

She caught her breath. Two miniature deer were feeding busily, and for the moment fearlessly, in the shrubbery. 'Muntjaks,' she breathed. (Years ago several of these had escaped from Woburn Park and their descendants were spread widely over the Midlands.)

'They've come out of the woods. Been here ages. Aren't they perfect?'

'Like fat little hoofed dogs. They're eating Robert's verbena.'

'They're hungry,' Maddy said indulgently.

They watched for a time in silence. Then Maddy went to the fridge, poured two glasses of grapefruit juice and rejoined Tessa at the window. 'Had to call you. I knew you'd like them.'

'Quite right too: I'd have been upset if you hadn't.' And she thought, It was me she needed to share this with. Their closeness seemed extraordinary. I love them both, she told herself; Nick *and* Maddy.

'Had breakfast?' asked Maddy after a time.

'Of course not.'

'I made some croissants last night. I could put some in the oven.'

'You made croissants for heaven's sake? What's wrong with the supermarket?'

Maddy shrugged and turned away. 'I was feeling fidgety. D'you want some or not?'

'Certainly do.'

Soon, heady perfume suffused the kitchen as yeasty buttery flour turned golden, and steam floated from the coffee pot. It brought Robert on the scene, beaming with anticipation. Luckily the muntjaks had gone, frightened away by a dog barking; it would have been churlish to draw attention to the chewed verbena.

'Poor old Nick, fusting in bed,' said Tessa, licking her fingers.

'Take him a couple of croissants, if you like.'

'Oh, thanks.'

Sunlight fell over the end of the table. She reached out her hand and watched it play over her spread fingers. Maddy and Robert went on talking.

A few words, and I could wreck this tranquillity, she thought. She imagined the startled silence, the gabbled words, Maddy's flight. And herself returning to Nick, snatching back the bedroom curtains, letting in the truth.

Truth be blowed! She turned her hand over and sunlight fell into her palm. I'll keep them both, she vowed. Blind, deaf, credulous, I'll hang on and keep them both.

11

On the journey into the city they fell silent, as though touched in advance by the pall which invariably fell over their spirits on entering Colin's house. Tessa thought of the days when the large Edwardian semi had cast a different spell, its chaotic rooms brimful with life, with children and their belongings, with Colin's and Lucy's friends. Pictures, sad as old photographs, flitted through her mind: the conservatory full of wine bottles and glasses and people stomping to jazz records; friends crammed elbow to elbow round the dining table while Lucy passed the food and voices grew argumentative; earnest talk in inappropriate places – on the stairs, over the kitchen sink, or in the bathroom as someone bathed the children. Colin, she remembered, had seemed always to preside, listening, saying little, looking lazily amused. Like a comfortable cat, Tessa thought. This was how she had painted him – nursing the current tabby in his tall-backed leather armchair, Colin's face feline, the cat's face Coline. The portrait had delighted him. He took it to his room at the university and hung it over his desk, where, Nick reported, it became quite a talking point. Cat-like, too, were Colin's sharp bits, usually safely retracted under purring amiability. His soft interjections (Colin never needed to raise his voice) were sharp enough to wound and might have done so were they not uttered smilingly with self-deprecation. Everyone listened carefully then hastened to incorporate Colin's view into their own line of argument; for Colin was one of the university stars, one of the few with an international reputation. Nick had often remarked what a fool Colin was to stay with the department, though Nick's prestige, like that of every other member of the department, had been enhanced by Colin's glory. According to Nick, Colin was self-sacrificing; too kind for his own good. Tessa thought rather that he liked an easy life.

It was the fact that the department was likely to lose Colin without Colin's volition that made recovering the papers he had been working on during these past months of illness so vital. Colin's signature on plans for the department's future was certain to impress the coming inspection panel and might ensure that the department did indeed have a future, an outcome which could not be taken for granted in today's climate of financial stringency with departments competing for scarce funds and some likely to go to the wall. The word 'redundancy' had been dropped during anxious deliberations. Such were Nick's thoughts as they drove along Marlborough Avenue and pulled on to the forecourt of Number 118.

They waited for some moments outside the front door, not looking at one another, until it was opened by a little fat dark woman with a faint moustache. 'Come in, please,' she said briskly, and then, indicating the drawing room: 'In there.'

It had the air of a waiting room. Colin was sitting in his fireside chair, a rug containing a curled cat over his knees and covering his legs to the floor. He smiled wearily but did not speak. Sophia was leaning forward on the sofa, her body hunched over the focus of her energy – a long, very thin cigar. Without stirring or looking up, she mumbled, 'This is Magda, my friend, who has come to help. I can do nothing. I am depressed.'

They shook hands with Magda. Tessa, touching Sophia's shoulder as she passed, went to kiss Colin and kneel by the side of his chair.

'Poor old Sophia,' Nick said, sitting bravely down beside her. She allowed him to take her hand. 'That's bad – depression.' She shrugged and withdrew her hand, and Nick shook his head ruefully at Colin. 'But it's good to see you in that chair again, Col, me old mate.'

With an effort Colin said, 'Good to see you two.' His clothes – they both recognized the sweater – and the familiar setting revealed an unwholesomeness about him that had not been evident in the asepsis-centred hospital. There was a greenish tinge to his skin and eyes. 'How's Paul?'

'Sick to be missing the rugby. You know he dislocated his knee?' Nick spoke rapidly as if offering an unnecessary reminder. 'We were looking forward to watching him play against our team next Saturday.'

'He sounds cheerful enough,' Tessa amended. 'Full of news about a revue he's written and directing for the end of term.'

'That's great. There's a letter from Annabel.' Colin's eyes went to an envelope propped on the mantelpiece. 'Read it, Tessa.'

She collected the envelope with the Australian post mark, opened it and began to read. Now and then she laughed and read passages aloud.

Bored with their interest in the doings of Colin's daughter, Sophia yawned. 'Darling, get these people some tea,' she urged Magda. 'Myself, I can't move. This depression is paralysing.'

Tessa and Nick took this in and carefully refrained from looking at one another.

'An old friend?' Nick enquired while Magda was out of the room.

'We met about six months ago. She, too, married an Englishman.' Sophia spoke as if their common misfortune had bonded them.

Over cups of tea, they talked generally and uneasily. Sophia and Magda shared long brooding glances. Colin managed to contribute a little, but Tessa recalled with alarm how much more talkative he had been over the telephone last Tuesday evening and how far stronger his voice had sounded. Instinctively, they avoided the subject of his supposed recovery, fearing it was too fragile a thing to mention and inspection might fracture it.

At last Magda rose to leave and leaned over Sophia to embrace her fulsomely. When Sophia did not rise, Nick saw Magda to the door.

'All right if I have a quick browse in the study?' he asked, remaining in the doorway on his return. 'There's something I'd like to look up in your Frei-hoffer, Col.'

Sophia got stiffly to her feet. 'I'll help you.'

'Oh, please . . .'

'It's no trouble.'

Colin sank his head and pressed a knuckle to his brow.

'Oh, don't bother today, Nick,' Tessa called urgently. 'Come and talk to Colin. Work can wait, for heaven's sake. Come on,' she insisted.

Nick returned and drew up a chair near to Colin.

'Academics!' Tessa said witheringly to Sophia, who lowered her large bottom on to the sofa's arm with an air of only temporarily settling herself, and lit another cigar.

It struck Tessa that there had always been tempor-ariness about Sophia's manner of comporting herself in this house, perching on chair-arms, squatting on the very edges of seats, standing in doorways as if hanging about for something better to turn up. She had made no impression on the place. Apart from Colin's familiar crannies – the area around the fireside chair and the study along the hallway – the rooms felt unlived in. It was the same upstairs. Once, in a temper because Colin had disparaged her frocks, Sophia had seized Tessa's arm and dragged her up to the large front bedroom. The bed and much of the floor were strewn with garments – frilly, drapey, silky stuff of the sort which usually encased Sophia's ample body. Further garments hung from open drawers and jutted through the gaping doors of the wardrobe. There was a suitcase on the bed, another on the floor, and in the bay window, stuffed carrier bags lay propped against the legs of the dressing table. The room appeared ravaged by someone in speedy transit. 'Look,' Sophia had cried, ripping off her dress and cramming her quaking flesh into another one very similar. 'He said it was tarty. What does this mean? I can tell you – it's too sexy; he's afraid of other men looking at me. Well, there was a time when he liked me sexy.' (No doubt, thought Tessa, when Sophia had been several stones lighter and had not bleached her near-black hair.) 'They can all go to Oxfam and then he'll have to buy me new ones. Serve him right, the bastard.'

Now, Sophia was expressing agreement with Tessa's comment. 'Uhuh – academics! Make your flesh creep. This morning that man John Elliott came round wanting Colin's help with his thesis.' She shuddered and drew deeply on her cigar. 'I threw him out,' she growled, exhaling.

'She certainly did,' confirmed Colin.

There was an awkward silence during which Tessa dealt Nick a look warning: For goodness sake forget about the papers for today; Colin can't stand another row. And Nick, with a grim smile, communicated understanding.

'Puss-puss,' Colin sighed, stroking the cat's head with a crooked finger. 'She feels jolly nice.'

'Bloody cat won't leave him now he's back,' said Sophia.

'I don't want her to,' said Colin.

Tessa and Nick contemplated the cat and, for want of a safer topic, commended its devotion. After a time, Tessa thought she ought to be sisterly. 'Poor you, Sophia. What's made you so depressed, do you think?'

But the question only infuriated. 'Do you hear her?' she demanded of the two men. 'She asks what makes me depressed! *He*' (she jabbed the cigar at Colin, looked scornfully at Tessa) 'is like a baby – he sicks, wets, poohs. But *I* am not a nurse' (the cigar returned passionately to her bosom). 'Remission – phh! They don't know what they're talking about. He should be in a hospital where they can take proper care of him and make him better. How can he get better here? This is a house, for God's sake. It's my house, where I live, and with all these messes and smells I can't forget this thing for one minute. I shall go mad with misery.'

Tessa leapt to her feet. 'Colin, come back with us,' she urged, crouching at his feet. 'You'll be fine at Holly House. I've nothing much on at the moment,' she said, flinching inwardly at promises she had made to her editor. 'Nick'll make you comfy for the journey. And there's a very good doctor in the village, if you're worried. Do come,' she implored, remembering to add diplomatically, 'and Sophia can have a good rest.'

Colin swallowed painfully. 'I couldn't. You mustn't worry. I'll pick up in a day or two. And if I don't – well, Sophia's right – I'll be better off in hospital.' He grinned. 'Anyway, I couldn't leave Puss.'

'Bring her. Tell him to come, Nick.'

'Look,' Colin said seriously, 'I really shouldn't like it. I want you and Nick to think of me' – he looked up and fixed his eyes on a photograph on the mantelpiece of a younger healthy Colin – 'like that.'

'When he was beautiful,' Sophia said bitterly.

Tessa looked across the room. 'Why don't I come tomorrow and sit with Colin while you go out somewhere? It might cheer you up.'

'I have no energy. Anyway, Magda will come.'

'Magda is very good,' Colin managed, and dropped his head.

'We're tiring you; we'd better go.' Nick rose and went to him. 'Give us a ring, old chum, when you're up to seeing us again. Make it soon.' As he clasped his friend there was a hurried murmured exchange – 'Sorry, Nick.' – 'Don't worry. Better luck next time.'

And Sophia, jamming the cigar between her teeth, summoned sufficient energy to haul herself to her feet and see them off the premises.

On a quiet stretch of road back to Wychwood, Nick

groped for Tessa's hand. She gave it to him and they grasped hands tightly until oncoming traffic obliged his to return to the steering wheel.

12

Half past eight on Monday morning and the exodus from Wychwood was virtually complete – the children gone off to school, most husbands and many wives departed for work. The Glebe was deserted save for Gloria Hennage in Number Three, whose inability to report for duty in the reception office of the Fetherstone doctors' surgery was due to a heavy cold. Only retired folk, leisured and unemployed folk, mothers of young children and those few workers who got their living from the land or worked at home (their own or in someone else's), remained in Wychwood this Monday morning.

Nick Brierley had left Holly House soon after eight, grumbling because he had a nine-thirty seminar.

'You won't be wanting dinner tonight, I take it,' Tessa had said.

'Er – that's right. Course team meeting this evening. Don't wait up; I expect we'll adjourn to the pub.'

Unusually, Robert Storr had gone from Jasmine Cottage. He would be away from Wychwood for a couple of nights attending a business conference.

The farms – Hilltop Farm, Thornton Lodge Farm and Elm Tree Farm on the outskirts of the parish, Manor Farm and Peck's Farm within the village proper – had been centres of industry since half past five this morning, drawing men from their beds in cottages and council houses to milk cows, feed pigs and start up tractors. In the village shop and post office, Brenda Varney was helping the postwoman sort letters and parcels, and in the Red Lion, a yawning Linda Maiden was chucking a bowl of soapy water over the floor of the gents'.

Rose Fettle and Dolly Cloomb had arrived at the Manor. They let themselves in through a door in the first of two extensions jutting at right angles from the ends of the original Elizabethan house. From the front, the property appeared unaltered, a long and beautiful building of cut grey stone and mullioned windows. The extensions were at the rear, the first arm containing domestic and farm offices, the second, at the far end of the house, a billiard room, a swimming pool and changing rooms for the tennis court. Most villagers were familiar only with the interiors of these modern extensions. People on farm business called at the first extension, people attending events got up by the Westbrooks in support of the Conservative Party or the local hunt were shown to the billiard room in the far extension. Some villagers admired these new facilities, particularly the swimming pool whose design reminded them of their Spanish holidays. Others were appalled. Tessa, learning some of the details, worriedly enquired whether the ancient interiors remained intact. Eleanor Browne had re-assured her: oak panels, oak beams and oak floors with Turkey carpets, were undisturbed – though perhaps dustier than in former days when Lady Hawthrop employed a full retinue of servants.

Members of both Dolly's and Rose's families had worked for the Hawthrops, men on the farm, women in the house, and both families had occupied tied cottages. When the Hawthrop family died out and the estate was sold to the Westbrooks, Rose and Dolly had been glad to secure work at the Manor. It was loyalty to a tradition – to the house and to their own forebears – rather than tender concern for Mrs Westbrook that made them always put the requirements of the Manor first and those of the Rectory and Holly House second. Mrs Westbrook, in fact, was a dreadful employer, always trying to detain them beyond the hours she was prepared to pay for with a bribe of a few dry sandwiches and a pot of weak tea. They had become wise to her ways.

'We has to go home for dinner, Mrs Westbrook. Dolly's got Mr Cloomb to feed and I've got to take in me washing' – or a neighbour's parcel or a delivery of coal. Such excuses served to indicate that they would depart at the end of the morning and oblige their employer if she so wished by returning in the afternoon for a set number of hours with clearly defined rates of pay. 'A bit bolshie' was how Celia Westbrook sometimes described Rose Fettle.

The trouble, from Celia's point of view, was a lack of village women both willing and able to serve. Besides Rose and Dolly there was only Debbie White (wife of the major's ploughman) who before her marriage had worked in the hotel trade and could be called in to cook or wait at table when the need arose (though lately the Red Lion, showing typically bad form, had seduced her from the Manor with exorbitant rates of pay), and poor old Mrs Bull who had given many years' service to the Manor but was now too fat and lame to tackle anything more arduous than silver-polishing and ironing. Every Wednesday afternoon Mrs Bull heaved her weight over the threshold of her cottage opposite Holly House and, propelling a shopping trolley for support, wobbled up Church Street to do duty at the Westbrook ironing board. Sometimes, when her lameness was particularly bad and the Manor desperate for laundered linen, Mrs Westbrook called to collect Mrs Bull in her car. Tessa had stood at her kitchen window to watch and marvel as Celia man-handled Mrs Bull, who, unable to bend her swollen knees, required pushing and hauling on to the back seat of the car. As Celia heaved and swore and ran round the car to do some shoving, there was always a moment when two trunk-like legs flew up airing prodigious lengths of knicker leg. The performance, presumably repeated at the other end and again on the return journey, appeared so exhausting that Tessa wondered why Celia did not find it simpler to do the ironing herself.

Sounds of disharmony reached Rose and Dolly as they took clean aprons from their shopping bags, put the halters over their heads and tied the strings in firm bows behind their backs. The noise climaxed in a volley of curses and Major Westbrook lurched into the corridor; he snarled at the two women and disappeared into the estate office. Rose and Dolly behaved as though he were invisible. When they were quite ready – boots off, indoor shoes on – they trooped into the kitchen and were just in time to catch Mrs Westbrook bowling a screwed-up dishcloth, overarm, at the sink.

'In a filthy temper,' she said of her husband. 'No clean bowl for his cornflakes. About time you two showed. Might have saved a bit of grief if you'd come earlier.'

'Half past eight's our time.'

'Well, buck up and wash me a bowl and spoon. Need my oats this morning if I'm to do any good with that horse.'

Rose surveyed the debris. 'I suppose there's plenty more in the dining room and the billiard room.'

'And in the drawing room. We squatted in there with our supper last night.'

'Right,' said Rose, rolling up her sleeves. 'We'll clear a bit of space in here first.'

'Cuppa?' asked Celia, waving the teapot.

'No, thank you,' said Rose, mindful that to accept more than a mug of 'Nescaf' for elevenses at the Manor was asking to be taken advantage of. 'Wash or wipe?' she asked Dolly.

Dolly elected to wash. It suited her stolid nature to lean against the sink and concentrate on the one task while Rose, who was nimble and tireless, scraped and stacked dirty crocks, dried and polished clean ones and put them away in the cupboards.

Soon, Mrs Westbrook left them to it. They worked largely in companionable silence, until, the kitchen being cleared, it was time to inspect the dining room. Here they allowed themselves a minute's breather, exclaiming at the mess, tutting at the waste, speculating over the identities of the guests and how the evening had gone. Then they loaded trays, carted them into the kitchen and began all over again.

After an hour, Dolly felt giddy. 'It's the steam,' she said, gripping the sink.

'Go and sit down, me duck. A few minutes won't hurt.'

Dolly obediently dried her hands and went to sit in a wooden chair at the table. Rose took over at the sink, her hands going more vigorously than ever, her thoughts flying to keep up.

Dolly had always needed looking after. Rose remembered her at school − a big daft lass − then leaving Wychwood in her teens to work miles away in some grand house; and returning for a holiday, suddenly and briefly beautiful. That were her undoing, thought Rose, that pink downy bloom of hers, fragile and overblown like a dog rose; it had caught the eye of Arthur Cloomb and think what that led to. She recalled − not censoriously but as further evidence of her friend's need for protection − Dolly's parting with Arthur at the end of her holiday, and then, four months later, her sudden return and hasty marriage.

In spite of Dolly's sturdier frame and freedom from the illnesses which had undermined Rose's childhood, in spite, too, of Dolly's greater comeliness, Rose knew she was the luckier. For she possessed two things Dolly lacked: sharp wits and will power. Rose could never decide which of her two blessings she valued the most. Sharp wits had prompted her to steer clear of village ne'er-do-wells like Arthur Cloomb and to pursue instead the meek, hard-working carpenter, Jack Fettle; will power had assisted her to make something of him and even more of their two children. Their son,

John, had amazed Wychwood by getting to university and marrying the lively Gail Bultitude (to the great sorrow of Mrs Bultitude who had taken some persuading of the notion that a university education mitigated the stigma of an Orchard Close upbringing). For the past twenty years her son had worked as a well-paid oil executive in Calgary, Canada, where Rose had visited on two occasions. Jack Fettle, still living at the time of Rose's first visit, had declined to venture across the water, so Rose went alone and thoroughly enjoyed herself, secure in her mind that she had left Jack with eight pages of written instructions and Dolly's promise to cook for him. Their daughter, June, had also made a success of her life. Having trained as a teacher and married one, she now taught in Leamington Spa where she lived with her husband and daughters in a four-bedroomed semi with a nice garden, a fitted kitchen, a car in the garage and another in the car-port.

Totting it all up, Rose decided it was mostly down to will power. She recalled staring into a wartime blackout, willing her husband to stay safe and come home; leaving the baby with her mother and grabbing the chance of earning good money at the munitions factory; standing over the kids while they did their homework, finding the courage to go with them to daunting places like museums and libraries, never for one moment allowing her mind to stray from her goal of a better life for them. Poor Dolly, on the other hand, didn't know the meaning of will power. She took what came and let folks trample over her. Especially those useless sons of hers – Barry, with his second wife expecting his fifth child, still a farm-hand for Major Westbrook; Mick, whom the local newspaper frequently described as being 'of no fixed abode'; and Pete, who lived in a caravan somewhere and didn't believe in work but thought his mother ought to provide regular hand-outs from her own wages.

'Feeling better yet?' she asked Dolly when the draining boards were full. And when Dolly heaved herself up, 'Do you want to dry this lot or go on washing?'

'Go on washing. You dodge about quicker'n me, Rose.'

At half past ten, Rose judged it was time for a break. They made themselves a mug of coffee each and sat down at the table.

'Thought I'd catch you,' cried Celia, coming in. 'I could do with a drink, myself.'

'Water's just boiled,' said Rose, not moving.

'Finished in here?' asked Celia putting a spoonful of coffee powder into a mug.

'Not done the floor or the tops. We've only just finished the washing up.'

Celia sighed. ''Spose there was rather a lot of it. Look, change the beds next will you? I'd better stick something in the oven – a friend of Giles's is coming to lunch. Can you do a couple of hours on the floors this afternoon?'

'I think we can manage that, can't we, Dol?' And Dolly nodded.

Celia brought her mug to the table, then reached into her jodhpur pocket for cigarettes and a lighter. Rose pushed an ashtray towards her. 'Good do, were it, on Saturday night?'

'Very. Sunday lunch wasn't much cop, though. Rather a thin party. I suppose you didn't go for a constitutional on Sunday afternoon?' The negative phrasing belied her expectation of an answer in the affirmative, for the older generation in Wychwood still liked to promenade after their Sunday dinner. The traditional walk was the Wychwood 'round', which encompassed the length of Church Street (with possible diversions to admire gardens in Peck's Lane and Honey Lane), the portion of Manor Road as far as the stile, the footpath running across two fields and the side of the wood to Fetherstone Road and from there, going left, back into Church Street. It was considered a great way in the old days of exchanging news, of keeping tabs on other people's garden or curtains, of parading new status such as betrothal or parenthood, of showing off new clothes.

'Dolly were too tired after hauling that wood on Saturday. But me and June went for a walk. She brought the girls over from Leamington.' Rose mentioned this fact casually but with secret pride.

Celia peered into her mug. 'Notice any comings and goings at the Rectory? Any parked cars?'

Rose thought about it. 'No. Mind you, if they was parked behind the trees you wouldn't see 'em from the road. Why?'

'No particular reason.'

They lapsed into silence until Rose asked daringly, 'Mrs Addinbrook any better? You said she were a bit down, what with her trouble an' all.'

'Oh, much perkier. Got a new man in tow. Mind you, this ghastly newspaper business – it's so unfair: they can say what they like it appears, and one has simply no redress – has had a terrible effect on her stomach. Pig sick a lot of the time. Which reminds me: you'd better give the downstairs lavatory a thorough overhaul.' She took a few sips of coffee and found it lacking. 'Think I'll take this into the other room and have ten minutes with the newspaper before I start cooking,' she declared, and ambled off in the direction of the drawing room drinks cabinet.

They swilled their mugs under the tap, then Dolly followed Rose upstairs. 'You strip 'em, I'll sort out the clean,' said Rose.

On the landing, Dolly turned left and went down the corridor to Giles's room. (Giles was the Westbrooks' younger son who had recently completed his agricultural course at Cirencester and was now living at home and running part of the estate. The elder son, Piers, had left home some years ago to farm in Queensland.)

Rose turned right and went to a walk-in airing cupboard at the end of the landing. She selected two double and four single sheets and six pillowcases, carried them back along the landing and placed them on top of a tallboy in the master bedroom. Although many of Mrs Westbrook's accoutrements were housed in this room – an armoire full of evening clothes, a dressing table smothered in jars of face cream and bottles of scent, Mrs Westbrook did her sleeping elsewhere – in fact, in a poky little boxroom along the corridor containing only a single bed, a po-cupboard crammed with whisky and gin bottles and a ramshackle wardrobe stuffed with her everyday clothes – stained jodhpurs, holey sweaters, check shirts. 'Major Westbrook snores,' she had once felt it necessary to explain. 'Makes the dickens of a row; I can't stand it.' And Rose thought that if the noise passing the lips of a fully conscious Major Westbrook were anything to go by, she for one did not blame her.

She stripped the major's bed, retrieved a cigar butt and deposited it in the waste paper basket, then, expecting Dolly's arrival any second, went to the window to gaze over the lawns, beyond the ha-ha, into fields full of sheep with rumps stained indigo by recent tupping. On the window ledge stood a pair of binoculars. (Major Westbrook kept binoculars at strategic points in several upstairs rooms for the purpose of spying on his workers however distantly they were occupied.) When her hand came in contact with these, she was immediately reminded of Dolly's non-appearance. Sucking in her breath, she bustled from the room and down the corridor, popped her head into the boxroom and found it empty as she had suspected, and continued to Giles's room at the corridor's end.

'Just as I thought,' she declared. For the guilty one stood at the window, queen of all she surveyed. Dolly was like a child with the major's binoculars. 'He'll catch you with 'em one of these days. Come on, you should've stripped Mrs W's by now.'

'There's someone sitting in the field over there. Hang on.' Dolly adjusted the focus. 'There. It's Mrs Brierley.

She's painting summat. Not much of a view, though, jammed up against that hedge.'

'Give 'em here,' Rose said. 'You're right. She's painting the rosehips, you lummox. Should make a very nice picture.'

'She's trespassing. Major Westbrook caught her once and asked her if she knew she were trespassing. I heard her telling Mrs Storr about it – they fell about laughing.'

'Can't see what's funny about trespassing, even if she ent doing no harm. Come on, Dol, for heaven's sake. It'll soon be dinner time.'

They went back to the major's room and unfolded a clean double sheet.

'Smells nice, don't it?' Dolly remarked as they smoothed it over the mattress, pulled it taut and made hospital corners. 'Better'n drip dry.'

'Very nice, I'm sure. Specially if someone else does yer ironing.'

'Poor old Clara Bull. Don't know how she stands it with her legs big as tree trunks. Cor, I ent half hungry, Rose. Are these the pillow cases?'

'Yes – pass us one over. We'll pop into Brenda's on the way home and pick up a couple of fancies. We deserve summat nice after all that washing up.'

'And working extra this after. I'll buy 'em. It's my turn.'

'You hang on to your money, Dol. My treat.'

Methodically, Tessa pinned the four sketches she had chosen down the edge of her drawing board. She was conscious of the way her hands moved, slowly, deliberately, as if they were a separate part of her, the assured part. Her stomach was full of delightful butterflies, for this stage of her work was the culmination of days of preparation, of thinking, planning and sketching. Now, the finished work established in her mind, ahead of her lay the unique pleasure of execution.

In other compartments of her life she could be

100

haphazard, easily swayed and distracted. As a painter she was a different person, organized, single-minded. Filed away in a cabinet behind her were hundreds of sketches ready for use – paintings done openly out of doors and surreptitious drawings made of her neighbours. The work now under way would feature Mrs Bull as a berry gatherer; she had made a study of rosehips for the purpose this very morning. Mrs Bull who lived in the cottage opposite had been drawn many times, a stout figure leaning over her gate to chat with passers-by, or hobbling down the road with her trolley to the village shop. Tessa had an excellent memory and could store away unexpected sightings to commit to paper on her return to Holly House. Once, spying Dolly Cloomb and Rose Fettle scurrying along arm in arm one moonlit evening, she had hurried home to incorporate them in paintings to illustrate a witch story.

But now, Tessa was thinking only of the work in hand, setting out her tools – brushes, pristine and shapely, clean water, new paint, soft cloth – as meticulously as a nurse preparing an operating theatre. Then, taking up a brush and moistening it, she painted a swathe of water and watched as the paper swelled and became receptive. She loaded the brush with paint and drew the first horizontal line.

Somewhere, at the very back of her mind, she knew this pleasure could not last, that eventually she must go down from her studio and re-enter the muddle of life; knew, even, that life was more than usually besetting at the moment. But she could treat this knowledge callously, temporarily disregard it. All that mattered now was her work going well and the brilliant feeling accompanying it – a feeling she thought of as happiness.

The moment the light faded, Maddy went over her house closing curtains. Then she laid out the clothes she planned to wear and ran her bath. She was glad

Robert was away; alone, she could concentrate on delicious preparations undistracted by a need for petty deceits, such as waving a notebook about for the 'creative writing' lecture, false chat about fellow students, pretending to wonder whether she could be bothered to go. She stepped into the bath and flopped back; squashed foam flew up and mounded round her body and between her limbs. She closed her eyes. Her mouth was dry as dust, her stomach squeezed by excitement. *Only two more hours,* she breathed. After all the counting and desperate sense of time staying still, it seemed unbelievable that the moment was truly close, close enough to believe in, to anticipate.

God, this had never happened to her before – shouldn't have happened now, couldn't go on happening much longer. But she had to hang on to it for a while, couldn't give it up yet; it was too addictive, too dreadfully wonderful . . . She supposed it must be happiness.

13

In his head and his heart, the Reverend Timothy Browne had been singing continuously since Thursday evening's choir practice. Now and then a joyful line or two escaped out loud:

> 'Come ye thankful people, come, sing the song
> of Harvest-home.
> All is safely gathered in 'ere the winter storms
> begin.'

As soon as he heard himself, he clamped his lips together, mindful of the need to preserve his voice for the greater glory of Sunday morning's Eucharist.

This Saturday afternoon, the church full of willing workers, he ceased thumbing through his prayer book and went over to consult the lectern Bible. He found he was obliged to negotiate the legs of Mrs Storr who was kneeling on the floor attending to her arrangement. Stepping back to admire her handiwork, it struck him as so attractive, so evidently inspired by the Holy Spirit, that he was unable to suppress a joyous outburst. 'Ta te tum ta tum tum tum. My word, Mrs Storr, what a beautiful job you're making of the lectern.'

The rector's approval attracted several jealous glances, particularly from Mrs Burrows who considered she was working wonders with 'Autumn Sun' rudbeckias round the pulpit and from Jane Bowman and Sarah Grace who were building vegetable pyramids on window ledges in the nave.

'Everyone's working *splendidly*,' Eleanor called diplomatically, clasping her hands beneath her chin and beaming round.

A pungent odour of chrysanthemum wafted from the rear of the church, where, over a trestle table, Mrs Frogmorton and Mrs Bultitude were snipping and stripping blooms donated by their husbands. Briefly, for the beautification of Wychwood church, the 'Korean Sunrise' lay with the 'Yellow Ragamuffin' and Mr Frogmorton's dahlias twined with Mr Bultitude's ornamental ferns.

Tessa Brierley came into the church carrying between her two hands a decorative, tall-handled basket stacked with colourful fruits.

Eleanor spotted her and hurried forward. 'Oh, Tessa, my dear. Timothy, do come and see. How clever!'

'How *delicious*,' said Timothy.

'Yes, won't they rejoice in the old folks' home when that arrives on Monday morning? And it's such an eye-catching piece for our festival. Where shall we put it?'

'On top of the font?' suggested Timothy.

'Yes – then people will see it as they come in through the door. Come, bring it, Tessa.'

All the ladies crowded round to admire, for, not being a flower-arranger, Tessa presented no threat and, indeed, her fruit basket was a most unusual and attractive idea. 'So different,' they enthused.

'Simply lovely,' said Maddy Storr.

'Oh, good. Well,' – Tessa moved away to look at other people's handiwork – 'I must say it's a wonderful display.'

'Come and see my vase in the sanctuary,' urged Eleanor – rather shamelessly, Timothy thought, misunderstanding his sister's motive which was not to secure personal praise but to draw her favourite closer to the place of benediction. (She had sensed a heavy heart beneath Tessa's cheeriness when she had gone to tea at Holly House on Thursday.)

Tessa admired Eleanor's vase and said she was sure she and Nick would attend tomorrow's evensong. Overhearing her, Timothy's spirits soared even higher. What matter if the Brierleys were infrequent churchgoers? At least they were moved to support the harvest festival. And he thought he knew why – and he gave thanks, for it was all grist to God's mill. 'Such resounding hymns, the harvest anthems,' he cried, and burst vigorously into a tuneful demonstration:

'"Lord, we know that Thou wilt come,
And wilt take Thy people home . . ."'

Eleanor put an urgent hand on his sleeve. 'Do guard the voice, old boy.'

Chastened, Timothy retreated through the choir stalls to his desk.

While Eleanor chatted, Tessa turned and looked down into the church – at Richard Grace up a ladder, manoeuvring corn dollies into place round the lip of a pillar; at all the bowed, stretching and kneeling figures hazed by slanting October sunlight; at Maddy in the chancel whom she hadn't seen or spoken to since last Sunday morning. When someone called for Eleanor's advice, she took the opportunity to move away, and went slowly down the aisle to stand for some moments watching her friend weave ears of corn and tiny blue aster flowers round the column of the lectern.

Maddy, her head bent over her work, glimpsed Tessa's approach. She became acutely aware of her standing there and of the silence between them. Yet she could not speak. A few minutes ago when she had joined in the praise of Tessa's fruit basket her voice had jarred in her ears, sounding falsely hearty. Not trusting herself to find a right note, she affected fierce concentration. To her horror, her dexterity suddenly deserted her. Her hands seemed to swell to an alarming size. The stem of a flower she was manipulating would not go neatly into place.

'I don't know how you do it – all this work in here and then organizing the supper tonight.'

It was a relief to let her hands fall on to her knees. She looked up and said quickly, 'You know me – never happy unless I'm rushed off my feet.'

'Well, then – happy times!'

Maddy dropped her eyes.

'See you tonight,' said Tessa.

When Tessa returned to Holly House, the telephone was ringing. Scrap hurled himself at her legs, barking to express disapproval of her deserting him. 'Silly,' she said, stooping to fondle his ears, 'I was only gone a few minutes.' Still, the phone went on ringing. Evidently Nick, wherever he was, did not intend to answer it. She pushed the dog away and went to pick up the receiver on the kitchen window sill. 'Hello?' she said – and her heart stood still.

The sounds on the line were unearthly. It was a few seconds before she could identify them – weeping, ratchety breath, incoherently blurted words overtaken by sobbing.

She swallowed, then began, 'Who . . . ? Um, can I help?'

A name was gasped out between sobs.

'Sophia! Whatever is it? Tessa, here. Is it about Colin?'

'Hospital' was the next word she caught. 'He's gone into hospital? Is that it, Sophia?'

There was a trumpeting noise as Sophia blew her nose. 'Went back this morning. Couldn't stand the pain. I couldn't do anything for him.'

'Perhaps it's for the best, then. You said yourself he'd be better off in hospital,' she reminded her – and then worried in case this was tactless when she had only meant to be comforting.

'But it's for more tests,' wailed Sophia. 'More bloody tests.'

'Look, we'll come over . . .'

'I don't want you,' Sophia screamed. 'I don't want anyone. I'm just telling you, for God's sake.'

'Well, thank you. Are you sure you wouldn't like us to come? What about Colin?'

'No visitors allowed today.'

'I see. Well, I'm so very sorry, Sophia.'

'I bet you are. With Colin out of the house, your husband won't find it so easy to get hold of Colin's stuff. You're all the same, you university people – all you care about is your jobs. They cut Colin's money – you know that? They'd like to stop it altogether, even before he's dead. I hate your bloody university – it stinks.' With which, she slammed down the receiver.

Oh hell, hell, moaned Tessa to herself, crouching and hugging her knees. Scrap butted her, and when she ignored him, turned to present an enticing view of his rear. She pulled him against her and buried her face in his furry back.

This was how Nick discovered her. 'Whatever's up? Was that the phone? I was in the bog.'

She looked up at him. Appalled, he pulled her to her feet, and asked again, 'What's up?'

'Colin's back in hospital. More tests.'

'That was . . . ?'

'Sophia.'

'Oh, God.'

They put their arms round one another and hugged

tight. Death was going to get him after all, Tessa thought – Colin, their friend and contemporary.

Eventually, they separated. 'More tests, eh? More surgery, do you think?'

She shrugged.

'Do you think he'll stand it?'

'Who can say?'

Nick made them a pot of tea and they sat at the kitchen table to drink it. 'Ought we to go in, do you think?'

'Sophia doesn't want us, and the hospital's barred visitors for the time being. She's on to you about those papers, by the way.'

'Stuff the papers. It's Col I care about.'

'I know, love. So do I.'

At half past five, Tessa went upstairs and opened the door of her wardrobe. She looked gloomily at several frocks hanging inside and began to mount a mental argument against them. A harvest supper, she reasoned, was a close relative of a barn dance. She invoked a hall dotted with bales of straw and jolly yokels sitting on them; people galloping about in pairs or scampering sideways in hand to hand circles. Many of the women, if she was not mistaken, were wearing jeans. So convinced did she feel that she almost closed the wardrobe door, until she remembered that in point of fact a harvest supper is not a barn dance, especially not the Wychwood harvest supper. She had attended many of these and the men had always aimed for a clean and smart look and the women for a pretty one. Sighing, for she could not bear to embarrass or disappoint, she reached out and dislodged a dress of navy corduroy velvet. It had a high neck and leg o'mutton sleeves, a nipped-in waist and a gathered skirt; she was certain it would be approved of. Leaving it on the bed, she went off to run her bath.

Nick came into the bedroom while she was drying her hair. 'Wearing this tonight?'

'Yes. It's OK, isn't it?'

'Sure. You look great in it.'

And when it was on and she went to study herself in the mirror, she saw that its demure style and rather voluptuous fabric suited her. Nick, she decided, pinning Aunt Winifred's cameo in the centre of the high neck, had not exaggerated.

The team for the harvest supper campaign was hard at it in the village hall. The most dedicated members – Mrs Storr of Jasmine Cottage, Mrs Burrows of Old School House, Mrs Dyte of Number Seven, The Glebe and Mrs Joiner of the Old Forge on the Green – were at action stations by five o'clock and had since been joined by members with a shade less backbone – Miss Browne of the Rectory and Mrs Grace of Pear Tree Cottage, Old Road. Earlier that afternoon, Ken Tustin had directed the men – notably, Robert Storr, Malcolm Joiner and Roy Peck – in the task of setting out the chairs and tables and decorating the hall with bales and sheaves from Peck's Farm; and at this very moment Jane and Derek Bowman were driving from cottage to house collecting contributions of prepared food and loaned equipment to ferry to the village hall. Three times a year the village mobilized in this fashion – for the summer garden fête and barn dance, for the Christmas bazaar and whist drive, and for the harvest supper. There were other minor events during the year, but these were the three great Wychwood occasions which those keen to avoid the label 'not a proper village person' would break a leg to attend.

Eleanor was already tired when she arrived in the village hall kitchen, blinking in the strip light after her walk through the dusk. It had seemed hard turning her back on the prospect of an evening by the fire, especially after working so hard to make the church festive this afternoon. Pangs of regret for the need to turn out smote her quite often these days, particularly on Tuesday evenings when, as the sole female representative of the Rectory she felt it her bounden duty – particularly in view of the Manor's laxness – to attend the WI. (In the past, ladies from the Manor or some other big house were WI presidents as a matter of course, and even nowadays it was thought correct that they should sit on the committee or at least take an interest; Celia Westbrook's attitude was that she would rather be dead than spend her evenings with such ghastly types.) Of course, things had changed; it was no longer plain which ladies should lead and which follow. Some changes were for the better – a livelier atmosphere and a greater range of interests – and some, in Eleanor's secret estimation, not. She felt very dismal when certain women rose to report ('Little did your delegate suspect when she left Wychwood at the unearthly hour of five o'clock last Friday morning, what a momentous day lay in store . . .') and even worse when she had to sit through sessions on 'How to decorate an egg' or Dusty Dean's complete repertoire of folk ditties. But she bore it bravely as a true daughter of the established church and only wished Winifred were still alive; dear Winifred who, out of friendliness rather than the dictates of her position as village school mistress and the only lady capable of playing the piano accompaniment to 'Jerusalem', had gladly shared her burden. Such a comfort it had been to indulge in a little moan afterwards, secure in the certainty of it never travelling an inch further.

Happily, things were not so dire as they were a decade ago. Dusty Dean and one or two eccentric enthusiasts apart, a more sensible class of speaker was usually invited to address the meeting, and this Eleanor attributed to the influence of Mrs Storr. She was not close to Maddy Storr, indeed, could not imagine being close to anyone so eternally on the go, but she did applaud her style; there was a twinkle in her eye which suggested a shared horror of egg decoration endured purely for the sake of members like Rose Fettle who adored fiddling with bits of tinsel, pots of glue and heavy helpings of stardust. (All the more strange, thought Eleanor, that her cleaner, Mrs Fettle, should betray such animosity towards the president.) Maddy Storr could be quite fierce in securing fair do's for less dominant members: Eleanor always silently cheered when she insisted on a respectful hearing for Phoebe Peck and sought the opinion of Dolly Cloomb.

For these reasons, Eleanor was glad this evening to discover Maddy in charge. Not that Maddy would have agreed openly with this perception of her present role. 'You'll have to ask Mrs Burrows about that – she's in charge of the food,' she protested when Jane Bowman, arriving with the pies, wanted to know whether they should go in the oven. 'But I should think it's a bit soon – what do you say, Edna?' And Edna Burrows felt Maddy Storr had read her mind precisely. Eleanor's relief at the sight of Maddy was prompted by the knowledge that no-one would ask for Miss Browne's opinion with Mrs Storr present and so capable of providing one instantly; nor, in the event of a dispute of the sort which sometimes broke out among the church flower ladies, would she be called upon to adjudicate. Maddy Storr's tact was legendary.

Jane Bowman, who had returned to her car for Molly Whitton's trifles, came back into the kitchen, looking dubious. 'Gosh, I hope they're all right. Poor old Molly – either her eyesight's worse or she's going ga-ga. She wouldn't let me in at first; insisted I was the window cleaner come for my money. "I haven't got it, young man; you'll have to come back next week."'

'Oh dear,' said Maddy, peering at the trifles. 'I did suggest she might like to give them a miss this year, but you know how it is.'

'Oh yes – "But, Mrs Storr, me dear, I *always* do the trifles."'

'Exactly. And we can't hurt her feelings. Actually,' – she raised each of the three glass bowls in turn to inspect the contents from below – 'they look fine. Just

110

jelly and bits of fruit, custard, cream and hundreds and thousands. Not much you can do with a trifle, fortunately; though to be on the safe side I've made a couple myself – she was so vague at WI last week, I wasn't sure she'd remember. Did you get Mrs Erskine's tablecloths, by the way?'

'Yes. Derek's taken them in to Ken Tustin.'

'Good. Then I'll just pop through and check the tables.' She pulled off her overall, revealing the red culottes and silk shirt ensemble, and strode down the corridor into the hall. She had selected the red outfit after careful thought. Its virtues were, firstly, that no-one had seen it save WI members (and it was not these she was seeking to dazzle this evening), secondly, that having worn it previously she could look Robert in the eye and swear to its being an old thing which only husbandly blindness had prevented him noticing.

'Hello, there!' she called gaily to the male members of the workforce, suitably adjusting her manner to suit – and at once became the focus of attention.

Teasing them a little, admiring the layout of the tables – two long arms and a crossbar at one end – her eyes roamed the room and quickly lighted on an impediment. 'Roy, your sheaves look lovely this year – oh look, Phoebe's wired in some paper poppies – gorgeous! But surely they should be at centre stage? They're wasted in that corner. Let's try it.' She vaulted athletically on to the stage. 'Can one of you give me a hand?'

And before Ken Tustin had time to remove the pipe from his mouth, his workers had rushed to assist the lady. This was not the first time a decision taken by the chairman of the parish council was undermined by the president of the WI. He remained below, pouring as much cold water as he could muster. 'We've got to leave room for the Cottiswick Singers, remember. Might get knocked over there. Could even be dangerous – those singers do a fair bit of running around.'

When the poppy-strewn sheaves had been rearranged, Maddy jumped down and ran to view the effect from the back of the hall. 'That's more like it – it's the focal point. Don't you agree, Ken? We don't want to waste Roy and Phoebe's good work. Come on, chaps – let's put out Mrs Erskine's tablecloths.'

At twenty minutes to seven, the telephone rang in Holly House. It was Derek Bowman who was manning the taxi service for the infirm. While driving Molly and Dan Whitton to the village hall he had learned of Mrs Bull's declared intention to give the supper a miss due to her legs being past walking on at the moment and her awkwardness getting in and out of cars. He had thought at once of Nick, the owner of a large battered Volvo and a neighbour of Mrs Bull's.

Nick readily agreed to collect her, though Tessa, in fact the Volvo's owner, suggested Nick use his own small car. 'I've had trouble getting her in mine before. It's too high. She needs to be able to flop in.'

While Tessa crossed over the road to Mrs Bull's gate, Nick got his car out. They went together down the path and knocked on the door. Tessa guessed they were expected, for Mrs Bull was wearing her best frock – a familiar garment at village events – and her coat and handbag lay close by on a chair.

'I told 'em I wasn't coming,' she protested. 'I don't like bothering folk.'

Nick was firm. 'Nonsense, Cinders, put your coat on; you *shall* go to the ball.'

'Ooh, and I suppose you're me fairy godmother.'

'Prince Charming, Mrs B; come with your coach and horses.'

She allowed him to help her into her coat. But on her way to the door, she hesitated, as if trying to remember something.

'Come on,' said Nick, reading her mind, 'you don't need your trolley.'

This tickled Mrs Bull. She was still laughing when they upended her on to the back seat.

'I'll leave you to it,' Tessa announced. 'Don't get

112

lost.' And she set off down the street to Jasmine Cottage. Nick tooted as he passed, and Mrs Bull's hand fluttered at the rear window.

Perhaps Robert had been watching for her, for when she turned in at the gate, the front door opened promptly. 'No Nick?' he called.

'He's giving Mrs Bull a lift.'

'I see. Well, come in for a minute, Tessa.'

'We ought to go in case Nick needs a hand getting her out of the car.'

'There'll be plenty of people about. Come in,' he insisted. He went into the sitting room. She followed, slightly uneasy.

'Drink?'

'No thanks. There'll be lots to drink later on.'

'You mean that disgusting plonk?'

'Maddy says the red's not too bad.'

'Ah – Maddy,' said Maddy's husband, looking thoughtful.

Tessa looked away. She longed to go, wondered how to insist.

'Have you noticed anything about Maddy lately?'

She stared at him in a stunned sort of way, thinking, that's torn it, if *he* knows. 'No,' she told him firmly, 'I haven't.'

Now it was Robert who looked away. Tessa became eager to disarm him; she didn't want him to know the truth; things would not be helped by Robert blundering in precipitating a crisis. 'I can't think what you mean,' she went on lightly. 'She seems the same old Maddy to me.'

'A bit frenetic? Wound up?'

'No more than usual.'

'You should see her here. Can't sit still for two minutes. The other night I was woken by a tremendous clatter. I found Maddy wasn't in the bed, so I went downstairs and there she was, turning out the kitchen cupboards. At half past two in the morning!'

'Heavens,' said Tessa, unable to recall having ever

113

turned out her own cupboards, 'that does seem excessive. But I'll tell you one thing, Robert,' she added slowly, desperation spawning deceit, 'I know she feels bad about all those bills she ran up. She told me you'd put her on a budget. Perhaps she's trying to be superwoman to make up for it. After all, she can't clear out the cupboards during normal hours, she's got too much on.'

'Do you think so? Does she really feel bad?'

'Gutted,' said Tessa, sufficiently carried away by her powers of invention to borrow a word from her son.

'You surprise me. Come to think of it, though, she was pretty defensive about tonight's outfit. Swore it wasn't new.'

'There you are, you see? Come on, it's time we were over there.' She walked to the door.

Robert followed, ruminating. 'You know, I think she feels it rather – not working. She's always saying how useless she is, that she ought to get a job. I don't want her to get a job. Not after last time. You know she had a breakdown before we came here?'

'Yes, she told me about it,' said Tessa, waiting for him to close the front door behind them.

'She practically ran the place. She was splendid, Tessa.' His eyes gleamed in the light over the door. 'And then that young fool . . . Hell, I used to fantasize about barging in and punching his nose. Once I even got as far as his office car park.'

'You were going to hit him?' She was thinking so hard she couldn't move, just stood looking at him.

'I suppose I was. But he came out with a couple of women and got into a car – saved by the bell.'

'You must love her very much.'

'Well, of course.' He seemed surprised. 'Coming?'

Dumbly, she walked on. Robert had forced a new perspective on her, and suddenly she was fearful for her errant husband. At the gate Robert offered his hand, but instead of taking it, she slid her arm, comrade-fashion, around his waist. His arm fell over her shoulders and thus they ran across the road to the light and buzz of the village hall.

14

The system was this: on receipt of a supper ticket at the bar just inside the main door, a free glass of wine (choice of red, or white medium-dry or medium-sweet) was handed over. Further glasses and full bottles were available for purchase. As a consequence of this arrangement the area between the bar and the waiting tables was chock full of merry quaffers downing free drinks as mere preliminaries – indeed, many men were already clutching a purchased bottle. Seated at the table, however, their free glass of wine chastely untasted before them, were those who must be thrifty – the older folk and the rather poor, those for whom a single glass of wine was a treat. Here sat Rose Fettle and Dolly Cloomb, Annie Seymore, and Molly and Dan Whitton. Davey Partridge, co-leader of the bell ringers and a retired gardener from the Rochford Estate who still put in a few hours on some of the Wychwood gardens, came up with his glass of wine and sat down beside Dan Whitton. 'Dan,' said Davey; 'Davey,' said Dan; both considerately averting their eyes from the strangeness of the other's appearance. They sat, shiny-faced, in constricting and rarely worn best clothing, staring with bemused expressions at their slender-stemmed wine glasses, wishing, no doubt, they were pints of Bass. Nearby, Nick was installing Mrs Bull. A distinguished-looking elderly man came and sat beside Annie Seymore. This was the retired physician, Dr Erskine. The willingness of the Erskines to join in and become as lesser mortals was much admired in Wychwood and often cited by people hoping to disparage the Manor. They lived in the former ancient farmhouse of Home Farm in Old Street which was considered by many to be the most attractive house in the village. While her husband paid old-fashioned courtesy to the seated ladies, Mrs Erskine stood and chatted with Mrs Sam Peck and her two daughters-in-law, Rachel and Phoebe. Phoebe did not enter into the conversation but stood to one side, smiling on it. Sometimes she gazed round, casting her smile more widely, and Tessa who was observing her as she sipped her wine, saw that Phoebe's smile was not so much a social response as a reflection of inner excitement. Her eyes were the most intensely bright spots in the room.

'Hello, Phoebe,' she said, walking over to her. Briefly, Phoebe's hand lay in Tessa's, and when it was withdrawn it scratched faintly like a dog's paw. 'You look tremendous,' said Tessa truthfully. Phoebe's straight dark skirt and cream silk blouse starkly emphasized her outdoor complexion – a disconcerting effect at first, but soon seen as stunning.

'It's great, innit? Me and Maddy went shopping. She spotted it in Dickins and Jones.'

'Gosh, did she?' said Tessa, hoping Peck finances weren't reeling as a consequence. 'Looks expensive.'

'Was a bit. But Roy wanted me to get summat good.'

'And he likes it?'

'Oh, yeah,' said Phoebe. 'I'm reading me poem tonight.'

'I know. I'm looking forward to it.'

'So'm I. Makes 'em real, somehow – saying 'em to people.'

'I suppose it must.'

'I spoke it to Maddy when we come home from shopping. She wanted me to practise, like.'

'What did she think of it?'

'Reckoned it was good, 'cept for the bit where the dog gets a rabbit. I said I'd leave that bit out, seeing as folks'll be letting their suppers settle.'

116

'That's thoughtful. Haven't you got a drink, Phoebe?'

'Mine's over there.' She nodded towards a lone glass of orange juice on the table. 'I can't drink wine cos of me pills.' She spoke without embarrassment. 'Oh – don't Maddy look nice?'

Tessa turned. Maddy, moving away from one group – and trailing an arm to indicate reluctance – seamlessly and radiantly accosted the next. She is in her element, Tessa thought, arranging us, encouraging us, making sure that we all go on as she has planned and have a thoroughly good time fulfilling her expectations.

Maddy, glancing about the room to gauge how quickly it was filling up, caught Tessa's gaze. She waved cheerily; the inhibition she had experienced briefly this afternoon utterly gone, confidence in her ability to cope with anything and everything never higher.

Rose Fettle, too, had her eyes on Maddy. She dug her elbow into Dolly's ribs. 'Look at her – swanning around likes it's *her* do, like she's *giving* it – 'stead of which we're paying good money. Cheek!'

'When it's our do at Christmas, folks won't be paying,' said Dolly.

'Ay, me duck. That's what makes it a party.'

'Have you tried yer wine yet?'

'Not yet, Dol,' snapped Rose, seeing through this innocent enquiry. 'If you drink it now you won't have none left for your supper. I wish they'd get a move on. Me belly thinks me throat's been cut.'

As if on cue, a warm-looking Mrs Burrows opened the hatchway between hall and kitchen and stuck her head out to catch Maddy's eye. Maddy broke off her conversation and went to murmur in Ken Tustin's ear.

'Ladies and gentlemen,' called Mr Tustin, rapping a spoon on the table, 'kindly take your seats.' And when the scraping of chairs subsided, 'Rector?'

The rector closed his eyes and tilted up his face.

117

Silence fell and everyone lowered their heads – except Maddy, who took the opportunity to check the numbers.

'Bountiful Father, we thank Thee for these Thy blessings – good food, hearty fellowship, Thine abiding love. Amen.'

'Amen,' they chorused gladly.

'Shall I?' mouthed Maddy to Ken Tustin, who graciously nodded his agreement that she should explain the feeding arrangements – which was just as well in view of his ignorance of the matter. She rose and described the dishes available – baked gammon and pineapple with an assortment of vegetables, courgette lasagne for vegetarians – and explained how people should go to the hatch in groups at a given signal, but could rely on helpers to collect their dishes should they prefer not to queue. All went smoothly under Maddy's jokey supervision; no-one went up before their turn and wants were satisfied with reasonable speed.

Nick went round with one of his purchased bottles, replenishing the glasses of unaccompanied ladies. Dolly saw him coming and quickly drained her glass. 'Very nice of you, Mr Brierley, I'm sure,' she said demurely.

'Thank you kindly,' said Rose, watching the filling of her own half-empty glass and thinking how quick off the mark Dolly could be when it suited her. She leaned over sideways and said softly, 'You're not so much daft as pudding-looking.'

Dolly applied herself to her supper with blank innocence.

When most knives and forks had been laid to rest, the team rushed round gathering plates and Maddy supervised the queue for dessert – a choice of Molly Whitton's trifle or Mrs Frogmorton's fruit pie. The trifle proved popular, and many plates of the wobbly stuff were borne to the table. Mrs Frogmorton settled down to a portion (to have chosen her own pie would have been very bad form, almost as bad as proposing herself for the WI committee) but very soon put down her spoon and clasped her throat. Maddy was going by with her own plate of trifle; Mrs Frogmorton whirled in her seat and caught her arm. 'Don't eat it,' she hissed.

Calmly, Maddy inclined her ear.

'It looks like peach but it's . . . carrot,' whispered Mrs Frogmorton, almost gagging on the word. 'It's not fruit salad in the jelly – it's macédoine of vegetables.'

'Oh, my goodness,' said Maddy, glancing quickly to where Molly Whitton was placidly tucking into Mrs Frogmorton's fruit pie (having been moved in her choice of pudding by a similar delicacy of feeling). 'She must have opened the wrong tin. Give it here,' she said out of the corner of her mouth, and quickly took the two plates back to the kitchen. 'Quickly, Jane. Dump Molly's trifles and get mine out – the ones with cherries on.' Hastily, she scraped the plates into a gaping black bin bag, spooned a dollop of her own trifle on to Mrs Frogmorton's and returned to the hall. 'You'll find that's all right. I made it,' she murmured, setting down the plate. Then, exhibiting a serene smile to forestall hysteria, she began to patrol the tables. Those swallowing chopped vegetables with every sign of satisfaction she left undisturbed, but at the first look of consternation on a diner's face, whisked away the plate promising not to be a sec, and rapidly returned with a radiant smile and an air of coming up with a desired second helping. Thus was the damage contained. And she comforted herself that even if someone did make a fuss, Molly's proven blindness would save her from noticing.

At the end of the meal, the rector called upon Mrs Roy Peck to propose a vote of thanks. Maddy did not line up with the other ladies modestly receiving thanks, but stood alone near the end of the tables in front of the stage – a position from where she could set an example. Phoebe rose, thanked the tireless workers, then announced a poem composed for the occasion. At this, Maddy swept her eyes over the company in a pleased sort of way and then fastened on Phoebe with interest and attention. The poem began well, but the second stanza brought a moment of peril. When the poet described how, astride her horse, she felt his rippling muscles and impetuous strength, Martin Smith of The Glebe said something behind his hand to his neighbour at which they both sniggered; luckily, Martin's wife kicked him and Martin's neighbour's wife looked daggers, and the theme soon developed a more universal appeal as horse and rider entered the harvest field and beheld the reaper's progress. The applause at the poem's close was generous. Phoebe bumped down on to her seat looking pleasurably stunned. Husband Roy nodded to his neighbours with pride, and even old Sam Peck, who was reputed to have uttered harsh words against his daughter-in-law, blinked in the limelight and perhaps adjusted his opinion.

When the tables were cleared and glasses replenished, Ken Tustin called 'Ready!' into the corridor, and in jigged the Cottiswick Singers – old and young but mostly middle-aged, the men in smocks and criss-cross tied trousers, the women in kerchiefs and dirndl skirts. They were led by a fat ringleader; an accordion player and a fiddler brought up the rear. 'Green grow the rushes-o,' they sang, beckoning the audience to join in the chorus.

As the singing got under way, the ringleader produced a chamber pot which he filled from a flagon of cider. This he presented to Gloria Hennage, assisted her to partake and then to pass it on to her neighbour. As the pot was passed round, groans of dismay rose up and shrill shrieks of glee; many who were only faintly merry on a glass or two of wine felt tipsy as a lord after sipping from the chamber pot, uproariousness being particularly marked in Mrs Bull's vicinity. Some, like the Erskines, were manifestly courageous, obediently sipping and passing the thing on; but Eleanor Browne kept her hands in her lap and steadfastly refused to notice it. There was something about her expression – the look of a prim child accidentally present when adults start making fools of themselves – which deterred both her neighbour (Mr Burrows) and the ebullient ringleader from pressing her. The rector leaned over to relieve Mr Burrows of his embarrassment and, though forbearing to taste himself, handed the vessel with some ceremony to Mrs Frogmorton, correctly judging her equal to the occasion.

'Who hired this lot?' Tessa asked Derek Bowman who was sitting on her left.

'We did – the village hall committee. Lucky to get 'em – they're very popular.'

Earlier on behind the scenes, the ringleader had taken soundings as to the man and woman most suitable for making fools of. Mr Tustin and Mrs Burrows had been nominated and marked out. Now, stout Mrs Burrows was dragged to the fore, pulled on to the ringleader's knee, serenaded and made spurious love to. The laughter greeting this was not untinged with malice, for Mrs Burrows was known to give herself airs; that she entered into the spirit of the thing with unsuspected gusto, served to increase the hilarity. Then it was Mr Tustin's turn. Tricked into rising to his feet, he was deemed to have volunteered for the part of the deficiently attired soldier in the song, 'Soldier, soldier, won't you marry me?' At the conclusion of each verse he was handed a new article of clothing to put on. The old ladies went into fits over Mr Tustin in voluminous drawers and a horrible hat, and others, like Tessa, rather enjoyed the old ladies. Maddy caught her eye and winked. There was a call for requests – 'The Ash Grove', 'The Londonderry Air' – and now, thoroughly in the mood, company and audience sang their hearts out.

After the singing, people got up from their chairs and

stood about talking, but gradually, in twos and threes, they departed, and Derek Bowman began organizing the return taxi service. Nick hauled Mrs Bull to her feet. 'I'm taking you home, Mrs B. Aren't I the lucky fellow?' Tessa came up with Mrs Bull's coat and they stuffed her into it. Mrs Bull was stiff from sitting too long, also she had drunk several glasses of Nick's white wine; going down the step, she lurched perilously. Nick caught her and held her tight. 'Ooh, me dear, I do feel queer,' he sang, pinching the fleshy dewlap over the top of her corset, making her screech. Tessa grinned at Maddy who had joined her in the doorway. 'Robert,' said Maddy, grabbing her husband. 'Go with Nick. I'm sure Mrs Bull will fall easily enough *in*to the car but it'll be the work of two men getting her out of it.' Somewhat apprehensively – for he lacked Nick's insouciance with the fairer sex – Robert duly went.

When the tables were cleared, Ken Tustin's team started folding them and sliding them away into the space under the platform. In the kitchen the same workers who had slaved to produce the supper, were now clearing up after it. Eleanor Browne was as pop-eyed as a sleep-walker. Tessa, who had stayed to lend a hand, forbade her to so much as pick up a tea cloth. 'Go home, Eleanor. You've been on the go all day.'

Eleanor hesitated. 'Would it be dreadful if I went? As a matter of fact, I should like to make sure that Timothy has an early night. It'll be such a demanding day for him tomorrow.'

'Exactly. I'll ask Nick to run you home as soon as he gets back from taking Mrs Bull.'

'Certainly not. It's only a step.'

At that moment the rector looked in – but not too far. (He was too old a hand to venture near ladies up to their elbows in hot water or vigorously wielding tea cloths; dark things might be going on under the surface. In the past he had often barged into the Rectory kitchen with helpful intentions only to be rewarded by instant silence and a gathering atmosphere; when Eleanor cryptically suggested that he see to things in the drawing room or the vestry, he had bowed to her informed judgement and very thankfully retreated.) 'Ah, Eleanor . . .'

'I'm coming, Timothy. Goodnight, everyone. I do hope we shall see you tomorrow,' she added, lightly reminding them of the religious side of the festival. Inwardly thanking God for a timely release, they went down the corridor and out of the side door into the kind night air.

'They're wonderful,' said Sarah Grace. 'How old would you say?'

'In their seventies. I know that for a fact,' said Mrs Burrows. 'Rector's seventy-two or three and his sister's a couple of years older. Isn't that right, Tessa?'

Before Tessa could reply, Maddy spoke up. 'It isn't how old people are that matters, but how they go on. No-one could take a more energetic interest in village affairs than the rector.'

'Oh, I agree. The young these days haven't the same stamina.'

'Edna, do, please, leave age out of it,' Maddy insisted, frowning. 'There's a stupid pressure on parsons to retire at seventy nowadays, and we don't want to precipitate that, do we?'

There was quickly expressed agreement.

'So less of the "aren't they wonderful", eh? Careless talk costs lives.'

Tessa smiled to herself. Maddy was such a politician, always making connections and foreseeing consequences, eternally wary of blunderers who lacked her own perspicacity. 'You do realize,' she had once told Tessa, rocking herself in the kitchen chair in Holly House one morning following a parish council meeting, 'that the Reverend Timothy will be the last incumbent to live in the Rectory? Oh, yes; when the Brownes go the Church will sell it. It'll become "The Old Rectory" like the one in Steeple Cheney, and some business tycoon or London stockbroker will buy it and tart it up. Like the Eltons in the Steeple Cheney Rectory. I suppose the Eltons are all right in their way – letting the Horticultural Society use their garden and so forth – but they hardly make up for a rector. Or if the Church can get planning permission it'll become another Glebe. They could build a dozen executive homes or twenty starters on that site. These are golden days, Tessa – mark my words. We should cherish the Brownes.'

Mrs Burrows had evidently felt herself unfairly rebuked. 'But I didn't mean . . . I merely said . . .' Her voice petered into petulance, and Tessa saw that she was overtired and very possibly, after the attentions of the ringleader of the Cottiswick Singers, overwrought. Her face was pudgy, her pink-pearl make-up had long ago melted from the promontories of her cheeks and settled into lines round her nose and jowly chin.

'I think you deserve to put your feet up,' she told her. 'That was a fantastic meal for all those people. All that after decorating the pulpit this afternoon! I don't know how you do it.'

Mollified, Mrs Burrows agreed that she was rather done in, and Tessa went in search of Mr Burrows in the main hall. 'Your wife has performed over and above the call of duty. Take her home, Mr Burrows, and make her a nice cup of cocoa.' And with feelings akin to the Brownes before them, the Burrows left the village hall and walked the weary few steps to Old School House next door.

Ken Tustin, Malcolm Joiner and Peter Dyte came into the kitchen to report that everything was now shipshape in the main hall. Derek Bowman confirmed that he would stay to lock up, and a relieved Mr Tustin departed. Nick and Robert returned to help with the washing up and stacking away. Maddy, trying to spur everyone on, announced, 'Coffee at our place when we're through.' Tessa, who was handing Robert a tea cloth at the time, caught his resigned expression and laughed in his face. Robert laughed too, at her knowingness.

'What's tickled you two?' asked Nick.

'Oh, nothing,' said Tessa.

Robert said, 'In which case, it might be a good idea, my sweet, if I were to go home and put the kettle on.' His wife graciously conceded the point.

'Want a hand?' called Nick.

'I'll manage,' Robert said, disappearing.

When at last all was done, they trooped to the door. Tessa waited outside as Derek Bowman locked up. Ahead of her, the others – Nick and Maddy, Sarah and Richard Grace, Jane Bowman, the Dytes and the Joiners – were crossing the road to Jasmine Cottage which was lit like a moored ship, the street lamp pale in comparison. Further up the street beyond the lamp's beam, were the shadowy shapes of houses and cottages – black, lying low, waiting. Derek stuffed the keys in his pocket and they followed the others across the road.

Vivaldi's *Gloria* was coming softly from the record player in the sitting room where Robert had the coffee ready. They sprawled on settees or the carpet, kicked off their shoes, and looked upwards to the exposed roof rafters. The bare stone and the room's great height and the driving artless music combined to slightly intoxicate Tessa. She felt that her perception was more than usually acute. For instance, Maddy seemed never to notice Nick, whereas Nick watched Maddy obsessively. It was ridiculous; his eyes were mesmerized by her. She feared Robert might notice. But Robert, of course, was only feigning attention to his guests; really he could hear and think of nothing but the music. Did Maddy sense how intensely she was regarded? Did it disturb her? Yes. Maddy's fingernails were thrust into the carpet, her hands stiff as hawk's talons. She affected relaxation – half-lying with her back towards Tessa, propped on an elbow beside an untouched coffee cup – but Tessa knew it was a pose. If I were to reach out and tap her shoulder, she thought idly . . . And, as if in a dream, did so. She was immediately vindicated by Maddy shooting out of her skin, sending the coffee cup flying. 'Sorry, sorry. My God, I'm so sorry,' Tessa wailed as people rushed about with cloths and water to prevent a coffee stain. She couldn't move, just sat there blinking, shocked to think she had behaved like a callous child with a captive insect, pricking it to watch it jump.

'There – no lasting damage,' said Maddy when the panic was over.

'I had been going to say that if I don't go home I shall fall asleep on your comfy sofa.'

'Feel free.'

'No, no. Come on, Nick. Take me home.'

Part Two

NOVEMBER

15

Maddy put the parish council meeting notes for Major Westbrook into her basket and let herself out of her house. A gunpowdery smell from last night's Guy Fawkes celebrations hung in the dank November air – a pitiless odour which increased her gloom as she went down the garden path, through the gateway and along the street to the cutting where her car was parked. All yesterday she'd felt dreary. She'd worked with a furious energy – cleaned out the garden shed and driven sacks of rubbish to the council tip, gone round to Ken Tustin's to discuss arrangements for the Christmas bazaar, called to see how Annie Seymore was feeling and stopped to help her turn her feather mattress (a chore which Annie, since her operation, had been unable to manage unaided), prepared one of Robert's favourite dishes and hurried over to the village hall for the parish council meeting. Each of these tasks she performed wholeheartedly, but none was as real to her as the memory at the back of her mind of how, early that morning, she had avoided Tessa. The memory made the day stale before it was over, and every achievement seem second best.

After breakfast yesterday, finding herself short of one or two supplies, she had set off for the village shop. Rounding the bend near the Green, she saw Tessa on the opposite corner chatting to Mrs Bull. Tessa had her purse in her hand and was evidently also on her way to the shop. Maddy turned instantly into Peck's Lane and almost raced the long way home. Back in her kitchen she stood gazing out into the garden, rerunning the scene, fearing lest Tessa had spotted her, asking herself again and again why she had done it. The answer was starkly obvious, but even more unsettling than the incident. Her eyes fell on the garden shed and, picturing the soily jumble within, she resolved to clear it out forthwith. It was a horrid job and would be a suitable punishment. Also, it might take her mind off Tessa.

None of the day's tasks proved able to do this. November the fifth remained a dismal day, culminating in her being the unlucky parish councillor detailed to call on Major Westbrook with a report of the meeting he had been unable to attend.

In the morning, because she loathed calling at the Manor, she decided to drive there rather than walk. A few steps run from her car door to Major Westbrook's office and back to her car were all she envisaged. Unluckily, the visit did not go as planned.

Maddy drove briskly along Church Street (looking straight ahead and carefully not at any of the houses lining it, especially not at Holly House), turned left into Manor Road and immediately right into the Manor driveway. The car scrunched over the gravel. She came to a halt near Major Westbrook's office door, gathered the notes from her basket and jumped out of her car. Before she had gone many paces, an outburst of demented barking stopped her in her tracks. Three golden retrievers came flying from the vicinity of the stables, their manner unappeasingly hostile. The leading dog leapt at her. She shrank against the car's bonnet, inadvertently encouraging canine hysteria.

Hands in jodhpur pockets, cigarette in mouth, Celia ambled on to the scene. 'Quiet, sir!' she cried from the back of her throat without moving her lips. The dogs backed off and barked with a shade less conviction. 'I said "Quiet"!' bellowed Celia. 'Orff!'

The dogs bounded away with valedictory yelps.

Maddy felt sick. For a moment, when Celia strolled closer, squinting at her over her cigarette, she could not speak.

'They're quite harmless, you know,' Celia told her with pitying amusement.

'Then all I can say is,' she managed shakily, 'they've got lousy manners.'

'They're dogs. If you show 'em fear, they get excited.'

'I do hope, Mrs Westbrook, that next time I drive past when you're out riding I don't forget to slow down and allow you plenty of room. I hope I won't be so discourteous as to give you a close shave and frighten your horse. Consideration for others does make life pleasanter, don't you think?'

Celia took the cigarette from her mouth and tapped it with a forefinger. (An unnecessary act, since a worm of ash had already spilled over her jacket.) Her eyes darted. Dimly, for she was not a quick thinker, she perceived that this female had somehow bested her – and Celia did hate to be bested. Her mind roved over various well-tried methods of putting uppity types in their place. A brief display of manorial splendour ought to do it. 'They tell me you're artistic. Eleanor Browne speaks well of your flower-arranging and so forth. Come inside and take a look at m'new pictures.' She chucked her cigarette on to the gravel, trod stones over it, and strode confidently towards the house.

After a moment's hesitation, dazed by the aftermath of terror and triumph, Maddy followed.

Celia led through her house, through oak-panelled rooms full of dusty light from mullioned windows, over Turkey carpets, beneath moulded ceilings, pointing nonchalantly to an antique tapestry, grumbling at the carved balustrade ('*dretful* dust trap'). The 'pictures' Maddy was about to view had been bought to cheer up a corridor leading to a newly built conservatory, she explained. 'In here,' Celia proclaimed, opening a door on to a modern passageway with clear glass windows set in a cream-coloured wall. At intervals on the windowless wall were hung half a dozen blameless paintings.

'What do you think of 'em? Frightfully expensive, but they're absolutely correct – approved by the botanical johnnies.'

Maddy's heart sank. She had viewed botanically exact paintings before and found them unfailingly depressing. Now, peering at a tulip, she wondered why so precise a representation of life should strike her as essentially lifeless, the colour parched-looking, the leaves rubbery and curled back as though exhausted by intense inspection. And it came to her that it was a study made without emotion, employing a cold eye. Art didn't come into it.

'Well?'

'Nice frames.'

Celia was not put out. 'Oh, do you think so? I wondered if they were rather plain. You don't think gilt ones?'

'Lord, no. Gilt would finish them off. I'm afraid this sort of thing isn't my cup of tea, though I don't doubt they're good of their kind.' She looked at her watch. 'I must dash. Look, will you give these to the major?' She thrust upon Celia the parish council notes. 'There's something in them he should think about before the next meeting. Are your dogs likely to behave themselves?' she called over her shoulder, starting back through the house.

'I'll come with you,' Celia said, feeling miserably outmanoeuvred.

'I suppose we can rely on you as ever to give the milk for the Christmas bazaar?'

' 'Course you can,' she snapped, and added (in the manner of every other Wychwoodian, high or low, if only she had known it); 'We always give the milk.'

Maddy drove fast over the gravel, braked, turned and turned again, in a tearing hurry to reach Holly House. She couldn't wait to tell Tessa. Already she was describing the scene – the beastly dogs, Celia's nasty amusement, her own inspired riposte about courtesy, the hideous 'pictures', the thwarted look on Celia's face . . . Already she was savouring Tessa's reaction, her sympathy over the dogs, her delight at Maddy's victory. Tessa's anticipated laughter was tingling deliciously in her ears as she braked outside Holly House.

Whatever was she thinking of? Things had changed – remember? She fumbled into second gear and accelerated away; parked her car at the gate to Jasmine Cottage and hurried indoors.

In the kitchen she made herself a lonely cup of coffee. She sat drinking it at the table, feeling flat. The morning's incident had lost its point now that she couldn't share it with Tessa. Her mind flew back, roved over the countless times when she or Tessa had arrived breathless at the other's door with a titbit. Life seemed suddenly darker, as if the sun had gone in.

Abruptly, she rose. You can't have it both ways, she told herself, and tossed the sour-tasting coffee into the sink.

Another week went by and still she had exchanged no word with Tessa. They hadn't spoken since the harvest supper over two weeks ago, she recalled, surprised that she should feel this so keenly when other strongly felt happenings preoccupied her. In particular, seeing Nick. (They tried hard to ration their meetings; never-theless, these were becoming more frequent, and in between times she was heavily engaged in reliving and anticipating them.) There was plenty going on in the village, too. In fact, she could see a power struggle looming between herself and Rose Fettle over the Christmas bazaar teas. Come to think of it, it was time she put Tessa in the picture about this; that is, if Tessa still intended to act as her assistant.

If she were honest, the prospect of a feud with Mrs Fettle keyed her up. It gathered her wayward mind; focused it. The harder she concentrated on Rose Fettle's shortcomings, the less was she disturbed by more intractable problems – such as the danger of losing Tessa, the shame of betraying Robert, and the desolation which overtook her whenever she contemplated giving up Nick.

She was going down her garden path on her way to Tessa's to explain the problem with the bazaar teas, when she changed her mind. I'll phone her about it instead, she decided, and turned back and went inside.

16

Pinned on to a notice board in Tessa's studio were chopped-up pieces of text. Some of the sentences were underlined in green ink. This was Larry's work for the new book – each separate piece would be placed somewhere on a double-page spread, according to Tessa's design. It was their practice to develop a book's theme together during long telephone conversations, then Larry would work on the text and Tessa on some preliminary sketches. When the finished writing was ready and divided into readable sections, it was left to Tessa to match the key sentences with illustration and design the completed book. Every day before settling to work she stood in front of this display, reading, thinking, imagining. This morning she had taken down a section of writing and pinned it beside her paper on the drawing board.

Tim crept to the window. He parted the curtains and looked down into the street.
He saw patches of moonlight and big black shapes.

Hours passed. It was Church Street she was painting, the way it had appeared to her one night last month when she stood gazing down, trying to suppress her suspicions about Nick and Maddy. A face painted at an upstairs window, tremulously indistinct, greenish and round like a dim mirror of the moon, might have been her face; but it wasn't: it was the face of the boy Tim, the book's principal character.

Last month, did she say? The thought, idling at the back of her mind, suddenly pushed to the fore and made her heart turn over. She put down her paint brush and swivelled on her stool to look at a calendar. Heavens, it was five weeks ago. If she added on another two for the time it had taken her to become aware of the affair, the six weeks she had given it were more than up. Yet there was no sign of its waning. Quite the reverse; as well as their contrived Monday evenings, Nick came home late or disappeared inexplicably at all sorts of times, and a remark of Robert's led her to suppose that Maddy's comings and goings were equally unpredictable. When questioned, Nick was unpleasantly defensive, so she affected not to notice any more. This was not a problem: her work absorbed her; she focused on it fanatically. Apart from a weekend visit to Paul, undertaken so that she and Nick might reassure themselves as to their son's recovery from his rugby injury, and regular visits to Colin in hospital, she had done nothing but work for the past three weeks. She had sometimes reflected that Maddy never called, but without regret, for she no longer relished her company. Not just because of the deceit lying between them, also because Maddy seemed to be losing her sense of humour; she would fasten on silly things, harp on them endlessly, boring Tessa and making her rather uncomfortable. At the moment Maddy had a bee in her bonnet about poor Rose Fettle – something to do with the Christmas bazaar teas and the refreshments for the whist drive which would follow it in the evening. She had rung Tessa up about it twice. Luckily, on the last occasion, Tessa had been able to tell her truthfully that she couldn't stop to listen because she was just setting off to visit Colin. 'Right,' had said Maddy grimly, 'I'll come round early next week and put you in the picture.'

Tessa blew her cheeks out impatiently. I can't be

135

bothered with such pettiness, she thought, turning back to her work, picking up her paint brush.

Scrap was asleep on an old couch near the studio door. Without stirring, he growled.

'Shut up,' she said. 'You're at least two hours too soon.'

The furry heap on the couch continued to reverberate, but she no longer heard. She was floating moonlight over the slanting roof tops, stippling it on the leaves of a tree.

Maddy ran up the steps of Holly House and tapped on the door. There was no answer, but a radio was playing inside. She turned the handle and found the door unlocked. Confidently expecting to find Tessa in the kitchen, she pushed it wide and flung in her brightest smile. No-one was there to see. Her smile didn't just fade; it vanished like a removed mask leaving a true reflection of her feelings – tight mouth, strained little frown.

As she waited there uncertainly, her eyes fell on an abandoned woolly pile on the settle which she recognized as Nick's old blue sweater. Her pulse quickened. Half-terrified by her foolishness, she stole across the room and gathered it up, buried her nose in it and drew in such an endless breath of Nick that her lungs strained against her ribs and rose painfully in her throat. Shakily, she cradled it into her waist, and finally, resenting the necessity, returned it to the settle.

In one movement, Scrap uncurled and jumped to the floor. With an air of a dog who supposes he really ought to do his duty, he went to the door and stood with his nose towards it in a pointed fashion. When no response came from his mistress he gave a single sharp-voiced bark.

Now she did hear; it was no grumbling anticipation of a dog's dinner, but a clear warning of someone about. 'Are you sure?' she asked, peering over the

136

drawing board. He barked again, flashed her an apologetic look, and returned fixed attention to the door.

'Well, you'd better be right.' She got up and went to open the door. Scrap shot into the corridor and scampered downstairs, snarling like an over-heated engine.

Help, he means it, she thought; perhaps she would discover something worse down there than just someone knocking at the door. The sensible part of her mind reasoned that she had probably left the snib up when she returned from the shop early this morning, and a friend, Maddy or Eleanor or Mrs Frogmorton, finding it unlocked had stepped inside. But the more nervous part of her envisaged an intruder, and her legs going downstairs were heavy with dread. Then, crossing the hall, she heard Maddy yelling, 'Be quiet, you little idiot!'

She put a hand to her throat. 'Oh, God, it's you. I thought for one hideous moment . . .' Nevertheless, she leaned down to stroke her dog approvingly. 'I keep doing that – leaving the door unlocked.'

'And you left that on.'

Tessa switched off the radio. 'I'm a bit preoccupied at the moment.'

'And I'm interrupting. You're busy.'

'Well, I've stopped being busy now, so you might as well have some coffee. Though it's almost lunchtime. How about soup?'

Maddy hesitated. She abhorred tinned soup – which, as she correctly guessed, was the type on offer – on the other hand she was bursting to secure Tessa's co-operation over this business of the Christmas bazzar teas and the whist drive refreshments. 'Thanks.'

Tessa went into the scullery and opened a tin of cream of asparagus. She poured the contents into a saucepan and put it on the stove. 'Like a roll with it? They're nice ones – wholemeal from Laye's.'

'Oh – yum.'

While the soup was heating, Tessa put the rolls into the aga to warm. Maddy, who was on familiar terms with the Holly House kitchen, collected plates and bowls from the dresser and put knives and spoons on the table.

When she had got her soup down and finished her roll, Maddy took a sip of water and looked sternly across the table. 'I hope you're going to support me in this business.'

Tessa sighed. 'What's it about, exactly?'

Maddy detected half-heartedness. 'Look, if you've got too much on ... Maybe I should find another lieutenant for the bazaar teas.'

'Of course not.' The very thought of bailing out of a job she had done for the past five years was enough to shake Tessa out of her work-induced myopia into a proper appreciation of village matters. Such things as who does what for this or that event were of compelling importance, and the least deviation from accustomed practice attracted comment and speculation. Some jobs were associated with particular houses. For instance, when Tessa moved into Holly House it was rapidly explained to her by a member of the garden fête committee that 'Holly House always runs the produce stall', which job Tessa had since unfailingly undertaken. When a task had been performed successively for two or three years a tradition was held to have been established, and the phrase 'Mrs X always does so and so' was guaranteed to brook no argument. Another favourite, equally clinching, was 'We always do it like that'. When Maddy first came to Wychwood, the lady in charge of the Christmas bazaar teas, finding herself in need of an assistant and taking a liking to the newcomer, had offered her the post. For five years Maddy served under Mrs Bowles, learning all there was to know about the Wychwood sandwich (including how to make a mock crab filling – a wartime invention too well-loved and revered to abandon – and how to cut a sandwich round into thirds, rather than halves which were considered ungainly, or quarters which were too small to sell for 10p, or 6d as formerly). Five years later, when Mr and Mrs Bowles retired to a bungalow on the south coast, Maddy became bazaar tea captain and her best friend her lieutenant.

'Certainly, I'm going to do it,' Tessa now insisted; adding like a true Wychwoodian, 'I always do.'

'Well, it's time we made a stand over this business of the so-called "left-overs". You remember how it happened? First Ken Tustin decides to hold the December whist drive on the evening after the Christmas bazaar. Then it seems a good idea to let the card players eat up any left-overs from the bazaar teas. Next we get Rose Fettle actually suggesting we collect extra food to accommodate the whist drive, and now it's a foregone conclusion – we're providing teas for the bazaar *and* refreshments for the whist drive. They're counting on it. It's become a tradition.'

Tessa shifted in her chair. 'I know – does it matter? We laughed about it last year.'

Maddy frowned. 'Look. We go round cadging – right? We ask people to give us stuff – cakes and cheese and milk and so forth – on the understanding that we're going to sell it in aid of something. It's clearly understood: we're giving our time, they're giving the produce, and people are buying it to help pay for a new church roof. The point is, they *don't pay* for refreshments at the evening whist drive. They call them "left-overs" but ask us to be sure and make enough. It's dishonest. It's probably fraud or something.'

'Oh, Maddy . . .'

'All right. Tell me, why should Rose Fettle and Dolly Cloomb throw a nice little party at the expense of the rest of us who provide stuff free?'

Tessa thought of the sort of people who regularly attended the monthly whist drives – older, less well-off folk, usually those associated with the land, born and

139

bred in Wychwood and their parents before them. 'It seems fairly harmless to me.'

Maddy turned pink. 'I disagree. I'm sorry Tessa, but you may as well know: I've spoken to Ken Tustin about it. I've told him that unless he charges for the refreshments in the evening we'll only prepare sufficient food for the afternoon teas. Dammit, Tessa, I should've thought you'd see that it's a bit thick for us to go round blatantly cadging free scoff for Rose Fettle and her mates. Where's the *objection* to charging? The whole point of the exercise is a new church roof.'

And to enjoy a village occasion, Tessa almost added, but decided she'd wasted enough time. 'I suppose you're right,' she conceded, not wholly convinced but fed-up with the argument.

'So you'll support me?'

'Mm. Yes. OK.'

Maddy let out her breath.

'Tea? Coffee?' Tessa asked, standing up.

'No thanks. Got Phoebe coming round this afternoon. She's in a stew about something or other.'

That would make two of them, Tessa thought, studying her friend curiously, noting the red patch at her throat and the stiff skewed line of her mouth. Why was she making such an issue of this? The old Maddy would have come up with an ingenious solution, not lost her sense of humour over it. 'You've got to laugh at those two,' Tessa suggested timidly. 'They've created a nice little role for themselves – gracious hostesses of the Christmas whist drive. I bet they revel in it.'

'The two witches,' Maddy commented spitefully.

'That's a bit strong.'

'That's how you painted them.'

'No, it isn't. My witches were nice witches. You make them sound evil.'

'They look evil – it's the way they huddle. They bustle down the street arm in arm with their heads together, muttering and glaring . . .'

'Not glaring.'

'All right – *huddling*. They get on my nerves.'

'Evidently.'

Heavens, we're rowing, thought Tessa, feeling hot and prickly, confronting Maddy's blazing eyes. All this passion over Rose Fettle and Dolly Cloomb? She dropped her gaze.

And Maddy hastened to check that the tiff had not damaged her recent achievement. 'Well, I'm glad you agree with me about charging for the refreshments. We'll have to start collecting promises soon. I expect Brenda will give the ham. I'll make a Dundee cake, by the way.'

'I'm certainly not baking. I'll give the tea bags.'

'Super.' Maddy was all smiles as she stood up and smoothed down her skirt. 'Shall I help you wash this up?'

'Gracious, no. It can stay where it is till I'm too tired to work.'

'Well, thanks for lunch. Don't forget; if you see Ken Tustin, be firm.'

'Right. Cheerio, then.'

'See you, Tessa.'

When Maddy had closed the door, Tessa stared at it for a moment, then walked over and dropped the snib.

17

'Blummin heck, Dol – you know what time it is?' asked Rose, stepping in at the Cloombs' back door and finding Dolly, not in her coat and scarf and outdoor shoes, but still messing about with her hair and standing in her down-at-heel slippers.

'Sorry, Rose,' Dolly said through a mouthful of hair pins, 'I had a bad night.'

'I'm not surprised. The row he made coming home last night! Give you some bother, did he?' She asked this cautiously, with reluctance, for she felt herself unfairly demeaned by Dolly's propensity for getting herself hit; deep down, Rose wondered whether close friendship with a victim of marital violence did not cloud her own superiority in domestic matters. To guard against this, she was fond of remarking that Jack Fettle, dead these nine years, had never in all their married life raised a hand to her.

'No trouble as such,' said Dolly, yanking out the last curler (she meant that on this occasion Arthur had not struck her), 'but I nearly ruptured meself getting him up the stairs.'

'Should've left him at the bottom, the pig. Do hurry, Dol. We don't want her keeping us today, not if we're getting the twelve o'clock bus.' (They were going to Fetherstone market to choose material for the new outfit Rose had promised to run up for Dolly in time for the Christmas whist drive.)

'Does that look all right?' Dolly asked hopelessly. There was no time to check in the hall mirror.

'It'll do. You ought to have a perm. Tell you what — I've booked Maisie to come and give me one just before the whist drive; she can perm yours at the same time. She might do us a special rate. Now what's the matter?'

'Lost me bag.'

Rose looked round. 'Here it is,' she cried, grabbing it from a chair seat under the table. 'Now, come on.'

Dolly, fastening her coat buttons, hurried after her friend.

Phoebe was darting about the village shop with a wire basket. Dangling from an elbow was her own brown shopping bag; over a shoulder was her shoulder bag. She was as happy as a workhorse let out to grass this morning, and making the best of it; for at any moment misery might smack her down, down and further

142

down until she felt like she did yesterday when she imagined a file thrust into her throat, grinding and rasping through the centre of her body, shooting pain to her extremities. Perhaps taking those extra pills this morning had done the trick. The doctor had warned her not to, but she didn't care; she felt great – daft as a pup, light as duck-down, bubbly as a cow's belly after clover-gorging. Grinning, she reached for a tin of ratatouille. 'Rata-what?' she chortled, and chucked it recklessly into the basket. She swung round muttering, 'I know what I fancy – one of them chocolate oranges,' and squinted at the confectionery shelves behind Brenda Varney's head. Yes, there were some there, all right. She'd ask for one when she went to the counter for some ham. Meanwhile, better think of something for the kids' tea and Roy's supper. Carelessly, she tossed down packets – small ones, tall ones, squashy and sturdy ones; and a few tins; oh – and a jar of coffee.

'There!' Brenda Varney rushed round the end of the counter. 'I knew it, and this time I've caught her. Come here, Mrs Partridge – I hope you'll bear witness. And you, Mr Whitton.' She wrenched open Phoebe's shopping bag, put in her arm and drew out a tin of salmon. 'See? She's been robbing me for weeks only I couldn't catch her at it. Well, now I have,' she cried, brandishing the salmon.

The door opened and Mrs Frogmorton came in. 'Whatever is the matter?' Hesitation caused her to leave the door unclosed.

Before Brenda could answer, Phoebe had gone leaving a little heap on the floor – wire basket, shoulder bag, shopping bag – where a moment since she had stood rooted to the spot while all her happiness fled.

Maddy was preparing Robert's lunch when the pounding came at the door. Startled, she wiped her hands and ran to answer it. Phoebe fell in and stood opening and shutting her mouth.

'Come into the kitchen. Sit down. Now — is it something you ought to tell me quickly or do you want to get your breath back?'

Phoebe scarcely knew, but a few words blurted painfully persuaded Maddy to press her.

'You mean just now, in the shop? Phoebe, you do mean here in the village, not in the supermarket in Fetherstone? Well, that's a relief. Look, have I got this straight? Brenda found a tin of salmon in your bag and accused you of stealing it.'

Phoebe clutched her heart. 'Couldn't think. Didn't know what to do.'

'You did the right thing exactly. You came to tell *me*.' She went to the kitchen door and called loudly up the stairs. 'Robert, will you come down quickly please? Phoebe,' she said, returning, 'I must go and see Brenda. You stay here. Robert will make you a drink.'

A bemused looking Robert came in. Maddy had already grabbed her coat.

'I want you to stay with Phoebe, Robert.' Robert stepped back making dumb pleading gestures, but she continued heartlessly. 'Make her a drink of something. There's been a bit of bother in the shop; it's imperative that I catch Brenda before she closes.' Passing him, she brushed deliberately close. 'And don't let her out of your sight,' she added in a threatening undertone.

All the way along Church Street, Maddy cursed Brenda Varney. Stupid peasant — don't you know anything? Christ, there was that terrible case of poor Lady Whatshername — drowned herself after they'd accused her of shop-lifting. I suppose, if it saved you the odd tin of salmon, you'd quite like Phoebe to do the same, you grasping bone-head . . .

Mid-rant, she stopped herself. She had reached the Green, and for some reason the sight of Holly House across the greensward, calm and solemn with its windows winking, made her sharply aware of the heat

144

coursing through her and the driving wrath which did not necessarily arise solely from this incident. Anger gathered in her quite often these days – just grew out of nothing, obliging her to cast round for some handy thing to pin it on. It was so wearying, this constant expenditure of useless energy – and 'useless' was the apposite word. For instance, whatever was the use of haranguing Brenda Varney? Would it solve Phoebe's problem? Of course not. She was losing her touch, she thought, and with sudden acuity saw her former self dealing with the problem. The vision armed her. She arranged a confidential smile over her features and approached the shop.

Brenda was turning the door sign to 'Closed'.

'How glad I am to have caught you!'

'I'm shut.'

'Would you rather I went round to the house? Only we must talk. I've come about Phoebe.'

'I haven't made up me mind . . .'

'Oh, good,' Maddy said soothingly, and stepped inside. Phoebe's belongings and the wire basket still lay on the floor where she had abandoned them.

Maddy came home with Phoebe's bags tucked under her arm. Robert heard her step and hastened to open the door.

'Hush, she's asleep.'

'Where?'

'In here.' He led the way back into the kitchen where Phoebe was sitting with her cheek on the table, her mouth squashed open, snoring faintly. 'How did it go?'

'All right, I think.'

They sat down in adjacent chairs on the side of the table opposite to Phoebe, watching her while they spoke in whispers.

'She won't report it to the police. In any case, I don't think Mrs Partridge and Mr Whitton – who were in the shop at the time – are prepared to speak up as witnesses. You know what village people are like – won't say a word against anyone to their face, but don't mind if it's behind their back and they won't be quoted. That's going to be the trouble, of course – the gossip. Brenda wanted to ban Phoebe, but I said I didn't think she could. Finally we agreed that in future I'd accompany Phoebe to the shop, at least until she's over this bad patch.'

'That's quite an undertaking.'

'I expect Tessa will help. And I must have a word with Roy. They get the bulk of their shopping at the supermarket in Fetherstone. He'd better make sure he goes with her for the time being. I'm sure he will. He doesn't say much, but he's always been good to her, in spite of his family.'

'Oh, Roy's a nice chap.'

'Yes, that's what I think.'

Phoebe stirred, half-raised her head, then sank down again.

'She does quite a bit of that, apparently,' said Robert. 'I wonder if it's the drugs? She told me she'd had a terrible day yesterday and took extra pills this morning to make sure of a better one. Poor kid – the way she feels sometimes sounds like a perfect nightmare.'

'Oh, Robert.' She took his hand, which was lying on the table, and kissed it.

'What's that for?' But he knew. It was for being brave, for having sufficiently stifled his distaste and fear of human misery to allow Phoebe to talk about it. He was rather proud of the achievement himself, felt warm and enlivened as if he'd indulged in vigorous exercise – strangely tender towards Phoebe, too. Sitting hand in hand with Maddy, watching over – it seemed – their big problem baby, he thought, This is what we've missed, this sharing. Parenting must be a powerful cement.

'I'll help you take her home when she wakes,' he offered.

*　　*　　*

146

Later that afternoon Maddy dialled the Holly House number.

'Tessa – sorry to disturb you.'

'That's OK.'

'I need to ask a favour.'

'Yes?' Tessa said calmly, carefully disguising the wariness which, when she was working, shrank her more instinctive sociability.

'It's for Phoebe, really. This morning there was some unpleasantness in the village shop. Somehow a tin of salmon ended up in Phoebe's bag instead of in one of Brenda's wire baskets. Brenda pounced on it – whether others in the shop saw what happened, I can't say – but there was quite a to-do and Phoebe came charging over to me. Robert looked after her while I went to calm Brenda. She's not going to take it any further – "this time" is how she put it – but she's not keen on Phoebe continuing to use the shop.'

'Oh dear. I don't like the sound of that.'

'Neither do I. It would be a source of endless nastiness in the village and very bad for Phoebe. So I got round it by promising to go with Phoebe when she wants to shop there. And privately, I'm determined to encourage her. Don't you think that's right, Tessa?'

'Yes, I do.'

'The favour is this: if for some reason I happen to be out when Phoebe needs to go to the shop, may she call on you? I shouldn't think it'll happen often, because she and Roy are going to do their main shop together in Fetherstone. But in an emergency . . .'

'Never mind an emergency. Tell her I'll be glad to.'

'Well, I already did. I was sure you'd agree. Thanks.'

'Fine. And – Maddy?'

'Yes?'

'What a blessing she called on *you* for help.'

There was a pause. 'Let's hope so,' said Maddy in a rush. 'Goodbye.' She rang off.

Tessa and Maddy had observed, but had not entirely

147

understood, the traditional caution of the native Wych-woodian when it came to speaking out. This reticence was for a very good reason, namely, that most natives of Wychwood – probably all if one delved back far enough – were related. Their perspective of the village was very different to that of the incomers. They did not think of it as a site of owner occupation ranging from substantial houses to pokey cottages with rented property tacked on to the lower end, nor of the inhabitants as well-educated or ill-educated, poor, comfortably off or downright flashy; rather, they carried always in their consciousness an image of their own kind as an interwoven stratum composed of close kin and cousins to the nth degree, in-laws, and neighbours who for centuries had once shared the same privy; above and below this significant stratum (though mainly above) were the newcomers, whose length of residence – be it four years or forty – was of little consequence or interest.

Many of these Wychwood people had relatives in nearby villages. So it was that when several branches of the WI held a get-together, members who were comparatively new to the area were surprised by all the shy hugging and calling of pet names and old jokes that went on. Mrs Edie Partridge, for instance (who with her second cousin, Dan Whitton, had been present at an awkward moment in the village shop this morning), had a sister married to the VG shopkeeper in Steeple Cheney. Her brother-in-law was Davey Partridge, the master bell ringer who for forty years was considered Wychwood's most eligible bachelor. Furthermore (and fatal to Brenda Varney's cause), Edie's mother had been a Peck. So it had caused Brenda no surprise, though it had bitterly annoyed her, when Edie and Dan proved dumb and blind this morning. In her heart of hearts she acknowledged the impossibility: no Partridge or Whitton would cast doubt on the name of Peck.

Edie lived at Number One Orchard Close, a corner

position affording a commanding view of movements in and out. Her daughter, Gail (the unmarried mother of five), lived at the top end of the Close in Number Twenty, which was why Partridge children were so often to be seen there, moving between mother's house and grandma's. At this moment, Edie was stationed behind a net curtain in her living room. Her embarrassment this morning had turned swiftly to anticipation; for what could not be acknowledged openly in public could be savoured delightfully in private. She had not had such an enjoyable morning for years, and now, having hoarded her treasure over the dinner hour, was impatient for a chance to show it off. Watching the comings and goings, she was sick with dread lest there should be intercourse between this end of the village (hers) and the top end (Dan's); luckily, all the passers-by so far had been Orchard Close dwellers. When Mrs Meers went past she was sorely tempted, but managed to restrain herself. Stella Meers was an insipid woman; it would be a waste to let her have the hearing of it, first-hand and brand new. Rose Fettle was the one Edie most fancied telling her tale to, for Rose thought herself sharper than most and would be mad as a bull to be on the receiving end instead of lording it. Edie was quite worn out by the time the Fetherstone bus drew up at the corner and Rose and Dolly got off.

They'd go to Rose's house, she guessed, for Rose's house didn't have a man in it cluttering the place up. She watched them do as she had anticipated; saw Rose put in her latch key and lead the way inside. Now they'd drop their parcels on the living room table and go into the kitchen to put the kettle on. Edie allowed the kettle three minutes to boil.

Rose was filling the teapot when the knock came. She and Dolly exchanged looks of annoyance.

'Go and answer it, Dol. Try and get rid of 'em.'

But lax-willed Dolly was no match for Edie's impending eruption. 'You *should*'ve been in the shop this morning,' she cried, making straight for her quarry in

149

the kitchen. 'It were shocking, me dears; I nearly died.'

'Cup of tea?' Rose offered.

Edie was determined to save her piece until they were seated cosily in the living room. 'Can I help? Shall I sugar 'em, me duck? You two been on the market?'

They answered her shortly. They knew the form. 'You can spit it out now, I can see you're busting,' said Rose when at last they were seated.

Edie was heard out in silence. Dolly would have made encouraging and sympathetic interjections were it not for Rose's bleak expression. 'Well I never,' she said nervously, when Edie had exhausted herself.

'She's wild, that one. Wouldn't surprise me if she ended up in quod.'

'Oh, Rose, you don't think she might? How terrible for poor Roy.'

'And for those kids. What sort of life can they have with their mother a criminal?'

'You remember that fire at the stables?'

'That's not all of it. Remember those plates vanishing from the village hall?'

'You mean . . . ?'

'I'm not saying. But who else round here's been caught red-handed?'

'Dear me, it don't bear thinking about.'

And so it went on, with Phoebe slipping further and further into recidivism.

When Edie had gone and they were swilling out the cups, Rose gave vent to her strongest feelings in the matter. 'Trust us to go to Fetherstone the one day summat actually happens. If we hadn't been rushing for the bus we'd've gone into the shop on our way home; we always go in for doughnuts on a Friday.'

Dolly, for whose sake they had undertaken the trip, feared Rose was blaming her. 'But we did enjoy the trip out.'

'We could've enjoyed it just as well another day when Phoebe Peck was behaving herself.'

Dolly said no more, but allowed silence to smooth away Rose's crossness. And soon it did. 'I think it'll suit you,' Rose remarked.

'What? Oh, you mean the material. It will. It's lovely.'

'I'll cut it out tonight. When I've made your dress I've got to make them dolls for the bazaar – I promised Mrs Burrows a few for her toy stall.'

'You are clever, Rose. I'll give a pot of me piccalilli.'

'Better not let Arthur see you then, the skinflint.'

'No,' Dolly sighed. 'I ent half looking forward to it, though.'

'Me an' all, Dol. Me an' all.'

18

Sunlight blazed through the uncurtained half of the window and cut the room in two. The lighted half was full of restless dust-motes disdaining to settle on the plastic surfaces of floor, chairs and trolley-table. The shrouded half, where Colin lay and Tessa sat, was devoted to the fundamentals – breathing, easing thirst, avoiding discomfort. As we begin, so shall we end, thought Tessa, observing Colin's chapped mouth and wondering whether it was worth disturbing him to offer again the teacher-beaker. He would nod in agreement if she held it out to him, for he had been instructed to drink frequently, but the effort would be exhausting and probably distressing. She glanced at the wrist watch abandoned days ago on top of the bedside cabinet and decided to postpone the ordeal for another ten minutes. Hand in hand, they endured the passing time in silence.

The far end of the room, where the glare obliterated underlying details and busy dust-specks swam, seemed to Tessa a representation of life as we blithely, recklessly live it, and this dim end suitable only for life's start and close, for bodily fixation. Her most urgent longing was to escape into the light; his was to pass the wind ballooning his stomach.

The last time she was here, four days ago, Colin had talked without pause for half an hour, having carefully thought out what he had to say beforehand. His children and his first wife, Lucy, were on his mind: they had spent such wonderful years together; he couldn't believe this didn't *mean* something. He asked Tessa to talk about him to his children when they next came to England, especially to recall their early years, which they may have forgotten – years shared with Tessa, Nick and Paul. Also, he wanted her to write to Lucy and pass on a friendly message – 'that I remember our time together with happiness and often think about it – something like that, Tessa.' She had heard him out and solemnly agreed to do as he wished, relieved, on this occasion to be able to give her promise without hesitating. At an earlier stage in his illness, he had asked her to befriend Sophia. Luckily, when she had pointed out the difficulties, particularly that Sophia might not welcome this, he had laughed and let her off.

Today he had no spare breath for talking. His self-absorption made her feel intrusive; she wondered whether her company was a comfort or a hindrance.

Out of the blue, before she had time to consider and repress the impulse, her desire for light brought her to her feet. She let go of his hand and went to the window which, from the top floor of the building, overlooked a grim quadrangle where starlings were scrapping. 'The noise these birds make!' she exclaimed as a cover for her sudden action. 'You should see them, Colin, squawking and swooping out here. Must be dozens of them. The wind's ruffled their feathers and made them look cross and slightly barmy. Their colours show up well in this light – flecks of iridescent purple and green.' Her hand went up to the curtain, but this time she checked her instinct – which was to snatch it back and let light pervade the room and perhaps arouse him to an awareness beyond his body. She dropped her hand and looked back to the bed. He smiled thinly. Did he wish she would go? Or did she want to believe that he wished she would go? 'Time you had another drink,' she declared, returning heartlessly to the bed-side cabinet. She slid an arm under his head and raised it, and put the beaker's spout to his red-raw mouth.

A nurse came in and saved her. 'Sorry to break this up,' she said archly, 'but doctor's on his way. Going to make you more comfortable,' she confided to Colin; then, looking at Tessa, 'There's a sitting room on the second floor if you want to wait.'

'No, no. I'll go now.' She looked into Colin's eyes and said (pretending to a certainty which neither fully believed in), 'I'll see you again in a day or two. Bye-bye, darling.'

Gathering her belongings and going without a backward glance to the door, she affected casualness as if these visits would go on indefinitely; but she was acutely aware of him watching her, perhaps for the last time.

In the car park someone was calling. She only half heard, assuming herself unconnected with anyone or anything here. Then, startlingly, the anonymous call became her own name, and when she turned and scanned the car roofs, there along a concrete corridor was Viv hurtling towards her. 'Tes . . . sa . . . I'm . . . so . . . glad . . . to . . . see . . . you!' – the running cry ended in a bear-hug. Then Viv stepped back leaving her hands gripping Tessa's arms, and looking stern demanded, 'How is he?'

'Worse. In great discomfort, I thought. As I was leaving, the doctor arrived, so I don't suppose they'll let you see him straight away. But there's a sitting room on the second floor.'

Viv shuddered. 'Gee, I'd rather wait out here. I do admire you, Tess,' she went on as Jerry came lumbering up, 'for coming here on your own. I couldn't do it without Jerry.'

You mean Jerry couldn't do it without you, thought Tessa.

Jerry looked careworn – as well he might after twenty years as the director of one of the more volatile university departments; he also looked sheepish which was his customary expression when faced with emotions not arising from academia. A sheepish expression had been his response to the news that Lucy had deserted Colin, also to Tessa's public weeping over Nick's affair with Janet Wainright, the departmental siren. Viv, on the other hand, thrived on passion and disaster, having metamorphosed from a dreamy Californian layabout into a devoted mother of three and a tireless worker for causes, notably, nuclear disarmament, a pollution-free environment and the release of political prisoners.

'Have you heard from Lucy?' Viv wanted to know.

'Not since Christmas. We had Annabel to stay in the summer, and I think Simon plans to fly over at the end of term.'

'Whether that'll be in time to see his father . . .' she shrugged. 'But I'm real glad Colin saw Annabel. He misses those kids. You don't think we ought to persuade them to come right now?'

'Not really. They're at college. Anyway, Colin hates a fuss.'

'I wonder about Lucy, though.'

'Impossible,' Tessa thought.

'She's wrapped up in husband number three,' Jerry pointed out.

'Number three!' echoed Viv, shaking her head at her number one and only. 'Say – d'you reckon we lack initiative?'

Jerry ignored her. 'And if Lucy did come, Sophia would have hysterics.'

154

They all sighed, and Viv nuzzled her head on Tessa's shoulder. (Tessa knew exactly what she would say next.) 'Where does the time go, Tess? We should *see* each other.'

Laughing both at her predictability and her dishonesty (the truth was, Viv had no time to spare from her causes), Tessa reflected that the long gaps between their meetings didn't really matter, for whenever they did bump into one another it was as though they had never been apart, so instantly were they at ease. Though I could never make her a true confidante, she reflected; I should feel so guilty pinching time from Amnesty International. 'I know. It's sad. Look, when things have settled down, you must come for Sunday lunch.' Guiltily, she knew they would assume that by 'things settling down' she meant Colin's illness, whereas it was the ending of Nick's affair with Maddy she was thinking of, for until that happy time she preferred not to have Viv's sharp eyes roaming her domestic scene.

'So long as it's in the pub. You mustn't dream of cooking.'

'Done. Look, I must go; I've a ravenous dog to feed.'

'That surly little beast?'

'Scrap,' Tessa said reproachfully.

Viv and Jerry each took one of her arms and walked with her to her car.

'I rather think,' confided Jerry, who could not for long keep his mind off life's importances, 'we may have found a solution to our problem with those papers. Do you know Roger Delzine? He was at Birkbeck with Colin where they collaborated on a series of books. Well, he's visiting the department next week – and coming to see Colin, obviously – and he's promised to look in on Sophia. Apparently, he is unique among Colin's friends in that she likes and approves of him. Colin had already told him of our little difficulty. A smooth operator, is Roger; he may well succeed where we rougher types failed.'

'Then Nick will be relieved.'

They stowed her into her car as if she were precious cargo, and stood waving until she had driven away.

Waiting at traffic lights on her way home, Tessa looked across and saw Maddy waiting in the opposite direction. It was the car she recognized first, then, familiarity fleshing out what she barely perceived, the driver. When the lights changed, she drove off slowly, watching to see whether Maddy had noticed the Volvo. But the little white car shot eagerly forward and Tessa, in one flashing second, gained a vivid and encompassing view of her friend who, without a doubt, was oblivious of all but a skimpy impression of her surroundings. She was jigging her head and mouthing words – presumably to music. She looked larky, all set for fun. Tessa wanted to pull into the side, to turn and zoom after her, to yell, Hang on, wait for me. That Maddy was racing to meet Nick did not at this moment occur to her, for the image had triggered a memory of a day last year spent with Maddy in Oxford.

Maddy was the driver, singing gaily to one of her tapes (of the sort which she never played in the house but only in her car). They went round the shops and tried on clothes they would never dream of buying, then took a late lunch at Gianni's and became so merry they had afterwards to walk for miles in the sun, through the botanical gardens and Christ Church Meadow, until sufficiently sober to drive home.

'Fifty pounds? You spent fifty pounds on lunch?' Nick had repeated when Tessa let out this fact.

'Fifty pounds *between us*, silly boy,' Maddy emphasized to reassure him. 'But don't tell Robert.'

'God Almighty, you must be mad.'

'It was a special occasion, wasn't it, Tessa?'

Nick was suspicious. 'What special occasion?'

'It was a special occasion of itself,' Maddy told him coldly, her tone implying little hope of comprehension from such a dolt.

Tessa, feeling a grin spreading over her face at the memory, checked it by recalling that it was the self-same dolt Maddy was now driving to meet. The ache in her heart was like a bud unfurling.

The phone was ringing as she ran up the steps. She did not hurry to unlock the door; paused, even, to fondle Scrap. 'Yes?' she said at last.

'Sorry, love. Got caught up in something. Shan't need dinner.'

'Somehow I thought you mightn't.'

Silence. Then: 'What d'you mean?'

He knows perfectly well what I mean, she thought; he just pretends to himself that I don't – blasted hypocrite. 'Oh nothing. I'm despondent, that's all. Spent the afternoon with Colin.'

'Bad was it?'

'Wretched.'

'Look, I'll try not to be too late.'

Foolishly, irrationally, picturing Maddy bouncing at the wheel full of eagerness, she hurried to forestall her friend's disappointment. 'No need to hurry, I shan't wait up – I need an early night.'

'Right. Hugs and kisses, then?'

'Yeah. 'Bye, Nick,' she said, and laid down the receiver.

Afterwards, she performed several tasks most calmly, fed the animals in turn, emptied the waste bin, scrubbed at burnt-on dirt on the cooker, even ran up two flights of stairs to examine the work she had completed this morning (and found it still satisfactory). But she did these things in a half-dream, all the time carrying at the back of her mind an insidious conviction of Nick's unworthiness. This conviction had attacked her in the past and was most effectively dispersed by single-minded concentration on his good points. She would conjure up telling pictures – Nick the charmer, Nick the sympathetic, Nick the sensitive and funny; and should goodness prove inadequate, she would invoke pity as well, dwelling on the

157

tragically orphaned eleven-year-old Nick until her heart was once more safely and properly engaged.

Somehow, this evening, she was too tired to be bothered with these mechanisms. Coming down from her attic studio, she paused on the first floor landing and looked out of the window at the dusk-cloaked Green. (The waviness of the ancient window panes slightly distorted the view. As she tilted her head gently from side to side, shadows thrown by the street lamp undulated like cautious worms, becoming still when she did, waiting for her next move.) Why it should be shaming to love someone who was less than perfect suddenly struck her as ridiculous. You are overwrought because of Colin, she told herself, and in no fit state to start altering decisions. Much better trust in the one already taken. It was true that the affair had gone on for longer than she had anticipated, but it would end soon. It must. All she had to do was to go on believing this.

19

Really and truly, for she was an old-fashioned thing, Eleanor confessed she would prefer luncheon at the Ram in Fetherstone. So here they were in the dingy oak-panelled dining room where everything – waitresses and menu included – wore an air of having conceded their better days to history. With regret, Tessa thought of the bright interiors, the professional service and admirable cooking now available in several local establishments; but Eleanor beamed round with satisfaction. 'So long since I was here. Let me see . . . Timothy and I came for luncheon on my birthday. Last year? No, the year before that. Do you know, it's two years last June?' She seemed to be mourning all the lost luncheons in between. 'Of course, Winifred and I used to come often; but that was a long time ago.'

The food, as Tessa had anticipated, was dreadful, but Eleanor ate with relish, and was particularly delighted when the waitress belatedly scurrying up with mint sauce suddenly claimed her as a fondly remembered patron. And when, as she raised a spoonful of gooseberry tart to her lips, she spotted Canon Topping and his wife at a distant table, her pleasure was complete. 'Canon and Mrs Topping,' she reported to Tessa in significant undertone, and nodded sagely as if to say, You see, my dear, we have come to the *right place*.

Stirring her cup of muddy coffee, Eleanor remembered a piece of news she intended to break. 'Do you recall, Tessa, all those things we got up last year in aid of the organ fund – the coffee mornings and the jumble sale, and that delightful painting of the kissing gate you gave us for the raffle? Well, as there was quite a sum left over when the work on the organ was done, the committee decided – and I know this will please you, my dear – to commission a small plate commemorating Winifred's years as our organist. A very discreet and tasteful brass to be put on the organ front. Timothy will dedicate it one Sunday at evensong towards the end of this month – I'll let you know precisely when, for I'm sure you will wish to be present.'

'Er – mm,' Tessa agreed absently, depressed by a prevision of herself at the service obediently submitting to having her heart wrung; and moving from thence to similar pictures of herself being and doing as she ought, and not as she felt inclined. With mounting panic she saw herself adrift on a sea of other people's needs and desires, and began to long most urgently to be back at work in her studio, in control, self-directed, alone. 'I'm not sure whether Nick . . .' she began prevaricating.

159

'Oh, never mind that. You must sit with me in the Rectory pew. After all, you and I shall be the two people there who were most close to Winifred.'

Tessa raised her head and shot a smile across the table. 'So we shall,' she said.

Rose Fettle sat at her table sticking pins into a doll – in fact, it was not quite yet a doll, but would be when she had replaced the pins with stitching. She took pins as she required them from a beaded pincushion which had once won her first prize for handicraft in a WI competition. When perfectly satisfied as to the rudimentary doll's shape and line, she rummaged through a collection of bobbins in an old Oxo tin, found the one she required and snapped off a length of thread which, by licking its end and rolling it between her fingers, she managed to entice through the eye of a needle. Then she shifted herself in her chair and settled down to sew.

The position she had settled to – shoulders back against the chair, elbows supported by the chair-arms, work raised near her face – was very familiar to her and very comforting; it was the one she had adopted as a child bidden to darn the family linen and as a young woman earning her bread with her needle. As her body relaxed into this customary posture, it was very easy with her eyes narrowly confined to her work to imagine herself in other settings where she had sat thus. Increasingly these days she thought back to her early years in Back End Row, as she did now, translating herself into a small girl with the sheets to mend seated by the family table.

The old cottage cajoled her senses. Behind her, a fire glowed and water moaned in a blackened kettle. In the muddy street outside, a horse and cart spattered by; calling children ran past the window. Out of the corner of her eye she glimpsed her mother – sighing and complaining – rise up and light the lamp, for the window was small and the daylight dismal. As the kettle began to splutter, her mother removed it from the fire, and Rose, her nose twitching, caught the pungency of hot sooty iron – it mingled with the starchy smell of the linen she was darning. This last made her think of Mrs Lamb in the end cottage who possessed a copper and took in her neighbours' washing. It were all right for her, a widow living on her own, thought Rose, but what with Mother, Father, Bobby and me, and Father's sheep dog in the kennel and the pig in the sty by the back door, there weren't no room for a copper. Just think: there were us lot in the middle cottage, five Tubbinses on one side of us, and Dolly's lot with their daft lad Jim on the other; then all them Partridges at one end of the row and Mrs Lamb at the other; the lot of us crammed into what *she* calls Jasmine Cottage.

Immediately, the scene in Rose's head changed to the village shop. She was waiting her turn to be served from the bacon slicer, while in front of her stood Maddy Storr loudly airing her notion of what life must have been like for the poor souls who once inhabited her newly reordered home. 'Simply cheek by jowl, the poor souls – the agent told us at one time there may have been fifteen or sixteen – a communal privy and Lord knows how many to a bed! No wonder there was disease and inbreeding.'

Mrs Storr's version of her early life had shaken Rose. She dwelt on the words, reran them obsessively in her head, applied them tentatively to her memories. There was disease right enough, she thought now; two of them Partridge lads coughed their lives away and Mrs Tubbins never walked again after her fifth. And she pondered uncomfortably over the case of Dolly's brother Jim, for she had heard there was some connection between idiocy and inbreeding. But the suspicion that Mrs Storr's words were rooted in fact only served to strengthen her sense of outrage and resentment. It was money she blamed, the money that had enabled a woman with scant knowledge of country ways to buy her way in and change everything to her own liking and disparage all that had gone before.

Her needle flew furiously as she mounted a counterattack in which she totted up the many good things about those days, the neighbourliness, the cosy companionship, the fun got from simple things. We didn't have to throw pots of money around and rush about disturbing and upsetting everything to get pleasure from life, cos our sort knows how to take what comes and make summat good out of it. Like me and Dolly fer instance, giving folks a party outta the bazaar tea leftovers.

The doll was made. She broke off the thread and put away her needle. Now she must decide how to dress it. She looked to the sideboard where there was already a row of completed dolls for Mrs Burrows' toy stall, and then back down at the naked one, considering. An idea came to her, and a lop-sided grin altered her face; she began to hunt through a mound of fabric scraps, picking out pieces of cloth in every shade of red.

Tessa and Eleanor were sitting in Tessa's car outside the Rectory gate. Tessa was talking animatedly, for the sun had come out after the morning's downpour and her spirits could never resist the light. Brightness lit Wychwood as though it were newly born and the lanes, still with puddles here and there, gently steamed and sparkled. The leaves in the Rectory shrubbery shone glossily. Tessa could not but feel that, whatever her troubles, on the whole life was pretty exhilarating.

Driving through the village they had passed several people exercising dogs and standing about gossiping. 'The sun soon brings them out,' Eleanor had remarked. 'Your little dog will be listening for you anxiously.'

'Oh, look,' she said now. 'There's Phoebe Peck stationed outside Mrs Bull's. It is her Land Rover, isn't it? I wonder what she can want with that old talebearer. Which reminds me: Mrs Frogmorton said some very harsh things about poor Phoebe the other day. I was not surprised to hear Rose Fettle speak unkindly when she told me about the incident in the village shop, but really, from Mrs Frogmorton! Such a revealing lack of charity. Thank goodness Brenda was persuaded to show discretion. I believe we have Mrs Storr to thank.'

High and low, thought Tessa, they all love to dish the dirt in this place. While Eleanor was speaking, Tessa had been watching the Land Rover which she now perceived to contain several occupants. It occurred to her that though Phoebe was parked outside Mrs Bull's, since the vehicle was pointing in this direction it could just as well be considered to be waiting outside Holly House. 'Do you know, I've a feeling Phoebe wants *me*,' she told Eleanor.

'Then you must go. Thank you, Tessa, for a lovely lunch. It was so kind of you to take me.'

'We'll do it again,' Tessa promised before the passenger door closed.

She drove up the street. Drawing level with the Land Rover, she leaned her head out of the window. 'Hello. Waiting for me?'

Phoebe nodded. On the passenger seat beside her, two little girls bobbed and craned their necks to peep at the newcomer.

'I'll just put the car away,' Tessa called.

Phoebe had got out of the Land Rover and her children were running up and jumping down the Holly House steps when Tessa returned. 'Come in,' she invited.

Phoebe looked embarrassed. 'I wanted a favour,' she admitted. 'Maddy's out, and . . .'

'Oh – you want to go to the shop. Of course. Let's go.'

'It's these two,' Phoebe explained as they went towards the Green. 'I was late picking 'em up from play-school and I promised 'em lollies when we got back to make up fer it.'

'Lollies, eh?' said Tessa to the little girls, who squirmed delightedly.

163

Silence fell over the shop as Phoebe and Tessa entered. 'Go and choose 'em, then,' Phoebe said, shoving the girls forward.

'Good afternoon, Brenda,' Tessa called. 'Good afternoon, Mrs Meers.'

'Afternoon,' echoed Brenda grudgingly. 'I'll just serve these if you don't mind,' she said confidingly to Mrs Meers, and might just as well have added to be rid of them quickly, so plain was her meaning. Mrs Meers was only too glad of the excuse to delay her departure and take in every detail of the lollipop transaction. Brenda walked round the counter and threw up the lid of the refrigerator. 'Red, orange, or chocolate?'

'Red,' they chorused shyly.

'*Please*,' Phoebe added, attending to etiquette as a means of emphasizing her position in the village as Mrs Roy Peck.

'Please,' her children whispered.

'That's 30p.' Brenda held out her hand.

Phoebe counted out the money. 'Thank you.'

'Thank *you*, I'm sure,' said Brenda sarcastically.

Tessa, pulling open the shop door and gulping, discovered she had been holding her breath. Bitch, she felt inclined to comment as they walked back to Holly House, but decided, in deference to Phoebe's feelings, to pretend not to have noticed Brenda's rudeness. 'Come in and have a cup of tea,' she suggested.

'They'll only drip their lollies.'

'Never mind. We'll stay in the kitchen.'

'They can play on the steps while they lick 'em,' Phoebe said. 'You'd like that, wouldn't yer?'

With that settled, and Scrap silenced with a bowl of dinner, Tessa made a pot of tea while Phoebe sat staring thoughtfully at the drying flowers in the inglenook.

'She's nice, int she?' she said suddenly as though Tessa by osmosis had followed her thoughts.

'Er . . . Maddy?' Tessa hazarded.

'Yeah,' said Phoebe, surprised there could be any

doubt. 'And sort of funny. She don't half make me laugh sometimes – when we're out shopping and that. She tries on daft hats.'

'Yes, she does,' Tessa agreed, remembering.

'Never buys one, though.'

'I don't think she likes hats.'

'Neither do I. And pretty, int she? Fer her age.'

Tessa smiled.

There was a pause, then Phoebe said, 'She's been very good to me over my trouble.'

'I know. Are you feeling any better, Phoebe?'

'Sometimes I am, sometimes I ent. Depends. A good gallop perks me up – usually.'

The girls came in and had their faces and hands wiped in the scullery. They tried to play with Scrap, but he proved disobliging and so Tessa showed them some lavender bags she had made for the Christmas bazaar.

'You and Maddy doin' the teas again?' asked Phoebe.

'Of course.'

'Me and Roy'll give the cheese for the sandwiches.'

'Thanks. I'll put that down on my list.'

'Come on you two, better get you home before your gran thinks I've drowned you or summat.' She grinned awkwardly at Tessa and added, 'Thanks for – you know.'

'Any time. Bye-bye, girls.'

They ran down the steps calling goodbyes and scrambled into the Land Rover.

Tessa watched them go and worried whether Maddy was aware of Phoebe's growing dependence on her.

Rose was watching from her window when Arthur Cloomb, dragging his feet and only half-alive at this time of day before his evening drink, went through his gateway and set off to the end of the Close. She pulled on her coat against the wintry nip in the air, put up the snib on her door and hurried over the road. 'Dolly?'

she called, opening the Cloomb back door. And again, stepping into the kitchen, 'You there, Dol?'

Dolly was hugging the living room fire. She had been longing for her chance to do this for the past hour, becoming colder and stiffer with every passing minute. Even so, when Arthur left, she had added only one small log to the glow, not liking to build a large blaze for just herself. 'Yes?' she answered grudgingly. 'I'm in here.'

'He's gone, ent he? Come back with us; I've summat to show you. Dear me – call that a fire? Put the guard up, girl, and come and get a proper warm.' She went into the hall and took down Dolly's coat from a peg.

They scurried across the road, hunched in their coats. Gail Partridge, turning into the Close, caught sight of the shadowy pair and thought they looked up to no good.

'Ooh, that's more like it,' Dolly cried, spying the fire. 'Arthur's mean with the logs, specially when he's off out for the evening.' She ran forward holding out her hands.

'Sit down, me duck,' Rose said, generously shoving her into her favourite chair. She waited to allow Dolly time to thaw into a receptive frame of mind, then rose and went to the sideboard. 'Here. What d'you think of this?' she asked, returning with the latest doll. She held it up with one hand. As Dolly stared – for the doll did not possess the blank simpering expression of the standard Fettle creation, but had a distinctly mean look – Rose put up a finger of her free hand and passed it slowly between the doll's legs – not with any lewd intent, merely to demonstrate that the doll's red skirt was divided.

Dolly gasped. 'Oh, law, Rose, you've gone and made *her*.'

'Madame President,' confirmed Rose softly. 'Fancy a cup of cocoa?'

20

Maddy, tapping her glass of water with a biro, called the meeting to order.

Dutifully they fell silent. Those felled in mid-chat hastily promised to tell the rest later, those who had been unable to get a word in edgeways sadly abandoned their pent-up comments. They looked towards the table on the platform where the president, flanked by her officials, was taking a sheaf of papers from her executive-style briefcase. Mrs Davenport, the secretary, was called upon to read the minutes of last week's meeting, which she duly did, earning herself a vote of approval. Then the treasurer was asked to report. Mrs Joiner rose and rendered simple sets of figures complicated by describing her state of mind and the doings of various members of the Joiner family at the time she had reckoned them. Maddy leaned across helpfully now and then, elucidating and clarifying for the benefit of members. When it was the president's own turn, Maddy rose with her sheaf of papers and told them all they needed to know of her correspondence with various WI bigwigs. Also, she chivvied them about their competition entries, recommended certain courses and excursions and asked them to support a new WI venture to aid isolated mothers in the city. Discussion followed. The president, it was felt, rather hurried them along. Mrs Burrows took exception and protested that Wychwood was not a large institute and members should think very carefully before taking on further, particularly outside, commitments. There were murmurs of agreement. Mrs Fettle opined that folk in the country had their problems, too, and was robustly applauded. With regret, Maddy let the city mothers go: her priority tonight was that they should just get on with it, cut the cackle, stick up their hands at appropriate moments, and allow her to be gone by half past nine precisely. Of course, the tricky part would come with the guest speaker. Happily, as tonight's talk was to be illustrated with slides, darkness would allow her surreptitiously to bring things to a close, should the need arise; and she would not scruple to do this, for tonight's speaker was a mere 'fill-in', a cheap, expenses-only booking hoping to drum up business for his garden centre near Fetherstone. The express purpose of inviting these people who would address them without a fee was to save funds to spend on expensive speakers and demonstrators, and on favourite causes. One thing Maddy knew she could rely on tonight was the prompt circulation of coffee and biscuits. 'I want to get off sharpish,' she had confided beforehand to Jane Bowman and Sarah Grace, whose turn it was to be hostesses – young capable women who would serve up and clear away quickly and without fuss. Furthermore, Jane Bowman was a key-holding member of the village hall committee and could be left to lock up afterwards.

The speaker – on Alpine plants – was introduced, and when his equipment was set up and working, the lights were extinguished and he began; which was the signal for several in his audience to turn to private reflection, or, like Phoebe Peck, to switch off altogether.

Eleanor Browne surrendered to the remorse besetting her – an acute sense of failure, a mental picture of God's disappointment. Earlier in the day Edie Partridge had called at the Rectory to request a pastoral visit for her ailing father-in-law in Number Two the Almshouses. As Timothy was out at the time, Eleanor had promised to pass the message on. Unluckily, before she could make a note of the request on the pad kept for the purpose on Timothy's desk, the telephone rang and a series of further items to be logged drove poor Mr Partridge out of her head. Forgotten he remained until she arrived at the village hall this evening and found Edie regaling members with an account of her father-in-law's bad turn. (Useless, then, to dash home with the news, because Timothy was taking his confirmation class.) Eleanor feared that she was becoming pathologically forgetful. Forgive me, dear Father, she prayed, her eyes misting on an over-lit mound of edelweiss, and – if it be Thy will – let me not become as poor Auntie Bo, – and to erase any suggestion of having deprecated her unfortunate relative, she added, grant Auntie Bo Thine eternal peace. Her guilt disposed of, she turned to the next item – atonement: how to keep Mr Partridge in mind until she was safely in the vicinity of the Rectory notepad. She required a means of jogging her memory. There was a pencil in one of her pockets, and several scraps of paper; however, should she write herself a note, could she rely on herself to read it when she got home? Might she not pull it out of her pocket days later when, in Partridge circles, Timothy's name was already mud? Of course, she could tie a knot in one of the many handkerchiefs stowed about her person, but, again, there was no guarantee of her noticing it. What *must* she see on her return? She imagined herself going in through the back door and through to the cloakroom to remove her coat. And then it came to her: she would tie something on to the ring of her coat zip – there was bound to be a piece of string or thread in one of her pockets. Furtively, she began to hunt.

By now, Phoebe Peck was faintly snoring. Rose Fettle, sitting on her right, nudged Dolly Cloomb. Mrs Frogmorton, to the left of Phoebe, murmured 'Dear, dear,' grimly in Mrs Bultitude's ear, and Mrs Bultitude tutted in reply. Then, finding the Alpine flowers rather tame, all four ladies lapsed into private contemplation of Phoebe's famous misdemeanours.

Sally Grace was glowering at the screen as if the Swiss mountainside were hateful to her; but it was her child's teacher she saw illumined there – a mean-spirited woman who this afternoon had remarked unfavourably on little Pippa Grace's attitude.

Nor had slides of Alpine flora captured Madame President's attention. Maddy was gloating, inwardly slavering and hugging herself over a particular miracle – that this time *he* had rung *her*. It was a sharply erotic little fact: she crossed and uncrossed her legs as her mind constantly returned to it. Other thoughts and feelings intermingled: amazement at the risk she was taking (she who had always been open and predictable, keen to be thought well of and much given to rallying weaker souls) and a new appalled self-knowledge that if she wanted a thing badly enough she would take it. Her excuse was that being new to it, lust had knocked her sideways. Hitherto, mild sexual pleasure had been the limit of her experience. When girls at school and in the office had mooned and swooned and thrown hysterics she had thought they exaggerated out of a wish to dramatize themselves. She had never dreamed of a force so powerful. It astonished her how passion could flourish in the face of prejudicial knowledge, for she was well acquainted with Nick's record of treachery. Robert, if he like herself had been confided in, would have called Nick a rotter, and on the whole, thinking back over Tessa's troubles, Maddy thought it an apt word. (Not that she dwelt on Tessa's confidences, for they prompted very uneasy feelings.) Nick was charming, witty, sensitive, clever, but not a man, she warned herself lightly, for a smart lady to become involved with. She even guessed it was the unlikeliness of their rather antagonistic friendship suddenly bursting into attraction that had gripped him in the first place, and a sense of power for having sparked her late awakening that kept him enthralled. 'You're like a wild little cat,' he had marvelled in a self-congratulatory tone; 'no-one would ever suspect it.' Sometimes she envisaged his obsession for her turning to hate as his fear of losing

170

Tessa grew and he took stock of Maddy's betrayal of her best friend. It would have to end somehow, but, please, not violently. And not yet – ah, God – not yet.

This bloody man would go on for ever. By the light of the projector, she squinted at her watch. It was five past nine, dammit. Smoothly, she rose, waited for him to take breath, then lent her lips to his ear. For herself he could go on for as long as he cared to, she whispered; sadly, time was getting on and some of the ladies were elderly. He readily agreed to very quickly skip through the last few slides.

When the lights came on, Phoebe sat up. She had the startled look of a prematurely roused child, staring-eyed and tousled. Mrs Bultitude hauled herself to her feet by pulling on the chair in front of her, and proposed a vote of thanks which was roundly applauded. Then the hatch door opened and coffee and biscuits circulated.

It was nine-thirty. The moment had come. Maddy's legs, though turned to the consistency of marshmallow and scarcely able to bear her weight, carried her across the room to Jane Bowman's side and, when Jane had repeated her promise to see everyone off the premises and lock up, supported her as she seized her shoulder bag, co-operated as she turned to flee. Once she was seated in the car fumbling for her keys, however, they threatened collapse, wobbled violently, almost jibbed at depressing the pedals. Nevertheless, within seconds she was gone from Wychwood.

'Where's Maddy?' wailed Phoebe, a lost waif. 'She can't just have gone.'

But she had: Mrs Davenport had seen her. 'She dashed off.'

'Strange.'

'Not like her at all.'

'I wonder if she wasn't too well. She seemed restless – a bit fidgety,' Mrs Joiner reported.

Mrs Frogmorton was vexed. 'Blow! I wanted to tackle her about a WI stall for the Christmas bazaar.'

'What WI stall?' asked Mrs Burrows, who was running a toy stall and wanted no dilution of effort. 'We didn't have one last year.'

'But we always used to,' Mrs Bultitude remembered.

'That's true. Maisie ran it one year, didn't she, Pat?'

'Mrs Grieves ran it for years.'

'And Dolly's made some of her piccalilli for it, special,' protested Rose.

'You see?' Mrs Frogmorton cried in triumph, precedent having negated the need for further argument.

'She's left her case,' yelled Phoebe, grabbing and embracing it as though it were a limb of the lost Maddy.

As one, they turned and stared.

'I'll take it,' Mrs Joiner said calmly. 'I'm going past her door. I'll drop it in.'

'No, I will,' said Phoebe.

Embarrassment shrank the air. Uppermost in every mind was the incident which had most recently enlarged Phoebe's reputation.

'Now, now, Mrs Peck,' Mrs Frogmorton said reasonably, advancing and laying a hand to the briefcase.

Phoebe dealt with her as smartly as she would a frisky stallion – 'Shove off – *I'm* taking it!' While Mrs Frogmorton fell back into the arms of her companions, Phoebe raced out of the hall and across the street to the haven of Jasmine Cottage.

Nick had not come home; nor had he telephoned. Tessa had taken his dinner – which was fettucini and would not keep – into the scullery and scraped it into the waste bin. Then she had gone upstairs to her studio to sort through sketches and notes, planning tomorrow's work. For the next two hours she did not think of him. Nor did she allow the thought to enter her head that for the fourth evening in succession he had snatched time to see Maddy. Coming up here had been on purpose to pre-empt such thoughts. She was working; hence she was inviolate.

172

The phone, when it rang, jolted her; she put aside her notes and stared at the noisy thing – unlikely to be Nick; it was probably Paul. 'Oh – *Robert*,' she answered after a hesitation, her voice made unsteady by a quick fierce pulse in her throat.

'I'm sorry to disturb you,' he said, for she had taken an age to answer and sounded flustered. 'You don't happen to know the whereabouts of my wife?'

'No. Why? Have you lost her?' The quip produced in the midst of her panic was masterly, she thought.

He laughed politely. 'It's WI night, of course. She said she had to go on somewhere afterwards. I could swear she said to Phoebe's, but just now Phoebe arrived with Maddy's briefcase. Apparently Maddy left the meeting in a terrific hurry and drove off without it. I wondered if I'd got it wrong, and you and she had arranged to go somewhere together. I quite expected Nick to answer . . .'

'No, we're just having a lazy evening. I shouldn't worry if I were you, there must be a thousand and one things Maddy could be doing. I bet it's something to do with those blessed Christmas bazaar teas – she's quite worked up about them. She thinks I ought to get equally heated, but you know me – anything for a quiet life.' Her voice ran on unperturbed and idle-sounding. It amazed her. All this time she had possessed a talent for deviousness and never suspected it – a shame it wasn't *she* who was addicted to love-affairs; she would be so much better at covering them up than poor old Nick.

Then Robert rather upset her complacency. 'Tessa – do you mind if I ask you something?'

'That depends,' she said lightly, putting a hand to her throat.

'You and Maddy haven't quarrelled, have you?'

'Good Lord, no. Why ever should you think it?'

His groan was exasperated. 'I don't know. Forget I mentioned it. It's just that she's behaving oddly. Inconsistently. One moment she's sweet, the next sour

173

as hell. And it struck me that your name seems to make her jumpy.'

'How . . . strange. But it's, um, it's probably what I said, Robert – you know – she's fed up with me for not feeling properly roused over this refreshments business.' (Heavens, how lame it sounded. She must make it more convincing.) 'I won't bother you with the details, but there's pressure on us to cadge sufficient contributions for the whist drive supper as well . . .'

'Don't bother, I've heard it all before. You're probably right. I'm sorry to have disturbed you both. Apologize to Nick for me.'

When they had said goodbye and rung off, his mention of Nick hung in the silence. She sat hunched over the telephone thinking of how Nick – blast him – would somehow have to be coached into showing no surprise if Robert referred to this call. How was she to do this coaxing without unleashing Nick's potentially havoc-wreaking insecurity? And what, if Robert chose to repeat them, would Maddy make of Tessa's excuses on her behalf? How she longed to have the time over again, to do it differently, to be cool, brief and non-committal, to express truthful ignorance of Maddy's whereabouts, to ignore any mention of Nick.

It was fear that had precipitated her rush into prevarication; fear of what Robert might do to Nick. Fear, too, of having her game-plan upset, for Robert was most unlikely to be persuaded by her 'be patient and it will soon end and we can pretend it never happened' argument. Rather, his instinct would be to snatch Maddy back if Maddy would let him and put an instant end to all communication between the Storrs and the Brierleys. Tessa he would view in the same poor light as her husband. Dear and kindly though he was, she knew him to be a conservative man who would feel intuitively that Nick might not be such a bounder if his wife made a proper job of keeping him happily in line. She sighed and thought how very often in men's eyes, woman's fault lay at the root of their ills.

While her thoughts ran on she had risen and was now standing with her back to the pinboard, staring at a reflection of her head and shoulders in the black window glass. She seemed to have been there a long time. In the way that a dream can seem one's permanent territory only temporarily abandoned for the pursuits of the day, so her face seemed always to have been there, remaining on the window when she left the room, fading when the day dawned, but still there – hidden as daylight hides the moon. The image, utterly still and greenish-waxen, was gazing at *her*, not she at it. It transfixed her with its great eye-hollows and made her perceive a deeper fear than those she had already faced, which was that she could not rely on Robert to play her waiting game because she herself was no longer sure of it.

In the car park in front of the village hall, Phoebe was sitting sideways in her Land Rover, bottom to passenger seat, feet to driver's seat, arms linked round her shins. She was watching Jasmine Cottage. Light splayed over the front door and glowed softly behind many a curtained window. Robert might complain at the money Maddy spent on clothes, thought Phoebe, but he didn't seem too bothered about the electricity bill. Earlier, when he had assured her that Maddy was out, had not returned, in fact, from the WI meeting, she had been unable to take it in. For she had been so sure of falling into Maddy's arms, of handing her the briefcase and receiving her grateful thanks, of pouring out her hurt feelings at the nasty suspicious manner of the WI women – all this anticipated so keenly during her flight from the village hall that her mind could not grapple with its abrupt cancellation. She stood blinking on the doorstep. Lowered voices reached her from across the street. (They had been watching, of course, to make sure she handed in the briefcase – God, she couldn't go back and face them.) When Robert rather promptly closed the door, she dived under his sprawling *rosa mundi* bush and crouched there in the dark, waiting for their voices to fade, for footsteps to lead off, for cars to start up and go. Once or twice her sharp ears caught her name amid the 'Ooh's and 'I know's and 'Brenda said's and 'Poor Roy and those kids'. Mean cows, she thought, bloody old witches; should've really walloped Mrs fuckin' Frogmorton, kicked a few shins while she was at it, an' all. Soon, Wychwood became night-time muted. Cars droning distantly along the main road, secret rustles, sudden cries, faint bellows from a far-off heifer in labour: these were the only sounds. She unravelled herself, stood up stiffly, then, on sure noiseless feet, trod across the street and climbed into the Land Rover.

She was waiting for Maddy; thoughts and emotions suspended, waiting. For two hours she sat there, checking off the quarter chimes from the church clock (which would cease between midnight and seven in the morning when only the hours were struck). Once, she became so uncomfortable that she got out of the Land Rover and went to squat by the wall. Even then she would not take her eyes from the cottage but crouched in a place where she could maintain her vigil while micturating. Before climbing back inside, she arched backwards over the vehicle and stretched her limbs.

She was sitting in her sideways position when Maddy's little car at last arrived and turned into the driveway a few feet from the cottage. Maddy's was the car usually parked in the drive outside, Robert's the one safely garaged. As Maddy drew up, Phoebe slipped out of the Land Rover and crossed the street.

Maddy switched off the engine, unbuckled the seat belt, took her shoulder bag from the seat beside her and began to get out of the car.

'Where've you been?' demanded Phoebe from the shadows.

Maddy, in the act of standing, sat abruptly down. 'Oh-my-God! You *silly* girl. You terrified me.'

'Sorry. Where've you been?'

Breathing carefully, Maddy got out of the car. 'What are you doing here?'

'Waiting for you. You left your case. I found it and took it to Robert. Them old cows thought I was going to pinch it. You should've seen 'em, Maddy, looking all nasty. That Mrs Frogmorton tried to grab it, but I give her a shove. As if I'd pinch summat of yours! – not that I meant to pinch from the shop; it were me pills.'

'Shh. Look, get into the car. We'd better think, I mean, talk.'

'All right.'

Phoebe walked round the car. Maddy got back in and leaned over to unlock the passenger door. Phoebe climbed in beside her.

'What about, then?'

'Mm?' Maddy asked, distracted.

'What we going to talk about?'

'Ah – well; if, as it seems, there was a bit of bother after I left, I'd better know about it. Tell me, by the way: you took the case to Robert?'

'Yeah. He seemed rattled. He said, "Oh, she's not with you, then?" – or summat like that. Where *were* you, Maddy?' And when she gave no answer: 'Hey – you ent been with a feller, have you?'

'What a thing to say! No, no. A friend of mine is very upset and needed to see me. Robert obviously got muddled and thought I meant you.'

'Oh – because *I* get upset and need to see you,' Phoebe said simply, having taken absolutely no offence.

Maddy was abashed. 'I didn't mean . . . You know what men are, they simply never listen. Now tell me what happened to you tonight. You didn't really push Mrs Frogmorton?'

'Yes, I did. It was horrible, the way they was looking at me. When you'd gone, I was upset; me head was sort of banging. Then, when I found your case, I grabbed it. I'll take it to her, I thought; p'raps she was dying for the toilet, I thought, or remembered she'd left the oven on. If I take it to her, she'll tell me why she dashed off and then I'll feel better.'

'Oh, Phoebe – you are a chump.' Touched, she put out her small smooth hand and took Phoebe's large rough one. It felt like a man's. Disconcerted, she let it go and put her own in her lap.

The brief contact had been quite sufficient to please and soothe Phoebe. She lolled back. 'It's all right now,' she mumbled comfortably, then yawned hugely and dropped her head.

'Phoebe?' said Maddy after a while. When there was no answer, she leaned over and fastened the passenger's seat belt, then her own, and started the car.

Bumping over the ruts in the Peck's Farm driveway, Phoebe stirred. 'Where we going?'

'I'm taking you home. Roy can fetch the Land Rover in the morning.'

Roy was standing under the porch, having heard the car. 'Thought she'd be with you,' he said. 'Rachael phoned to say there'd been a bit of bother at WI and Phoebe had run over to your place.'

'Yes, well, Robert spoke to her. I was out, briefly. When I got back, she needed to talk. We sat in my car for ages. It does her good to get things off her chest – though it seems to have exhausted her, I'm afraid.'

Between them, they hauled her out of the car and led her into the house.

'I'd better go. Robert will think I've absconded.'

'It's very good of you, Maddy.'

Thanking her stars for Phoebe Peck, Maddy drove home with restored confidence.

Robert, who had been sitting listening to Bach and planning how with reticence and cunning he would startle the truth out of his wife, found, when it came to it, he could not hold back. Perhaps it was her look of spurious virtue – a bright, weary-with-doing-good sort of air – that proved too much for him. 'Phoebe was here,' he blurted wrathfully, 'so I know you haven't been with her.'

'I most certainly have,' she retorted, flopping into a chair and holding a hand to her forehead. 'God, I'm whacked. I've just helped Roy to get her upstairs. The Land Rover's still parked across the road. Roy will have to collect it in the morning.'

Robert sat down in a chair opposite to her. 'She said you'd gone off. *You* said . . .'

'Do stop barking, dear.' Her eyes fell on the briefcase. 'Oh – the source of the trouble. What a fool I was to forget it. I dashed off to see Mrs Knight – she's poorly, but she was anxious to know whether they'd agree to the Sandringham excursion, and I promised to pop in afterwards and let her know – I did tell you this, darling – if only you'd listen – and I said I *might* go on to Phoebe's. Of course, I didn't get that far. Mrs Cottrill called at Mrs Knight's, all breathless with the news that Phoebe had assaulted Mrs Frogmorton and run off with my briefcase. Imagine! I drove straight back and found poor Phoebe cowering by our garage. Took me an age to calm her down. What the hell am I going to say to Mrs Frogmorton? Phew, I've had it. Give me a drink.'

'Scotch?'

'Lovely. Had a nice evening?' she idly enquired, picking up a record sleeve. 'Oh – a new band. Any good?'

'Mm. Nice bright tone. Not sure about their tempi.'

'Thanks. Oh, well, back to good old Christopher, eh? – and the brilliant Academy.'

'They're certainly hard to beat. Er, Maddy?'

'Yes, dear?'

'You're not getting out of your depth with this Phoebe business? I mean, the girl's sick; she needs professional handling.'

'She needs friends, too, Robert, and they seem to be in short supply. I'm just doing my best.'

'I know you are, sweet. But you do too much. Let's eat out tomorrow.'

'Bliss! You are a pet.'

*   *   *

Tessa was not in the bed. This fact, when he discovered it some twenty or so minutes after arriving home, seemed to stop Nick's heart. He ran back downstairs to check the living and dining rooms. The dog caught his excitement and followed at his heels. 'Where is she, you blighter?'

Scrap, who knew, looked cunning.

In her studio, of course, he thought with relief, and set off back upstairs. After two flights he arrived in the attic corridor. The studio door was ajar, showing a wedge of wan light. This proved to be cast by an anglepoise lamp near the drawing board. On the rickety couch behind the door, Tessa lay fast asleep. He was relieved to see that she appeared to have fallen asleep by accident; uncovered and fully clothed, she had evidently not taken a decision to abandon the marital bed. Her head lay on an old patchwork cushion, one hand curled beneath her chin, the other hanging over the side of the couch. She even still had her shoes on.

Darling – oh, love, he said silently, falling to his knees beside her. Her face was pale; dark lashes curled in the bruised hollows beneath her eyes; her dark hair spread over cushion and couch as if she had tossed back her head and instantly dropped asleep.

Scrap pushed against him, staking his prior claim. Idly, Nick fondled his ears, but the dog remained tense and watchful. 'I love her too, you know,' he muttered resentfully, seeking, by including her pet, to lighten the heaviness settling over him. But he soon forgot Scrap, becoming lost in the sight of Tessa and the terrible tenderness she evoked. That was the trouble with loving her so much; it hurt badly; it had overtones in it of the love he had borne his mother, which had not died when she died, merely cracked and warped through lack of nourishment.

Timidly, he wrapped his hands round her trailing fingers. 'Love,' he whispered, 'wake up. You'll have a stiff neck if you lie there much longer.'

180

Scrap whined and butted the couch.

She groaned as she woke. 'What time is it?' she asked thickly.

'Gone midnight. I've been in ages,' he lied. 'Didn't want to wake you, but then I thought you'd be better off in bed.'

'I feel . . . horrible. Oh, I hate sleeping anywhere but in bed. I must have sat down for a minute and dozed off. You'll have to help me.' She held up her arms like a child.

'Pull.'

'Where've you been?' she asked as the evening came back to her. 'I made you a meal.'

'Sorry. Got caught up. Bad news, I'm afraid – or possibly good: they're going to operate again on Col.'

'No,' she said vehemently, sitting down again. 'They mustn't. It would be obscene.'

He sat beside her, less sure than she was. 'But surely, if there's a chance, Tess . . .'

'There isn't. We know there isn't.' But when his arms were round her and she felt his heart beating against her shoulder, she lost her certainty. Despite her knowledge of Colin's condition and its hopelessness, the thought of *not* Colin – Colin, who was so alive to her, finished, gone – was an enormity too gross to be possible. She pushed Nick away. 'You're right, of course; they should try everything. Is that where you were tonight – with Colin?'

'Yes,' he said truthfully, for Colin's bedside was where he had passed the time before meeting Maddy. Trimming the truth, for he had only called briefly at Jerry's, he continued: 'Then I went to Jerry's. He was terribly upset in a guarded sort of way, and as Viv was out, I stayed on for a bit. I should have phoned you, though.'

I've misjudged him, she thought, taking his face between her hands and searching his eyes. As if seeking forgiveness, she pressed her lips solemnly to his forehead.

He flinched under her touch, understanding it and

knowing himself to be Judas – though suffering rather than giving the kiss. She was too trusting, always too trusting. Perceptive and quick in so many things – she seemed to guess every nuance of an affair once he had confessed its existence to her – she was always prepared to believe in him until the next disillusionment. He must divest himself of Maddy, he thought urgently; though carefully, for unlike his other affairs, she lacked experience. Maddy was vulnerable, brittle as thin silver. God, what a heel he was! Here were two women he'd thoroughly mucked up, and the worst of it was they were close and supportive friends.

'Come to bed,' he pleaded.

She sighed. 'If I were religious I'd stay up all night praying for him – at least then I'd be doing something.' She rose clumsily and trod on the dog. 'Scrappie-scrappie-scrap!' she exclaimed, kneeling and gathering him up. 'Oh, baby! And you such a loyal little pooch. Look at him,' she invited, as Scrap, his yelping abandoned, coyly lowered his head and rolled up his eyes. 'Doesn't your heart melt when he looks like that?'

'We can't all have four stumpy legs and a fluffy tail,' Nick complained; 'some of us were born handicapped.' Which she loved, of course – pealing with laughter, hugging him for his funniness.

Cheered, arm in arm, Scrap stolidly following, they went off to bed.

21

'I knew it,' cried Rose vindictively, glaring at Dolly's black eye. 'I guessed there'd be trouble when I heard him come home last night. What a racket!'

Dolly, her back against the kitchen wall, said nothing.

'It's a good job you've only got Holly House this morning. If it was the Manor . . .' She cast round for Dolly's coat and handed it to her. 'Mrs Westbrook said if it happened again she'd tell the major, and he's on the bench, remember.' She made this sound ominous, but in their hearts they could not imagine either Westbrook bestirring themselves on behalf of an employee. 'You are coming to work this morning, I hope,' – Dolly had put on the coat but had made no further improvement – 'seeing as I've booked you that perm. It'll cost you a tenner, so you don't want to go losing wages. What about your shoes?'

Dolly kicked off her slippers, and Rose groped into a cupboard for Dolly's outdoor footwear. 'I only hope it fades in time for the whist drive. You're too soft with him, Dol; always were, always will be. Is your bag ready?'

Dolly reached for it over the table.

'Come on then; buck up. Mrs Brierley won't push you too hard – not when she sees that shiner. It's not as if she's a slave-driver, anyway, not like some we could mention. Mind you,' she added (apparently disqualifying Mrs Brierley from the slave-driving rights allowed Mrs Westbrook), 'she's the sort who'd have to do her own cleaning if people didn't pay her for them pictures.' She nudged Dolly through the doorway. 'We'll ring up your Barry after work. He may be idle, but at least he can handle his dad.'

Tessa was in the kitchen when she heard Dolly mounting the steps. She pulled open the door. 'Oh, Mrs Cloomb!' she exclaimed in a shocked voice, as Dolly, looking sheepish, took off her coat. 'You poor thing. How simply dreadful. Can I get you a cup of tea?'

Dolly brightened. 'Yeah – all right.'

'Sit down.' She rushed about putting the kettle on, rinsing the teapot, taking mugs from the dresser. She also grabbed the biscuit tin. 'Help yourself. Sweet things are supposed to be good for shock,' she urged, forgetting that it was she who was shocked; Dolly had had several hours to get used to her injury.

'Ta. I heard that, too,' said Dolly, selecting a chocolate digestive. She slumped back in her chair and munched, and when Tessa poured out the tea said, 'That feels better.'

Tessa was encouraged. She intently watched Dolly drinking her tea, as if every sip possessed healing properties. And perhaps they did; for certainly Dolly grew pinker and less clammy-looking; she had slept fitfully with her fists clenched; this was her first moment of true relaxation since Arthur's homecoming.

Tessa wondered what to do, for the man could not be allowed to get away with it. She would phone Eleanor presently; also Maddy. 'Don't get up before you're ready,' she protested when Dolly made to rise. 'Relax for a while. Let me give you another cup.'

Dolly settled back.

Tessa tried to think of a cheerful topic. 'Nearly the end of the month. And then, I suppose, it'll be one mad rush for Christmas. And there's the bazaar coming up . . .'

'And the Christmas whist drive.'

'That too.'

'I 'spect you and Mrs Storr are busy collecting stuff for the teas. I know Rose hopes there'll be plenty leftovers for our do in the evening. You'd be surprised how folks look forward to it. We don't usually have refreshments at the whist drives – well, only coffee – so the Christmas one makes a nice change.'

'I suppose it must. Um, Ken Tustin hasn't had a word with you about that?'

'No,' said Dolly, surprised. 'Was he going to?'

'I think so. Mrs Storr is rather anxious to make sure everyone knows where they are – about these refreshments and so forth.'

'Oh, Rose knows where she is, don't you fret.'

'Another biscuit?'

'I couldn't,' said Dolly, drawing daintily back from the tin. 'Maybe for elevenses. I feel better now, so I'll get on.'

'Take things slowly,' Tessa advised unnecessarily, and went upstairs to use the telephone.

After all, she decided to postpone calling Eleanor until Rose Fettle had left the Rectory. Instead, she rang Maddy's number.

'The monster!' cried Maddy when she had heard the news. 'Ought to be locked up.'

'I know. But what can we *do*? It's much worse than last time, a full-blown black eye.'

'Nothing, probably,' Maddy said glumly. 'Though a woman I worked with on the Oxfam stall in Fetherstone market is married to a probation officer. Perhaps I should get in touch with her.'

'Oh, do, Maddy. It makes me so mad. By the way, Mrs Cloomb mentioned the teas. Hoped there'd be plenty of "left-overs" for the whist drive supper. It doesn't sound as if Mr Tustin's said anything about charging for them yet.'

'Damn. Another useless bloody man. Scared to say "boo" to Rose Fettle, I'll bet. You're still with me, I hope?'

'Of course.'

'I'd better go and sort him out, then. Ta-ta.'

Putting down the receiver, Tessa wondered whether she would have done better to have kept her mouth shut.

Celia Westbrook was making one of her rare visits to the village shop. Provisions for the Manor were largely acquired at the cash and carry, for which Celia had wangled a ticket. She went there once a month, taking with her a farm-hand to draw the cumbersome trolley up and down the aisles of the concrete and iron warehouse. Packs of tinned dog-food, packs of boxed breakfast cereal, packs of soup tins, packs of frozen cod fillets were stacked with a score of similar packs

185

into the Range Rover; for the Westbrooks did not aim to eat healthily, graciously, imaginatively, or excitingly, but as cheaply as possible with the minimum trouble. Of course, their diet was enhanced by game shot on their land, and by their own farm meat, eggs and milk. Now and then, however, Celia discovered a small deficiency in her store cupboard – pointless to purchase the cash and carry's pack of packaged walnuts when all that was required was a mere quarter pound. At such moments, full of fury and cursing the world for its lack of servants, its insistence on walnuts and its harbouring of bolshie village shopkeepers who wouldn't deliver, she abandoned her kitchen and bowlful of well-mixed flour, fat, eggs, sugar, dates (everything, in fact, save the blasted walnuts), leapt on her bike and tore round to Brenda's.

'Morning, Brenda,' she said today, striding confidently towards the counter. 'I won't hold you up. Just four ounces of walnuts – chopped.' By 'won't hold you up' she indicated her expectation of Brenda's dropping Mrs Joiner's requirements and rushing round the counter to lay hands on the nuts. She was not disappointed. Brenda would apologize and complain about her later to Mrs Joiner but not until Mrs Westbrook was out of earshot. It had taken all Brenda's courage ten or so years ago to explain that she could no longer dash to the Manor with a single item whenever the telephone summoned. Afterwards, Brenda had suffered palpitations; and Mrs Westbrook out of pique had done without her chopped walnuts, the odd jar of Marmite and the occasional tub of glacé cherries for at least six months.

'By the way, Brenda. I hear you caught a pilferer red-handed. Well, it was a great mistake to let her orff. The major sees too much of that sort of thing on the bench and he'll tell you, it doesn't pay to be sorft. Another time, I hope you'll do your duty.'

'Let's hope there won't be another time.'

'If you people would be more public spirited, we shouldn't have to rely on just hope. How much? *78p*? – it's a wonder you stay in business.'

'Thank you, Mrs Westbrook. That's twenty-two change.'

Snorting, Celia snatched up money and walnuts, and without further ceremony, swept out.

Ken Tustin, retired gas board official, keen gardener, chairman of Wychwood parish council and of the village hall committee, was comfortably seated in the front room of his bungalow in Fetherstone Road, a cup of coffee to hand, seed catalogues heaped on his knees. He was preparing an order for spring-sowing cabbages, studying the form, hovering between 'Wheeler's Imperial' and 'Myatt's Early Offenham'. Hearing the click of the front gate, he put the catalogues aside, rose and peered through the ruched net curtains. What he saw on the path galvanized him, turned a ponderous man into a sprinter: through the hall he bounded, through the kitchen ('I'm out,' he growled to his wife), down the garden path and into the garden shed. Mrs Tustin, rolling out her pastry, was dumbfounded. When the door chimes called their cheery 'coo-ee' summons, she panicked – dropped the rolling pin, wiped her hands on her apron, peeped across the hall at the shadow on the frosted glass in the front door, went to the back doorstep and stood wringing her hands in an agony of confused indecision. 'Ken?' she called in a stage whisper. 'Front door – shall I answer it? Oh, *Ken*.'

At the front door, Maddy was listening intently. Her ears persuaded her to try the back.

Ken was looking cautiously out of the shed and waving crossly at his wife when Maddy came round the side of the bungalow. 'Ah, there you are,' she cried advancing. Not wishing to be backed into the arms of his lawn mower, he stepped out and met her on open ground.

'I rather think you've not kept your word, Mr Tustin.'

'Er?' said he, searching his pocket for the comfort of his favourite briar. Finding the pipe, he put it into his mouth; bit it and sucked hard.

'I fear so. Mrs Fettle is still going around talking about "left-overs" for the whist drive supper.'

'Ah.' He brought out his tobacco pouch and looked carefully at the contents.

'You undertook to make it quite clear to Mrs Fettle that if I am to provide refreshments for the evening as well as for the afternoon, they will have to be paid for on the same basis. Otherwise, I'm not prepared to have any more to do with it. I hope you're not trying to acquire my services on false pretences.'

'Heaven forbid, Mrs Storr,' said he, stuffing a large pinch of tobacco into the pipe's bowl.

'Well, then, let's be clear about it. Are you or are you not going to charge for the evening refreshments?'

'I am.'

'And will you inform Mrs Fettle?'

'As I said before, leave it to me,' he said placidly, prodding the tobacco with a matchstick. 'I'll, er, pop round there next week, I dare say, and have a word with her.'

Maddy squinted at him through narrowed eyes. 'You "dare say", Mr Tustin? And what's wrong with *this* week?'

'Where's the hurry? It'll be done.'

Maddy sighed and turned to go, then swung back with a final warning. 'This is a matter of principle, you know. The point of the exercise – the reason why people are good enough to give contributions – is to raise money for the church roof. Any back-sliding and I shall wash my hands of the whole affair.'

'Like I said, Mrs Storr – I'll see to it.'

'I'm pleased to hear it.' This time she did leave him. Passing the kitchen and catching a glimpse of Mrs Tustin, she called out in her friendliest voice: 'What a wonderful smell you're making!'

Mrs Tustin smiled and bobbed her head, and hoped she was not about to catch it from Ken.

A feeling grew, during the short walk along Fetherstone Road to the corner of Church Street, of slight misgiving. To counteract this, Maddy prohibited herself from looking across the road to Orchard Close and strode out with particular jauntiness, her chin up, her hands in the pockets of her yellow donkey jacket. The feeling persisted; she became quite cross with herself. As she approached the corner, a car hooted. Its driver, Derek Bowman, waved and grinned. 'Hi,' she mouthed, smiling and twirling to avoid the necessity of taking her hands from her pockets. The exchange made her feel gay and youthful. People like Derek and herself worked their socks off for Wychwood, she reflected, uplifted by a sense of camaraderie, whereas people like Mrs Fettle were little better than scroungers.

By the time she turned in at her gate she had ground to dust the small seed of doubt. In any case – and here she recalled Mrs Fettle's flint-hearted opposition to the WI project for aiding city mothers and many similar obstructions over the years – the woman had got it in for her, had taken a dislike to her from the moment she moved into Jasmine Cottage. 'Well, duckie,' she said under her breath, conjuring a witch-like Rose on the path ahead of her, 'rest assured – the feeling's mutual.'

Watching the rosy-red fire, Dolly said dreamily, 'I hope that Mrs Storr ent up to summat.'

'What d'you mean?' Rose asked sharply.

'It were what Mrs Brierley said this morning – had Mr Tustin said summat to us about the refreshments for our do? I said "no, he hasn't", and she said Mrs Storr told him to make sure we knew where we was. Funny that.'

Instantly, Rose's idle afternoon with cups of steaming tea and toasted muffins squelching with butter was ruined. She couldn't sit still. She leapt to her feet, went to the sideboard, snatched up her sewing.

'What's the matter?' asked Dolly as Rose began sewing.

'She's out to spoil it for us, Dol, that's what's the matter. She don't reckon our ways are worth tuppence.' She stitched as if her life depended on it. When she ran out of thread, she looked up. 'But she's not going to. Let her send Ken Tustin: I'll soon put him straight. She's not going to spoil it, cos we won't blummin let her.'

22

The garden was mouldering. Funereal plumes of dry buddleia hung over the border where soggy mounds of greenery rotted and spent flower-heads of aster and hydrangea turned, brittle-brown, to dust. A few late roses bloomed, but there was no freshness in these end-of-the-year buds; they were born world-weary and, Tessa felt, might just as well not make the effort, for the decaying garden was beyond cheering. There had been grey mist or black rain for days. The darkness seemed to wrap round her so that it was an effort to move her limbs, an effort even to think. Inside herself she carried a great weight of despair. 'Why do you turn your mouth down like that?' Nick had rounded on her yesterday evening – his quick drink in the Red Lion evidently having made him irritable.

'Do I turn it down?' Puzzled, she had put her hands up to feel, and discovered he was right: the corners of her mouth were pressed tautly down against her teeth. Try as she might, she could not release the grimace, and now that her attention had been drawn to it, she could feel the strain on her facial muscles.

'Christ, you look grim. Why don't you stop it?'

'I don't seem able to. Maybe I should take up yoga again – it always helped me to relax.'

'Well, do something, for God's sake.'

Now, standing at the garden window in the sitting room, she put her hands to the sides of her face and tried to ease the tautness. It surprised her that misery could exert such mastery, pull her face down and make a badge of her. If only the weather would brighten – but there seemed little chance of it; it would take a gale to clear the fathoms-deep clouds. As she gazed outside, it was sunlight she yearned for rather than an end to her troubles: wishing for the sun seemed a more sensible course than wishing for a change in people.

There had been a change, albeit a small one. Nick was now at home more often. The first evening he stayed in, she felt encouraged. Then, on the second evening, the telephone rang. 'I'll get it,' he cried, leaping from his slumped position in front of the television. (He had sat deliberately close to Tessa – wedged her between himself and the arm of the settee – on purpose to annoy the dog, obliging Scrap to lie on the floor if he wished to be near his mistress.) But instead of picking up the receiver on the Pembroke table, Nick ran upstairs to the extension in the bedroom. When he returned he was restless – turned off the television (which Tessa was not watching), picked up a book and flicked through the pages, read bits aloud sneeringly, threw the book down, went to make coffee. The telephone rang briefly again. Presumably he answered it in the kitchen. The conversation could only have been brief, for ten minutes later he was back with the coffee tray. A little later it rang again. When he made no move, she put her book aside. This galvanized him. 'Don't bother. I expect it's for me.' She listened to his feet on the stairs, turned and looked at the ringing phone. When it fell silent, the air above seemed to tremble as though it could barely contain the intensity of their voices. Speculating, she imagined

191

them: entreating, recriminating, pledging, disavowing. It had been all she could do not to pick up the receiver and listen. She grew angry. How *dare* Maddy intrude into her peace like this. Wasn't it enough that she had stored away intimate knowledge of Nick, which Tessa had trustingly confided, to use for her own greedy satisfaction? Wasn't it enough that she repeatedly and deceitfully drew him away? Must she insist on his attention even when he decided to withhold it, thereby unsettling her home? Looking about her, Tessa saw that the room had shrunken into itself. The whole house was on edge; nervy.

The next evening had brought a further change. Now it was Nick who made repeated telephone calls. Opening the sitting room door (which she had been surprised to find closed), she discovered him with the receiver to his ear. 'Oh – sorry,' she said when he quickly replaced it, 'don't let me disturb you.' But without a word he left the room. A similar thing happened an hour later when she ran up to the bedroom to fetch a book: he jumped up from his perch on the side of the bed and dropped the receiver as though it were scalding. Half an hour later she found him beside the telephone in the kitchen. 'Oh, for heaven's sake!' he snarled, as if she were deliberately spying on him. To keep out of his way, she had gone to bed to read, guessing that he would keep on ringing Jasmine Cottage until Maddy answered instead of Robert. (She hoped most fervently that Robert was not becoming suspicious.) Later, Nick had come upstairs with a black face and announced that he was going to the pub for a swift half. Hating herself, she had gone over to the window to see that he did indeed go across the Green to the pub.

This Saturday afternoon, her reverie at the sitting room window was interrupted by Scrap making 'there is someone at the door' signals. She went through the hall into the kitchen and opened the street door. Phoebe Peck stood there.

It was almost as if her wish for the sun had been granted, so radiant was Phoebe's face. 'Gosh – you look happy!' she burst out. 'Come in.'

'I am. I had a fabulous time last night. Me and Maddy went to the pictures; the film were terrible – really stupid – but we killed ourselves laughing. Afterwards, we went for a Chinese. Then coming back we had this music on real loud; and we sang – oh, it felt fantastic – Maddy in such a great mood – speeding up the motorway . . .'

'Well! Sit down. What was the film?'

Phoebe sat in the wooden rocking chair and tried in vain to recall the title, then to explain why watching a terrible film had proved hilarious. This was unnecessary. Tessa knew perfectly well how Maddy's company could have a similar effect to gulping champagne. She listened with only half an ear, nodding and smiling, reflecting on how odd it was of Maddy to go with Phoebe to the cinema. Perhaps Maddy intended to create a precedent – after all, her most plausible excuses must be pretty well used up, but now, after last night, Robert would not be too surprised if she used an evening excursion with Phoebe to explain an absence. She was also thinking that it was no wonder Nick was edgy yesterday evening. None of his persistent telephoning could have been answered by Maddy. No doubt he had gone to the pub to prevent Tessa witnessing his perturbation. (What Tessa did not guess was that Nick had swallowed his beer in three minutes flat, then gone through the rear of the pub into the car park, out into Peck's Lane and thence into Church Street near Jasmine Cottage where he had soon discovered the absence of his lover's car from its accustomed place in front of the garage doors. Maddy, he saw, was out; and her husband, he knew, was in and diligently answering the telephone. Where, the blood in his veins screamed to know, had the little minx gone? What the hell was she playing at? Sullenly he retraced his steps: through the pub – to the great surprise of Linda

Maiden behind the bar – and out of the front door, across the Green to his home. Later, in the bedroom, Tessa's unpleasantly grim expression had provided a handy excuse to vent his feelings.)

'So I wondered,' Phoebe was saying, 'could you help me think of summat she'd really go for?'

'Er – yes. I'll try. How much do you want to spend?' Tessa's mind rapidly replayed what Phoebe had been saying – that she wanted to buy Maddy a present because Maddy had insisted on paying for nearly everything last night. 'I shouldn't go too mad, though, or she'll be embarrassed.'

'About a fiver?' Phoebe wondered.

'No more. Now, let's think.'

'Flowers is a bit boring, and I don't suppose she eats chocolates.'

Tessa, hearing the sudden noise of a sports commentary, knew that the sitting room door had opened. Nick came quickly through the hall and scowled into the kitchen. His face cleared when he saw Phoebe – 'Oh, hello!' – and his fists unclenched; he put his hands in his pockets. After a few pleasantries he returned to the television.

It was hard applying her mind to Maddy's present, only Phoebe's wistfulness persuaded her. 'Something unusual,' she thought aloud. 'Something small and attractive. Mm. How about . . . You remember those lavender bags I showed the girls the other day – the ones I've been making for the Christmas bazaar? As well as those patchwork bags, I've made two rather special ones from some antique lace my aunt left me. One is to be a present.' (This was for Eleanor; she planned to give it to her tomorrow after evensong when the organ plaque to Aunt Winifred had been dedicated: the other lace bag she had made for herself.) 'But you can have the other one, if you like.'

'I'd have to buy it, then.'

'All right. You can pay me and I'll put it in with the bazaar money. Three-fifty?'

'Ooh, are you sure?'

'Positive. Hang on, I'll go and fetch it. And I've got some nice tissue paper you can wrap it in.'

As she was going upstairs to her studio, the telephone rang. The sitting room door flew open. 'I'll get it,' yelled Nick to forestall her. She did not look down or reply, but continued running upstairs and almost at once heard the sitting room door reclose. From a drawer in her studio she took one of the lace lavender bags and examined it with a tinge of sadness – the ivory tracery over peachy satin, the slippery, scrunchy feel – and from another drawer, a sheet of brown tissue paper and a length of shiny brown ribbon. With these she returned to the kitchen.

Phoebe was enraptured. 'Cor, she'll *love* it. She's got ever such good taste. I was scared of getting her something – you know – in case it was wrong. You are clever, Tessa. That'll suit her down to the ground.'

'Shall I wrap it?'

'Please!' Phoebe watched her.

'There you are.'

'Oh, thanks, Tessa. Thanks ever so. I'll take it to her right away.'

'Will you?' asked Tessa doubtfully, mindful of Nick on the telephone. But just then she heard his step in the hall. 'No time like the present,' she agreed.

Phoebe was already in the doorway. She seemed to float down the steps. ' 'Bye.'

'Goodbye, Phoebe.' She turned to face her husband.

'It was Sophia.'

'Oh?'

'He's not too bad. We can go and see him tomorrow afternoon.'

'Oh, Nick.'

'Don't get your hopes up,' he warned, his eyes so full of hope that they were watering.

23

Tessa sensed that Maddy and Nick had turned a corner, were no longer simply carried away by one another and prepared to suspend all else in the pursuit of passion; old loyalties had intruded, bringing regret, even guilt, and made each seem less wholly delightful, less sweetly accommodating. This was purely surmise; but she felt sure of it. She tried to stay her own gathering impatience.

It was raining again as they drove to the hospital. The windscreen wipers grated on Tessa's nerves; they whined complainingly; their jerky action implied that their task was arduous, that they were underpowered and put upon. Perhaps the battery was low, she thought turning her head away to stare out of the side window. On the outskirts of the city the houses lining the road – of red brick or mucky-grey stucco – were dreary. Not a single light showed at their windows. Presumably all living was done in the back rooms or else conducted in the half-light.

'Bloody Sunday afternoon,' said Nick, echoing her sentiments. 'Bloody miserable country. Always bloody raining.'

'Not always,' she said pedantically. 'Do you think these wipers need attention?'

Sophia was with Colin when they arrived. 'He's cured,' she cried. 'Look at him. It's a miracle!'

Tessa wondered if she were drunk. Colin's pink and puffy face was scarcely recognizable. Tubes came out of him into bags, as before. His arms still lay uselessly by his sides. A new feature since his operation was a saline drip, and this had relieved the dryness of his mouth which now wore the familiar lazy smile. But 'cured'? Tessa winced at the word. 'Let's give Sophia and Colin longer together,' she suggested when she had kissed them. 'We'll go for a cup of tea – come back later.'

'No,' said Sophia imperiously. 'I must go. My young man is coming to entertain me.' Her eyes grew large and saucy; she preened herself. 'You didn't know I had a young man? He is Dutch. His name is Pieter. A very nice boy; very correct, very attentive. I think he likes Colin's cognac – also my cigars. I like him to come to the house; it makes me feel good.'

'I'm glad, Sophia,' said Tessa, thoroughly embarrassed. She darted a look at Colin, who grinned amiably.

Wafting Chanel, Sophia waved kisses and flounced off.

'She met him at her club where she met Magda and the others. It's supposed to be a club for Eastern Europeans, so why a Dutchman was there, I'm not entirely clear. But he cheers her up. Good luck to him!'

They listened to him speaking with rapt intent. It was the most he had said for weeks. *What* he said was of secondary importance. 'Darling, you sound very much better,' said Tessa.

'They've done a good job, Col – obviously.'

'Early days,' murmured Colin. 'How's tricks?'

In rather desultory fashion they reported some of their various doings. Then Nick recalled a matter of importance. 'Did you hear, by the way, that the famous Delzine charm proved impervious? He went to see Sophia – that friend of hers, Magda, was there. Anyway, they were all getting along famously until Delzine mentioned that you had asked him to check those papers. Whereupon Sophia stormed upstairs with a migraine and ordered the formidable Magda to throw him out. It'd be quite funny, really, if poor old Jerry wasn't having the vapours over it.'

'Don't bother Colin,' urged Tessa.

'It's so ridiculous. I'll try and reason with her.'

'No worries. If the worst comes to the worst we'll have to convince the panel without them.'

Just then a nurse looked in. She gazed speculatively at Tessa, then beckoned.

Tessa rose. 'Me?'

'Can you spare a minute? It's Mrs Brierley, isn't it?'

'Yes. All right.' Somewhat dubiously, she left the men and followed the nurse into the corridor.

'It'll be something to do with Sophia,' Colin sighed. 'Could you feed me a drop of water, Nick?'

Going along the corridor, Tessa could hardly keep up. The nurse's feet overtook one another with astonishing rapidity, and all the time she talked. 'Mrs Petchel stopped to have a word with Sister. She was sort of euphoric. Sister tried to let her down gently – I mean, it's no good Mrs Petchel having false hopes – Professor Petchel's very poorly. She doesn't seem to understand – the operation was more to *relieve* him . . . That's her, in the room at the end.' They had turned a corner and dreadful sounds could be heard. 'We thought a woman friend . . .' (Oh dear, thought Tessa.) 'I'll leave you to it – Staff's with her.'

The sister had gone – Tessa did not blame her – and had left staff nurse to do her best. Sophia was bawling. Between howls, she threw her head back and gulped in air. Her hair was matted to her sopping wet beetroot-coloured face. Seeing Tessa, she stretched out her arms and flicked her curled up fingers. Tessa approached timidly, was seized, clasped, head-battered, thrust away.

Sophia's emotion was overpowering. Suddenly Tessa envied her, longed to follow her lead, to throw back her head and spew out all her misery. For that was what Sophia was doing – expelling her terror and sense of rejection, cleansing herself body and soul without a care for the damage caused to those who must stand by and watch. If only she could be like Sophia. You're too proper, too goody-two shoes, she scornfully told herself. 'Sophia!' she said sharply, and

Sophia suddenly quietened, stood panting and shuddering through an open mouth which had strings of spittle crossing it. 'Sit down,' Tessa ordered more kindly.

Sophia sat. After a moment, she looked round for her handbag. Staff nurse handed it to her, then mouthed to Tessa that she would go.

Sophia, taking out a mirror and some cotton wool and lotion, proceeded to cleanse her face. She did this thoroughly. Then, fiercely concentrating, she re-applied her make-up. Finally, she combed and teased and sprayed her hair. 'I must look a sight,' she mourned. 'And Pieter will wonder where I've got to.'

'I'll walk with you to your car.'

'Why?' she asked rudely, snapping her bag shut and getting to her feet. 'You've come to see Colin, so go to him. Goodbye, Tessa.'

Feeling wrung out, Tessa lay back in the chair and closed her eyes.

Nick had very quickly run out of things to tell Colin – university gossip was rather thin at the moment. He lapsed into silence, wondering why Colin was looking at him strangely. Or was it that Colin's baby-pink over-large face was unsettling?

'I hope,' Colin said at last, wearily, 'you're not up to your tricks again. Though I rather fear you are. You've been most diligent with your visits, old chum, nevertheless they don't quite add up to the magnificent sum Tessa fondly imagines you've made. One notices these things,' he said apologetically, 'lying here with nothing better to do.'

Nick made blustering noises.

'Don't for a minute imagine I'm complaining. You're a smashing bloke, but . . .'

'But?' In spite of himself, Nick needed to know.

'You never quite grew up.'

The silence beat in Nick's ears. The dying have an advantage, he thought resentfully; when they proffer their final thoughts, it somehow doesn't seem decent to yell 'balderdash!'

'I know it goes on all the time – seems to in our line of business, anyway. But for pity's sake, Nick – isn't Tessa worth better?'

'All right,' Nick conceded, after a pause. 'I've been an idiot. Trouble is, this one's . . . different.'

Colin groaned.

'I don't mean the situation's different, or that I'm different – oh no, I'm the same weak culpable fellow. I mean, she is. She could be hurt.'

'Madness.' He sighed deeply, turned his head towards the wall. 'Face it – you're going to hurt one of them. I do hope it won't be Tessa. In fact,' – his eyes returned to Nick – 'it would relieve my mind considerably if I had your word that it wouldn't be Tessa.'

Nick got up and put his hands in his pockets, walked to the window and back to the bed. He sat down again and said, 'OK, you've got it.' Then added hurriedly, as if giving away the key to his soul, 'I never could stand the thought of losing Tess, you know. It's my secret nightmare.'

'Then do yourself a favour.'

When Tessa came in, for different reasons, all three were careful to avoid the others' eyes. Tessa fussed with the things on top of the cabinet. Nick complained that there was fluff under the bed which could never have happened a decade ago. Colin countered that he was lucky to have a side room; a decade ago you had to die on the ward. This cast a tense silence until Colin dispersed it by describing how, when his father died, no-one noticed until a WVS lady complained that old Mr Petchel had not only ignored her offer to change his library book but had pulled a disagreeable face at her into the bargain.

A nurse breezing in to take Colin's temperature was shocked to discover them laughing. Then Colin confessed to being tired, and the Brierleys, rather shakily, took their leave.

In the car, their spirits rose – though privately. The rain had stopped. Tessa stared out of the window and

200

thought how glad she was to be going to church tonight with Eleanor. It would be a relief not to be shut in the house with Nick and the blasted telephone. Nick, invigorated by the thought of his impending sacrifice and of years thereafter spent in perfect fidelity, drove as though he were being examined in the art, signalling, overtaking, cornering with textbook precision. His fluency, his sense of control, helped to restore his rather battered self-image; he began to suspect that he was not such a bad chap after all. The reasonable thought took hold that, having committed himself to relinquishing Maddy, there would be no harm to anyone if he postponed the evil day in order to accustom her gently to the idea and make the best of their last encounters. Say, for a week or two. Come to think of it, Christmas would make a handy milestone with lots of festivities going on to divert her from any grief. Having already settled in his mind that he would do the right thing by Tessa, it seemed only fair, as far as circumstance allowed, to be sensitively considerate to Maddy.

Tessa was changing in the bedroom.

'Going out?' Nick seemed surprised.

'Yes – to evensong. The rector's going to dedicate that plaque to Aunt Winifred. I'm going with Eleanor. She's asked me in for coffee afterwards. Actually, she asked me for tea this afternoon, but I put her off because of Colin. I didn't think you'd be keen.'

'No, no – I shan't butt in. You go with Eleanor, darling.' He spoke as if he were forgoing a treat. He began to whistle, then broke off as though recalling some urgent matter and hurried off downstairs.

He's going to telephone her, she thought. Damn! – if only she'd thought about it more quickly, she could have estimated the time he would take to reach the sitting room telephone and have more or less simultaneously raised the bedroom receiver. For she had resolved to listen in when she got the chance, not seeing why, when she was directly affected, she should continue to remain in the dark. But there was no time now, anyway; the church bells were ringing.

She looked into her mirror, decided she needed a touch of colour and selected a pale bronze lipstick to smear over her lips. Then she lightly touched her cheekbones with it and smoothed it in. The effect was to brighten her eyes, which prompted her to further enhancement – grey eye-shadow, black mascara. Her face attended to, she repeatedly drew her fingers through her hair, making it billow. Her reflection was now so stunning, she wondered whether she had overdone things, got herself up more for a party than for evensong. If Nick thought this – fine; but she would hate to embarrass Eleanor. However, her plain black coat would tone her down, she considered, going to fetch it from the wardrobe.

When she arrived downstairs, Nick seemed not to notice how nice she was looking. He came out of the sitting room and escorted her through the hall to the street door – despatching her. 'Want a torch?' he called when she was already going down the steps.

'Lord, no. It's perfectly well lit.'

The door closed behind her and she forgot him. The Wychwood autumn smell – wood-smoke, dank air, an earthy mustiness – and the Wychwood bells calling, conjured her instantly to another time. It was as though she were eleven years old again, when sensation was sharp and evening gatherings magical, when hurrying to evensong at Aunt Winifred's side would be repeated – so it seemed – for an infinity of Sunday evenings.

Nick had been enormously cheered by Tessa's announcement. She ought to go out more often, he told himself duplicitously; she spent far too much time cooped up indoors. He waited three minutes – he stood in the hall watching the clock, timing them – then pulled on his coat and took up his keys. As he ran down the steps, Mrs Bull was coming through her garden gate with her daughter. 'Hello, gorgeous,' he cried; and to the younger woman – more restrainedly, 'Evening, Mrs Turner.'

'Come with us, me dear,' Mrs Bull roguishly called.

'No fear. I've led a sheltered life. Too late, now, to hit the flesh pots.'

'To church, you cheeky devil.'

'Oh. In that case, say one for me.'

'Come and say one for yourself.'

'Not tonight, love. You say one for me and I'll stand you a fairy cake at the Christmas bazaar.'

'Ooh – you're on!' she cried, laughing to herself with a catarrhal cackle as she hobbled away on her daughter's arm. 'He's wicked,' she complained, her voice a purr of satisfaction.

The spell persisted as she entered the church. Even responding as Mrs Brierley – to Mr Bultitude when she accepted a hymn book, to people who nodded from pews – she was at the same time Tessa the eleven-year-old child whom her aunt had dispatched down the aisle while she herself went into the vestry to don her organ-playing gown. Not even the strangeness of slipping into the Rectory pew beside Eleanor jarred the sensation – sensible though she was to the honour done her, to the exception made on this occasion; for the Rectory was wisely careful never to demonstrate favouritism.

When she closed her eyes feigning prayer, the passing of time was utterly obliterated: there, still, was the organ playing – calm, intimate, fluting, as familiar as her own voice; there, still, the sharp candle smell and the glance of cold air across her forehead; there the rustles, the creaks, and the particular closeness of bodies sharing silence; all there as last Sunday and a thousand Sundays before.

Eleanor smiled at her as Tessa got off her knees. The choir entered, followed by the rector. The service began to unfold, the familiar pattern, reliable, comforting. She felt enisled in this lighted church; outside in the dark was a churning sea – a restless dashing about – which meant nothing and had nothing to do with her. The sermon, and the preceding notices about doings in Wychwood, threatened to breach her containment, but after a time she overlooked the words, hearing only the lulling, mellifluous voice so perfectly attuned to the lofty building. But the concluding words before the blessing recaptured her, for they recalled and praised Winifred Hodson, and recited the inscription on the commemorative plaque. Deeply moved, she braced herself for the final hymn.

After all, there was no need to hunt through the hymn book. She recognized the first chord and knew what it was to be: 'The day Thou gavest, Lord, is ended.' It seemed to Tessa that the church must echo with these words and the swooping plaintive tune, for so long had they been sung here. Years ago, she had sung them with an aching throat, thinking of her father's car on its way to collect her, of the imminence of Monday morning and school, of no more Aunt Winifred, no more Wychwood, until next Saturday. Now she could not sing at all, her childish sadness overlain by an informed sorrow – for Saturdays that can never come again, nor ever again uncomplicated love, straightforward affection.

Afterwards, she stole into the chancel to peep at the brass plaque which stated the simple facts of Winifred Hodson's long service as church organist. Then she joined the departing throng in the aisle, queuing to hand in hymn books. Mr Bultitude took hers gravely. His manner permitted no relaxation from the knowledge of where they were and the occasion. His voice betrayed him, though. 'A lovely service; it would have pleased her,' he said brokenly.

'It would indeed,' smiled Tessa, stepping to one side to wait for Eleanor, for whom many detaining hands lay in wait.

At last, Eleanor reached her. 'Come – back to the fire! We shall have a glass of wine to celebrate.'

Outside, Eleanor switched on her torch and waved the beam towards the Rectory gate. They picked their way along the grassy path between the gravestones.

Eleanor sighed reflectively. 'I think it was as she would have wished. It was not showy; Timothy kept to the point. Yes, I think we can feel that Winifred gave us her blessing.'

'It was perfect,' said Tessa.

Part Three

DECEMBER

24

Down the church path and through the lych gate came Tessa, Scrap at her heels. There was something in her manner of walking that struck the watching Maddy as different. Usually, Tessa walked with an easy swing, constantly turning her head in a relaxed and interested way to note with pleasure how lichens glowed sea-green and amber on a grey stone wall or how light shafted through the beech trees. Today, she stared fixedly ahead, hands deep in her pockets, shoulders rigid. Only a breeze floating her long dark hair, timidly, like an afterthought, softened the extremity of her unwavering progress.

This grim-looking Tessa frightened Maddy. She couldn't face her. Having just come out of the shop, she could hardly re-enter it; instead she fled further along the Green into the Red Lion.

'Yes?' asked Linda Maiden behind the bar, bristling at what she took to be unfriendly censoriousness on Maddy's face.

Maddy's eyes moved from Linda to a display board covered with small packages.

'Peanuts,' she said desperately, 'please.'

Bending to clip on Scrap's leash brought Tessa out of her trance and allowed her a glimpse of the fleeing Maddy. The sight did not disturb her; rather, she felt relieved not to be obliged to speak to her. Her feelings for her friend were so mixed these days, a jumble of anger, impatience, pity, regret, that it was difficult to be sure whether any affection remained. Sometimes she wondered whether love had turned to hate, though still, every now and then, she caught herself longing with a wave of anguish for the old Maddy to confide in. (What wouldn't she give to express the horror of watching Colin decay from within like rotten fruit? Whom else could she tell it to? She would not distress Eleanor. Nick, like Jerry and Viv, was already shouldering as much of it as he could stand. There was only Maddy . . .) If it were not for being so full of dread and concern for Colin, she might have examined her feelings for Maddy more closely, might even have concluded, perhaps, that she wasn't worth all this pain and forbearance. As it was, she lacked the energy to think about it. She was simply living from day to day.

Rose, putting the finishing touches to her entry for the WI county competition (handicrafts section), a collage of woodland *objets trouvés* garnished with *appliqué* needlework, was enjoying the virtuous glow of finding herself ahead of schedule. Tomorrow she would hand in her collage. On the sideboard lay a whole row of dolls promised for the Christmas bazaar toy stall (the 'Madame President' doll prominent among them). The dress she had made for Dolly was pressed and hanging upstairs in her wardrobe. (It was not hanging in Dolly's wardrobe because Rose was determined to keep it until the day of the whist drive – a decision prompted by Dolly's account of how Arthur, after a skinful, had once mistaken the bedroom cupboard door for the door to the bathroom.) This morning her own hair and Dolly's had been permanently waved. Thus was everything done that had to be done in time for the WI county competition next week and the Christmas bazaar and whist drive eight days hence.

The light, tight feel of her hair was pleasing to Rose. Every now and then, reaching for scissors or looking up at the clock, she turned or bobbed or flicked up her head more exaggeratedly than was necessary, on purpose to note how nothing moved; not a curl, not a single strand. When she went into the kitchen to get a cup of tea, she made a detour to the hall looking glass to appraise again her crisp appearance. The perm, she considered, had made her more like herself; she was now, so to speak, Rose Fettle with knobs on. Alas, the same could not be said of Dolly. The familiar Cloomb look of hair just unrolled from curlers and hanging in disordered and independent clumps had vanished utterly. In its place was a fierce uniformity lending Dolly the incongruous appearance of a bald and bewigged infant. Her scalp showed pink through the waves, and several inches of face around the hairline, usually hidden from view, were now exposed to the air and seemed abashed by it. 'It'll soften,' Maisie had soothed, showing Dolly the results of her labours in a hand mirror. 'Gawd – I 'ope so,' Dolly said, aghast. Rose was confident of her own perm not softening. She had calculated carefully when to have it done – allowing long enough for the pong to wear off, but not so long to permit any laxness of curl.

She sat back. Her collage was finished; any more fiddling would ruin it. It had turned out well; even she, who was privately self-critical in matters artistic, awarded it high marks. She wondered about her rival's entry. Tomorrow, when she took her collage round to Jasmine Cottage, she would doubtless get a look at it. Sometimes Rose could tell at a glance whether it was she or Mrs Storr who had triumphed (as far as their personal rivalry was concerned); at other times their entries were too disparate to make a judgement. Her most treasured moments, almost as good as winning a prize, were those one or two occasions when Mrs Storr had contemplated Rose's work and conveyed, not the admiring interest it was only polite to award another member, but momentary envy, her silence betraying respect.

Rose did not often visit Jasmine Cottage. As far as possible she avoided the need to do so; just now and then it couldn't be helped. Mrs Storr, as WI president, often held committee meetings at her house and bring-and-buy coffee mornings; and whenever items were to be collected together (as, for instance, for this competition prior to their being taken by car to the county hall), invariably the president invited members to 'drop them in' when they were passing. It gave Rose quite a turn to stand in the space which had once comprised the ground floor of her family home, and a burning anger to see it function now merely as the Storrs' entrance hall. There was a small cloakroom at the far end and a staircase to the side, a telephone on an antique chest and some book-shelves in the cavity which had once housed the kitchen range, an expanse of silky blond floorboards and a pale-blue Scandinavian rug. Blatantly unused space was what the homestead had become, space just to look at, to walk through. It was as if the Storrs were crowing over her: 'see what we think of your puny cottage; so little, we just pass through on our way to more important rooms.'

Once, she had found herself alone in the hall. Mr Storr had answered the door and asked her to step inside while he fetched his wife. Rose stood on the pale-blue rug and closed her eyes. Ghosts jostled round her, elbowing themselves a bit of room to cook in, to eat in, to laugh, bicker, plan, hope, worry and cry in: for two minutes it was bedlam in Rose's head. When she opened her eyes she felt more than dispossessed: on behalf of her ghosts she felt insulted. Never before had she thought of space as a mark of privilege. She recalled, on a WI outing to Lincoln, wandering round the cathedral. There were no chairs or pews in the main body of the building, just vast empty space which had struck her as odd at the time. After the Jasmine Cottage experience she understood the matter; cathedrals were built so large, not, as she had thought, to accommodate a great horde of worshippers, but to accord God due lavishness of space.

Of course, her brother wouldn't allow that they should feel aggrieved. If the Storrs hadn't bought the place and done it up to suit themselves, it would have crumbled to rubble years ago, he maintained, like most of the old Wychwood cottages. The truth of this did nothing to assuage Rose's feelings.

She was not thinking of these things at the moment, however, but of her collage and how its excellence might rattle Mrs Storr. She started to clear the table of all the bits and tools she had used. When everything was packed away into polythene bags and tins, and these stowed neatly in the sideboard cupboard, she went into the kitchen to make a mug of cocoa. She was about to carry her drink into the living room, when a noise startled her. The letter box flap had clapped shut – not a sound she expected to hear so late in the evening. She peered down the hallway. An envelope lay on the doormat. What could it be? Rather apprehensively, she went along to pick it up.

Inside the envelope was a much folded piece of paper. As she unravelled it, a tobacco smell wafted, sickly-sweet.

Dear Mrs Fettle, [she read]
This is to confirm that the whist drive refreshments will be priced as per the Christmas bazaar teas.
    Yours truly, K. R. Tustin. (Chairman)

She stood stock-still with her heart thumping; dazed at first; then full of pain like a child having a favourite doll wrenched from her by a more powerful and ruthless schoolmate; and at last – and this restored her to herself – wrathful.

She forgot the cocoa cooling in its mug on the kitchen table. On leaden legs, she went into the living room and sat down. A second reading of the note, then a third, added nothing to her understanding, which had been complete in the first instant. She returned the note to its envelope and let this lie in her lap while she stared into the fire, too preoccupied to notice how low it was getting.

It was Mrs Storr, of course, who had powered Mr Tustin's elbow. Rose's first decision was to defeat her. It took her longer to work out how. She raked over her past life, hunting for pertinent examples, and fastened on how, when her children were small, she had assumed confidence when she felt none, particularly in dealing with teachers and librarians and officials. Often, to get respect for herself and the best for her children, she had had to bluff, to feign knowledge she did not possess. Now, it suddenly came to her, she would do the opposite; pretend blithe ignorance. Quite simply, she had never clapped eyes on the letter. For all Ken Tustin knew, she was tucked up in bed when he pushed it through her letter box (too cowardly to speak the message to her face) and it had lain on the mat until morning. Then, when Rose came downstairs and, without putting on the light and letting folk see her in her dressing gown, opened the door to reach for her milk bottle, as like as not a draught sucked the letter away leaving Rose none the wiser. (It was shocking how the wind in the Close jumped at you some mornings when you put your head out.) She smiled thinly to herself and nodded, imagining how she would sail through the bazaar and arrive at the whist drive blissfully unaware of any altered arrangements. And then, when it was too late to get anyone to stand in for her, she would simply refuse to charge for the refreshments, full of horror that Mr Tustin could dream of taking money for left-overs. And Mrs Storr, of course, would not be around to do a blind thing about it, her sort – the posh sort of newcomer – never having been known to patronize a whist drive.

When she had run through the entire scene in her mind and proved victorious, Rose tore the envelope into quarters and poked it into the hottest part of the fire until it caught, flamed, and turned to ash. Nevertheless, some of her joy at the prospect of the whist drive had also gone up in smoke; she must look forward to it now with a marred pleasure. Nor could she share the strain with Dolly, who, if she were confided in, would not be able to carry off the deception. Even so, Rose *would* look forward and she *would* prevail. She wasn't going to let *her* spoil it.

In the event, Rose did not take her collage round to Jasmine Cottage. Fearing some reference to the whist drive refreshments might be made, upsetting her plan of feigned ignorance – even though Mrs Storr was apparently relying on Mr Tustin to do her dirty work – Rose sent Dolly with it instead.

'Oh, I don't want to,' said Dolly.

'Well, ta very much. How often do I ask *you* to do *me* a favour?'

'Oh, Rose; it'll be awkward. She might ask why I haven't entered summat meself.'

'No she won't. She'll be too busy peeking at my collage. Mind you remember what she says about it.'

'I wish I hadn't got to,' moaned Dolly, stuffing it under her arm.

'Treat it careful! Tell her I'm indisposed.'

'Indis what?'

'Indisposed,' yelled Rose, shutting the door.

Maddy was surprised to find Dolly on her doorstep. 'Mrs Cloomb!' she exclaimed, then, noticing the fading black eye, added encouragingly, 'Do come in.'

'I won't, thank you, me duck. I've just brought Rose's thingy. She's indisposed.'

'I'm sorry to hear that. Nothing serious?'

'I can't say,' said Dolly mysteriously, uncertain as to what degree of calamity 'indisposed' referred.

Maddy was removing the wrappng paper. 'She won't mind if I . . .' She fell silent. 'God – that's good,' she said flatly, for it upset her idea of the world that artistry as well as technical facility should fall from the fingers of such a prosaic and disagreeable little body as Rose Fettle.

215

God-that's-good, Dolly repeated in her head, memorizing it for Rose.

'And how are *you*, Mrs Cloomb?'

'Oh, not so bad, only I've been a bit pushed lately, what with one thing and another. I s'pose you could have a pot of me piccalilli for it, only really they're promised to Mrs Frogmorton.'

Baffled, Maddy said, 'That's quite all right. And thank you for bringing Mrs Fettle's collage; tell her I'm sure it'll win a prize. And I hope she'll be better by Tuesday.'

'Right-oh, me dear,' said Dolly, thanking heaven her piccalilli was still safe for Mrs Frogmorton. On the way home, she practised saying God-that's-good with increasing enthusiasm.

'God, that's good!' she delivered at last, in an incredulous, awe-struck tone.

'Just like that?' Rose was suspicious.

'Honest – her very words. She said it would win first prize.'

'Yeah? Then she thinks mine's better'n hers.'

'Have you at least canvassed your list for promises?' Maddy persisted.

Tessa stared into her coffee mug.

'Oh, really! There's little over a week to go. I'd better do it. Give me your list . . .'

'No. I'll go out this afternoon.'

Tessa sounded so dull, Maddy became uncomfortable. 'I suppose you're weighed down with work.'

'No. As a matter of fact, the book's finished.'

'Finished?' Maddy cried, starting up; but Tessa stayed in her chair, and Maddy tried to retake hers as though she had never made to move out of it.

Embarrassment shuffled into the kitchen and hung round until they both felt too encumbered to speak. The same thought was disturbing both. For the past seven or eight years Tessa's announcement of a book's completion had sent Maddy scampering delightedly up to the studio, assuming, as Tessa had intended her to, that the announcement was an invitation to view. When the paintings had been thoroughly examined and discussed, Tessa would produce a bottle of wine and they would settle into a private celebration. Now, in a hurry to cast off their discomfiture, they both spoke at once:

'I'll do it when I take Scrap out.' – 'I don't mind in the least doing it for you.'

Their voices having collided, their sentences hung undeciphered in the air.

'Sorry.'

'No – you say.'

'I just said I don't mind doing your end of the village. I've done mine. And I know you're pretty tied up visiting your friend in hospital.'

'Not this afternoon. Nick and I are going tonight.' (For the past week, possibly because Colin's case had become hopeless, Nick had insisted on their visiting him together. Maddy, who already knew of Nick's intended movements, said nothing.) 'I promised I'd help you with the teas, so I will. I'll make a start this afternoon. It's too muddy, anyway, to go tramping over the fields.'

'If you're sure. It's all sorted about charging for the whist drive refreshments, by the way. I saw Ken Tustin earlier. He said he'd told Mrs Fettle. So we must be sure and collect enough stuff for the evening as well as for the afternoon. People at my end have been very generous – at least with their promises; and they're usually as good as their word.'

'That reminds me. Phoebe Peck promised the cheese. She's on your list, really . . .'

'Yes, I've got her down for the cheese.'

Silence fell. Maddy's eyes searched the table top as if for some safe thing to say. Tessa watched her dispassionately, marvelling at how flat she felt in her friend's company. 'I expect you want to get on,' she said abruptly, not caring how this sounded.

Maddy flushed and rose. 'Yes. Um, Tessa?'

'And I've got to phone Larry.'

When Maddy got to the door, she hesitated and turned. 'You are OK?'

'Of course. Just a bit pressed.'

There was nothing for it but to go. 'I'll, er, see you, then. 'Bye.' Going down the steps, she heard the door closed promptly behind her.

Round the corner from the Green came Phoebe. 'Oh, Maddy! Robert said you'd be at Tessa's or in the shop.'

Maddy frowned. Hardly a day passed lately without Phoebe appearing on her doorstep.

'There's a smashing film on next week.'

'Next week's a bit difficult – my creative writing class is on Monday, we're at the county hall on Tuesday, there's a sub-committee meeting of the parish council to be fitted in somewhere, and Saturday's the bazaar.'

'You're not busy every night, then,' said Phoebe, keeping count.

'Well, we'll see.' This was most unfortunate. She had planned, in fact, to use a visit to the cinema with Phoebe as an excuse to get out with Nick; Phoebe's habit of turning up at Jasmine Cottage and exchanging words with Robert threatened to jeopardize this plan – which was a shame, because excuses were proving harder to come by. 'I'll let you know. It'll be a spur of the moment job if we do go. But Wednesday may be possible.'

'Great!' Phoebe stood rooted in the street with her eyes shining.

'I'm going to the shop now. Want anything?'

'No, thanks.' Only her head moved as Maddy passed. 'Maddy?' she called, remembering something she had meant to say. 'I've writ a poem for that competition.'

Maddy turned back. 'The county competition? But I thought it didn't appeal to you – "My longest day".'

'But I thought of a good 'un – that day when you and me went to Leamington and tried on all them clothes.

Then, to make it longer, I stuck on about us going to the pictures in the evening and then to the Chinese – cheating a bit, but you're supposed to use your imagination. I'm going to copy it neat, then I'll drop it in. There's some ever such funny bits. You'll die.'

Maddy turned her head and stared at the Green – at the brewer's delivery lorry and the barrels rolling, at the shouting men and at Linda Maiden standing in the doorway with her hands on her hips showing off her bosoms; nothing came to her that she might say to dissuade Phoebe without upsetting her. 'I'll look forward to it,' she said, and, sighing to herself, went on over the Green to Brenda's.

Ken Tustin was also busy with the Christmas bazaar preparations. Certain little difficulties had been smoothed over, he felt, largely by his not saying too much about them. Problems were like dust – better not stirred up. When challenged by Mrs Storr this morning, he had chosen his words carefully, had not said he had *spoken* to Rose Fettle, rather, that he had 'communicated'. 'I have communicated with Mrs Fettle. She now knows the whist drive refreshments will be charged for, same as the bazaar teas.'

'Oh, good. That's all right, then. She took it calmly, I trust?'

Ken mumbled into his pipe and blew a bit. (Maddy was so relieved she scarcely noticed. Her question had been a mere politeness; she did not care if Rose had stamped her foot and driven it into the ground.)

It was now Ken's ambition not to bump into Mrs Fettle. (Though he was unlikely to do this, since Rose was very busily avoiding him.) Casting his eyes up street and down lane, he called at the homes of other volunteers, ensuring that the bran tub would be operational (Mr Bultitude), and that preparations for the various stalls were in hand: the toy stall (Mrs Burrows), the Christmas card and wrapping stall (the Brownies), the 'nearly-new' stall (Sarah and Richard

219

Grace), and the produce stall (or WI stall, as its superintendent, Mrs Frogmorton, maintained); also, that the Santa Claus costume would still accommodate Derek Bowman, that Mrs Dyte had received promises of good prizes for the raffle, that the Christmas cake was ready for its weight to be guessed (Mrs Joiner). He also briefed the men who would set out the stalls and do duty on the door, and called on the rector whose tasks included declaring the bazaar open, announcing the prizes, and arbitrating in any altercation. Talking to the rector, it did cross his mind to mention the little difficulty over the whist drive refreshments; but he decided against. Least said, soonest mended. Rose had not come angrily to his bungalow front door, nor had he heard a whisper of the affair on his trips round the village. Mrs Fettle, it seemed, had taken the whole thing lying down.

25

How everything stays the same, thought Tessa, flying down the street tugged by Scrap. The sameness seemed to leap at her – a hump in the pavement like a molehill with tar crusting it; the puddled edge of the road where cars and lorries had clipped the greensward; cow parsley grown up through the bars of the long abandoned Rectory gate – all unchangingly familiar; she had been treading over them or walking by for ever, it seemed. And there, still jutting provocatively over a garden wall, was the branch from which her ten-year-old son had once fallen during a trespassing raid for conkers. The sameness was only to be expected, of course; nevertheless, today it struck her as heartless. If a calamity were taking place at this moment in one of the cottages, or some long drawn out tragedy, the streets outside would show no sign. The village would still stare back dispassionately; people would carry on as usual, making the same witless comments – 'I must just pop over to Brenda's before she shuts' – 'Ghastly weather, but I suppose the farmers are glad of it' – 'Quite a good turn out last night, considering'. In the old days people had drawn curtains over their windows, tolled bells, shut up shop; imposed on everyday sameness, disturbed it, given it a kick. Her bleak view of the unchanged scene this afternoon felt like a dream, and this was not surprising; Colin was filling her heart and her head, though she was not actively thinking of him; he was just there, inside her, in abeyance. Suddenly her mind emptied, as Scrap, stopping abruptly, brought her up with a jerk. 'Oh, you!' she said, crossly comprehending, and resigned herself to a protracted inspection of a lamp post.

Once past the churchyard, Scrap had perceived what sort of walk this was to be. Not a scamper through the kissing gate followed by the freedom of the fields and the wood, but a promenade linked throughout to his mistress (save for a brief unclipping of the leash on rough grass at the village edge), passing gates marking other dogs' territory, tracing other dogs' walks, being fondled, even treated, by other dogs' mistresses. His own mistress put a strain on this sort of walk. Though he was working on it, she lacked a proper understanding of the ways of dog. For instance, if he was not vigilant, if he failed to dig in his heels, she would charge past sites of canine interest without a second glance. He had learned from bitter experience to bring her under control in advance, to halt her in her tracks well before the exact spot; thus, advancing slowly upon lamp or gatepost, she could be held at rest while he made his enquiries and added his own contribution to the fund of canine knowledge. Even then she acquiesced with bad grace. 'Oh, come on. Don't you dare do the other thing.' This last he treated with disdain, for it betrayed her ignorance. When he was ready he trotted onwards, bringing her after him, looking out for the next familiar staging post.

When Scrap had visited the rough ground a quarter of a mile out of the village along Manor Road, Tessa retraced her steps and began making her calls. She disliked the begging aspect intensely, even though it was expected of her and she was giving her time for a village cause. 'I myself shall be giving the tea-bags,' she always managed to get in somewhere. Her embarrassment was quite out of place; generally people fell over themselves to make promises. 'Oh, the teas. Well, last year I made my coffee sponge. Would that suit?' suggested Molly Whitton, leading Tessa to the rear of her tied cottage to show off her bantam chicks. The Manor could be given a miss, she thought thankfully, for Celia Westbrook, as was well known, always gave the milk. When anyone looked doubtful, she offered a let-out. 'I know it's difficult; I expect other people have been round asking you for things,' she said, having been comprehensively badgered herself. Several of the older folk mentioned the whist drive refreshments. 'For the teas? Oh yes, my duck. I'll send you up half a dozen eggs – there's nothing nicer than an egg and cress sandwich to my way of thinking. Mind you make plenty left-overs for the evening. Us old 'uns look forward to a bit of a do.' The expression 'left-overs' disturbed her. Evidently, the issue was not as straightforward as Maddy had implied.

It was late afternoon by the time she had completed her list. (Mrs Frogmorton had insisted on giving her tea and scones and finding a Good Boy Treat for Scrap; and Mr Bultitude – his eyes lighting at the sight of her – had led her into his greenhouse.) Rather wearily, she shooed Scrap into her kitchen and went on down Church Street to Maddy's.

She was rather surprised when Mrs Dyte admitted her – 'She won't be a tick. Come in.'

The usually spacious hall was cluttered with

packages. 'Our entries for the WI competition,' Mrs Dyte explained, following Tessa's stare.

A door banged, footsteps hurried, and Maddy appeared. 'This do?' She held out a bottle of Robert's best port.

'Oh, lovely.' Mrs Dyte took the port and turned to Tessa. 'It's for the raffle. I suppose you wouldn't like to give one of your paintings for a prize?'

'Well, no. But I'll give something else. What have you got besides Maddy's wine?'

'Oh, all the big prizes. It's the small ones we're short of. A nice box of chocs?'

'All right,' said Tessa coldly, miffed to learn that her painting would have featured as one of the lower ranked prizes. Maddy rolled her eyes in despair, and, to pay Mrs Dyte out, said slyly, 'Do show Tessa your cushion, Joan.' She took a large package from the pile of competition entries and thrust it at Mrs Dyte, who unwrapped it. 'Isn't it something?' Maddy asked innocently. It was of tortured red plush in the shape of a cat.

'Indeed. Very novel.'

Joan Dyte was all modesty. 'I don't suppose it'll *win*. But they're cute in the kids' bedrooms. And one has to show willing. Well, I'll leave you ladies to it. Shall I call by for the chocolates?'

'No, no. I'll drop them in when I'm walking the dog.'

When she had gone, Maddy slipped her arm through Tessa's and gave a squeeze. 'Cheek! I'm glad you didn't waste a painting on her. I'll show you something good, though.' She went to the pile of competition entries, found and unwrapped Rose Fettle's collage. 'What do you think?'

'Nice!'

'Yes. Guess who?'

'Mrs Fettle's?'

'The very same. That woman beats me – such a meanie, such a killjoy, and yet . . .'

'She probably thinks *you*'re a meanie.'

Maddy was indignant. 'I'm the one who's always trying to get us to be big-hearted at WI. And without fail, Rose Fettle puts the boot in – townies, foreigners, she's agin 'em all.'

'Probably because life in Wychwood hasn't been a picnic. That reminds me. Talking to people this afternoon, I suddenly saw another side to this whist drive refreshments business.' (Frowning, Maddy replaced the collage on the pile.) 'Some of those who are giving food for the teas – the older ones mostly – would be the very ones to benefit if it was free in the evening.'

'But most people who are giving food *won't* be going to the whist drive. So where's your problem? It's not a benefit, anyway; it's for the church roof.'

'I just think there may be more to it than we suspect. The old folk see it as a bit of a knees up . . .'

'At other people's expense – devised and presided over by Mrs Fettle. God, the woman *must* be a witch. Look at you – one scowl from her and you cave in!'

'I haven't been near Rose Fettle,' Tessa said indignantly. 'Orchard Close is on your list. Oh,' – she threw up a hand – 'forget it!'

Their eyes shied from one another and ranged over the packages, the floorboards, the rug.

'Cup of tea?'

'No thanks. Here's my list. You'd better check it in case we're going to be short of something.'

'For goodness sake! Stop looking so peeved and come and have a cuppa.' And without waiting for a reply, she went through to the kitchen. Half-heartedly, Tessa followed. 'Here; read this,' said Maddy, thrusting a sheet of paper at her, then going to fill the kettle.

The first few lines set Tessa laughing. Then she became uncomfortable, as if she were spying on a person she knew. When she reached the end, she put Phoebe's poem down on the table.

'I'd have thought,' said Maddy, bringing over two mugs of tea, 'you'd be splitting your sides. Bloody embarrassing for me. The "Maddies" are so prominent – an unlucky name: have you ever met any other Maddy? I'll make sure no-one in Wychwood has a look at it. But I'll have to enter it – it's for the competition – and there's bound to be someone I know on the judging panel. Ah, well,' she sighed, 'it'll brighten someone's day. Is that all right or do you want some more milk?'

'It's fine, thanks.'

'You might show a bit of sympathy.'

'I suppose,' said Tessa slowly, 'you've rather asked for it.'

'What the hell d'you mean?'

'You've given her a lot of attention. She liked it, wanted more of it, started to become dependent on it. That's quite a responsibility.'

'You sound like Robert,' grumbled Maddy, going pink. 'I've taken an interest in Phoebe ever since she joined WI – tried to encourage her, help her. I've stuck up for her . . .'

'And I admire you for it. It's just, well, lately it seems to have got more personal. Which is all right, so long as . . .'

'So long as?'

You're not using her was on the tip of Tessa's tongue; but she lacked the courage to say it. 'So long as she doesn't get hurt.'

'What a cautious attitude! Are we supposed to take lessons before making friends with someone a bit disturbed? Take a degree in risk-free chumminess?'

Tessa felt justly rebuked. Maddy had always given her time readily to anyone in need of it. Of herself, the same could not be said. 'Sorry,' she mumbled, sinking her nose into her mug.

With the fanaticism of one who likes to secure all her points, Maddy hastened to take advantage. 'And you do agree with me over the whist drive refreshments?'

'Oh, I'm sure you're right – you're the expert in village politics; I'm just the recluse who sticks her head out of the house now and then to stop people wondering.' She stood up. 'I must get on. I'm meeting Nick at the hospital at six. By the way,' she added on her way to the door, 'I told people to bring their contributions to you, though in one or two cases I've promised to collect. I presume we're making the sandwiches here, as usual?'

'Mm?' said Maddy, her mind on another matter. 'Oh, sure; yes, fine.'

As if parading a good deed, Nick ushered Tessa into the room. He couldn't say any more to Colin on the subject, but nor could he bear to end up in Colin's bad books; unable to protest his repentance, he presented it instead.

It was doubtful whether Colin noticed. Tessa sat beside the bed holding Colin's hand. Nick sat further back, hunched forward, jumping up with desperate eagerness at the least chance to give assistance. 'Pass me the beaker,' Tessa requested now and then, and once, 'Pass me a tissue.' When the nurse came in he bounded to his feet ready to move mountains if only she would ask.

'I think his mouth needs swabbing,' said Tessa to the nurse. Nick envied her that.

Sophia arrived, signalled Tessa to remain where she was, snatched the box of tissues and proceeded to sob and heave her way through them. Later, when Colin became restless, Tessa looked frightened.

Nick went to the head of the bed. 'Col? Are you in pain? Is it bad?'

Colin nodded.

Nick went out of the room.

'He's had all we can give him,' the staff nurse said. 'Only the doctor . . .'

'Then fetch the doctor.'

'But he's . . .'

'Fetch him.'

Twenty minutes later a houseman arrived with a nurse bearing a swathed basin. Tessa, Nick and Sophia left the room. When the doctor and the nurse came out, they filed back in and sat in silence for a time while Colin slept.

'Come on,' said Nick at last, enfolding Sophia, rocking her. 'We're taking you home. Say good night to him.'

She allowed him to lead her to the bed, and obediently kissed her husband. Nick took Colin's hand. Tessa kissed his forehead. They didn't linger.

'We'll go in yours,' Nick told Tessa. 'Pick mine up later.'

As they drew up in the Petchels' driveway, Magda opened the door. Sophia passed her without a word; she moved swiftly – her eyes screwed half-shut, her hands stiffly before her – like a blind woman fearing obstruction, and disappeared into the drawing room. Magda detained Nick and Tessa in the hall; without speaking, indicated her question.

'Someone should stay with her tonight,' Tessa said by way of an answer.

'I will, of course,' said Magda. She did not invite them to proceed further.

'I'll just . . .' Nick began, and edging past Magda made for the drawing room. 'Are you . . . ?' Tessa heard him begin. She waited. A moment later Nick returned, very red in the face.

'What was the matter?' she asked, driving back to the hospital to collect Nick's car.

'Nothing.'

'Something upset you.'

'There was a fellow in there. Youngish, foreign-looking.'

'Probably this Pieter.'

'Sitting cool as you like in Col's chair.'

They drove the rest of the way in silence. In the car park, getting out of the car, Nick said, 'I may go on to my room for a bit.'

He meant his room in the university, she understood. 'At this time of night? It's nearly ten.'

'You don't mind, do you? I just feel like – a bit of quiet.'

'You'd better go, then,' she said, putting her car into reverse gear.

'I'll get it,' cried Maddy – so sharply that she, rather than the telephone's shrilling, made Robert jump out of his skin. He was caught putting on a record and could not have countered her if he had wanted to. He turned the volume down, then went swiftly to the door and pressed an ear to it.

'Yes,' she was saying. There was a pause and her voice became low; 'I'll try,' were the words he thought he made out; then, more loudly, an unmistakable 'Yes'. When the phone suddenly clattered, he jumped away from the door, but at once her feet went running up the stairs. Three minutes later – it could have been no longer – she looked in and gabbled so quickly and urgently, he failed to make out the words – something to do with Phoebe and trouble? 'What did you say?'

But she was gone. He hurried after her and saw the front door close. 'What did you *say*?' he called, wrenching it open. He went outside. When he reached the alley where the cars were kept she was already backing out. Her face was in darkness until, as the car bumped into the street, the lamplight caught her. 'Maddy!' The window came down an inch. 'Back soon,' she yelled, and the car rushed forward.

It was very quiet when she had gone. After some minutes he had a hunch that the car had not turned right towards Peck's Farm, but left towards Fetherstone. He tried to recall the noise it had made travelling, but it was no good, he couldn't be sure. Cursing himself for not listening attentively at the time, he went back to the house, his footsteps on the gravel sounding inordinately loud.

The record had stopped; in its centre, the needle swung uselessly to and fro. He plucked it off and put the record away. Then he sat down and lit his pipe. At length, almost against his will, he rose, went into the hall and reached for Maddy's telephone pad. He found the name Peck and looked long and hard at the number beside it. Making up his mind, he snatched up the receiver.

'Roy — sorry to disturb you — Robert Storr here. My wife isn't with you by any chance?' The heartiness of his voice disgusted him. How honest and calm was Roy's drawl in comparison — 'Sorry, Robert. She ent here. Hang on; I'll ask Phoebe.'

'No, don't do that. It's just that Maddy gave me a message and I'm afraid I wasn't attending. No matter. Sorry to have disturbed you, old chap. Good night.'

Hot beads had sprung on his forehead. He went to the back door and stood in the sharp air watching bats make passing swoops of the garden. 'Sod it,' he said suddenly to the shrouded mulberry bush. He returned briskly to the hall where the pad was still lying beside the telephone. This time he looked up Brierley.

Tessa, arriving home, ran straight upstairs to run her bath. As she arrived on the landing, the telephone began ringing. 'Yes?' she said breathlessly, snatching up the bedroom receiver. There was no answering voice. 'Tessa Brierley speaking,' she prompted. Her eyes went to the window (the curtains still undrawn), to the blackness outside and her own reflection. She knew there would come no answer.

After a moment or two, in Jasmine Cottage, the receiver was very gently laid down.

'I'm sorry your friend died,' said Maddy, arriving at Holly House the next morning — Saturday — with a bunch of forced freesias. 'I, er, saw Nick getting his car out this morning. He said he was driving in to see if he could do anything for the wife.'

'Yes,' said Tessa, taking the flowers. She went into the scullery to put them in water.

'Forms to fill in, I suppose. There's always forms.

229

And just when you can least do with it. If there's anything I can do, Tessa . . .'

'Thanks, but I shouldn't think so.'

'I mean, don't worry about the teas. I'll ask someone else. You won't want to bother . . .'

'Yes, I will. Nick phoned just now to say the cremation's fixed for Friday, so I'll be quite free to pull my weight next Saturday.'

'Look, I didn't mean . . .'

'I want to do it.'

'Oh. Right.' After a pause, she said timidly, 'Fancy some lunch at my place?'

'Not really, Maddy.'

She nodded at this, then went to the door. 'See you later in the week, then.'

'Thanks for the, um . . .'

'Flowers? That's OK. 'Bye, Tessa.'

'Goodbye.' She went into the hall, leaving Maddy to let herself out.

26

Not by chance had Maddy observed Nick going into his garage this morning. She had spent twenty uncomfortable minutes peering between the churchyard yew trees on purpose to do so.

When, at half past eight, Brenda turned the shop door sign to 'open', she was surprised to see Maddy Storr on her doorstep already preparing to enter. Hand pressed to chest, Maddy announced an urgent need for indigestion tablets. Oh – and while she was at it, she told a bemused Brenda, she might as well take half a dozen eggs and a packet of butter. These items were laid tenderly in her basket; they gave her confidence, for they were visible proof of her housewifely innocence in being abroad so unusually early for a Saturday. However, she did not take her purchases home. She ducked in at the church gate and, grateful for the covering mist, swerved left along the path which ran through the more ancient graves and parallel to Church Street. Shielded from sight by tall fat yews, she kept watch on the Holly House garage. Cold damp seeped through her boots, stunning her toes; her eyes and nose watered; her breath sent out clouds. She thought of the madness of the night before and repeated silently, like a mantra, over and over, Please let him come out alone – please let him come out alone.

When he telephoned last night (so late, so unexpectedly; desperate, he said, to see her) his stated despair answered her own desperation which she had endured for the past five days. They had not been together since the previous Monday. (At least their precious Monday evenings had remained sacrosanct – she supposedly at her creative writing class, he at his spurious course development meeting.) He had told her then of Colin's rapid decline, and of their intention – his and Tessa's – to visit the hospital every evening together in order to support one another during the crisis. Clearly, Maddy had been in no position to protest. She had merely wailed, 'Oh, Nick!' – desolate, but almost sure he would not be able to do without her for long. As the days passed she became less certain, grew agitated. Then, last night, he telephoned.

Her first instinct was to enjoy her thrill of elation while sensibly rejecting the possibility of so late a meeting.

'God, I've bloody missed you,' he said. 'Have you missed me?'

'Yes,' she said, unable to risk saying more.

'Come in now, then, darling. You can manage it somehow. Please. I can't tell you how I need . . .'

'I'll try.' The weakness attacking her legs had evidently spread to her brain.

'Try? Come *now*.'

A rough edge to his voice decided her. She simply closed her mind, barked, 'Yes,' slammed down the receiver and raced upstairs where she took two minutes to get ready. Coming down, she was still far too highly charged to think of anything to say to Robert. She just opened the drawing room door, threw in a few garbled words and ran – ran in panic as though Robert were some cruel tyrant about to come after her, to catch and detain her. Her sense of escape as she wound down the window, yelled, 'Back soon,' and shot from his grasp, was so immense that, turning the corner, putting her foot down, she laughed repeatedly out loud.

In Nick's room they hardly spoke. They fell on one another greedily. Very soon afterwards they began to quarrel.

(Was that it? he asked himself, was that all? Hell, man, Col could have been dying at the very same moment!)

(I might have been happy *and* safe, she thought bitterly, if only I'd said it wasn't on – happy knowing that Nick wanted me, but safe still with Robert. Now I've got to face the music.)

Blame hurtled between them, accusations of disregard for the other's difficulties. Nick grew sullen, Maddy angry. He wanted her to go. She lingered, postponing the moment of peril. His expression (that of a peeved and yobbish adolescent was how it appeared to her) enraged her. She jumped into her car declaring she had no idea when or if ever she would see him again. All the way home she racked her brains for a convincing tale to tell Robert. Phoebe, the one person who might conceivably summon her so late at night, seemed her likeliest hope. But almost immediately Robert pulled this safety net away.

'Where have you been? Why couldn't you explain properly instead of dashing off like a maniac? I've been out of my mind. I rang the Pecks to see if you were there . . .'

'You did what?' She shouted, taking refuge in indignation. 'How dare you ring round my friends checking up on me. Who else did you phone?'

'Just the Pecks,' he said, too dumbfounded to mention Holly House, and too ashamed of having hung up on Tessa to confess it.

'Who the blazes do you think you are? You don't own me. Just because you're a stick-in-the-mud . . .' On and on she ranted until she arrived at the point where she could yell her intention, in view of the impossibility of spending the night with so objectionable a man, of sleeping alone in the spare bedroom. He followed after her in bewilderment, uselessly protesting, as she stormed from master bedroom to bathroom to spare bedroom and finally shut the door in his face and turned the key.

A few hours' grace! she jibbered thankfully to herself, sitting on the edge of the bed while she waited for her heart to stop thumping. But as her body calmed, her thankfulness evaporated. She grew stiff and cold; at last, like a fumbling old woman, undressed and climbed into bed. The need to pacify Robert lost its urgency as she lay staring into the darkness, displaced by the looming memory of her quarrel with Nick. She passed the night in a half-awake state of frantic dreaming. Bird-song woke her. At seven she got up and stole downstairs to make a pot of tea.

Got to see him, she thought, staring out of the window at the morning mist. Got to make it all right.

She recalled Nick's expectation of his friend not surviving the night, and of himself spending today helping the prospective widow to deal with the formalities. Would Tessa go with him? she wondered. Probably not. Tessa, she rather gathered, was not keen on their friend's wife, and in any case, Nick had mentioned that the wife had a woman friend – also a foreigner – staying with her. Nick, she grew convinced, would drive into the city alone. Encouraged by the veiling mist outside, she resolved to lie in wait for him after first calling at the village shop to legitimize an early-morning excursion.

When Nick came running down the Holly House steps – alone – she watched with the amazement of one who has carefully calculated the odds yet can scarcely credit it when her horse romps home. Stumbling back along the path, her legs gradually returning to life, she arrived, panting, in the Brierleys' garage. 'Hello.'

'What are you doing here?' he asked, not pleasantly surprised.

'I've been shopping,' she said, lifting her basket. 'I was coming back when I saw you, and I had to know . . .'

He frowned.

'About your friend?'

'He died.' He turned to unlock the car door.

'I'm so sorry.'

'I've got to go.'

'Of course. Nick – last night I was really scared to go home. I'd given Robert no explanation – still haven't for that matter. It was nervousness. I'm sorry, Nick.'

He looked into her strained face and softened. 'Don't worry about it.'

'I'll see you on Monday? It'll be all right then?'

'Yes,' he said soothingly. 'It'll be all right on Monday.'

'Oh, Nick . . .' She went weak with relief.

'Got to go.' But he was touched by her, and paused to press his hands reassuringly over hers which were wrapped round the basket handle.

'Monday,' she whispered.

'Monday,' he replied.

Smiling, she hurried home.

'My God, where've you been this time?' Robert bellowed.

'Shop,' she said shortly, putting her basket on the table.

He peered into it. 'Eggs and butter,' he sneered disbelievingly. 'It's Saturday. We're going to the market.'

'You can go where you please. I'm going to suck one of these indigestion tablets I got from Brenda's, then quietly sip a cup of tea, then drive to the garden centre and choose some really nice fragrant flowers for Tessa.'

'Flowers for Tessa?' cried Robert, as his world lurched from one improbability to another.

'If you must know,' said she, implying how much earlier she would have explained matters if only she had been granted an opportunity, 'their close friend – whose sad case I have often told you about – died last evening. It's all been . . . pretty dreadful.' With which, she popped a tablet into her mouth and left the room.

Robert sat down.

Was she honest? he asked, as many a better man before him. Did this tragedy explain her flight last night? Had the telephone call been a summons from Tessa? Ah – but Maddy had not driven in the direction of Holly House but very smartly away from it, he remembered, pouncing on his surmisings like a stage attorney. Could, then, he countered timidly, Tessa have telephoned from elsewhere – requesting a lift, perhaps? The attorney struck again: certainly Tessa could not have been ringing from the city hospital because he had heard her speak on the Holly House telephone not twenty minutes after his wife's departure. Well then, from somewhere nearer – where did these people live? Or perhaps Tessa's car had broken down. He tried to recall how Tessa had sounded – breathless when she first answered the phone, then, when she spoke her name, leaden, world-weary, as if knowing the call was a nuisance call. It was then that fear had flooded him. Nick's not at home, he had thought with sudden certainty, and an idea which had once briefly disturbed him, grew anew to outrageous proportions and beat in his head like the wings of a demented bird. Very gently – because unable to speak – he had put down the receiver.

Now he was no longer sure. If their friend had just died, Nick could not possibly – could not *possibly* . . .

She came back into the kitchen and filled the kettle.

'I'll make that if you're not feeling too bright,' he offered.

'Thank you,' she said with ironic surprise at his civility.

He made the tea and took her a cup. 'Shall I come with you when you go?'

'No thanks. I just want to choose some flowers for Tessa and take them round there. She's on her own at the moment.'

Ah – so Nick was away from home *altogether*. (The widow could not be left alone and no doubt required all sorts of assistance.) He began to perceive that he had been a heel. But if only she had taken the time to explain before dashing off. Nevertheless, he was feeling much better.

'Tea all right?'

'Wonderful.'

'Good.' He crept away as if she, too, were in mourning.

On her return from Holly House, Maddy made Robert a very good lunch – though she consumed little of it herself.

'Now,' she said, as if she could not take his continued reasonableness for granted, 'you do remember agreeing to me using your car this afternoon?'

Life was full of traps; anxiety had made him witless. He cast his mind back in trepidation. 'Did I?'

'To ferry all my stuff to the county hall – the WI competition entries.'

'Of course,' he cried. 'I say, why don't I come with you? If I give you a hand, the job will be done quickly, then we could go and have afternoon tea at the Swan Revived.'

'Oh, what a nice idea, Robert,' she said, weary longing stealing over her for the peace of an elegant sitting room, for a deeply luxurious sofa, for waitresses in caps bringing plates of fiddly sandwiches, for a pot of steaming Assam, for warm scones, jam, cream. 'That would be perfectly lovely.'

As they set off, the sun came out: it seemed a good omen. During the journey they found safe topics to talk about and by the time they arrived at the county hall, had completely re-established their habit of speaking nicely to one another. With Robert's help it did not take long to transfer the competition entries from the car on to the long table designated 'Wychwood' in an upstairs room. There were many similar tables, one labelled 'Steeple Cheney', another 'Erdingford', another 'Spinney Compton', and so on. The entries would remain on display for one week to delight visiting instituters and members of the public. Wychwood Institute planned a visit for the forthcoming Tuesday evening to replace the normal meeting. When everything was arranged to Maddy's satisfaction and she had exchanged pleasantries with various officials, she and Robert departed. They drove out of the city centre to the waterside car park of a gracious and ancient hotel, the Swan Revived.

Once through the revolving door, Maddy's feet seemed barely to touch the ground. She glided over the sumptuous carpet, nodding to the girl on the desk, left Robert there to order their tea, and went on to the flowery-smelling pink and green ladies' room. A little titivating, an appreciation of the expensive soap, and out again into the corridor where Robert was waiting. In the sitting room, dominated on one side by a row of tall sash windows and on the other by an Adam fireplace, the colours were yellow, grey and burnt-orange. She chose a settee, remembered to take off into it with a little backwards leap – for she was tiny and the settee large – and landed sunken in its blissful comfort. When the waitress arrived bearing a well-filled tray, Robert jumped up and collected several cushions to put behind her back and allow her to sit in a more upright position. He did this with enormous gallantry, emphasizing her petite size, sharing with the waitress an affectionate smile for her, making Maddy feel precious and protected and universally loved.

It was over a maid-of-honour tart that her complacent mood took a turn for the worse – when Robert said in a low sympathetic voice, 'How *is* Tessa?'

About to take a bite, she paused. 'Um – tired. Weary and sort of numb – as if it hasn't sunk in yet.'

This, he recalled, was a fair description of how Tessa had sounded last night. He put down his cup, guilt-stricken. 'I did a stupid thing. Can't think what came over me.'

'What Robert?' Taking a sudden dislike to the almondy tart, she pushed it aside. 'What did you do?'

'I phoned Tessa last night – don't look like that – I didn't speak to her. In fact – God knows why – I hung up on her. What a creep – intruding on her at a time like that – in such a way!'

She wondered whether she dare risk saying, Oh, was that you? But Robert didn't appear to expect it. He was simply staring dejectedly into the fireplace. How typical of him to care; how kind he was and . . . honourable. The word caused her pain. Tears welled and mounded perilously along the rims of her eyes. For a moment she couldn't breathe; when she did, she breathed in shudders which shook her tears free. Blindly, she groped in her handbag.

'What is it? Maddy, whatever's the matter?'

'Tissues,' she gasped.

He took her bag and found her one.

'Maddy?'

'Don't talk. Drink . . . your tea.'

The next five minutes were devoted to disguising the fact of her weeping from anyone near enough to notice. She dared not get up and walk to the ladies' room. When the waitress came and offered to replenish their teapot, she shot forward, pretending to examine her shoe.

'No, thank you,' Robert smiled, sending the waitress away. 'Darling,' he urged in great alarm, recalling her breakdown a decade ago, 'you must tell me.'

Since she could not begin to account truthfully for her emotion, she cast desperately about for some plausibly tragic explanation. 'It's their friend dying like that. I can't get it out of my mind. He was your age, Robert, that's all.'

'The Brierleys' friend?'

She nodded. 'And so dreadfully long dying, exhausting all that hope. Horrible.'

He took her hand. 'Maddy – my love.'

The long case clock near the fireplace majestically ticked away the seconds. She grew calmer. He adjusted her cushions and she sank back between them, exhausted. She's worn out, he thought. She won't spare herself. The bazaar teas, the WI competition, Phoebe's troubles, now Tessa's – not to mention all the exquisite food she prepares for me. In a moment I'll suggest a breath of air – a walk by the river; and I'll book us a table for dinner. She likes it here. A good rest, and she'll be more herself again.

And she, slumped in her soft cocoon, gazed at the moulded ceiling and thought, I was never meant to have affairs. I'm not cut out for it. She would not be at all surprised if going against her nature so violently brought on some terrible disease. In which case it would be entirely Nick's fault; with his wealth of experience he should have known she was not right for it. He should have left her alone – peacefully, healthily, blissfully, unawakened.

These are the worst weeks of my life, Tessa promised herself, looking from her bedroom window across the shrouded churchyard. Faith enabled her not to add the words 'so far', a faith still insisting that if she could just hang on, could just see these bad times through, never again would life be as bleak and thorny. This morning, the first morning without Colin, she was clinging on to her faith only by her fingernails.

The telephone rang so joltingly, she had to clutch hold of the window frame. It was Nick calling to say he was now at Jerry and Viv's: was she all right or would she like to come over?

'No. I'm all right. Tell Viv I'll phone her later.'

She went downstairs. Passing the hall table she was smitten by the scent of Maddy's gold and purple freesias. A sharp pain reminded her that she last ate at Mrs Frogmorton's at about half past three yesterday afternoon. She went into the scullery and opened a large tin of beans, cut a thick slice of bread, put the kettle on.

When she had eaten, the sun came out. Radiance poured through the kitchen window – she looked up from the newspaper propped over her unwashed plate and blinked at it. The light seemed to beam in on purpose to collect her. 'Scrap,' she called, jumping up to fetch her boots and jacket; 'walk!'

At the wood's edge, she looked back. Wisps of silver floated here and there; mist still lined the valley. She was glad to be full in the sun where the laden grass dazzled, and dark bare trees – drab and ill-defined when she had looked from her window earlier – now stood proud against the light. In the foreground the church gleamed like bleached bone; its window glass shimmered. On an impulse, on her return, she tied Scrap's lead to a boot-scraper by the church door, kicked off her boots in the porch and went inside. Noiselessly in her fisherman's socks, she padded to the font and turned down the central aisle. In the sanctuary the altar wore Advent purple. Light streaming through the stained glass window had spattered colour over the floor – blobs of red, green, blue and yellow were like watery jewels on the bare stone, fading, then glowing, and sometimes swimming giddily, as clouds

passed over the sun and wind shifted branches outside the window. Eleanor came out of a small ante-
room and was startled to see Tessa, in her socks and
jeans and forest-green corduroy shirt, her hair a fiery
mass in the sun's rays, evidently taken root there.
Tessa sensed she was watched. 'Oh – Eleanor! Come
here and see.'

The shifting pattern of colour amazed Eleanor. She
laid a hand on Tessa's arm. 'It has never happened
before,' she whispered. 'It's a miracle.'

Tessa laughed. 'You just didn't notice.'

Eleanor drew herself up with immense dignity. 'If
such an effect had occurred before, I should most
certainly have noticed.'

'Well, it's very striking. Hypnotic. I can't take my
eyes away.'

The door at the back of the church creaked open and
in came Mrs Dyte, followed by her eleven-year-old
daughter, with an armful of flowers. 'Oh – Saturday
afternoon,' Tessa murmured, waving discreetly to the
newcomers and recalling the routine from the times
when she had helped Aunt Winifred with the church
decorating.

'Good afternoon, Mrs Dyte. Good afternoon, Clare,'
Eleanor called in a subdued voice. 'It's her turn to do
the flowers,' she confided to Tessa. 'I'm going to
clean the brasses.'

'Can I come back and help you when I've taken
Scrap home and collected my shoes?' Tessa asked,
suddenly very keen for company.

'Of course. You can help me polish the lectern. I'll
start spreading out the newspaper.'

When she returned, the Dytes were unwrapping
flowers in the Lady Chapel and Eleanor was in the
chancel applying Brasso to the lectern eagle. The
Dyte daughter, in a piercing and self-righteous voice,
launched into an account of a schoolfellow's wicked-
ness. 'I'm not playing with Pippa any more, Mum.
She's been ever so bad. She got sent to Mr Ellis for

drawing rude pictures – I can't say of what – all over the blackboard. Mrs Miles was *furious* . . .'

'Hush, dear. Pass me the secateurs.'

Eleanor and Tessa, feeling very glad not to possess an eleven-year-old daughter, got on with their rubbing.

'Our friend died last night,' Tessa said softly, pausing for a moment with her duster-covered finger in a crevice of the eagle's wing. 'We were quite . . . glad in the end. It was such a relief, you see.'

'I know it can feel like that.'

'You don't like giving up hope for someone so young – young to die, I mean. But . . .' She sighed.

Eleanor's hand fell still, her eyes became unfocused.

'When the relief fades, it'll be a different matter. I shall resent it,' Tessa foresaw, and briskly resumed her polishing.

As they were packing away, Tessa, finding her need for company undiminished, asked Eleanor to return with her for tea.

Eleanor hesitated. Timothy had been called to old Mr Partridge's bedside and would come home tired and famished. On Saturdays she particularly liked to attend to his comforts and feel secure of his ability to get through Sunday in tip-top form. 'Later on in the week would suit me rather better.'

'Later on?' Tessa echoed doubtfully. The coming week loomed and filled her with misgiving. 'I'm dreading next week, as a matter of fact; there's so much on. Tomorrow we're driving down to see Paul. Of course, I'm really looking forward to that – he's written a revue and we're invited to watch a rehearsal. Then on Monday I'm going over to Larry's, my partner's house, taking my paintings for the new book. Friday's the funeral, Saturday's the bazaar . . .'

'That leaves a sizeable chunk in the middle.'

'So it does,' agreed Tessa, laughing, feeling caught out, thinking of the type of socializing she preferred – no hard and fast arrangements; people dropping in without too much warning and thus obliged to take her as they found her; herself phoning a chum to ask, 'All right if I come over later on?' 'Perhaps,' she wondered aloud, 'I dislike commitments.'

'But you're very committed,' Eleanor objected, 'to Nicholas and Paul, to your friends – as I myself am fortunate to know. And very committed to your work.'

'You're right,' she said, looking into herself with pleased surprise. 'Though I do shrink, rather, from the week ahead.' It was perfectly reasonable to be apprehensive about the funeral – Sophia throwing a fit, and everyone's stomach churning; but there was something else, more ominous . . . And then, like mist clearing, came the premonition that this coming week would see everything decided between Maddy and Nick – and consequently for Robert and herself – she was sure of it.

'Is something the matter, Tessa?'

She shook her head.

Eleanor, suddenly seeing how to accommodate both her friend and brother, clasped her hands. 'You must come back and have tea with me. I expect Timothy, you see, and I want to make sure he eats properly. But I know he'd be delighted . . .'

'Thanks,' said Tessa, quickly and gratefully. 'I'd be glad to.'

27

They gathered in the village hall car park, the car drivers and those requiring lifts. There was some polite holding back, some friendly pushing forward; and some feeling of desperation, for it was cold. The night was clear with stars and a three-quarter moon; a frost was expected.

'Oh, come on Sah; just get in,' called Jane Bowman to her friend, Sarah Grace.

As Sarah arranged herself on the front passenger seat, Maddy stuck her head in. 'Two seats in the back? Come on, Mrs Fettle, Mrs Cloomb – room here.'

Rose looked dubiously at Jane Bowman's canary-yellow estate. Mrs Davenport's elderly Rover struck her as more suitable; even, at a pinch, Mrs Burrows' Mini. She sniffed, then signalled to Dolly to run round the other side to get in behind Sarah, while she, with bad grace, took the seat behind Jane.

'All set?' Jane called. And Maddy signalled her to drive off.

Rose and Dolly sat straight-backed, knees together, handbags held to attention on their laps. They listened to the matey chat going on in the front with hard blank faces, like two old nuns forced to brush up against sin. Now and then the younger women remembered to include them in the conversation, but with scant reward. Dolly kept her mouth shut for fear of putting her foot in it, and Rose confined herself to formalities – 'Very nice, I'm sure,' 'I couldn't rightly say,' and 'Fancy!'

Phoebe Peck had hung behind. 'Can I come with you, Maddy? The Land Rover's so flippin' slow.'

'Of course. Who else is left? Only you, Eleanor? Well, let's catch up with them.' She pushed the driver's seat forward and motioned Phoebe into the back, then leaned across to unlock the passenger door for Eleanor. ''Fraid it's not very comfy back there,' she called, driving out into Church Street. But Phoebe was very content with her sideways perch on the hard seat. Chin propped on her knees, she sang softly to herself. After five minutes or so, she fell silent, and Eleanor remarked, 'That was a happy little tune.' Maddy had thought it plaintive, and supposed Eleanor had spoken for speaking's sake. When still no sound came from the back, she and Eleanor glanced round and saw that Phoebe, her head lolling and bouncing like a doll's, was lost in slumber.

'I feel rather like that myself,' said Eleanor, stifling a yawn. 'It must be the cold.'

'Me too. Though I promise to keep my eyes open.'

Eleanor acknowledged the joke with a gentle laugh; sighed about the traffic; lapsed into silence. For which Maddy was overwhelmingly grateful; she had wondered where she would find the stamina if chatting were required. Her own fatigue, however, did not dispose her towards sleep; it was edgy, nervy, born of eternally balancing on a knife edge.

Her thoughts flew to Nick and the previous evening. Selfish sod, she thought. Squalid waste of time. Shouldn't have agreed to see him tomorrow. Last night, as soon as their love-making was over he'd looked at his watch. She'd tried to ignore this, tried to rekindle the teasing banter they used to enjoy. Gracious! – not so long ago the greater proportion of their time together had been taken up with tender confidences and silly confessions and surprising one another with amusing little presents. He had looked down at his wrist for a second time.

'You keep looking at your watch.'

'I've been thinking – might be an idea to get home early. Tess has been at her partner's all day – Larry's place – it's quite a drive. If I got back in time I could have supper ready. I could say my meeting was cancelled. It'd be nice to chalk one up for a change.'

She'd hated him when he said that. Cheapskate, hypocrite: got what he'd come for, time in hand, so busting to rush home and show like a good boy scout. And never a care for what all this was doing to Robert. My God, how that poor man suffered last Friday and Saturday – and all because Nicholas Brierley had fancied a lay. At least, though, she hadn't hung about. 'Right,' she'd cried, jumping up and grabbing her coat. 'Go home and put your pinny on. Frankly, this stinky little room's getting me down. Those gross coffee rings!'

Their leave-taking was so laden with loathing,

neither felt it possible to mention their next assignation. Perversely, all the way home she worried about the omission and wondered whether it was bothering him also.

Robert had been pathetically pleased to see her. 'Darling! You're back early.'

'I know. I think I'm getting bored with these classes. Pour me a large one, there's a love.'

She downed her drink quickly, then devoted every remaining scrap of nervous energy to being sweet to Robert. She slept badly; woke early – it made her squirm, now, to recall her first waking thought: When am I going to see him again – oh my God, when? There was a raw emptiness inside her; a frightened insecurity. Hours stretched ahead of straining her ears for the telephone.

Nick eventually phoned in the afternoon. She rushed to snatch up the receiver. 'Yes?'

'Tomorrow night – same time, same place?'

'All right,' she said, slamming it down again.

Now, driving to the county hall with a slumbering Phoebe and a dozing Eleanor, she knew she could never be satisfied. Relieved (or was 'vindicated' the more accurate word?) by Nick having phoned to make a date, at the same time she flinched from the prospect, began to suspect its price was too high. Turning into the car park, she bit her lip in annoyance, thinking that she was behaving like some sort of addict – always desperate to know where the next meeting was coming from, knowing it could no longer bring her peace. And unable to break the idiotic cycle.

'Alight here, please,' she called gaily, 'terminus!' – as though there could be nothing more pressing on a president's mind than that the members had a good night out.

'Well, I don't think much of Steeple Cheney's,' Rose Fettle was saying when Maddy, Eleanor and Phoebe entered the exhibition room.

Maddy glanced round to see if anyone from Steeple

Cheney stood within earshot, then took Mrs Joiner's elbow. 'What's eating Mrs Fettle?' For Rose certainly looked disgruntled, her lips pressed together, her head faintly vibrating.

'She wants to know what you've done with her collage. It's not on the table.'

'It must be. I put it there.' She ran to see. But the collage was not in the Wychwood display.

Just then, Mrs Hesketh-Jones – a big wheel – a member of the national executive committee – came by. 'If you're looking for that marvellous collage, it's over there – see – on the central display board with the visitors' information. We hung one or two of the choicest items there; it's so important to leave people with an impression of *quality*.'

'Oh great! Now come over here, please, and repeat every word to Mrs Fettle. Mrs Fettle – this is Mrs Hesketh-Jones, our area organizer, who has something to tell you about your collage. And to think,' she added happily, turning aside to Mrs Joiner, 'we haven't even had the judging yet. I've a feeling we're going to do well this year.'

For the next two hours she was completely caught up in it all, and felt refreshed as a consequence when it was time to go. But first she drew Phoebe aside. 'Phoebe, my dear, the flicks are out, I'm afraid, as far as tomorrow evening's concerned. Ken Tustin phoned just before I came away to say we shall have to hold a sub-committee meeting tomorrow evening after all. Sorry, love. But if the film's any good it'll come round again. Another time, eh?'

'Oh,' said Phoebe crestfallen. 'Oh, all right, Maddy.'

It was a changed Rose Fettle on the journey home, relaxed, almost benign-looking. Dolly, who knew Rose as well as she knew herself, thought sneeringly that there was nothing like a bit of praise – praise for her kids or for the arty-crafty stuff she was always turning out – to soften her up and stop her being so sharp and down on the world. And sure enough, when Sarah

247

Grace started moaning about how Pippa's teacher had a down on her, Rose was all ears, craning forward, making ready to tell how she had brought up the Fettle kids to be blummin marvels.

Sarah Grace was in a ferment. Hardly a week went by without Mrs Miles summoning her to school to discuss Pippa's misdemeanours. The latest complaint was to do with some offensive pictures drawn on the blackboard. It had come as a shock to discover the episode was common knowledge. Mrs Dyte had referred to it as she and Sarah stood together eating quiche and potato salad off cardboard plates. 'I shouldn't worry too much,' had said she – the mother of a whole string of obligingly virtuous children, 'I expect Pippa's going through one of those difficult phases you read about.'

'If Mrs Miles has been gossiping to other parents,' she fumed now to Jane Bowman, 'I'm going to have it out with her. Trouble is, I get so mad with Pippa – the constant aggro, the humiliation – sometimes I feel like giving up, telling her she'll have to sort things out for herself.'

'Ooh, you mustn't do that,' cried Rose. 'If her Mum don't stick up for her, who else will?'

Sarah turned her head. The sentiment expressed her true feeling, despite the wounds to her maternal pride.

'I had terrible trouble with the teachers over my John at one time. They made out he were bad when I knew he was just bored. "You keep him busy," I told 'em; "then you won't get no trouble." They didn't like it, but I kept on. Made 'em set him homework, too. If she's playing up, me dear, you ask 'em why and what are they doing about it.'

'Thanks, Mrs Fettle, I jolly well will,' cried Sarah, inspired.

That's done it, thought Dolly. There'll be no holding her now. It'll be 'my John this and my June that' for days – rubbing it in about my lot not doing much for theirselves. When, back in the car park, Rose delayed to give Sarah one last word of encouragement, Dolly shuffled off without her.

Rose caught her up by the side of the Fetherstone Road as Dolly stood waiting for Mrs Davenport's car to pass on its way to Hilltop Farm. 'What's up with you, then?'

'Oh, nothing,' sighed Dolly.

In Number One Orchard Close, Edie Partridge sat hugging her coat round her shoulders and keeping watch by her window. The only light in the room came from dying embers in the grate. Outside it was brighter; under the street lamp, frost-speckles glinted. When Rose Fettle and Dolly Cloomb came within the lamp's orbit, she darted to her door and ran down the path. 'Psst, Dolly!' she hissed, 'don't go no further. Come in, me duck, while I tell you what happened.'

Doubtfully, they followed her into the house. Whatever it was, Edie would squeeze from it the last drop of satisfaction.

'There's been such a to-do. Your Arthur came home – and I don't think he were hisself,' Edie said delicately. 'When he found you were out, he went mad – banging on doors up and down the street, yelling and creating, and I don't know what he weren't going to do when he got hold of you. Our Gail had her friend over – that Tony from Fetherstone. He told Arthur to chuck it, cos Stella Meers – you know what she is – was having hysterics; she said someone ought to ring the police. Anyway, after a bit your Arthur went back in and quieted down – leastways, your front door's half-open so I suppose he's inside. But you'd best be warned, me dear; he's in a terrible paddy.'

Rose cut in. 'We're much obliged, thank you. And now you can get to bed, Edie, seeing as the fun's over. Come on, Dolly.'

'But Rose,' whimpered Dolly, hurrying to keep up as Rose set a terrific pace down the path and through the gate, 'what am I going to do?'

'Come in with me, quick, or they'll all be looking out their windows.'

This seemed to Dolly the least of her troubles. Darting frightened looks over the road for fear of Arthur watching, she hurried after Rose into Number Six.

'Put the telly on,' said Rose, calmly, pulling up the electric fire and pressing down the switch. She had let her fire go out, not expecting to sit by it this evening. 'I'll make us some cocoa.' But alone in the kitchen, she stood trembling and wondering what the dickens she would do if Arthur came roaring across the road. When nothing useful came to mind, she dealt with herself as sharply as she would some other dithering person: Stop mithering and make the cocoa, woman; then you can have a think about it.

In the living room, Dolly was standing in front of the television transfixed by a steamy scene in a foreign film. Hurriedly, as Rose came in, she switched it off. 'Nothing much on.'

'Never is. Here's your cocoa. Biscuit?'

'Oh, ta.'

The room was slow to warm. Rose leaned down and switched on the second bar of the fire. They stared at the rosy rods, their eyes growing heavy.

Twelve hoots from her cuckoo-clock woke Rose. She pushed herself out of her chair, went to the window and peeped through the curtain chink. It was quite black outside, for the street lighting always went off at midnight. 'Dolly, wake up,' she urged, turning off her electric fire. 'I reckon we'd better go over and take a look. He won't see us coming – if he's still watching, which I very much doubt – cos the street lamp's gone off.'

This offer to accompany her struck Dolly as so generous that she couldn't speak. She got up and dumbly followed Rose's cautious creeping progress through the doorway, down the path, and, skirting a few patches of quavery moonlight, over the road.

When they got to the Cloomb front door they found it was indeed ajar as Edie had reported. Rose put her hand to it and slowly exerted pressure. Dolly, unable to breathe, stuck a knuckle in her mouth. 'Won't move; summat's jamming it,' muttered Rose, and she stepped closer and peered round. 'Reckon it's him out cold on the floor. Let's go round the back.'

Dolly rummaged for her key. Rose snatched it from her and ran to the back of the house and unlocked the door. They crept in without a sound – dreading a suddenly resurrected Arthur – and stole through the kitchen and along the hall passage. Dolly switched the light on.

Arthur's jaw dropped. A couple of strenuous snorts, then his head rolled to one side and he breathed on, moistly but quietly.

'That's it, then,' said Rose, disappointed. 'He don't half stink.'

Dolly, seeing her dearest hope come to nothing, sighed. 'Give us a hand getting him upstairs,' she wheedled.

'No fear,' cried Rose, mindful of her position as the widow of Jack Fettle – a temperate man with reliable legs who had barely allowed Arthur Cloomb the time of day, much less laid hands on him. 'I wouldn't demean meself. Let the nasty pig lie.'

'I wish he'd never get up,' said Dolly bitterly.

For some moments her words hung there, provocatively. Then, with the air of one who has thought things out, Rose went forward. She gazed speculatively down at Arthur's head, then turned and studied the door. 'Put the light out,' she ordered.

Dolly flicked up the switch. Rose waited for her eyes to adapt to the dark, then crouched down and tugged at a corner of the door mat. Arthur moaned faintly as the mat came free of his head, but remained limply unconscious. 'If we leave this stuck out a bit over the step,' whispered Rose, placing the mat as she suggested, 'and then wedge the door over it like so . . .

there'll be a shocking icy draught. Feel.' Dolly put out her hand, then snatched it back with a shiver. 'And the beauty of it is, he'll be lying with his head in it *all night*.'

'Yeah,' breathed Dolly.

'Shouldn't wonder if it did for him – a man in his condition. Now, you come back with me – they all heard he was threatening to give you a hiding, so it makes good sense – and no-one can ever say you knew he was lying here. Then, in the morning, we'll get over sharpish and put the mat back.'

'Ooh, Rose, you are bright.'

'Come on, then; out the back way; and don't make a sound.'

Along by the side of the house and up the path they went, Dolly giggling under her breath, light-headed with the prospect of a dream coming true and the responsibility for achieving it comfortably resting on Rose.

At six in the morning they got up and hastily dressed and flitted like shadows across the unlit road. They felt their way through the house to the front door. 'Perishing,' said Rose with relish. She stooped down and pulled the mat in, told Dolly to lift Arthur's head, then returned the mat to its proper position. Finally, with a flourish, she reached out and switched on the light. 'There – we've come over and found him,' she proclaimed.

They surveyed him.

'He looks horrible, Rose. And his breathing's all rattly.'

'Aye – better get yer skates on. Run down to the call box and phone the doctor.'

28

'A pint of the best . . . and a G and T for the lady wife. That's one-eighty, please,' said John Maiden, placing the drinks on the bar mat, taking care to keep his eyes well away from Phoebe.

'Have one yourself,' said Roy, handing over a five pound note.

'Very kind, I'm sure.' He doled out the change, then pulled another pint. 'Your good health.'

'Quiet in here tonight.'

'Lively enough in the back,' he said, jerking his head at an eruption in the public bar – a hard smack and a clatter, raucous cheers. 'Ladies' skittles – our lot versus Spinney Compton.'

'You ought to go in for that,' said Roy to Phoebe. 'You've the muscles for it, and a good eye. Ever seen her throw darts?' he asked the landlord.

John, who had his doubts about Phoebe let loose in his bar with a fistful of potentially lethal weapons, made an indistinct reply.

Phoebe was smiling modestly into her drink. Watching her, Roy felt he had done the right thing, persuading her to come out this evening, sending the kids over to stay at his mother's. 'What d'you fancy?' he asked, pointing to the menu chalked on the blackboard.

'Steak, chips and peas sounds all right.'

'Yeah. Twice, John, please.'

'Steak, chips and peas twice . . . coming up!' he said, writing it down with a flourish and going off to tell Linda.

'Where d'you want to sit, love?'

Comfortably perched, the heels of her boots hooked

over a rung of the bar stool, she said, 'Let's stay here till it's ready.'

'Right-oh. Drink OK?'

'Yeah, nice.'

Her skin had a pale waxy look, he noticed, never a good sign; and her eyes, raised to a bottle of livid-yellow advocaat at the back of the bar, were darkly dilated. He hoped the gin would settle down peaceably with her pills. She had insisted on it – 'One won't hurt, not if I'm going to stuff food down me' – and he hadn't liked to argue.

John came back armed with cutlery and condiments which he set out on a table, then, uttering profuse apologies, he hurried off to satisfy the more lucrative demands of the skittle players.

The street door opened, was held in place by an arm, and Mrs Tustin came in, followed by husband Ken. 'Evening Roy,' said Mrs Tustin; and then, hesitantly, 'Evening Phoebe.'

'Well, this is nice,' said Ken. 'We didn't bank on having company, not on a Wednesday. What are you having, Roy?'

'No, I'll get 'em,' said Roy, bringing his hand down on the bar bell. 'Pint is it? What's yours, Mrs Tustin?'

'Oh, a sweet sherry, ta. How, er, how you keeping, Phoebe?' she felt constrained to ask since Phoebe's husband was buying her drink.

Phoebe ignored her. Her eyes under her scowling brows were fixed on Ken. 'You should be at the meeting.'

'Who? Me?' asked Ken, looking at the others. When she continued to stare unwaveringly, he gave a nervous laugh. 'Not tonight, love, I'm glad to say. Tonight me and the missus are treating ourselves, aren't we, Marge?'

Marge Tustin looked coy.

'Special occasion?' asked Roy.

'Wedding anniversary. Thirty-four years.'

'That's summat to celebrate, ent it Phoebe?'

'But he *should*. It's the sub-committee meeting.'

'Now, Phoebe. Ken knows if he's got a meeting or not. Ah, John: a pint and a sweet sherry. Ken was just saying it's their wedding anniversary.'

'Well, well, well!' cried John with overdone excitement, nervous in case a cry of 'On the house!' was expected.

Phoebe climbed down from her stool. 'I know he should,' she persisted belligerently; 'Maddy said . . .' And then her brow cleared. 'Oh – I get it! It's been cancelled. Crikes, I bet she's looking for me.'

'Phoebe!' yelled Roy, shooting his hand out to save her toppling glass.

But Phoebe was already yanking the door open. Half a second later she was gone.

To Robert, opening the door and finding Phoebe there was like drawing back the blinds on his worst, most secret fear. An hour ago, Maddy had left saying she was going with Phoebe to the cinema. Here stood evidence of her deceit. His instinct was to ward Phoebe off, to be rid of her. 'What are you doing here?'

'Meeting's cancelled. Maddy?' she cried, in her eagerness stepping past him.

'Now look,' he began.

But Phoebe was not interested in a sight of Robert; her big feet on the blue rug, she examined the hall. 'Where is she?' she demanded as if Robert had Maddy trussed up in a cupboard. Losing patience, she ran into the sitting room, out again, pushed past Robert and went on to the dining room. 'Maddy?' she yelled crossly, going through to the kitchen. When she ran back into the hall a second time, Robert grabbed hold of her.

'You can stop that,' he cried, curt as a school master with an unruly class. Her strength, when she dislodged his hand, was disquieting.

'She said we couldn't go to the pictures cos of the meeting. But there ent one. It's cancelled. I've just seen Ken Tustin.'

'Well, she's not here,' he snapped, barely keeping a grip on his self-control as he digested this confirmation of his wife's treachery. 'So you – you'd better go.'

His hostility translated to Phoebe as cruel determination to thwart her: she wanted to find Maddy; he intended to stop her. Her face twisted. She turned and tore upstairs – 'Maddeee.'

This was intolerable to Robert, full of rage and hurt, wanting his wife here, now, to take account of his passion and – pray God – appease it with an explanation; intolerable at such a time to have another's need for her thrust in his face, bawled in his ears. He charged after Phoebe and gripped her forearm as she stood hesitating on the landing. 'Come along,' he commanded, frogmarching her to the nearest bedroom – 'In you go. Take a look. Not here? Right' – and into the next – 'Go in. No luck?' – and kicked open the door of the bathroom – 'Try here. No? Come on then, we mustn't forget the study. Not here either? Well, that's the whole house, so . . .' he hauled her back along the landing and indicated the stairs – 'I hope you're satisfied.'

Phoebe's head was swimming. A corner of the wall, the newel post, a picture frame – all lost their sharpness, blurred a little. Meaning seemed to slip from her grasp.

Robert thought, 'My God, she looks dense.' His fingers dug deep into her arm; he swung her round to face him. 'Listen. You want her; I want her. Sadly' – he mouthed the words exaggeratedly – 'she's not here. Got it? She's *gone*.'

'Gone' was a terrible word. Her father had used it the day she came home from school to find a wrecked caravan and no mother. 'She's gone. Hopped it with her fancy man. Better roll your sleeves up, girl, and do something about this mess.' 'Gone' was a word often hurled at her during her unreliable childhood. It was said of her pony – 'He's gone. Bloke came and took him while you were at school' – and of her Alsatian

256

bitch – 'Bleeding dog got on me nerves, barking and whining all day. Don't ask no questions; she's gone.' She couldn't stay here in Maddy's house another minute with 'gone' ringing in her ears. She wrenched herself free and fled down the stairs; through the hall, out of the door, into the night, she hurtled – 'Maddy . . . Mam . . . Rocket . . . Jess . . .' – wailing a pathetic inventory of the lost.

Her dying wail was caught by Robert. It shocked him, filled him with dismay. Misery, he understood, had made him a tyrant. Very urgently he wished to make amends and be assured that she was safe. It was not in him to dash after her and run through the village calling her name – the idea occurred to him, but years of practising propriety had ingrained in his bones a wariness of public display; instead, he closed the front door and went to the telephone.

'Tessa – Robert here. Look, Phoebe may be on her way to you – I hope to God she is. I suppose she hasn't arrived? Well, if she comes, keep her with you; she's very upset. I'll phone back in a few minutes.' Then he sat on the wooden chest with his head in his hands, marvelling at the speed with which his most urgent desire had been overtaken. His sole concern while Phoebe was here was Maddy's deceit and her prompt return – so much so, that he had disregarded and abused Phoebe. Now, sickened by the memory of his fingers dug into her arm, of his voice barking orders, of his contempt, he cared more immediately, more franti-cally, for the distraught girl.

In Holly House, Tessa sat swaying forwards and back in the kitchen rocker, thinking, I can't stand it. On top of everything else, I can't stand it.

After a time she bounced out of the chair, having told herself tartly that she'd have to stand it, and reached for the telephone on the window sill. 'There's no sign of her, Robert. What's it all about?'

He sighed. 'Maddy, of course. I don't know what

she's playing at exactly, but she lied to me and let Phoebe down into the bargain. And then just now I behaved abominably – to Phoebe, I mean. If anything should happen to her . . .'

'I'm coming over. If she's on her way here, I can't help but bump into her. Be with you in a minute.'

Scrap was watching her. She stared down at him without speaking. He swung his tail – once – twice – hoping to dissuade her from restlessness.

'It's all right for dogs,' she muttered.

He flattened everything – tail, head, spine – but in vain; his mistress marched away, grabbed a coat from the scullery, keys from the dresser, went out and slammed the door. Disheartened, he stared at the door with unfocused eyes, ears pricked, head tilted, straining after her fading footsteps until his blood's singing drowned them.

'I suppose Nick isn't at home?' Robert said with careful nonchalance. They were sitting in the kitchen, where he had given her an account of Phoebe's visit.

Tessa hesitated. 'No, he isn't.'

'Ah.'

There was a suspenseful hush, then they both spoke at once – 'I wonder if . . . ?' – 'How long since she left?'

'Er – about twenty minutes,' said Robert.

'Phone Peck's Farm. If she's not there, at least you can warn Roy.'

But there was no answer. Robert held the receiver between them so that they could both hear how the telephone rang and rang.

'Tell me again – she said she'd seen Ken Tustin?'

'Yes, I'm sure she did.'

'Where would that be?'

'In the pub?' They both leapt to their feet.

'I'm sorry to have dragged you into this,' said Robert as they half ran along Church Street. 'I know it's a bad time for you. It's just that I couldn't think of anyone else.'

'Don't worry. I'm glad you did.'

In the lounge of the Red Lion, the Tustins were rounding off their meal with Black Forest gâteau and Irish coffee. 'That's right,' said Ken, smothering a belch – 'she ran off. She'd got a bee in her bonnet about some meeting. I told her there wasn't any meeting, and she just shot off. Didn't she, Marge?'

Marge, daintily conveying a large forkful into her mouth, nodded.

'Roy was pretty upset,' Ken recalled. 'He'd just ordered their meals. 'Course, he had to go off and look for her. That's two large steaks going begging, John said – a bit awkward for him, really . . .'

With hasty thanks, they left, and returned across the Green.

'I think we should drive to Peck's Farm,' Tessa said.

'I'll go. There's no need for you . . .'

'Of course I'm coming. I've got my keys; I'll drive.'

Still no sign of Nick's car, they both silently noted as Tessa backed out the Volvo. There was no sign either of Maddy's when they drove by Jasmine Cottage. She turned right on the Fetherstone Road and slowed to turn left at Peck's Farm. A vehicle was approaching from the opposite direction, indicating right. 'A Land Rover,' said Robert, deducing this from the closely set headlamps. 'Probably Roy's.'

Tessa pulled up on the track as the Land Rover drew up behind. Before they had unclasped their seat belts, Roy was already at Tessa's window. 'Phoebe in there?'

'Sorry, Roy. We're looking for her.'

Robert, leaning across Tessa said, 'She came to my place – oh, getting on for an hour ago – wanted Maddy – pretty upset. I'm afraid I wasn't as helpful as I might have been. She ran off.'

Resting against the car, Roy said, 'She's gone funny again. I've seen it coming; it's been building up for weeks. Still, I suppose we've had a pretty good run,' he sighed, as if talking about a change in the weather.

Tessa half-expected him to add 'mustn't grumble'. 'You mean she's ill?'

'Yeah; the pills aren't working, she gets mixed up, neglects the kids – the usual stuff. I drove home and there wasn't a sign of her, so I went over to me mother's in case Phoebe's gone there, worried about the little 'uns. Should've known better; she's more likely to think of her horse than her kids.'

'Horse,' said Tessa, pouncing on the word.

Roy straightened. 'I never looked in the stable,' he said, turning and running back to the Land Rover.

Hitting the ruts, they drove fast to the yard.

Phoebe was indeed in the stable. By the light of the yard lamp she was attempting to saddle her horse. Her appearance suggested that she had not taken the simple route home; twigs hung in her hair, her face was scratched and dirt-smeared.

'Hello, Phoebe,' said Roy. 'Leave him alone, love. You can't ride out in the dark.'

She ignored him and continued to grapple with a buckle.

'Please, Phoebe. Come on,' he cooed, approaching cautiously with outstretched hands as if she were an untamed animal. When he touched her, her arms flew up like pistons, sending him sprawling. She came after him at once, launched at him with fists and feet and head. The attack – the thudding and grunting – was deeply shocking to the pair watching and too divorced from any previous experience to permit interference. They blankly stared.

At last Robert roused himself, gathered his nerve and projected his body over her thrusting legs. Phoebe gasped. As Roy scrambled free, she fell limp.

When they had got her into a chair in the kitchen, Tessa ran a bowl of water and cleaned her up while Roy telephoned the hospital.

'They're coming for her,' he reported. 'I don't know how I'd've managed without you two, I really don't,' he went on brokenly. 'She doesn't mean it, you know.

She's gentle as a kitten, wouldn't hurt a fly. It's just when she's taken bad.'

Robert wrung his arm. 'Don't worry, old man. I'm thankful we found her. To tell you the truth, I can't forget my part in this. I was hard on her, you know . . . I hope, when she's better, she'll forgive me.'

'I blame meself. I should never have taken her out tonight; I knew she weren't right. Thank God you turned up when you did.'

Tessa, applying a towel to an inert Phoebe, thought, They sound like disaster survivors, endlessly recounting their guilt and thankfulness. 'I'll look at your face if you like, Roy,' she suggested timidly. 'Got any TCP? And Robert: make us some coffee – there's the kettle, there's the jar.'

'Oh – right,' said Robert, jumping at the chance to be useful.

On the short drive home, Robert's head lolled back and he closed his eyes. But when the car turned left into Church Street and slowed to stop outside his house, he looked quickly to see whether Maddy's car was standing in front of the garage. Tessa also glanced across. There was no little white car.

'Drive on,' he suggested. 'I'll see you indoors then walk back.'

She laughed at this and pulled up outside his gate. Light from the lamp on the other side of the street shone into the car. 'I have managed it before, you know – let myself into the house on my own. And you're exhausted. Go in. Go to bed.'

He unclasped his seat belt but made no further move. 'I shall dream about her,' he said gloomily.

'Maddy?'

'Phoebe.'

Reading in his face a determination to talk, she switched off the engine.

'It's a strange thing,' he began, as if ruminating for his own benefit rather than Tessa's. 'All the time she

261

was in the house I discounted her. My attitude was –
she's an irritant; be sharp with her, get rid of her, then
concentrate on more important matters. Yet, now,
every second of it haunts me. I see her; I see myself: I
see us both charging about on the landing – so vividly
it's more like a dream than a recollection. Poor kid; I
wonder where she is – what it's like for her? I hope it
isn't too harsh or clinical.'

'I don't think so. I remember Roy saying it's a homey
place.'

'Oh well – perhaps we can visit her, Maddy and I.'

There was a long silence, though neither noticed it;
and neither heard a sound like a child running,
halting, running, past the car and on down the street (it
was not a child nor the ghost of a child, but a turning
leaf bowled crisply along by the wind). Robert was
wrestling with his last three words – 'Maddy and I' –
and wondering whether such a thing still existed,
whether, by now it was 'Maddy and someone else'. But
his mind froze on the 'someone else'. He concentrated
on Maddy. What should he say to her? How would she
be?

Tessa was thinking, He's not an idiot, he must know.
Even if he's not sure, when Maddy comes home he'll
soon shake the name out of her. She thought of the
funeral to be got through. And of there being no Colin.
Loneliness hit her with such a pang that tears gathered.
Struggling with them, she prayed he would go.
'Robert?'

He started and turned.

'I'm . . .' Her voice shook. She forgot what she was
going to say.

'What is it?'

'I'm at the end of my tether,' she blurted as the tears
rained. She searched frantically for tissues.

Robert went cold. He knew it all. He'd known it
before, but hadn't wanted to. There was no shadowy
supposition; the 'someone else' was a fact, an identity.

'I'm so sorry, Robert.'

262

He pitied her. But a man in his sights changed everything. No need to pussyfoot: a man was something to focus on – to pin down, rail at, destroy. Even Maddy receded. His breathing quickened.

She blew her nose. 'What I want to say is – to beg of you – a few more days. There's the funeral on Friday. I couldn't stand . . .' But a fresh convulsion hindered her.

'How long have you known?' he asked curtly.

'What?' She wiped her eyes. 'Oh – weeks.'

'Then why the hell didn't you say something, do something – stop them?'

'I couldn't stop them,' she cried. 'Neither could you. Barging in and shouting the odds might have driven them into a corner – turned a passing affair into a complete smash-up. And I didn't want to lose them; either of them.' Relieved to be no longer crying, she went on more calmly. 'When things like this happen, we do have a choice. There are no rules laid down – "accuse, demand, issue ultimatums." If we want to, we can just . . . wait and see.' How lame, how feeble it sounds, she thought. He must despise me.

In fact, his acuity sharpened by the evening's drama, he was awed, having suddenly perceived what she had set herself. And he saw her point, for certainly he would die rather than lose Maddy. Come to think of it, he hoped for Maddy's sake that she could hang on to Tessa's friendship. Thinking along these lines, his chest grew less tight, his breathing eased; it was as if his anger stepped back. 'I suppose you felt, knowing them so well, it was a fair calculation.'

The new note in his voice gave her hope. She put her hands on the steering wheel and held tight. 'Nick will never leave me – that I do know. And I'd stake my life on it never crossing Maddy's mind to leave you. So, yes; I calculated on it fizzling out. Once or twice, I admit I've almost lost my nerve; but I've managed to hang on because I truly believe it'll end if we leave it alone. It's nearly over, now.'

'How do you know?'

'I just sense it.'

'So – you're asking me to do nothing?'

Her grip on the wheel tightened. 'You'll have to tell her about Phoebe; I can see that. But if you'd not *precipitate* anything. Give it a week – I can't stand much more of it myself. A few days?'

He sighed. 'Against my instinct – but, all right. I'll try and weather it for a few days.'

'Oh, Robert, thank you.' She began to shake, her feet knocked on the pedals, her teeth chattered.

'I shall see you home, after all,' he decided. 'In fact, I'd better drive.' He got out of the car.

She scrambled into the passenger seat and pressed her hands between her knees. Would she ever stop shivering? He drove to Holly House and into the garage. She got out and went up the steps and waited for him to bring her the keys. Reaching past her, he unlocked the door and held it open.

Scrap darted out, barking. They ignored him, and looked at one another in the light of the carriage lamp. When Robert leaned over to kiss her cheek, she clung to him for a moment or two. 'Thank you.'

'Good night,' he said in her ear.

As she raised her head, she saw a curtain move at a window of the cottage opposite. 'That's torn it.'

'What?'

'I've just seen Mrs Bull's curtains twitch.'

'Then we are sunk,' he said, going down the steps. At the bottom he turned and raised his hand to her and waited until she had closed the door.

In the morning, though jolted by the alarm bell and by Nick disturbing the bedclothes when he got up and went to the bathroom and, as usual, groaned and splashed and banged about a great deal, Tessa remained beset by sleep. She could not shrug her mind free of it, but drifted in and out of a dream while a great lassitude pinned her body to the bed. When the phone rang unusually early on the bedside table beside her, there was a hiatus. She came awake but was too stunned to move, and in the bathroom the noisy splashing ceased. Then, as she feebly drew an arm from the bedclothes, Nick – a towel round his neck – came bursting in, shouting (and 'shout' was the word, thought the shrinking Tessa), 'I'll get it. I'm expecting a call,' and raced downstairs.

Sophia? she wondered. Roy about Phoebe? Maddy – Oh, God, had Robert gone back on his promise?

She sat up. Suddenly, without thinking about it, she did as she had once resolved to do – picked up the phone to listen. In spite of her resolve she had not done this before; and her quick impulse, which did not allow for hesitation or dithering fingers, brought her instant success. As she took up the receiver she heard a clatter on the line and then Nick said, warily, 'Yes?'

'Oh, thank God – if it hadn't been you I'd have died. Nick, oh Nick, everything went wrong here last night.' (Tessa's stomach lurched.)

'What d'you mean "wrong"?'

'I told Robert I was going to the cinema with Phoebe. Well, she had some sort of breakdown last night – had to be carted off to hospital. Robert left me a note.'

'You mean he didn't ask you about it?'

'No. He'd gone to bed.' (Tessa breathed out in relief.) 'He's *never* done that before. I spent the whole night racking my brain for a good story and, blow me, Robert got up at six and cleared off. He put his head in before he went, offered me a cup of tea and said he'd got a meeting in London. First I'd heard of it. I'm scared, Nick . . .'

'I don't see what I can do . . .'

'You can bloody well *talk* to me.'

'Not now.'

'No, tonight.'

'Look, we agreed,' Nick said through his teeth (harassed, Tessa thought), 'not until Monday.'

'You've got to help me. I thought I'd say the car broke down and I had to wait for the AA.'

'Sounds dodgy.'

'See? It needs thinking about. I'm not going to be left on my own with this.'

'All right, then. A quick chat on my way home tonight. Half past six – The Bay Tree at Erdington.'

'Right.'

''Bye.'

His abrupt – and startlingly unfond – farewell almost caught Tessa off guard. She put down the receiver and lay back with closed eyes. When he came back into the room, she sensed him studying her.

He was not wondering whether she had eavesdropped, but how much she knew of this business about Phoebe Peck. 'You seem unusually tired this morning. Heavy evening? I thought the book was finished,' he remarked, trying to work round to the subject.

'Phoebe Peck ran off last night. Roy was worried to death. I helped search for her. We found her in the stables. Had to get her to hospital, though.'

'Poor old Roy.'

'And poor Phoebe.'

'Yes. Cup of tea?'

'Please. Paul rang, by the way. I think he's been brooding about Colin; he was very fond of him. He wondered whether he ought to come up for the funeral.'

'But he's got the revue on. Anyway, it might be a bit awkward. Doesn't look as if Annabel and Simon will make it.'

'That's what I thought. I told him Colin would want him to get on with his life.'

'Good.'

'Put the snib up, will you?' she called as he went through the doorway. 'It's Mrs Cloomb's morning; she might arrive before I'm dressed.'

But Tessa was dressed and making toast when Dolly

Cloomb arrived. Tessa heard her on the steps and pulled open the door. 'Hello!'

'I'm not stopping.'

'Oh.'

'Arthur's been took very bad. He's in hospital.'

'Then of course you can't stop.'

'It were yesterday morning. We had to get the doctor, and he sent for an ambulance. Mrs Burrows took us in her car – I was that upset, Rose had to come with me. So we didn't go and do the Manor like we was supposed to, and Mrs Westbrook says we've got to make up for it today cos of all them MPs coming to lunch – it's a big do; ever so important.'

'Oh, well,' said Tessa, spreading her hands in mock surrender. 'Who am I to protest? I'm very sorry about Mr Cloomb.'

'Yeah. They said they don't hold much hope.'

'Dear me! Well, if I can help in any way – with lifts and so on . . .'

'Ta, me duck. I'd better be off. Rose is just telling the Rectory.' (Eleanor and I both left in the lurch, thought Tessa, half-amused). Dolly turned to go. 'See you Sat'day.'

'Saturday?'

'The bazaar. You're doing the teas.'

'So I am. But what about . . . ?'

'Oh, I'll be there, don't you be feared. Can't let folks down.'

That puts you in your place, Arthur Cloomb, thought Tessa, closing the door. She ate her toast, drank her tea, considered doing the cleaning. Not now, she decided. Later.

Aimlessness gripped her. When Celia Westbrook jigged by on her hunter, Tessa was standing listlessly at her kitchen window. Celia, as usual, stared in frankly, possessively, as of right. Their eyes met, but neither smiled nor gave any sign of seeing the other. Beastly rude woman, thought Tessa, imagining how gratified Celia must be to have deprived Holly House

267

of its cleaner. She recalled Maddy's jokey '"Mornin' squire,' which seemed perfectly to sum up Celia's proprietorial manner. She enjoyed recalling it; turned away, grinning. Then, thinking of Maddy, she went abruptly to the door and pushed down the snib. All things considered, she preferred not to have the AA or any other excuse tried out on her this morning. To make doubly sure, she went round the house disconnecting the telephones. In the studio, having pulled out the phone's plug, she lingered over a pile of sketches. After a while she went to the door and closed it. Scrap, reading the signals, jumped on to the sofa and settled down, peering at her from under his hair. Sure enough, she took one of the sketches over to the drawing board, propped it up, and started to set out her paints. Heavily exhaling, Scrap closed his eyes.

29

There seemed nowhere left to park in Marlborough Avenue. Nick drove along slowly, naming the owners of cars he recognized, worrying when he failed to spot the vice chancellor's black BMW. Nearing the avenue's end, coming across one remaining space, he swiftly braked, and Tessa sprang out to guide him into it. Then, safely parked, car doors locked, they gripped their coat collars tight to their throats and hastened arm in arm back to Number 118. A sharp wind shook the laurels lining the drive. Sun dazzled the white gravel stones. Squinting towards the door, they saw someone waiting there; a young man with close-cropped hair and a black bow tie. (Bow tie? wondered Nick, then, recognizing Sophia's Dutchman, assumed his foreignness must account for it.) 'Thank you for coming,' the young man said gravely. 'Mrs Petchel is in the drawing room.'

They joined the queue to embrace the widow. The house was over-heated and stuffed with people in winter clothes. Sophia was more coolly attired in a shiny black frock with ruffles about the cleavage – more cocktail than funeral, thought Tessa, and Colin's sardonic grin flashed in her mind's eye. The couple ahead moved away, and Sophia turned upon them her huge watery eyes. It seemed strange to Tessa to be so formal all of a sudden. She pecked Sophia's proffered cheek. 'Is it warm enough in here?' Sophia wondered. 'This house is a bugger to heat. I want it to be cosy for the party afterwards.'

'Quite warm enough,' said Tessa, and stood back to make way for Nick – whom Sophia seemed suddenly to adore. 'Ah, oh,' she groaned, leaving him no option but to gather her up in his arms. Whose benefit is this for? he wondered, his nostrils stifled in a web of her hair, his hard chest made fluttery by the fleshiness suddenly clamped to him like a warm, faintly damp cushion. When he extricated himself, she latched passionately on to someone else – he did not pause to see whom.

'Who's the cove on the door?' asked a familiar voice in his ear.

'Oh, hello, Vernon. Boy friend of Sophia's, I believe. Dutch.'

'Very,' said Vernon. 'Good turn-out, I must say. You know Professor Stern's in the dining room?'

'A. W. Stern?' cried Nick, impressed. 'That's decent of the old codger. Must be pushing eighty. Wasn't he Col's tutor at Cambridge?'

'The very same. A vigorous old bean. Coming through to meet him?'

'Sure. Let's hope the VC turns up. I'd like him to register A. W. Stern's presence.'

'Wouldn't do the department any harm.'

Weaving through the throng in the hall, Nick put a

269

hand on Vernon's arm. 'Isn't that John Amery talking to Roger?'

'No, really? Good Lord, I believe you're right. Well, that is splendid.'

In the drawing room, Tessa had been seized by Viv. 'Hi, kid. Isn't this *creepy*? All the guys sizing one another up, counting how many luminaries Colin's mustered.'

'I know. They're on tenterhooks in case the VC doesn't show.'

'Oh, he's promised Jerry he'll be at the crem. Look, d'you see that terrified-looking woman over there?'

'With Howard?'

'Uhuh. The youth with the specs and the spots is her son. Well, she's Colin's sister. The only relatives here. Isn't that sad?'

'Thank goodness Howard's looking after them,' Tessa said, for they could be in no better hands; smooth, solid, lay-preacher Howard oozed reassurance.

'D'you imagine it's Sophia making her look like that?'

Tessa shrugged. 'Maybe. Maybe us lot.'

'Nonsense! It's Sophia – you bet. Oh hi, Liz!'

'Hello, Liz,' echoed Tessa to Doctor Elizabeth Court, a colleague of Nick and Jerry's. While Liz and Viv chatted, Tessa's eyes wandered.

Over by the french windows, Elaine, Colin's long-time secretary, was chatting to a man. Tessa raised a hand, and when Elaine waved back the man beside her turned to look at Tessa. He seemed to recognize her – nodded and smiled. Do I know him? she wondered. She could neither place him, nor give him a name. Suddenly, catching the striking blue of his eyes, she felt a leap of pleasurable recollection – nothing specific, just that she had once met him and particularly liked him. She was about to go over and speak, when Viv took her arm and said in an undertone, 'Liz looks a bit red around the eyes.'

'Does she?' Tessa glanced to see.

'Hardly surprising. You know she had a fling with Colin?'

'Ah, of course – after Lucy left him. Poor Liz. Poor all of us.'

Nick came back, having exchanged a few gratifying words with the great man in the dining room, and stood in the doorway examining the crowd, finding it necessary to look twice at people, everyone so strange-seeming in their sober suits, with their careful comments and subdued expressions. (All these academics and no row going on!) At length, satisfied that the psychology department had turned out in strength to honour its most illustrious colleague, he went to join Jerry who was standing by the fireplace with his hand resting along the mantelshelf beside the photograph of a boyish-looking Colin. 'Hello, old chum. Good turn-out.'

'Nick – thank goodness. God, I'm depressed.'

'Professor Stern's here. That's rather gratifying, isn't it? – for Col, I mean. Have you spoken to him?'

'No, I haven't; but David said he was here.'

'In the dining room. And John Amery's with Roger Delzine.'

'Oh, yes. He came to lunch.'

'I notice she's got the study door firmly shut. Still, you never know: with the house jammed full of people like this we may get lucky with those papers later on.'

'For heaven's sake,' said Jerry, looking round nervously, 'keep Sophia sweet at all costs. The VC may come back afterwards.'

'Then he is expected?'

'He's certainly going to turn up at the crematorium.'

'Good. And Delzine's giving the address?'

'Don't worry; he's been properly briefed. He understands we have a captive audience for once.'

'A nice little opportunity for the department – as Col would have been the first to recognize. Ah!' – they jumped slightly as a voice rose in the hall.

'Ladies and gentlemen,' the young Dutchman had called, and a hush passed through the house like an intake of breath as he continued, 'the hearse has arrived.'

'We'll go in our car,' murmured Jerry. 'Where are the girls?'

'Over by the window. I'll get 'em.'

The mourners shuffled to the door. In twos and threes and fours, they piled into cars and set off across the city for the crematorium.

It was airy in the chapel; benign with contemporary calm. Cream walls, blond wood, clear glass windows: a setting for a modern leave-taking.

They sat in silence. New arrivals tip-toed in, crept to seats. Whispers broke out as the place filled and seats became harder to find. Heads inclined when the vice chancellor arrived; 'He's here,' went the whisper along the rows, from the corners of mouths.

The coffin arrived. The congregation rose. Roger Delzine walked to the lectern. Colin was a free-thinker, he reminded them, consequently the ceremony would simply celebrate his life and afford remembrance. First of all, they would hear some music; one of Colin's favourite pieces.

As the first soupy notes sounded, horror broke out among the cultured, and puzzlement afflicted the logically minded. 'Christ, what's the VC going to make of this?' worried Jerry to Nick behind his hand.

'Why worry? He's a geographer,' murmured Nick, made comfortable by the thought that with such an upbringing the VC was unlikely to know his Bach from his Gounod. Even so, Nick was indignant on his dead friend's behalf. *Ave Maria*, my fanny, he fumed. This is Sophia's doing. And certainly, the music was affecting the widow; great racking sobs broke out in the front row.

Confidence among the colleagues was rapidly restored by Roger Delzine's address. Nothing was

272

overlooked; no published book, no paper read to international symposium, no contribution to erudite quarterly, but every item lovingly tabulated together with admiring comments from those eminent in the field and their predictions for the work's significance in the future. Gee wizz, Col, thought Nick to his dead chum, with a CV like that they'll be falling over themselves upstairs. I can hear Saint Peter now: 'Come in, me old lad – no need for the interview – Boss says the Celestial Chair in Metaphysical Psychology is yours!' As the excellence with which they had until recently been associated was accounted, many members of the department were deeply moved and fondly imagined the impression made upon others in the congregation. A tense moment followed when Delzine announced a reading from one of Colin's favourite pieces of poetry – quickly dispelled when this proved to be T. S. Eliot's *Burnt Norton*. The passage, read by a friend of Paul's in the English department, sounded well, everyone thought, until the bit about the door into the rose garden which proved too rich for Dr Elizabeth Court, the one-time lover of Colin's. Her stifled sobs were remarkably penetrating – Tessa hoped Sophia would not take offence. But soon, sniffs resounded from many parts of the chapel, for, at the verse's conclusion they were motioned to rise, a pair of curtains parted, and the box containing Colin glided into oblivion.

Now they could not escape quickly enough. There was a longing among them to leap and bound, to savour liveliness. Sadly they were obliged to shuffle in line to view the flowers, to shake Delzine's hand and kiss the wringing-wet widow. Outside, Tessa, for whom the ceremony had passed in a dream, was brought up short by the sight of a smoke plume. 'My God, look at that!'

'What did you expect?' Nick snarled, aching for a fight. 'Spontaneous combustion?'

'Oh, I know what Tess means,' soothed Viv. 'It is a bit . . . blatant.'

Driving towards the gate, they glimpsed Dr Court through the rhododendrons, breaking her heart in the arms of one of the department's young untenured lecturers.

Jerry braked. 'There's Liz. She's upset. We could squeeze her in with us.'

'Drive on, idiot man,' said his wife. 'What would she want with us when she's got him?'

Jerry drove out of the gates into the fumy traffic on the ring road. They sat in silence, nursing restlessness provoked by the thought of Liz Court and other forms of active life getting on with it, and they still bound by the conventions of death.

'Champagne!' shrieked Sophia. 'We must all drink champagne. It is a custom of my country.'

'And very civilized, too,' said Nick as he and Jerry joined the crowd round the table from where some other friend of Sophia's (not Magda or Pieter) was dispensing the prescribed liquid. They returned to their wives bearing two glasses apiece and all four began gratefully and quickly to drink.

Soon, the men moved away. There was business to be done, introductions to be made; it was important that certain people met certain other people, and that the department's message was adroitly hammered home. This message stressed the department's invaluable contribution to the university's prestige, and how vital it was, therefore, to fill Colin's vacant professorial chair forthwith and not allow it to wither away as had happened with vacancies in some other departments. So far as this appointment was concerned, natural wastage was most inappropriate.

'Don't know about you, kid, but I sure could do with some more of this stuff,' said Viv. 'Gimme your glass.'

'Oh, thanks,' Tessa said. She wandered into the drawing room, hoping to find the man with the striking blue eyes whom she had seen earlier talking to Elaine. Disappointed when she failed to discover him, she returned to the hall and went into the kitchen to introduce herself to Colin's frightened sister.

It proved hard going. Eileen, clinging to her son, referred constantly to her watch; and when Viv returned with Tessa's replenished glass and offered to go for further refills, she declined vehemently, one glass having been more than enough. 'We're not used to drink as a rule, and the taxi'll be here any minute. Our train goes at twenty past.'

When Howard came in and announced the taxi's arrival, Eileen nervously tapped Sophia's arm. 'Er, we must go, Sophia . . .'

Sophia whirled, cigar smoke streaming from her nostrils. 'Yes,' she intervened quickly, and not at all grieved, 'there is nothing for you here.'

'But, I – oh, dear,' said Eileen. Very gently Howard steered her away.

Watching, Tessa was filled with an urge to detain her, to beg, don't go, as if by hanging on to Colin's sister, she could keep a fragile hold on Colin. If only she had met Eileen somewhere else, in a different context; in Wychwood, for instance. She could imagine Eileen settling down very comfortably with a cup of tea in the kitchen at Holly House. Perhaps she should run after her and get her address? No – her relief to be going had been plain to see: let the poor woman escape cleanly.

'A very stupid woman,' said Sophia to those about her. 'Drink up, everyone; there are bottles and bottles. It's good – huh?'

Oh, yes, they assured her, most excellent champagne.

'And there is food,' prompted Magda from the sink where she was rinsing wine glasses.

'Food, too,' yelled Sophia, moving into the hall. 'On the dining room table. Somebody take off the cloth!'

The thought of Wychwood and her friendly kitchen had unsettled Tessa. A pang grew in her stomach like hunger – or was it homesickness? she wondered, as the ache spread to her heart. She opened her mouth and a great sob came out. Airlessness was the cause, she concluded, and was considering slipping into the garden when Howard returned to the kitchen, plumply placid and virtuous. 'Rather an ordeal for the dear lady, I fear.'

'We are instructed to eat,' Tessa told him. 'Also to drink up.'

Howard, a good Methodist, turned on Magda his smoothest smile. 'Might I trouble you for a glass of water?' And when with a 'Sure' and a shrug she had poured and handed him a glass, 'Delicious,' he pronounced; 'most refreshing.' He turned to Tessa, who was grinning at him over her champagne flute. 'Let us, then, repair to the dining room.'

Tessa discovered her pangs were definitely not of hunger. Half-heartedly, she ate a mushroom vol-au-vent, disbelievingly a caviar-smeared cracker. 'Caviar, darling, the best. This is a celebration, no?' Sophia had become very pink, and her décolletage, quivering excitedly with every shout and gesticulation, moistly glistened. To hell with the food, Tessa thought, this booze is the thing; she drained her glass and a profound sense of everything adding up and making sense came over her, and the strain and misery of the past few months slotted neatly, with a satisfying thud, into their proper perspective. Life, dear girl, that's what it is, she told herself, joining the huddle round the champagne table, something for which poor old Colin, given the chance, would have gratefully overlooked a dose or two of misery.

Ahead of her, Viv, already sipping from a newly filled glass, moved away from the table. She was with a fellow American, listening to him with an expression of incredulity which did not, Tessa felt, bode well. 'Whaddya mean, "freedom fighters?"' she suddenly snarled, almost pinning the man to the wall. 'You CIA, or somethin'?' Tessa turned her face from this scene and said to the woman next to her, 'Sophia is bearing up wonderfully.' 'Isn't she?' enthused the woman. 'And all this work someone's been to.' 'Mm, absolutely,' said Tessa, keeping a sharp eye on the champagne bottle going from glass to glass, valiantly masking her despair that it would run dry, trying to disguise the fact that she was quite ruthlessly pushing and was, now it came to it, deliberately thrusting out a long arm to secure her own glassful ahead of her dumpy little neighbour. No matter – she had her reward: her fingers round a cool glassful, her lips to the creamy top, prickles on her tongue, easeful warmth radiating inside her.

Moving away, she bumped into Nick. 'Hello, love. Let me know when you've had enough.'

He frowned at her as if she were mad. 'Had enough? We've only just come.'

Rebuked – and, after all, what was there to rush home to? – she wandered into the drawing room.

Here she found a hubbub of earnestness. Looking on, her focus shifted. She felt herself recede while everyone else loomed large; she was nothing, nowhere; they were all. Their voices filled her ears, drummed in her skull.

'At least the VC was there for the ceremony.'

'But he came back here – not for long, I grant you; he'd got a meeting at six. He and Stern had quite a good chat.'

'Delzine introduced him to Amery, I believe. Unluckily, Sophia barging in rather spoiled things – probably hastened his departure. One thing in her favour, though – this champagne. A nice little tipple, wouldn't you say, Brian?'

'Lacks the profundity of a Guinness, dear chap, but useful, useful.'

'Of course, the VC did point out the vacancy in Economics. A chair there's been going begging for months.'

'Not likely to be filled, either. What was it in – Third World something or other? No, no; our case is solid.

277

We're discussing Colin Petchel's former chair, let it not be forgotten.'

Howard, arriving on the scene and failing to attract due notice, experienced a quite violent need to establish the weight of his presence. 'The empty chair,' he intoned in his pulpit voice, nodding sagely, rocking gently on his toes. Their eyes followed his to the fireside where stood Colin's high-backed chair. They fell silent, rather discomforted for having dwelt so on professorial chairs when a more poignant chair perhaps merited their attention. David Yardley, a young and thrusting member of the department who made it a point of honour to demonstrate on every available occasion how unimpressive he found his senior colleagues, immediately sat down in it. 'The last time I saw Colin sitting here . . .' he began, lolling back and familiarly patting the chair arms. He got no further.

'You – in that chair!' screamed Sophia, scattering people aside to lunge at him. 'Out. *Out*. This is the last person, the very last person,' she apoplectically declared to the onlookers as David Yardley leapt to his feet. 'Can you believe this man? The very night before Colin's last operation he tricked his way to his bedside to demand a *reference*!'

'Sophia,' David remonstrated sorrowfully, backing away with his hands up, 'please understand . . . Colin urged me to apply for that job. He was most anxious – said if I wrote something he'd sign it . . .'

Sophia threw back her head. 'You people are *sick*,' she bellowed. ' "Read my thesis, Colin, give me a reference, Colin, put in a word for the department with old so-and-so, Colin" – on and on, all through his illness right up to his dying moment.'

'Now, Sophia, we're all Colin's friends here . . .'

'You've been through a terrible time . . .'

They failed to notice Colin's cat which came weaving between them, paused on the hearth rug to arch its back and stretch its mouth in a mute cry, then sprang into Colin's chair and curled down; only Tessa noticed, but the sight distressed her and she turned her back and went out of the room.

Her feeling of being diminished, of only nebulously existing while vigorous others loomed, strode, throbbed and completely dominated her senses, persisted as she stood in the hall. So many people. She hovered on the fringe of a group for a while until a female member of the department who was only vaguely familiar to her, began to interrogate her. 'And what are you working on now, Mrs Brierley?' Tessa, who could not remember, fortunately discovered a few hackneyed phrases on her lips. When her interrogator's attention was claimed from elsewhere, she moved away, joined another group, tried to become interested. Suddenly, the words, 'Give me a few days,' were uttered. 'Just a few more days and I'll have cleared the backlog,' someone near to her went on. For some reason the words filled her with panic. She turned as if recollecting something and walked purposely into the dining room. Here she paused at a loss. The old man they were all in such awe of was holding court on a settee in the bay window. His high-pitched whinnying hurt her ear drums. Perhaps, after all, she would eat something – at least it would be an occupation. Examining the remains of the food for an undemanding morsel, she selected a finger of iced sponge. Well, that's that, she thought when it was gone, striking her hands against one another to remove crumbs and stickiness, gazing aimlessly about. On the drinks table, an open and neglected bottle of champagne was bubbling quietly away to itself. Almost out of pity, she went towards it and, having lost her own glass, found another and began to pour into it, patiently allowing each rising of froth to subside before adding to the quantity in the glass. Really it was very harmless stuff, having had no effect on her whatever so far as she could tell, and might just as well be particularly nice lemonade. She was, however, feeling tired, and would sit down for a while on this dining room chair.

Viv, who was explaining things vigorously to a group in the hall, glimpsed Tessa through the doorway. She beckoned her. 'Tessa, come here,' she commanded. 'Tell them. Go on, you're an artist – Tessa's a proper artist, she makes money from it – go on, Tess, tell 'em.' But what she was supposed to tell when she joined the group did not emerge, for Viv hardly paused and others were too roused and combative to give way. Tessa simply smiled and sipped her drink.

'Of course, you're Tessa Brierley,' said a voice to her right. When she turned, the crowded hall swam a little, and people's faces passed by her own as if she were at the centre of a carousel and they at the periphery. Finally, she got to him. At last! – it was the man with the striking blue eyes. Peering closely, she found that his eyes really were of the most startling blue, also that he possessed black lashes and eyebrows and, at a slightly further distance, black curly hair (thinning, it was true). Such a potent combination, blue and black. (Even as she remarked on this to herself, she knew it was not a fresh thought but one she had dwelt on before when standing before an oil painting done entirely in blocks of blues mixed to a greater or lesser extent with black, producing a night-darkened view of warehouses – hypnotic, enfolding, intense.) While she was recalling this, the man went on talking. 'It's your portrait of Colin, isn't it? – the one hanging in his study at the university. "Colin and moggy," he called it. Very amusing; a lovely piece of work.'

'I remember you!' cried Tessa, as the components suddenly jelled and formed a whole. 'We were at dinner here once. Ben . . .'

'Goodwin. I was a colleague of Colin and Roger's at Birkbeck.'

'Yes – Ben Goodwin,' she agreed, as if glad he had produced the right answer. 'You were with Julie . . .'

'Past history, I'm afraid.'

Why, she wondered were his hands hanging emptily by his sides when all other hands hereabouts held plates or glasses? It gave him a sad disengaged air. 'Have some of this,' she suggested, holding out her glass. 'There's an open bottle on the table.'

'I was about to go for the London train.'

'Oh, don't. There are trains to London any old time.'

He laughed, and for a moment returned her scrutiny. 'Right. Let me renew yours. Don't go away.'

But he went too abruptly. She lurched as if her eyes staring at him had been propping her entire body and there was nothing in the void he left behind on which she could focus. His return was a relief. I shall paint him, she thought, the idea kindled by a warm impulse, a desire to express something. Gratitude? Appreciation? No, more – a yearning, almost like love. She drank excitedly, and began to examine and commit to memory certain details: fans of lines at the sides of his eyes, raspberry-coloured veins in his cheeks like threads, the relaxed set of his mouth. And all the time talking – how wonderful to come across someone at last who was perfectly comfortable to speak of Colin. Time stretched. The present, *now*, became hugely dominant; before and after dimly unreal. It seemed she had been talking to him half her life when a sudden stirring in the crowd jostled them into one another. His hand flew to her arm. It remained there. Now they were no longer talking, but laughing; breathing one another's breath, allowing the pressure of passing people to repeatedly rock them against one another as if they were dolls with no means of resistance. A trembling crept over her, and a secret prickling gathering energy. She thought: This is what holds Nick and Maddy in thrall. The idea, springing from nowhere, shocked, but perversely excited her. 'Oh dear . . .'

'Oh dear?'

'Oh dear, if only . . .' she began, then half-aghast,

attempting to remove his image which seemed to have filled her universe, hid her eyes with her hand.

'If only?' He put his glass down on a ledge over a radiator and pulled her hand away, while his hand on her arm moved slowly into the centre of her back. 'What were you going to say, Tessa?'

Turning, looking round, she heaved in air, and her breasts rose and brushed across his arm. 'If only we could go somewhere,' she mumbled in a rush.

He became thoughtful. 'If, I mean, since people are so animated, if we were to edge towards the stairs . . .'

'Go upstairs?' Picturing it, she burst out laughing. 'You mean hand in hand, or ducking and running? They'd have to be animated indeed to miss that.'

'Oh, Tessa.'

'Oh . . . Ben.' (She hit on his name just in time.)

His fingers pushing down her spine gave her voice a will of its own. 'There's the study, though,' she gabbled, 'which appears to be out of bounds today.'

'Yes?'

'At the end of the passage round the corner. Not many people are down there. Perhaps, if we very casually made our way, we could just . . .' In a swift movement, needing to know what it would feel like, she trailed her mouth over his.

'Yes,' he said decisively, and took her empty glass and placed it beside his own.

In a dream, she turned to lead the way; fastened her hand over his which was resting on her hip; went forward, paused, edged forward; turned the corner, at last arrived.

Their backs to the study door, they surveyed the corridor. Tessa put her hand on the door handle.

'Ready?' he murmured.

She pushed down the handle and backed inside.

In a single movement he backed in after her, closed the door, caught her to him and smothered her mouth.

Belatedly, it occurred to her that the room was lit. 'Just a minute,' she gasped, struggling to turn in his arms. The source of the light, she discovered, was an anglepoise lamp by the fireside where Nick was kneeling, his hand in the act of removing papers from the bottom shelf of a recessed cupboard. Then the door flew open and Sophia stood on the threshold.

'Thief!' she cried, having switched on the overhead light and taken stock. 'See, everyone! I have caught the thief . . .' – she ran forward and snatched the papers – 'redhanded! It was she, his wife, I had my eyes on – sneaking through the hall, dragging this man after her. Bringing him in here to copulate.' (At this, Tessa leaned against the wall and closed her eyes, Ben checked his watch and began to edge back into the hall, and Nick began to walk over to Tessa.) 'Unluckily for her, her husband was already here, rifling through my property. He is a thief. She is a whore,' Sophia ended triumphantly, having defined the Brierleys with exactitude and economy.

With difficulty, Nick turned from his wife. 'Now look here, Sophia,' he said unsteadily, 'those papers belong to the department. Colin told me they were here and he made it abundantly clear I was to collect them. If you hadn't been so damn cussed about them, there'd have been no need for all this cloak and dagger stuff.'

'That's quite right,' Jerry said judiciously, stepping forward and putting out his hand. 'Let's have them, Sophia. Do be reasonable, for poor Colin's sake.'

Sophia clasped the papers to her breast. 'For poor Colin's sake, huh? Poor Colin, poor Colin,' she mocked. 'Yes,' – her eyes narrowed and she nodded sagely to herself – 'with you people it is always poor Colin and terrible Sophia. Good Colin, kind Colin, clever, wonderful Colin – shame he married that bloody awful pain-in-the-arse bitch. Well, my dear friends,' she said (sounding not at all friendly), 'wait here a minute; I will show you something – a little surprise.' Breathing strenuously, she marched on the staircase.

The draught from her sweeping progress was warm

283

and scented. Their eyes followed her, fascinated by her high-heeled sandals pounding the stairs, her flashing black-stockinged legs, her bouncing silk-sheathed behind. When she passed out of sight, grunts and bangings overhead kept them in touch.

(Only Tessa, slumped in a study chair, and Nick who was shaking her and hissing the same question again and again with variable phrasing, and Ben who had fled to catch the London train – only these three were ignorant of Sophia's present doings.)

She was not long out of view. 'You see,' she cried, pausing breathlessly on the small landing at the turn in the stairs, clasping a great pile of magazines, 'while poor, good Colin is lying in hospital I have to try and do something with this place. I have to live. I think I will let rooms, maybe. So I turn out the back bedroom. Papers everywhere, boxes and boxes of them. And in one of them . . . these!' She tossed down an item. 'Take a look. See how your wonderful Colin liked to spend his time. Oh yes, here's a good one. And another. More, more . . .' One of the magazines fell face upwards, very clearly entitled *Miss Whiplash*. Losing patience, Sophia abruptly cast down the remainder (including, Jerry gasped to see, those precious and elusive departmental papers). 'Go to hell,' she bawled. 'Pieter – throw them out. I'm tired; I'm sick to death; I'm going to bed.' With which, she turned and stomped up the remaining stairs and out of sight along the landing. This time, they heard a door slam.

Only Jerry moved – darting to snatch up the departmental papers. For a moment, no-one seemed willing to speak: all this incongruous literature lying about was disconcerting. Thank goodness the VC's gone was the private reaction of many, and some went on to ask themselves whether their sterling afternoon's work had been undermined. For if this got about . . .

To the general relief, that polished operator, Roger Delzine, stepped forward, leaned down to gather up *Miss Whiplash* and ran its pages through his fingers while regarding the work with a benevolent smile. 'Of course,' he murmured, 'Sophia has not properly understood the matter. I do not accuse her of deliberately seeking to mislead, but you should all be aware that Colin and I have for years been researching the masochistic personality.' Languidly, he retrieved another of the magazines. 'Yes, yes, this is all very familiar; quite useful in its way – for research purposes . . .'

'Research – ah, *research*,' they told one another, the word's susurrant sound as cooling to the fevered atmosphere as an incoming tide to hot sand. Now they understood. 'Research' explained all; was a reliable, weighty, wholesome word, denoting integrity and honourable toil; they repeated it often and with every utterance became more confident.

Quietly as a cat, Pieter arrived with an armful of coats. 'Thank you. Good night. Mrs Petchel is tired.'

Jerry collected his coat but did not put it on. Holding it to his chest, he ran back to the study. More leisurely, Viv followed.

'Stop badgering me, will you?' Jerry heard Tessa say, and cleared his throat. 'Nick? I've got 'em,' he hissed, opening his jacket a few inches to show the retrieved papers pressed to his heart. His habitually dull eyes were shining. 'You missed a terrific carry-on out there. She tossed a load of rubbish down the stairs and these papers with it – in too much of a paddy to know what she was doing, I daresay – then cleared off to bed giving me the chance to grab them. I'm off, now. Just thought I'd let you know.'

'That's wonderful, Jerry. Nice work,' said Nick in a flat voice.

Jerry went, but Viv hung back. 'Tessa – you OK? Nick,' she said, drawing him to one side. 'Don't be hard on her. More than any of us Tess saw Colin through this thing. She didn't spare herself, and she's not over it – you saw at the crematorium how that smoke upset her. Another thing,' she whispered, 'she's

285

been knocking back the booze. Boy – haven't we all! So go easy – huh? Take her home. 'Night, babe, I'll call ya,' she raised her voice to tell Tessa. 'Oh – 'night, Roger,' she said, bumping into Delzine in the doorway. 'Fine address you gave.'

'Thank you. Good night.' Having urged the majority of the guests safely over the threshold, Delzine now proposed to see off the Brierleys and depart himself. 'I've brought your coats. Sophia has retired somewhat overwrought.' He sighed and put an elegant hand to his temple. 'I fear she has a tiresome habit of misreading situations; we must endeavour not to let her unsettle us.'

'Quite,' said Nick, helping Tessa into her coat. 'Strikes me, she's pretty damn tiresome altogether. I say, though, that was commendably quick thinking on old Jerry's part.'

'Indeed,' murmured Roger as they went into the hall. And to Pieter who was holding open the front door he said, 'Do give Sophia our fondest love.'

Pieter gave a small bow and wished them good night. Then he closed the front door and went back through the hall into the drawing room.

'You want to eat?' called Magda indistinctly from the kitchen, her mouth full of smoked sausage.

'No, thank you.' At the drinks cabinet he poured some brandy into a goblet, then carried the glass to the fireside where he shooed the cat from Colin's chair and himself took possession of it.

Upstairs, the floor of the master bedroom was strewn with clothes – scattered sandals, snaking bra, a twist of shiny frock, a heap of tights and pants. In the bed she once shared with Colin, Sophia lay with her face in a pillow, sobbing and dozing, starting, subsiding, dreaming.

'I'll say nothing about the fool you made of me in front of the entire department – not to mention in front of certain eminent blokes whom I might otherwise have

regarded as potentially useful on my behalf; I'll say nothing whatever of that. I simply want to know . . .'
He paused, having arrived at the slip road which gave on to the motorway, glanced in the driving mirror, nipped in behind a lorry. 'I simply want to know,' he repeated, cutting across into the fast lane, 'would you have done it with him?'

She spluttered and clamped a hand over her mouth, her throat full of rumbling laughter.

'Would you?' he yelled, snatching a look at her. His face was thunderous, he beat on the steering wheel. 'I bloody well want to know!'

This finished her. She laughed so hard she had to hoist the seat belt from her aching ribs. 'Oh, Nick,' she gasped at last, 'you're so . . . *funny*.'

30

'Please, Maddy – the other night I fell in when you needed to talk, so it's the least you can do. I've had a hellish time; I'm desperate. I've been undermined . . .'

'Not now. It's late, and we've taken too many risks lately. In fact, I wish you hadn't phoned . . .'

'I had to – don't you understand? Look, I'll give you the gist of it: Tessa misbehaved herself in front of the entire department.'

'What do you mean?'

'With a bloke is what I mean.'

Silence.

'I don't believe you. Not Tessa.'

'Yes, Tessa.'

'But, oh God!'

'See? I'm desperate to talk about it.'

'Not tonight, Nick. Tomorrow. I'll be dead after the bazaar but I suppose I could manage an hour or so.'

'Bless you. Er, Maddy?'

'Yes?'

'You don't think the line sounds funny – hollow – kind of . . . expanded?'

'I hadn't noticed,' Maddy said cautiously.

Nick became brisk. 'Right. Eight o'clock tomorrow. Same place as before.'

'All right. Good night.'

They hung up, then, in their respective rooms, stood still for a moment, listening. (In *their* respective rooms, Robert and Tessa had also hung up with hands made nervous by Nick's remark.) Maddy, going downstairs, heard music in the sitting room and was relieved to find Robert just as she had left him – settled in an armchair, pencilling ticks and circles in December's edition of *Gramophone*. He looked up when she came and stood before him.

'I think I'll go to bed now.'

'So soon? I suppose you've a pretty demanding day tomorrow – all those sandwiches to cut.'

But she made no move, just continued to stand there, fiddling with the belt of her trousers. 'I wonder how Tessa is?' she said suddenly.

'Tessa?'

'It was that man's funeral today.'

'Ah, yes.'

'She could be feeling a bit low. Do you think I should ring her?'

'Surely she'll be wanting to rest. Anyway, she'll be round here first thing.'

'That's it,' she said eagerly, jumping at the excuse. 'Perhaps I ought to tell her not to push herself to come too early.'

He pulled a quizzical face. 'And you don't think she can decide that for herself?'

'Mm. Good night, then, Robert.' She darted forward and kissed his forehead.

'Good night, my love.'

Returning to the bedroom, she went to sit down at

the dressing table. In the looking glass, her grey-green eyes stared back. Every hair on her head was in place, holding the shape and angle set it this morning. Her make-up was a little stale looking, though; it had settled rather in the lines round her nose and mouth. She exercised these features vigorously, flexed them from side to side, then peered closely at their reflection. There was an annoying shadow under her nose: she leaned to one side and turned on a low lamp, instantly obliterating the shadow and becoming elfin-sweet, glowing. But the image wearied her, her face as delicate and empty as a china figurine's. She conjured Tessa's face instead, enviously superimposed it upon her own – its rougher surface with a smattering of blemishes, a blotch and some freckles; its pallor dramatized by trailing dark hair lending a dangerous bruised look. How misleading are looks, she thought; for it was she who was dangerous, never Tessa. Yet if Tessa ('She's artistic, you know, a bit – what's the word? – *Bohemian*') were to be revealed as an adulteress, the village would not recoil with the same horrified surprise which would greet similar revelations concerning herself. If she, Maddy, with her 'groomed-to-go-anywhere', 'Madame President-with-flair', 'so-clean-you-could-eat-off-her' style and looks, were to let people see what she really got up to, she would set off a whirlwind; people would never be done with scuttling from house to cottage to shop to pub ('My dear, have you *heard*?').

'What happened to you, Tessa, this afternoon?' she asked the ghost in the looking glass. The thought of her friend 'misbehaving with a bloke', as Nick had put it, was incredible. During their long and close friendship, she and Tessa had often discussed such matters which had arisen naturally from long post mortems on Nick's love-affairs. Tessa had admitted to having more than once felt the urge; also to there having been several opportunities. 'But when I thought it over, it jarred with my view of myself,' she explained. Which had greatly amused Maddy. 'Perhaps you think things over too much,' she suggested. This habit of reflection was the essential difference between them. When Maddy wanted something badly she deliberately snuffed out hindering thoughts. The other week, for instance, when desire for sand-washed silk trousers and tunic smote her in the middle of an economy drive, she had simply pulled down a shutter over the bank balance. It had been the same with Nick. Suddenly she had had to have him and consciously closed her mind to the consequences. For Tessa, on the other hand, desire had always to withstand deliberation. When she fell for something (and here Maddy recalled Tessa's reaction to a vastly becoming outfit in Anna Belinda's) she reckoned up, considered all the implications and whether the role it would play in her life was sufficiently important to offset its price. And unlike Maddy, Tessa was capable of forgoing those things she strongly desired without excessive heartache (as had proved to be the case with the Anna Belinda outfit).

So what, in heaven's name, had turned Tessa into a reckless hedonist this afternoon? True, she would have been low after her friend's cremation and the harrowing months of his illness. Even so . . . The idea of Tessa 'misbehaving in front of the whole department' with some man was more shocking to Maddy than any aspect of her own recent behaviour. It was the thought of Tessa going against her own nature which alarmed her. Under any other circumstance, if Maddy had learned of such a thing she would have gone immediately to Holly House, no question; but the news having come from Nick made this impossible. And if something disturbing *had* happened to Tessa, how strange that she hadn't come hastening round to Jasmine Cottage for comfort (as she had done so often in the past – when she found out about Nick's affair with a colleague, for instance, or when her Aunt Winifred was taken ill) – very strange . . .

Her hands flew to her face. A thud inside her was

like a stone dropping. Of course Tessa hadn't come running to Jasmine Cottage with her troubles for the very good reason that she, Maddy, was the cause of them. Nonsense, she told herself, snatching up a jar of cleansing cream, unscrewing the lid, slapping the stuff on. The funeral unhinged her. People often go haywire at funerals – it's a well-known fact. She ran into the bathroom and dowsed her face, then took off her clothes and got into the shower.

When she was scrubbed clean and rubbed dry and her teeth were brushed and tingling, when all that remained was to climb into the neat bed, she fell into a panic, knowing sleep was impossible. Recalling that Robert kept some sleeping tablets for emergencies somewhere, she snatched open his bedside table drawer and rummaged for them. With a pill on her tongue, she ran into the bathroom and swallowed a mouthful of water – funny, she thought, that she had never taken one before, not once, despite all the recent trauma. With the faith of inexperience, she then flew about the room tidying things away, fearing to be overtaken, before she was properly settled in bed, by Mogadon induced slumber.

At seven in the morning, Maddy awoke with a thump. She sat up and looked at the clock, then lay down again. She could not recall ever having woken so abruptly – from sleep to full alertness in an instant. Then she remembered the sleeping pill and supposed this to be the cause. Her reason for taking the pill – worry about Tessa and Tessa's out of character behaviour and what may have prompted it – then returned to her and she sprang out of bed and began very rapidly to dress.

'Wha – what's hurry? What's time?' Robert asked groggily.

'Seven.'

He lay assimilating this. Then, 'It's Saturday,' he protested.

'Bazaar day,' she said, pulling a sweater over her head.

A bizarre day? he wondered muzzily. How did she know? 'It's only just begun.'

'Oh, go back to sleep,' she snapped, and closed the bedroom door behind her.

'My goodness, you've made a good start,' said Tessa, wincing at the sound of her own voice. 'Sorry I wasn't here earlier.'

'I expected you to be much later. You must be shattered. How'd it go yesterday?'

'What do you want me to do?' She hoped for the sort of job which entailed keeping one's head still.

'You spread the butter and I'll spread the filling?'

'Right. This knife OK?'

'Yes. The butter should be nice and soft now. So – it went off all right yesterday?'

'He was successfully cremated if that's what you mean.'

'Sorry, Tessa.'

'Don't be daft – it was me; I was tart. I'm glad it's over, that's all.'

'You look a bit peaky.'

'Do I? You don't look so hot yourself.'

At once Maddy flew to an ornamental mirror at the end of the kitchen – which made Tessa chortle. 'It's just that I thought I was a bit baggy round the eyes this morning,' Maddy said defensively. 'Is that what you meant?'

'Not particularly,' said Tessa, peering up slyly without raising her head; and they both burst out laughing.

A tractor came chugging down the street and stopped outside. 'Celia Westbrook's man with the milk,' cried Maddy, flying to the door. 'Not in here,' she yelled; 'over the road. Side door of the hall – it's unlocked.'

'She said here,' called the man doubtfully.

'Well, she said wrong. The hall kitchen's where we want it, which she'd have known if she'd given the matter half a second's thought.'

'Right-oh.' He jumped the churn up against his thighs and jog-trotted with it across the road.

'She did the same thing last year,' said Maddy coming back into the kitchen, 'and her man left it here before I could catch him.'

'How many more of these loaves do you think?'

'Oh, keep going. Now that they're charging for the whist drive refreshments we'd better make sure they've got plenty to sell. Oh, my goodness, here's Mrs Partridge coming down the path. If she comes in, we'll never be rid of her.' She darted away, pulling the door to after her.

Tessa continued to butter bread while listening to the voices coming faintly from the front doorstep. She hardly noticed Robert's entry into the kitchen, so quiet it was. 'Hello, Tessa.'

'Oh, Robert – hello,' she replied, flustered. Her hand doing the spreading took on a furious pace.

'Cup of coffee?'

'Yes, please.'

He put the kettle on; shook muesli into a breakfast bowl, poured on milk, sat on a stool and began to eat. When the kettle boiled, he rose and made the coffee. 'Sugar? Milk?'

'Just milk.'

'Tessa – are you all right?' he asked, putting the cup down beside her.

She paused and stared at the cup. Then, raising her head and looking at him levelly, said, 'As a matter of fact I've got an almighty hangover.'

'Poor you. Taken anything for it?'

'Vast amounts of water, a slice of dry toast.'

'Just a minute.' He went out and returned with a brandy bottle. 'One slurp,' he said, pouring a little into her coffee. 'There. That'll steady you. Help you through the morning.'

His smile was kindly, she saw. He seemed most unlikely to start reminding her how time was getting on.

'Sit down and relax for a few minutes.'

'Well,' said Maddy, coming back and finding them idle, 'this is nice! Where's mine?' But she went and got her own coffee. 'Edie Partridge brought a nice looking cake; a big chocolate one.' She did not sit down with her coffee but stood it on the table beside her and began very vigorously to grate cheese.

When the entire wedge lay in shards, she said to Robert – scratchily, Tessa thought, 'Isn't it time you went over the road to give them a hand? All those stalls to set up, goods to lug in – they'll be run off their feet.'

He sighed, rose, put down his empty cup, and left them to their preparations.

It was ten minutes to three. Tessa, in the village hall kitchen, looked up at the clock on the wall and thought it would be ten minutes to three for ever. On the counters against the walls were rows of heaped plates – two plates of cheese and chutney sandwiches, two of ham, two of egg and cress, and two of the Wychwood favourite mock crab; plates of chocolate cake, coffee cake, date and walnut loaf, fairy cakes, scones and fingers of shortbread; all swathed in polythene. On the floor beneath the counters were baskets containing further supplies. Cups and saucers were laid out beneath the hatchway, together with bowls of sugar and jugs of milk, plastic teaspoons, piles of paper napkins and a box of loose change. Behind her, the giant urn chuntered.

After so much spreading and cutting and running hither and thither, after her scratch lunch and all the little interruptions – 'Yes, isn't it a wonderful spread, Mrs Tustin?' – 'Oh, Mrs Meers, what a scrummy looking cake!' – now, standing perfectly still, awaiting not Prince Charming's kiss to spring her to life but the rector's announcement on the other side of the hatchway that the bazaar was well and truly open, Tessa felt the moment could never come; it was too long anticipated and over-prepared for. The kitchen, its contents and she herself were frozen in expectancy.

The door opened and Maddy came in looking very managerial in a kingfisher-blue jump suit over gold satin blouse. (Tessa hadn't changed, self-knowledge having prevented her: before the last tea was served, her clothes would bear ample evidence of her afternoon's activity; much better, she had reasoned, stay in her jeans which were easy to wash and in her son's old rugby shirt – navy with white collar – purloined years ago because it was fetching; chosen today because it brought Paul – whose loyalty she could be sure of – comfortingly close.)

'They all seem ready in there,' Maddy reported. 'There's some rum stuff about – crochet-work egg-warmers to name but a dozen, and some rakish looking dolls made by Rose Fettle. And if you ask me, Mr Bultitude's been over-enthusiastic with the bran tub; there's sawdust everywhere, and the kids haven't had their hands in it yet. How's this urn coming along? I hope the brute's going to behave this afternoon.' She gave it a masterful slap.

'It wouldn't dare not.'

'What?' Holding a cup under the spout, she turned on the tap, and the urn hissed like a dragon about to lose its temper. Tessa resolved to stay well clear of it.

'Dolly? It's five to. You ready?'

'Nearly. I'm looking for me headscarf.'

Rose stepped in at the back door (for in spite of Arthur's remove to hospital, out of long habit she and Dolly still ignored the front entrance). She went into the living room and found Dolly rummaging in a sideboard drawer.

'Where is the darn thing? I'll ruin me hair cramming a hat on.'

At the mention of hair, Rose put up her hand and

295

patted beneath her hat. Her waves felt crisp as corrugated card, her curls tight as curtain rings. 'You go too mad with the hairbrush, Dol; that's your trouble. Still, it's an improvement on what it was.'

'Here it is,' cried Dolly, yanking a tangle of pink nylon from a jumble of old letters and knitting wool. She shook it out and laid it carefully over her head. 'I'll take it off soon as we get there.'

'All serene at the hospital, was it?' Rose asked cautiously.

'I didn't stop long. I told our Barry I'd have to be back by two. Arthur was much the same. Still got that tube thing in his mouth. Looks 'orrible.'

'Don't know why they don't take it out and end his misery.' And ours too, Rose thought but did not add. 'You coming, then? If we go now, we'll arrive just right: someone'll have shut the rector up and the teas'll be in full swing. I want to make sure they've made enough for us tonight. Oh, and Dolly, keep your trap shut about the refreshments. Whatever's said, just play dumb.' She laughed – a harsh sound like a corncrake: 'Shouldn't give you no trouble, girl, not with your practice.'

Single file they went down the garden path, Rose leading, Dolly pausing to latch the gate. She hurried to catch Rose and take hold of her arm. 'Brr. Sharp, innit?'

'Mm,' said Rose, too keyed up to hear. This is it, she was thinking, keep yer wits about yer, girl. She ran through all that she must do – breeze in, buy presents for the grandchildren, check that the women serving the teas were holding back enough food for tonight's refreshments and at the same time keep off any mention of charging. If the worst came to the worst and charging *was* mentioned, well then, she'd have to be shocked and surprised and lay down the law there and then instead of saving it for tonight. She had the advantage because she knew what was coming, whereas they, poor fools, thought she'd given in like a lamb.

*　　*　　*

Eleanor was hard at work, 'circulating'. 'Do not forget to circulate,' she had admonished her brother on their way to the hall; for Timothy was inclined to relax and enjoy himself, to forget their prime purpose in being there. And so it proved. Timothy had opened the proceedings with a charming little speech, hitting all the right notes, lending considerable grace to the occasion – Eleanor would have been surprised if he had not – and now stood about joking with a group of men. At a look from her he would presently wander away to tease the nearest lady stall-holder, or join the queue for the bran tub and over-excite the children. And he would, of course, make an enthusiastic meal of his tea. But so far as purposeful circulation was concerned, Eleanor knew it must fall to her to forestall that dreaded calamity: someone going home feeling slighted by the Rectory. From stall to stall she wended her way – as, in other parishes, her mother and aunts had wended before her – finding a thing to praise, a thing to wonder at, trying to recall every personal particular to be enquired after. As well as doing her duty by the stall-holders, there were a great many individuals milling freely in the hall to be greeted, some of whom would wish to draw her aside. But Eleanor never forgot where she had got up to. Keeping, as it were, a finger on her place, as soon as the diversion was satisfactorily completed, back she went – as she did now to the 'nearly-new' stall, manned by Sarah and Richard Grace, assisted by daughter Pippa who was, Eleanor had learned from a confiding Mrs Dyte, 'going through a phase'.

The 'nearly-new' stall in fact displayed some goods of considerable antiquity. (It was so named to discourage people from giving jumble: there were whole attics in Wychwood given over to housing left-overs from past jumble sales.) Eleanor admired several objects on display, though she did not buy any. (To buy from one stall entailed buying from all, a thing the Rectory budget did not permit.) She expressed wonder at their having collected such a variety of goods together, then did her best with the subject – daughter Pippa – she guessed to be of most pressing concern to the Graces at the moment. 'I did enjoy your recorder solo at the school concert, Pippa,' she remarked. 'I said to the rector afterwards, "we must ask Pippa to play during the Festival of Nine Carols and Lessons". Do you think you could accompany "Away in a manger"?'

Pippa flushed pink but looked excited. Her mother was ecstatic. 'Oh, she would love to, wouldn't you, darling? I think she's going to be musical,' she told Eleanor, pinning a world of hope on this one point conceded by Pippa's teacher in Pippa's favour.

'Look – there's summat yer Mum'd like,' said Roy Peck, pointing to a silver tie pin embellished with a horse's head.'

'Oh, hello, Roy. Hello Alice and Melanie.'

'Say "hello" to Miss Browne,' Roy urged, but the little girls pressed against his legs and turned thumbs in their mouths. 'They're looking for a present to take Phoebe. We're going to see her later. Can they look at it?' he asked Richard, pointing out the tie pin.

Richard handed it over, and Phoebe's small daughters, their long lank hair falling, peered at it.

'Nice?'

They nodded solemnly.

'Right, we'll take it.' He reached into his back pocket. 'How much?'

'We thought a tenner, Roy. It's hallmarked, look. But seeing as it's for Phoebe . . .'

'No, no; a tenner's all right. Yer Mum's worth it – ent she girls?'

'How is Phoebe?' asked Eleanor.

'Coming along nicely, thank you. She should be home for Christmas.'

'I'm so pleased. Give her my love. I'm sure your mummy will be delighted with her present.'

Mrs Davenport, who had been smiling benevolently

on this exchange, drew her friend Mrs Wilkins aside. 'Did you hear that?' she hissed. 'Only ten pounds for a hallmarked silver brooch! And they were going to reduce it! It's what I always say – you're better off giving them money. It'd kill them to ask proper prices.'

'I know; they'd rather give stuff away. That cake I made for the summer fête – six eggs, half a pound of butter, not to mention the electricity – and they stuck three pounds fifty on it! I told them – "it cost me that to make it," I said. "Oh, we can't charge shop prices, Mrs Wilkins," they said. "Why ever not?" I said. "Home-made's better than shop, any day; you could charge a premium." That shocked them.'

'It would. But that's the village for you.'

A crush of WI members had formed in front of Mrs Burrows' toy stall. 'Seen Mrs Fettle's dolls?' Mrs Burrows had leeringly enquired of Brenda Varney. 'Take a look at the red one. Go on, pick it up,' she urged, her eyes keeping a darting look-out in case of Madame President's unexpected arrival.

'Oooh!' breathed Brenda with glee. 'Hey Pam, take a shufty at this.'

Soon, quite a crowd of ladies were jostling to peek at the doll, to snigger at the culottes, to speculate coarsely as to the cause of the doll's pained expression. 'Quick, rector's coming,' hissed Mrs Burrows; and the doll was rammed back into line, and pink-faced matrons fell over themselves to coo over stockinette teddybears and bead-filled frogs.

Rose and Dolly had reached the head of the tea queue. It was Mrs Brierley who was serving at the hatchway, Rose was glad to notice; Madame President was at the back of the kitchen, battling with the steaming urn. 'Damn!' they heard her swear. 'Pardon me!' Rose commented, raising her eyebrows, then, lowering them to address Tessa: 'Lovely selection you've got, me dear. I hope you've kept us plenty for tonight.'

'Good lord, yes, Mrs Fettle. There's enough to feed an army.'

'Ta, duck, that is kind. We'll have two cups of tea, please. And what else do you fancy, Dol? Mock crab, egg and cress? Two of each, please. Cake?'

'Are there any of them cherry cakes like last year?' asked Dolly, squinting at the mounded plates.

Tessa joined in the search. 'I'm not sure. Do you mean these?'

'No, they was round, not sliced. Ooh, these look good. What are they like?'

'How d'you expect Mrs Brierley to know?' cried Rose. 'D'you want one or not?'

'Go on, then.'

'Two?' asked Tessa. 'That's one-twenty, then, please, Mrs Fettle.'

Rose carried the tray and Dolly carried their handbags to the table area set out on the platform. 'One-twenty!' exclaimed Rose. 'I'm glad folks ent expected to fork out that sort of money tonight.'

Dolly, who had not done the forking out this afternoon, said nothing.

There was a lull in the kitchen. 'You know, Maddy. I think you've maligned Mrs Fettle. She was perfectly sweet buying teas just now. Asked if we'd made enough for tonight. "Ta, that is kind," she said, when I reassured her – right as ninepence and not a trace of sour grapes.'

'Did she now?' said Maddy thoughtfully, staggering up with a large refilled teapot. 'Here you are – though of course, now I've made it, there are no takers.'

But just then Mr and Mrs Dan Whitton arrived to be served. While Tessa attended to them, Maddy considered Rose Fettle's remark. 'Kind' seemed an inapposite word in view of the proposed charges. She untied her pinafore. 'Back in a sec.'

The rector was watching Ken Tustin trying his luck in the bran tub. 'Excuse me, Mr Tustin,' said Maddy. 'Might I have a word? When you spoke to Mrs Fettle

300

you did leave her with a clear understanding of the matter – that the whist drive refreshments are to be charged for?'

Ken shook his prize and blew off some sawdust.

'Well, did you or didn't you?' cried Maddy, becoming excited. The rector looked concerned, Mr Bultitude gaped, one or two people came nearer to listen.

'Shall we, er, shall we discuss it in the kitchen?' Ken suggested, inviting her to lead the way.

Maddy marched back with a very black face. 'Well?' she demanded, closing the kitchen door. 'A straight answer, please. When you spoke to her . . . I suppose you *did* speak to her?'

Ken felt for his pipe. 'I wrote to her,' he said at last and put the pipe in his mouth. He took it out again and looked at it. 'Whether she understood the matter, I can't say.'

'For two pins,' said Maddy threateningly, 'for two pins I'd come to the blasted whist drive and sell the refreshments myself . . . But I can't.'

No, you can't, remembered Tessa, thinking of the telephone conversation she had listened in to last night.

There was a moment's silence.

'Two teas, please,' called Edie Partridge through the hatchway.

Tessa, who had turned her back on the hatchway while she observed the discussion taking place in the kitchen, whirled; but before she could move a hand to the teapot, Maddy had run across and slammed the hatchway door. 'Sorry, we're closed,' she snapped through the crack.

'Maddy!' Tessa protested.

'No, listen, Tessa. You heard him.' She threw a contemptuous look at Ken Tustin whose pipe was now clamped between his teeth with a hand to support the bowl. 'He's got us to do all this work under false pretences. He knew our terms – we'd make the food if they'd charge for it tonight. He gave me his word on it.

301

Well, I'll tell you what: I'd rather pay for the whole damn lot than be beaten by that crafty witch.' She seized an empty basket and began to cram food into it.

'Hey, Maddy, what are you doing?'

'Packing up the food. Then I'll tot up what it's worth and slap down the money.'

'You can't. People out there are wanting to eat it.'

Maddy was tearing off a piece of cling film with her teeth. 'Too bad,' she said, tipping a plate of sandwiches on to the wrapping. 'He can whistle for his teas.'

The door opened, and the rector looked in. 'Is anything the matter?'

Motioning him outside, closing the kitchen door, Ken joined him in the corridor for a hasty consultation.

Tessa, watching and listening to Maddy raving, aware of a press of people on the other side of the closed hatchway, could only tell herself that this was a turn-up and as such required careful consideration in order to discern what her own course of action should be. There was one chair in the kitchen. She sat down on it.

'Do you want any of these cakes?' Maddy wanted to know. 'Some of them'll freeze beautifully. This chocolate sponge, for instance.' She turned, sucking a chocolaty finger. 'Want it?'

Perhaps Tessa shrugged or shook her head – she could not say how she reacted, only that Maddy said, 'Oh well, if you change your mind later you'll know where to come. Christ, when I think of that sly smug-faced creature . . . What did she say? "Ta, that's kind"? I'll say it was kind – what she had in mind was so kind it was a steal!'

Fascinated, Tessa watched as Maddy, pink-faced and still ranting, grabbed a carving knife and deftly sliced a Dundee cake in two. 'I made this, so I'm giving you half – OK? But what the hell we're going to do with all these sandwiches . . . I can't see Robert tucking into mock crab. I'll wrap them, anyway. As long as that witch doesn't get them. We touted for them, we slaved

302

for them, and Rose Fettle is *not* going to play lady bountiful with them.'

In a minute I shall wake up, thought Tessa.

Rose, who had mislaid Dolly, spotted her coming away from Mrs Burrows' toy stall. 'You've never bought that?' she cried, seeing Dolly with the Madame President doll – Maddy Storr's effigy.

'I thought it'd look nice on me mantelpiece,' said Dolly, shamefaced. 'And it'll give us a laugh.'

'You lummox. I'd've given it you if you'd said. How much she charge you?' But she never learned. She had glimpsed the approach of Ken Tustin and the rector, and was seized by a terrible premonition.

'Mrs Fettle, er, might I have a word?' Ken said, taking her arm.

Rose, dislodging him, grabbed at her friend for support and accidentally laid hands on the Madame President doll.

'Over here if you just wouldn't mind.'

Rose could not help but be led to one side; in her intense dread, the anticipated show-down having arrived prematurely, she snatched the doll to her breast and stood squeezing and working it with her fingers.

'You recall, um, my note, Mrs Fettle – detailing the charges for tonight's refreshments?'

This is it, girl, thought Rose, collecting her wits, adopting a look of scandalized surprise. 'Your note? I never got no note. And I don't know what you're talking about – charging for the refreshments,' she cried, her hands thoroughly throttling the doll. 'We never charge. It's just left-overs to have a bit of a party with, summat the old folk look forward to for weeks and weeks. If Mrs Cloomb and me had known you was thinking of charging, we'd have told you straight out we couldn't oblige. Cos it's against our principles, ent it, Dol? We couldn't do it, not see poor old folk go without when there's left-overs. You'll have to get someone else; someone hard-hearted.' As Dolly, to whom this had come as a shock and a blow, began to snivel, Rose lowered her voice and confided, 'And I must say, I'm very surprised at you, Mr Tustin, upsetting Mrs Cloomb like this, and her with Mr Cloomb in intensive care, likely to breathe his last any minute.'

'Mrs Cloomb – I beg your pardon; I wouldn't dream of adding to your grief. And, Mrs Fettle, I do know how people look forward . . . Believe me, you two ladies have lent a real festive spirit to our Christmas whist drive over recent years. It's just, well . . . Oh, dearie me, rector, it's a ticklish one.'

'A dilemma indeed,' said Timothy, pressing his fingertips together. 'Might I make a suggestion?'

'Oh yes, do.'

'Mm. Let me see if I understand the matter correctly. An entrance fee is charged for the whist drive, I take it?'

'Oh yes. People pay at the door.'

'And traditionally, during the Christmas whist drive, refreshments are served?'

'That's right.'

'Then I think it can be said that refreshments are included in the price at the door.'

'Ah, ah . . .'

'Yes,' he smiled to himself, thinking his words worthy of a Jesuit. 'Be very careful how you put this to Mrs Storr, Kenneth; but my advice is, go to her and say: "refreshments tonight will be paid for at the door." No more; merely that.'

'Wonderful,' cried Ken, and rushed away with the phrase as if delay might weaken its potency, down the corridor to the kitchen. On the threshold, he paused, drew himself up with dignity, and announced in stentorian tone: 'Refreshments tonight will be paid for at the door!' And when there was no reply but they simply stared at him, he said it again.

'You mean, Mrs Fettle a-agreed?' stammered Maddy.

Mindful of his instructions, Ken merely nodded. 'Now, do you think, ladies, we might have some more tea?'

At last Tessa found her voice. 'Of course, Mr Tustin.' She ran to the hatchway and flung it open. 'Normal service has resumed,' she called cheerily. And without looking round, 'You'd better get that lot unwrapped, pronto.'

In the hall, the buying and selling had died down. On Mrs Frogmorton's produce stall, only some chutney and a pallid-looking fruit pie remained – the chutney sunken in the jar and crusty on top thus betraying its age; the pie an embarrassment which, if Mrs Frogmorton had had her way and her stall been designated the 'WI' stall, would not have passed muster in the first place. The depleted toy stall and Christmas card stall had joined forces under Brown Owl while Mrs Burrows went for her tea and the Brownies, formerly neat little sales persons, ran amuck, red-faced and quarrelsome. The bran tub, as several irate children had discovered, was exhausted; Santa was removing his beard in the gents; and the 'nearly-new' stall was missing five pounds with Pippa nowhere to be seen.

People were not, however, inclined to go home, but lingered over tea or stood about gossiping. Customers at the hatchway were now, in the main, tired and hungry stall-holders. Serving them and chatting to them – people like Mr Bultitude whom she had known all her life – restored Tessa. She began almost to enjoy herself. Earlier, it had been a case of spurring herself on to do her duty. Then had come Maddy's tirade when she had seemed to suspend existence. Now she felt renewed, as if awakened from a satisfying sleep. Life goes on – of course it does, she told herself gratefully – the banality springing at her with the freshness of discovery.

Not so Maddy. Like a piece of wound-up clockwork

she could not desist. Having, as she imagined, won a great victory, she continued to rant and rave; only now she was triumphant. Washing up at the sink beneath the window, she maintained a steady stream of self-congratulation and wonder at other people's duplicity, pausing only to swivel her head now and then to ensure that Tessa alone was there to hear her. Whenever a customer arrived she fell quiet, and resumed instantly when they moved away. 'It just shows, you have to dig your heels in. But I was absolutely determined not to be beat. I couldn't have lived with myself if . . .' (Silence, as Tessa poured Mrs Burrows a second cup of tea.) 'Of course, they imagined we'd lose our nerve – they were depending on it. They thought, once we'd made the stuff we wouldn't feel able to do anything about it. God, when I think of it . . . But we showed 'em. We damn well showed 'em. I'd like to see her face now . . .'

Tessa walked across to the rubbish bag and scooted into it a half-eaten sandwich. 'Shut up,' she said.

Maddy looked round, presuming Tessa to be warning her of another's presence; but the hatchway was blank, the kitchen door closed. 'What?'

'I said "shut up",' growled Tessa, tossing the dirty plate into the washing up water and not caring in the least if the resultant splash gave Maddy an eyeful of soap-suds. Dislike was making her nerves twitch. I'll crown her if she says another word, she thought, and left the kitchen to search for dirty crockery in the tea area.

Dolly and Rose were hurrying home with Ken Tustin's blandishments still in their ears.

'You two ladies off already? We'll see you tonight? Good, good, that's a relief. I've had a word with . . . a certain lady, and I can assure you our procedure tonight will be the same as usual. You take my drift? Good, because it wouldn't be the same without you two ladies brightening us up, oh, dear me, no. See you later on. Here, let me open the door . . .'

'It were nice, weren't it, what Mr Tustin said,' Dolly remembered dreamily.

Rose felt not quite up to replying. What she needed, she had just discovered, was a good bawl. For this she required privacy, never having given in to tears other than when quite alone.

'Want to come in for a bit?'

'No. I want to be quiet if it's all the same.'

'You are all right, Rose?'

'Of course I am. But I want to recover for tonight. I'll call for you at quarter to eight.'

'Right-oh,' said Dolly, leaving her and crossing the road.

Rose unlatched her gate and went down the path – a small grey figure in the moonlight – feeling spent, old.

Now they were clearing away. Why must they all come in here? thought Maddy, when I'm dying to make it right with Tessa . . . Her ears were still scalding. She's gone off me, she thought with slow, widening amazement.

'Such a wonderful tea, my dears,' cried Eleanor, putting things away in the wrong place, trying to be helpful.

In the corridor, a melodious booming laugh rang out. 'I hope Timothy isn't tired,' said Tessa, 'with Sunday tomorrow.'

It worked instantly. Down went the tea-cloth, up went a hand to her throat. 'I had forgotten! My goodness, what am I thinking of? And he has been tiring his voice all afternoon. You won't mind if I go? Oh, look – here's good Jane to give you a hand.'

Dammit, thought Maddy. Any minute now someone will say Tessa's tired and ought to go home and there'll be my last chance gone. Not that she looks tired; she looks positively revitalized. It's deliberate. Her way of showing that she couldn't care less if our friendship's ruined. What did I *do*? She knew how I felt about charging for the refreshments; she agreed with me; she saw how they did the dirty on me. So why go against me?

'Actually,' Jane Bowman was saying, 'I'm worried. Pippa's vanished and Sarah's at her wit's end. Would you mind awfully . . . ?'

'Of course not; you go. Sarah needs you.'

'Thanks, I will. Good night.'

That seemed to be the end of the procession into the kitchen. Men's voices and a few bangs could be heard in the hall as the stalls were dismantled and tables set out for tonight's whist drive. Maddy removed her pinafore, folded and smoothed it. 'Tessa?'

Tessa frowned. 'Yes?'

'Tell me what I've done.'

Can I be bothered? wondered Tessa, bending to stow the last pile of plates into a cupboard. Straightening, looking at her squarely, 'I don't know you,' she said.

Maddy put a hand to her mouth. 'Don't know me?'

'Nor do I much want to. I'm sick to death of you – what you've become. Could you *hear* yourself this afternoon – blackening that poor old woman, gloating over her? Determined to beat her, were you? Well congratulations, what a fine ambition! Fancy being desperate to beat someone with so little, on her own tiny patch of territory! It's unspeakably mean.'

'Mean?' Maddy blinked. 'If we're talking "mean", how about applying it to Rose Fettle? – out to con the church roof repair fund, not to mention everyone giving the food.'

Tessa smacked her hands down on the counter top. 'If I hear you say that once more! Look,' she cried, trying not to shout, 'your logic's impeccable, no argument – but it doesn't *feel* right. No-one's convinced; people just wish you'd shut up about it. Surely you see? It's one of those illogical village things – doesn't make wonderful sense, but it's what people do, what they *want* to do. And so what, if a few old-age pensioners have an unofficial knees up at other

308

people's expense? Nobody's bothered. There's only you honking like a lone goose. If you really begrudge them, your remedy's plain – go to the whist drive and bag your own share. God – why do I need to tell you this? A few months back we might have argued about it, but you'd have seen the point and laughed. "Batty old Wychwood," you'd've said.' She sighed, turned, and flung herself back against the counter. 'You've changed, Maddy,' she went on in a quieter tone. 'These days you're blind to everything but your own wants. You ride roughshod . . . use people. Look what you did to Phoebe.'

'I'm not having that. I've been a good friend to Phoebe, which is more than most people can say in this village.'

'A very good friend, I agree – in the past. A good friend to Phoebe, to Annie Seymore, to scores of us – but not any more. You harmed Phoebe for your own ends – yes, you *did*!'

Maddy, gone very white, had opened her mouth. But no sound came. The kitchen was intensely hushed, a tap dripping the only sound. She turned to the wall and gripped the counter's edge.

'That energy of yours,' said Tessa in a low voice, 'marvellous, life-enhancing. You made people feel good. I loved you for it. But you perverted it – channelled it into a single-minded pursuit . . .' She stopped – she was getting too near. Another minute and she'd blow it sky-high. She leaned down and fished under the counter for her handbag. 'Do you think they'll find everything tonight?' she asked, casting her eyes over plates of film-covered cakes, over plastic boxes full of sandwiches, all set out for Dolly Cloomb and Rose Fettle.

'What? Oh, yes, I'm sure,' said Maddy, still hanging on to the counter.

'That's all right, then.'

'Um . . . Tessa?' said Maddy slowly, and turned.

But Tessa had gone.

31

Robert was growing alarmed. Maddy had lain in the bath for nearly an hour. Half an hour ago he took her a cup of coffee, thinking then that she was rather over-doing the soaking, yet still she hadn't stirred. He went to the foot of the stairs and stood there, gazing up, thinking, Can't very well take her more coffee. Isn't she supposed to be meeting Nick at eight? Earlier today she had muttered some excuse about meeting some WI official.

Underpinning his alarm were those last few minutes in the hall this afternoon. He had been helping Ken Tustin and the others set out the card tables for tonight. Going into the corridor between the main hall and the kitchen he heard raised voices – Maddy's he thought, and certainly Tessa's. He'd backed away; then, five minutes later, seen Tessa sprinting out of the side door, not stopping to close it, and when Robert hurried after her she had dashed out of sight down Church Street. Maddy was still in the kitchen. 'Coming home?' he'd asked, and might, to judge from her expression, have asked her to fly to the moon.

And really, now he came to think about it, she'd done and said very little since – flopped into a chair, kicked off her shoes, watched the television news, scrambled some eggs. 'I'm not hungry; I've seen nothing but food ever since I got out of bed this morning.' And, leaving him to eat alone, she had gone upstairs for a bath.

'I've trusted you, Tessa Brierley,' he warned under his breath; 'I hope you haven't miscalculated.' In his mind's eye he saw her – the dark mass of hair, the white face, the steady almost sorrowful eyes – and he found he trusted her still. Even so, Maddy was taking an age up there. He ran upstairs and called outside the bathroom door. 'You haven't drowned, have you?' – keeping his voice light and easy.

There was a start of water as if she had suddenly sat up. 'Be out in a minute,' she called; and water, with a great shout, went rushing down the waste-pipe.

The moon was high and brilliant. Frost glinted on the pavement. Dolly and Rose linked arms and scurried to the top of the Close. Their breath rose in clouds under the lamplight on the corner. They waited for cars to pass, then crossed over Fetherstone Road and turned into Church Street. And there it was – the village hall with its windows ablaze like a golden ship in a dark sea. Awaiting them.

'Ooh, it's going to be lovely, Rose.'

'Lovely, Dolly.'

He was in the kitchen, scouring the egg saucepan when she came downstairs.

'Robert?'

'Mm?'

'I'm going to Tessa's. Can I have a bottle to take – something nice?'

'I thought you were going to see this area organizer woman?'

'I've put her off. Please, Robert. Tessa's on her own. Something a bit special to cheer her up.'

'All right.' He dried his hands, went away, came back with a bottle of his best brandy. 'She happened to mention a hangover this morning, so I shouldn't risk wine if I were you. A drop of this won't hurt.' He put the bottle on the table.

'Gosh, Robert, thanks.'

'Bring back what you don't drink, mind.'

She laughed and reached up to kiss him. 'You're a sport. What are you?'

'A sport,' he sighed.

311

'Told yer!' She pulled on her coat, seized the bottle, went to the door. 'Don't expect I'll be late.' Then she paused and looked back. 'I've been thinking. You were right when you said I take on too much. In future I'm going to do a lot less.'

He didn't trust himself to answer, simply followed after her.

'Just look at it out here,' she exclaimed: 'bright as day!'

'You're sure Tessa's in?' he called as she went down the path. It stopped her in her tracks.

'Oh, she must be,' she gasped, and went rushing through the gate and down the village street as if in pursuit of salvation.

He gazed after her – a dart in the moonlight. Please be in, his mind called to Tessa, like a prayer.

The only sound in Holly House was the hall clock's ticking – resonant, measured, reassuring, thought Tessa, who was attending to it. Scrap lay at her feet on the sofa, so tightly curled it was impossible to imagine him stirring ever. The left side of her body leaned against the sofa's back; she lolled forward, her arms round her knees. Only the clock and the dog for company, she thought, picturing Nick and Maddy in the pub car park at Erdington, or else inside with glasses of beer set out on a table. She conjured the picture deliberately, trying to stir up loneliness – to feel anything at all would come as a relief – but continued to feel nothing but blankness.

Tock, tock, went the clock stolidly. Then it gathered itself and whirred – In a moment we shall have some excitement, it promised, for I shall strike eight times. Tessa waited. Here they came: eight bell-like calls – rather hurried calls, Tessa always felt, for so dignified and ancient a timepiece.

Suddenly, in an instant, Scrap became a furious streak across the carpet.

'All right, all right,' she called, scrambling to her

feet, pulling down her shirt, going through the house to the street door.

Maddy stood on the doorstep, waving a bottle of brandy.

'You'd better come in,' said Tessa.

In the Bay Tree car park, Nick sat hunched in his car. She's late, he thought, because I came early – it's always the way. He had half-expected it; it had been that sort of day.

Tessa had gone over to Jasmine Cottage very soon after they had risen this morning. He had seemed to spend the day looking at his watch. They'll be having coffee now, he thought at half past ten; and at half past one he pictured them carrying baskets of food across the road. His counting the hours was due, not to a longing to be with Tessa, but to talk about her. For this reason he had telephoned the Marchmonds, hoping for a word with Viv, hoping, even, that she would invite him round there to discuss Tessa's behaviour yesterday at length.

'Viv's in London,' Jerry said cheerfully. 'On a demo. I say, Nick, those papers of Colin's – they make our case unanswerable. Come over and take a look, why don't you? You could be in line for his chair yourself.'

'Sorry, Jerry, too busy. I just wanted to check something with Viv. It'll keep.'

He then drove into the university to do some work, but soon discovered that he was too hungry, having omitted to eat any lunch. There was nowhere open on campus, of course (miserable place), so he drove to the city centre and parked in the multi-storey; nowhere to eat there, either, except for a desolate-looking café where they were already stacking chairs on the tables. Finally, in desperation, he went into a hamburger place full of adolescents pursuing Saturday afternoon tomfoolery. He took his food to a table in the window and tried to ignore the excesses going on around him by staring outside. But the larking around seemed to

313

have spilled on to the pavement: ugly kids were chasing one another with squirt cans, shooting endless squiggles of violently coloured goo. Too much pocket money, he thought, recalling more straitened times. He bolted the plasticky food, gulped the lukewarm coffee. On the way out, he caught sight of himself in a chromium panel – a seedy-looking party, irritably thrusting through a mob of kids.

By now, he was so miserable, he could imagine Maddy letting him down altogether; it was already ten past eight. 'Good food, real ale' a display board announced across the car park: he decided to put it to the test. Maddy knew his car and would guess where he was; nevertheless, he would leave a note under the windscreen wiper. He pulled out a pen, found a scrap of paper: 'Gone inside for a beer' he wrote.

Maddy, having flown to Holly House dreading Tessa's absence, found, after her initial relief, she was unable to lead up gently to the things she was bursting to say. 'I want to make it up,' she blurted.

Tessa looked at the brandy bottle. 'What's that for?'

'Us. I asked Robert for some wine, but he suggested this because of your hangover.'

'So, we're to drink, you and I?'

'If you agree.'

'Come on then. Let's find some glasses.'

She led into the dining room where she collected two goblets, then into the sitting room where she put the glasses on a low table and retook her place on the sofa.

Maddy poured the brandy, handed a glass to Tessa, then took her own to an easy chair opposite. 'I've been a bitch,' she said in a low voice, staring into her drink. 'Everything you said was right. I'll do anything, Tessa,' she said, glancing up, 'anything to wipe the slate clean.' Then she sat very still, re-examining her brandy.

Tessa sipped hers slowly. Scrap, having decided that the excitement was over, jumped up, turned round and round and flopped at her feet – a perfect circle. The hall clock, whose ticking grew louder with a hint of irascibility, was quite the most animated thing in the house.

'I've been thinking,' Maddy went on after a while. 'Ever since, I've been thinking. I lay in the bath . . . All I want in the whole world is for us to be friends.'

'Perhaps,' said Tessa at last, her thoughts evolving as she spoke, 'we could think back to where we were. When was it before things went wrong – September? Pick up from there.'

Maddy's breath came shuddering out as if she had not properly exhaled for some time. 'Oh, can we?'

'We can try. Everything's possible.'

They began to drink more purposefully.

'Did you have any supper?' asked Tessa. 'I didn't, and I'm famished.'

'Me too. Starving.'

'Let's go and get something,' said Tessa, jumping up, Maddy following her example. 'There's a pizza in the freezer. Or we could have an omelette. Do you fancy welsh rarebit?'

'Let's see what you've got,' said Maddy.

The food at the Bay Tree proved more than passable. 'I must bring my wife for a meal,' he told the landlady. 'That vegetarian moussaka would be right up her street.' He mentioned Tessa with confidence, having no qualms, now it was past nine o'clock, that Maddy would walk in and accost him and thus wreck the picture he had implied of marital orderliness. Maddy had stood him up and he found he did not mind this in the least. One way and another the evening had developed surprisingly well. At the bar, a bit of an argument had sprung up among the regulars over proposals to sell a local property to a charity for the mentally handicapped. 'I know how you feel,' he interrupted sympathetically, 'but they're a first-class

315

organization, I happen to know. Ever visited one of their places?' His engaging manner, his evident knowledge and willingness to share it in the friendliest possible way, removed any scope for bitterness and quickly drew them under his spell. 'A very pleasant evening,' he complimented the company when he got up to go. 'See you again.'

Driving to Wychwood he felt refreshed, as though he had taken a holiday from his fears. They came creeping back, but were now accompanied by a piece of common sense which, all unbeknown, had been worming its way into his mind while he was setting other folk to rights. It went as follows: there was only one person worth discussing Tessa with, and that was Tessa.

'I really and truly hope,' said Maddy, waving her fork over her plate of tuna risotto which she had cooked with items found in Tessa's store cupboard – miraculously and deliciously cooked in Tessa's opinion – 'that Rose Fettle and Dolly Cloomb are having a wonderful evening. Enjoying themselves as much as we are,' she said, flashing Tessa a glance.

Tessa gave her a broad smile to indicate that, yes, she was enjoying herself and her agreement with the sentiment was total.

'I can picture them,' Maddy went on, 'and, by the way, I can quite see that having to handle money would have ruined it for them; I can see them in their best frocks going from table to table, pressing dainties on everyone. "Another mock crab sandwich, Mrs Tustin?" "Oh, Mr Whitton, you must try one of these almond squares." "And how about a fairy cake, Mrs Bull?"'

'Funny you should say that,' said Tessa with her mouth full. 'This afternoon Mrs Bull was most put out not to find Nick. Said he'd promised to buy her a fairy cake.'

After the tiniest hesitation, Maddy took this mention

of Nick in her stride. 'Poor old thing, I bet it ruined her afternoon. Still, she's probably making up for it now, rolling her eyes at Ken Tustin.'

'Tessa,' she said as they were washing up, 'do you remember when we went to yoga classes?'

'Gosh yes, they were fun.'

'Shall we take it up again? They have yoga on Monday nights at the health centre in Fetherstone.'

Monday nights! thought Tessa, and said, 'Yes, let's. I'd enjoy that.'

They were drinking coffee in the sitting room when Scrap growled softly and the garage doors banged. Maddy went white. Tessa went on talking.

Footsteps came quickly through the house and stopped abruptly in the doorway. 'What's she doing here?' Nick asked belligerently, as if whatever they said he would deny it.

Tessa frowned. 'Maddy and I have been having supper together. It was good – like old times. We're planning to take up yoga again. Apparently there are classes in Fetherstone on Monday nights.' This absolutely took the wind out of his sails, she was not displeased to note.

'I must go,' said Maddy.

'We'll walk you back – won't we, love?'

'I suppose so. Whose is the brandy?'

'Robert's,' said Maddy, managing to speak to him. 'He lent it. We must take the rest back.'

Maddy and Tessa went to the scullery to collect their coats. 'Coming Nick?'

'In a minute,' he called, going into the downstairs cloakroom.

Maddy went running down the steps with the brandy bottle. At the top of the steps Tessa waited for Nick. Across the road, Mr and Mrs Dan Whitton were hoisting Mrs Bull out of Davey Partridge's old car. The scene was lit like a film set, Tessa thought – the jutting shadows, the brilliance flooding, the figures made strangely tiny, shown up in God's perspective, or the

317

moon's. She turned, hearing Nick's approach, wanting to include him.

'Did you have a good whist drive, everybody?' Maddy was calling.

'Yes, ta, me duck,' replied Mrs Whitton, 'and I must say, the refreshments were better'n ever. Weren't they, Dan? Though it was a pity that couple from Steeple Cheney had to win first prize. I'm not complainin' nor nothing, but they're always winning; they take it too serious.'

'Never mind,' said Dan, puffing. 'You got the booby prize, didn't yer, Missus?'

He was addressing Mrs Bull it emerged. 'Booby prize!' she scoffed. 'They can call it what they like; fer me it's a bar of chocolate.' And she turned, raucously laughing, to be sure they had all marked her triumph. At the top of the steps, Nick closed the door behind him. 'There he is,' she yelled: 'there's the rascal. What happened to me fairy cake, then?'

'You promised her one at the bazaar, apparently,' murmured Tessa.

In mock despair he clapped the heel of his palm to his head. 'Mrs Bull,' he cried, running down the steps, 'can you ever forgive me? I'll make amends. Tell you what: I'll call for you tomorrow before lunch and buy you a stout in the Lion.'

'On the Lord's day?' she cried scandalized. 'Never! But you can take me to the pub on a Saturday night any time you want. And mine's a sweet sherry,' she added slyly.

'Anything you say, Mrs Bull.'

'Don't you forget.'

Arm in arm, Tessa and Maddy set off. He could hear them laughing at him. 'Hang on,' he called, catching up. He linked his arm through Tessa's free one.

'She caught you there, lad.'

'Yes, it'll be steak and chips and chocolate gâteau before she's done with you,' Maddy prophesied.

Bathed in moonlight, they walked down the centre

of the village street. Tessa drew them close against her and thought it a miracle. The moon had its chuckling, fat-faced look. Laugh all you like, she silently told it. See if I care!

A few stragglers still lingered by the village hall. 'Good night – good night,' people called.

Jasmine Cottage had every window blazing. Maddy saw that the front door stood ajar, and remembered running out earlier without her key. Robert was so thoughtful. Then, suddenly very frightened, for here she came bringing Nick of all people, she broke from the others and ran down the path as if her suspenseful fright were unendurable. 'Robert, Robert,' she called, her voice thin with false brightness.

Guessing her friend's fears, Tessa dawdled in the gateway, glancing about her at the moonstruck shrubs. Moonlight tipped her hair with silver.

Looking at her, Nick, too, was prompted to meet his worst fears head-on. Never mind delving into that business yesterday – get to the nitty gritty – quick. 'Tessa,' he said urgently, catching her arm, 'you're not going to leave me, are you?'

She stared in amazement. 'No, I'm jolly well not,' she said – thinking indignantly After all the trouble I've been to!

He was filled with a warm rush. He wrapped his arms round her, buried his head in her shoulder, safe, secure. Now he could tell her, now he could embark on a purging confession and make everything all right again. 'Love – I've been such a sod. I've got to tell you: Maddy's not the good friend you think she is . . .'

'Stop!' she cried fiercely, pushing down his arms. 'I don't want to hear – understand? Not now, not ever. And if it hurts keeping it to yourself – well, tough! There are things in this life we have to keep to ourselves – because they're too damn painful to burden others with. It's hard, but it's time you learned. It's called *growing up*.'

He stood very still, hearing Colin's voice as well as his wife's.

'You two coming in?' called Robert amiably from the doorstep. 'This bottle could take some more punishment.'

She held out her hand. 'Coming?'

He took it, and together they went down the path and stepped in at Jasmine Cottage.

THE END